Virginia Baily holds a PhD and MA in English from the University of Exeter. She founded and co-edits *Riptide*, a short-story journal. Her debut novel, *Africa Junction*, won the McKitterick Prize in 2012. She lives in Exeter, Devon.

www.virginiabaily.com
@VirginiaBaily

ALSO BY VIRGINIA BAILY

Africa Junction
Early One Morning

THE FOURTH SHORE

VIRGINIA BAILY

FLEET
2020

FLEET

First published in Great Britain in 2019 by Fleet
This paperback edition published in 2020 by Fleet

1 3 5 7 9 10 8 6 4 2

Copyright © 2019 by Virginia Baily

The moral right of the author has been asserted.

A CIP catalogue record for this book
is available from the British Library.

ISBN 978-0-7088-9852-9

Typeset in Bembo by M Rules
Printed and bound in Great Britain by
Clays Ltd, Elcograf S.p.A.

Papers used by Fleet are from well-managed forests
and other responsible sources.

Fleet
An imprint of
Little, Brown Book Group
Carmelite House
50 Victoria Embankment
London EC4Y 0DZ

An Hachette UK Company
www.hachette.co.uk

www.littlebrown.co.uk

For my mother, Jill Baily

Caelum non animum mutant qui trans mare currunt.

They change their sky, not their soul, who rush
across the sea.

HORACE

PASTA WITHOUT SALT

Items: Sheets of paper torn from a notebook. Pressed between them are three varieties of flower: the bluish-purple of Salvia *or sage; a cluster of creamy yellow buds from* Lawsonia inermis, *commonly known as henna; the red and spiky head of the plant* Ricinus communis, *whose crushed seeds produce castor oil. Each of the flowers is labelled in black ink handwriting, with pencil notes beneath. The page is dated May 1929, Tripoli Oasis.*

Here she is – Liliana Cattaneo, nearly eighteen years old, on her first day in Tripolitania. Brimming with anticipation and the hot African sunshine.

It is not even two hours since she disembarked in the port of Tripoli, the capital of the Italian colony of Tripolitania, after a seven-day voyage across the Mediterranean Sea from Naples. Now she is in the oasis on the city's north-eastern edge, whisked there in a trice by her big brother, Stefano. And he, trying to keep an eye on the borrowed car that he has left at the side of the road, is spinning and turning as he walks beside her, swivelling to look back the way they have come, skipping backwards for a few steps and then facing about again, and each time he turns he is hooking and unhooking his arm from hers and laughing, because they haven't seen each other since 1925, four years ago, and now here they are again, on a different continent and with the sense of having shrugged off things that had sat heavily on their shoulders. Or that is her sense. She cannot tell what his is, but anyone would know that he is pleased to see her.

They would see it in how he picked her up and swung her around at the port, sending her hat flying. How he borrowed this extraordinary racing car to fetch her. In the ridiculous breathless freedom of the drive, like a promise of things to come. That he has taken the morning off work to spend time with her. They would see it in the daft grin on his face, and the way he wants to keep telling her about everything around them, as if she needs to know it all now, right now. And already, just on the stretch of road from the port along the sea front, and only out of the corner of her eye as they shot by, she has seen the castle and the theatre, arches, towers and minarets, the high-domed tombs of holy men, heard the cry of the muezzin calling to prayer, seen the white-robed men on their bicycles and the ones squatting by the roadside brewing tea.

Bowling down the corniche in the extravagant racing machine with her brother, she felt she was roaring along the rim of the world, clutching her hat to her head, smelling the sea, feeling the dry salty air tickling the inside of her nose and whipping her hair away from her face.

She is here at last. She has arrived.

The two of them walk through the fringe of eucalyptus trees and down a sandy path in between gardens, orchards of almond and apricot. Fields full of crops and vegetation, peanuts and beans, stretch away on either side. It is lovely and lush, with all gradations of green, from the pale silvery-green of the olive trees, to the shiny dark green of the leaves on the lemon trees. 'Back home, in Italy, there are people who call this country the "big box of sand"!' she says.

'Well, they are right,' he concedes. 'This is an exception. It's an oasis and a highly cultivated one. Most of the country *is* a sandbox.'

They wander on. Pale clusters of berries drip down from overhanging branches. Mulberries, he says. 'Can you eat them?' she asks.

'Yes, they're sweet and delicious, but these ones aren't ripe yet. They'll be bright red when they're ripe.'

'Do we have mulberries?' she asks.

'Do *we* have mulberries?' he echoes, doing his dancing backward skip again and holding out his hands to point them out, the plenitude of their mulberries. 'Look how many we have!'

'I mean at home in Italy.'

He shrugs. He neither knows nor cares. 'This is home now, Lili,' he says and for a moment she thinks she catches a shadow passing across his face, but then he continues in such a jolly voice she realises she must have been mistaken. 'The mulberry trees are with an eye to silk production.'

'Aha,' she says.

'Little worms will munch their way through these leaves.' He wriggles his fingers to imitate the movement of worms. 'So they're hoping to produce silk and that it will be one of the colony's exports in the future.'

Liliana bends and she pinches off a flower from one of the little sage bushes scattered along the side of the path. Scything the stem between thumbnail and forefinger and cupping the flower head in her hand. The sun on her back, her hat sliding forward on her head, still hooked to her brother's arm, hanging from him, the soft burr of the leaves, the flower scent, the buzz of insects, the hot sandy earth.

She feels richly layered and fruity and puffed up and full, like a *mille foglie* cake. She is raspberries and cream, she is sponge and spun sugar and she is shot through with something else, a darker layer, a subsoil of mystery because, unbeknownst to anyone, she has an assignation in two days' time, with a man she met on the journey, Ugo Montello. A very dashing and charismatic man, a colonel in the air force, no less. 'I can't believe I'm here,' she says and squeezes her brother's arm again. She loves it that she is with Stefano, by whom she is known in a way that no one else on earth knows her, and that, at the same time, he does not know about Ugo Montello.

They pass a field full of henna bushes. The leaves are used for dye, both of hair and of cloth. The women here paint patterns on their feet and hands with it for ceremonial occasions. She picks a few flowers and holds them softly in her hand with the sage.

'How come you know such a lot?'

He has been on a walking tour of the oasis, he says. With his friend Alfonso, who is an agriculturalist and knows all sorts.

'Oh, the famous Alfonso,' she says archly. Stefano has mentioned Alfonso often in his letters home.

'We'll cut back through the palm grove and down that other path,' he says.

'So what can you tell me about palm trees?' she asks.

'Oh, you will be sorry you asked,' he says. 'I'm a palm tree expert.'

She laughs.

The trees are laden with golden bunches of dates in the autumn. They are the main food of the people here. The stones are removed and the fruit compressed and stored in sacks made of sheepskin. A family can go on eating them for a whole year, eking them out to last until the next harvest. He has heard that in some parts of the country the poorest people eat nothing else.

'Is that possible?' she says, 'Wouldn't they eventually starve? They must be exceptionally nutritious.'

'It does sound far-fetched,' he agrees. 'But I think it is probably true. There's terrible poverty here. Dates can be brown, green, black and red. The red ones are sometimes called horse-dates and are fed to horses, while the stones are given to camels. The organic matter around the trunk is used for ropes and mats. The leaves are used to make the roofs of rural huts or can be plaited to make baskets. When the tree dies, the wood of the trunk is made into rafters for houses.'

'Very useful trees,' she says.

'Look up there.' He points out a deep incision in the top of the trunk. 'They do that to let out the liquid. But then they mark the tree as the fruit will not grow again for three years. One tree can produce two gallons a day and some trees can be tapped five or six times. The juice they extract is whitish, thick and sugary, and they call it *lagbi*. In summer it is thirst-quenching and if you leave it to ferment it turns into a sort of strong and frothy wine. Quite tasty,' Stefano says, 'and very intoxicating.'

'I'd like a glass of *lagbi* now,' she says. 'To celebrate.'

'I suppose you're old enough to have a drink,' he says playfully.

'I certainly am.' She remembers the glasses of champagne she tossed down her throat in Rome the night before she sailed, the night she met Ugo Montello and found herself unravelled.

On the way back to the car they pass a field of red flowers. The plants have big glossy star-shaped leaves with red veins and red stalks. 'What's this one?' she asks, reaching out and plucking one of the blooms for her small collection.

He doesn't answer straight away. 'That's ricin,' he says eventually. 'They call it the golden nectar.' Something has altered in his voice.

'Why is it called golden when the flowers are scarlet?'

'Because the oil, the castor oil, is yellow.'

'What is it used for?'

'Apart from torture?' he says.

'Pardon?'

He makes a little shake of the head, as if his hands are tied and he's shaking off a drop of water that has landed on his nose. He blinks in a slow way. 'All sorts of uses. In the manufacturing of soaps, lubricants, hydraulic and brake fluids, paints, dyes, pharmaceuticals and perfumes.' He turns to look at her as if to say, Satisfied now? Is that what you wanted, for me to reel off a list? 'The idea is that the colony will become a net exporter,' he adds.

She doesn't want to ask. She'd rather not, but she does it anyway. 'What do you mean, torture?'

'You must have heard of the golden nectar. The thing the Blackshirts do. Force-feeding people castor oil.'

'That's just a story,' she says.

'Why do you think I was sick?' he says, 'Before I left Italy?' And then he laughs again.

'You shouldn't joke about things like that.'

'You're right, Lili. I shouldn't.'

Later, when she is alone in her room at his apartment and

has unpacked her clothes, she presses the flowers between the pages of her notebook, carefully labels them in ink and marks the date. She takes out a pencil, and underneath the *Ricinus* flower she writes 'poison?' She sits on the bed and she remembers the winter night, back in Italy four years ago, in 1925, when her mother came into her room and shook her awake.

~

'Get up,' her mother said. 'I need you to move.' She pulled back the blanket and Liliana lay in the chilly night air uncovered, her nightgown rucked up around her thighs, before she tugged it down and slid from the bed. Her mother's face in the yellow light from the oil lamp she was carrying was thin-lipped and grim. 'Go and lie on the daybed,' she said.

'Is it Papà?' Liliana said, her cold legs trembling. Her father had had an accident at the railyard where he worked. He had been bad at nights sometimes since.

'It's not Papà. No. It's your brother. He's sick and I'm going to put him in here. Come on, now.'

'What sort of sick?' Liliana asked.

'Stomach sick. Didn't you hear him crashing around when he came home?' Her mother ushered Liliana out of the bedroom, lighting her across the hall.

'No.'

'You and your father would sleep through a hurricane,' her mother said and gave one of her long-suffering sighs. No one knew the trouble she had to put up with. She transferred the lamp to her left hand and made the sign of the cross.

'But is he bad? Where is he now?' Liliana opened the living-room door. 'Yuck. It stinks in here, Mamma.'

'Don't make a fuss. I can't be doing with your fuss now

on top of everything. I've cleaned it up and I've opened the window to let in some air.'

She pushed Liliana into the dark, fetid room and shut the door.

Liliana felt her way across to the daybed and climbed under the blanket that had a faint scent of engine oil. That was Stefano's scent. He didn't use to sleep here in the living room on this bed her mother had taken to calling the daybed, as if it were an elegant addition to the furnishings, where genteel ladies might sometimes recline. Before he went to Milan to work for Fiat Motors, she and her brother used to share a bedroom. Then, when he visited on his day off and stayed the night – he didn't always because it was only a short train journey back to Milan, where he had a room in a boarding house – he took to carrying his mattress in here, not to wake Liliana if he came in late, and respectful of her being 'a young lady' now. He had learnt these new ways in Milan. When he moved back home full time in 1923 because he had a job at the new race track, Liliana was nearly twelve, and he shifted his whole bed in here, against the side wall. Their mother made some cushion covers in the flowery material left over from when she had upholstered the sofa, and they were all told to refer to it as the daybed when people called.

He hadn't minded it in Milan, but he preferred it at home, he said. Alfa Romeo wanted him to work for them, on their design team, and their father had advised him to leave Fiat. 'Follow the money, son,' their father had said, but Stefano developed his own motto that he confided to her: 'Follow the gleam.' He said Fiat was good enough for him and he was glad to come back to Monza. 'Never follow the money,' he had told her, 'go with your passion.' He was courting now. Teresa Puricelli wore her brown hair in a shiny bob. Her father was an architect and they lived in a large apartment near the park. Teresa's family went up to Foppolo in the mountains every weekend in the winter and Stefano had gone with them. They allowed her to ski and she did it brilliantly, he said. Like him, she loved speed.

Liliana pulled her brother's blanket up to her chin, held one of the flowery cushions to her stomach and shivered. When the smell in the room died down, she got up again and closed the shutter and then the window. All the while she was listening to the sounds beyond the living room: running water; the front door opening and closing – that must be her brother coming back in from the toilet; the murmur of her mother's voice, perhaps explaining the new sleeping arrangement; heavy shuffling footsteps that sounded neither like her mother's quick pitter-patter nor her brother's springy bounce.

The footsteps made Liliana think another person, a lumbering kind of fellow, was in their home. They put her in mind of the men who came back after the war, injured men in the streets of Monza with bandages around seeping wounds, on crutches or with missing limbs. When her father, and the men on the radio, talked about the mutilated victory she used to think they meant that the soldiers who had come back from the fighting were mutilated. She knew better now, because she had learned about it at school. They were actually talking about the Treaty of London, which Italy had signed with the Entente Powers, America, France and Britain, before the war. In exchange for a military alliance Italy was promised that, in the event of victory, she would be given certain territories, but these had not all been awarded afterwards. It was the poet Gabriele D'Annunzio who had come up with the phrase 'mutilated victory'. Italy had fought on the winning side. She had lost hundreds of thousands of men and spent all of her money and more but had not received what she rightfully claimed. Liliana's father spoke bitterly of the 'unredeemed lands' and directed his rage most particularly at France, a country he had previously loved. He liked to declaim from D'Annunzio's 'Letter to the Dalmatians', about when 'we armed ourselves to save France and the world', but instead of being rewarded were left with an enfeebled Italy.

Since her father's accident, his rage at the injustice was even more easily ignited. As if France were to blame for the crane hook that had swung into his face and cost him the sight in his right eye. As if his injury were a war wound.

She heard her mother's voice again and she could tell from the sing-song tone that she was praying. Then came the clunk of the other bedroom door, and then silence.

Everyone gets sick sometimes, but they manage to get as far as the toilet before they let it out, Liliana thought. Smelly old Stefano.

As she was dozing off, there came a terrible groaning. She got up quickly and went and opened the door. It was dark, but she could make out the outline of her brother half-slumped in the doorway opposite. He was wearing his big coat and he was groaning from deep in his chest. Before she had taken a step or even thought what to do, their mother appeared carrying the lantern. 'Back to bed, Liliana,' she said. She hooked her shoulder into Stefano's armpit and they made their way to the door with him leaning on her heavily. Liliana saw that it was this combination, her big unsteady brother and her sturdy little mother moving together, that had made the heavy shuffling, uneven footsteps. She trailed behind them in her bare feet, following them out and along the outside landing to the toilet that the three apartments on this floor shared, charting their lopsided progress. She had never seen her brother needing help to walk before. Their mother elbowed the toilet door open and in the wavering bands of light from the swinging lantern Liliana saw Stefano stagger into the smelly little room, like a drunk man, or like a man who has been beaten in a fight and knows he is finished.

The noises that followed, the farting, squealing, retching, grunting, bellowing, the plopping and the splattering were so dreadful, so primitive and shocking, that they sent Liliana scurrying back inside.

Her Papà was only just recovered enough to be up and walking about. And now it was Stefano's turn. First Papà and now Stefano. Liliana lay awake but with her eyes squeezed tight because that was the only way she could keep them shut, and she started to think again about the mutilated men. She couldn't help it. They just presented themselves in her head and paraded there in their broken way. There were so many of them after the war ended. They used to gather outside Santa Maria in Strada on Sundays, begging for alms. She had to walk past them on the way in and again on the way out, and her mother used to hold her hand tightly. There was one who had been there first, before any of the others, and who was always in the church's vicinity, even when you went for evening rosary on a weekday or came back for Benediction on a Sunday afternoon. She wondered what had become of him, this man who had no legs and got about on a little wooden trolley with wheels and had a strange beard that only grew out of one half of his chin. He was sometimes difficult to spot among the more recent jostling crowd of beggars who were able to stand and to push forward. She used to worry about him. With so many newcomers competing for donations, his tin was often empty.

Liliana never had anything to put into their outstretched

hands and caps. On the rare occasion that her mother gave her a coin before mass, it was strictly for the collection plate.

One time, Liliana pretended to put the coin in the plate but actually kept it in her hand, and after mass, as they were passing the crowd of beggars, she looked out for the trolley man, thinking she would drop it in his tin. But he was too far back, and her mother had hold of her hand, so she didn't.

She hid the copper coin in her drawer with the intention of giving it to the man the following week. She took it out a few times and thought of the paper twist of sugared caramels she could buy for herself, and every time she put it away again and kept it back for the man she felt a glow of compassion and kindness inside. But, before the time for mass came round, her mother found the coin. She smacked the back of Liliana's legs and called her a thief. She didn't care that Liliana wanted to give the money to the beggar. She made Liliana go to confession and told her the words she needed to say. She had stolen from the Church, which was like stealing from the priest, which was tantamount to stealing from God. Even if her mother hadn't found the coin, God would have known it was there, stashed away by a wicked, sinful girl who thought she knew better than her own mother and the Holy Church. It was a blessing that her mother had found it, because now these smacks and Liliana's contrition and the penance from the priest would absolve her from her sin, which otherwise she would have carried with her as a stain on her immortal soul.

She sat up in the daybed. There was a shaft of light coming in under the shutters. It would be morning soon. She had only been a little girl when she had taken the coin, seven or eight years old, but she was thirteen now.

She pictured the beggars again and she saw her papà in

12

among them with the patch over his eye and a forlorn look, and now her brother joined the throng too, all hunched and rickety, making terrible inhuman noises.

Since her father's accident he hadn't worked, and the household depended now on her brother's wage. Without him, Liliana wouldn't be able to stay on at school. Without him, they would be on the street, her mother said.

She slid out of bed and knelt on the floor. She said an Our Father and a Hail Mary and a Confiteor. She prayed for humility and asked God to look favourably on her brother and let him be well again.

When morning came, she opened her eyes to her mother's grim haggard face. 'How is he?' she said.

'He'll live,' her mother said and pressed her lips together. 'Be a good girl now and jump up quickly. I want you to write a note for his boss at the Autodrome and then deliver it before school.' Usually Stefano dropped her off at school on his bicycle before he went to the race track.

'Do we need to fetch the doctor?' Liliana said. The doctor cost money.

Her mother shook her head. 'He just needs to let it go through his system,' she said. And then, 'Pray with me.' She flipped over the edge of the rug and they knelt on the double layer. Her mother's knees were swollen and she couldn't kneel on the bare floor. 'Dear Lord, forgive my son Stefano for his trespasses and help him learn and stay on your path from now on. Forgive him if he has strayed. Let him be well again. He is a good boy. He has learned his lesson. Amen.'

'Amen,' Liliana echoed. 'What lesson, Mamma? What has he done? Can I see him?' she asked. Her mother held on to the table edge to hoist herself back to her feet.

'No, you can get dressed quickly, write that note and carry it to the track.' She went into the kitchen to make the coffee.

Liliana crossed the hallway and opened the door of her bedroom a crack. The shutters were still closed and it was dark in there. The room stank. She could hear her brother's heavy breathing but could only dimly see him. She turned her face back to the hall, filled her lungs and then tiptoed in, feeling her way about in the gloom for her clothes and shoes, holding her breath. She came out gasping for clean air, and pulled on her things quickly in the living room. Her mother came in with the coffee and bread and shoved her father's books out of the way to clear a space on the table. Her father read all the time, mostly poetry. D'Annunzio and Ungaretti were his current favourites, since he had gone off Baudelaire because of him being French. Her mother hovered at Liliana's elbow. She never sat down at meal times but liked to bustle in and out of the kitchen and then eat standing up by herself in the kitchen afterwards. 'What shall I say is wrong with him?' Liliana asked, picking up a pen.

'Put that he's got an infection in his stomach.'

'He will get better, won't he?'

'He certainly will. Or he'll have me to answer to,' her mother said and she paused a moment to tighten her apron, then stood with her arms folded, ready to do battle.

'Who's that?' Liliana's father said, sidling into the room. 'Who has incurred your wrath?'

Her mother sighed and went into the kitchen to fetch his coffee. She was probably cross with him for having slept through everything.

Her father turned his head to watch her mother go and smiled faintly. He was a man who looked taller than he was because he was narrow and thin and long-legged, and because his shoulders were hunched as if he needed to lower his head to listen to you or as if he were in the habit of stooping to get through doorways. His hair was thinning but was still dark and he wore it combed back from his forehead and tucked behind his ears. His hair had been black and his eyes a bright and unusual blue. Like a brigand, her mother said, although she had no experience that Liliana knew of brigands, and he was not a very brigandish sort of man. The blue of his good eye had faded, and this Liliana rightly or wrongly associated with the accident, but the other eye, the damaged one, which now had a white blob in the middle where it should have been black, retained the depth of its colour. The mismatch of his two eyes was disconcerting and, to Liliana, once she had got used to it, eerily lovely to behold. Neither she nor Stefano had inherited his blue eyes.

He tended to go about now with his head always twisted slightly to the right, so that his good eye was more central and better placed to do the work of two. 'Who has incurred your mother's wrath?' he said, looking down at Liliana where she sat at the table, his head cocked like a curious bird's, as if he could hear better with his left ear too, as if the whole right-hand side of him had been demoted. He had always expressed himself with a literary flourish, but this habit had become more marked since the accident. It was as if he took refuge in these poetic turns of phrase. He seemed to slip away further from Liliana when he spoke like this, and she didn't know how to stop the slide, but her instinct was always to touch him.

She reached up now to give him a hug, and when he ceded to her grasp she gave him a kiss on his cheek. 'Stefano is ill,' she said. 'He's been very sick all night.'

'Oh, poor lad,' her father said, straightening. 'Has he been drinking that rough wine again?' He gave a little laugh. 'One should always be drunk. That's all that matters . . . with wine, with poetry, with something else, dum dum . . . ' He was quoting one of his poets.

'Nando,' her mother shouted from the kitchen. 'Can you come in here?'

～

Nando is in the kitchen waiting for his wife to stop sighing and speak to him. He watches her putting her hands up to her wiry grey hair and pinning a stray tendril into the bun on the back of her head. He takes a step backwards and lowers himself onto the stool in the corner. Agata presses the palms of her hands together. She is a pious woman, his wife, and something is bothering her. He closes his good eye so that he can't see how drawn and unsettled she looks. He keeps the blind one open. There are all sorts of colours and strangely moving shapes behind it. It isn't all black. Sometimes there are purple swirls and waves of lit crimson.

She knows the boys in the fascist youth squads, the *squadristi*, can be rough, and that sometimes there needs to be clean, tough action to get rid of the rot, she says. It's like lancing a boil, draining the pus. Isn't that what he, Nando, has told her?

'Yes,' he says cautiously. 'That is to say . . . ' He doesn't want to agree too wholeheartedly until he better understands her point. On occasion he makes a powerful case for something about which in reality he has doubts, to put Agata's jumpy, fearful mind at rest. He does have mixed feelings about these gangs of armed young men. When they first appeared with their skull-and-crossbones banners, roaring about in their borrowed army trucks, taking the law into their own hands, beating and crushing their opponents, he was alarmed at their thuggishness. But back then, in 1920, when the socialists and the communists were holding the country to ransom and the Bolshevik fever was spreading, brutal measures were needed. There was no denying it. They broke up the strikes for the factory owners in the towns and for the landowners in the countryside. Yes, tough action was needed and the *squadristi* were there to deliver it where the weak liberal government utterly failed. So, even back then, there was something glorious about them. But now that they are state-sanctioned, it is a different matter. 'They do have backing from the state now,' he hazards, aware that Agata is making the faint whimpering noise that sometimes preludes an unholy shriek. A state, what is more, he thinks but does not say, that has not shied away from the task of forcibly restoring order in these difficult times, of doing what needs to be done to restore Italy to its former glory. He has come to see the *squadristi* as a necessary evil. This is not a time for mixed feelings. 'They are almost an extension of the police and army, really,' he says. 'A more zealous arm,' he adds. They might be overzealous, but there's no denying that they are patriots, fighting the Bolshevik influence, guarding Italy from going the way of the Soviet Union, breaking the spell of the red terror. Yes, indeed, they embody the martial spirit that Italians need to regain. 'Live dangerously' is one of their mottos. 'Better one day as a lion than a hundred years as a sheep' another. He envies them. If he were young again. If he were able-bodied. 'Yes,' he says, more certainly. 'The *squadristi* are an instrument of the state, albeit a blunt one. They're a cleansing force in this corrupt society.'

He cannot see Agata, because he has turned his blind eye to her, but he can still hear her faintly moaning. He doesn't know why she has called him into the kitchen for a political discussion, nor why she should be taking it so personally. He wonders if she has heard some news of which he is ignorant. She was very upset when the *squadristi* beat a priest to death in Ferrara, but that wouldn't happen now that the Church and the Fascist Party are becoming closer. The *squadristi* are still unruly, it is true. They don't always discriminate. Sometimes innocent people might get hurt, but that is the price that has to be paid.

Agata doesn't speak. He makes himself turn his head and look at her with the good eye. Her hands still pressed together as if in prayer, she is looking at him with such anguish.

'What?' he says.

Now this cleansing force has picked on her son, their son, she says. They have singled him out to hurt and humiliate.

Nando's heart stops within his chest and then starts to thunder. 'Who has picked on him? What has happened?' he says.

Stefano knew the men who did it, she says. The black-shirted young men who tied him to a chair, tipped the chair onto its back legs and force-fed him castor oil, and who left him to crawl home, spewing and soiling himself in the street.

His son.

If you didn't have your head in a book all the time you would have noticed that he was in trouble. Our son. He is not pus to be drained. He is a good man. A well-meaning man.

'What exactly has he done?' But he can already imagine. He thought he had put a stop to all Stefano's socialist non-sense. That it was all left behind in Milan.

It is not what he has done. It is what he hasn't done. He has not joined the *squadristi*. He has refused to join them.

'Can that be all?' he asks. If so, this might yet be remedied.

She does not know if that is all. Stefano knew the men, but they are not from his work, she says. At least that. They don't know about this, the people at the Autodrome.

They will, though, he thinks. They will come to know.

She never cries, Agata. Sometimes, when crossed, she might let out those piercing shrieks as if being stabbed. But now she is crying.

Nando swivels his head away again and tries to gather his wits. 'Stefano will have to pledge allegiance. There is nothing else to be done,' he says. 'He will have to join them. Not the *squadristi*, not go as far as that. But the Fascist Party. He will have to learn to keep his mouth shut. A public gesture is needed. He can sign up as soon as he is sufficiently recovered, and over time it will quieten down, it will be forgotten.'

She cries more loudly. She is trying to say something, but the crying is getting in the way. She is wiping the tears from her face with her palms, as if she's slapping her own cheeks.

'What?' he says again. 'Spit it out, woman.' His voice is harsher than he intended.

She lowers her hands. He would rather die. Stefano says he would rather die.

'It is a mistake,' Nando says. 'They must have got the wrong man. They are out of control, these *squadristi*.' He himself will go to the party office and he will make a complaint. 'An official complaint,' he says, nodding.

The way she looks at him then is more than he can bear.

He turns his face to the side again, so he doesn't have to meet her unbelieving eyes, and keeps it there until she stomps out of the room.

He sits in the corner, half blind and useless and unemployed and he cannot think what to do. He cannot earn a wage. He cannot keep his son in line. He cannot protect

19

him. He cannot punish his tormentors. He cannot ensure his children's future. He used to be someone. He used to have his own office and command some respect in the workplace and beyond.

Down at the railway yard there is a disused dead-end siding where goods trains used to be kept but which has long since become a dumping ground for broken pieces of machinery. That's where he belongs. A little Ungaretti poem comes to him. 'Let me be / Like a thing / placed in a corner / and forgotten.'

Agata is back and she is shaking him. Sit up, she is saying. No use to anyone slumped in the corner like an old sack of borlotti beans. Her grip on his shoulder is pincer-like.

He puts his hand over hers.

Breaks my heart, she is saying. Breaks my heart, but it has to be done.

He turns to look at her, fierce, indomitable little woman that she is. She has one hand on her hip and the other on his shoulder, like the handle and the spout of a jug, and she is tilting towards him as if she were about to pour some bracing tonic from her jug into his vessel, his crumpled goblet. He straightens his spine in preparation.

Stefano is going to have to fit in, she says. He has to play the game like everyone else. Does he think that all the people who make the fascist salute believe in what they're doing? He is going to have to knuckle down and fit in.

Nando doesn't want to remind her that Stefano said he would rather die.

It's not just about him. He puts us all in difficulty. He makes us a target. What about his little sister? Was he think-ing of her when he got on his high horse?

'His high horse?'

Saying he'd rather die! She takes her hand off his shoulder

so that she can throw it up in the air with the other one. No room for martyrs here, she says.

'And if he refuses?'

He'll have to go. He'll have to leave.

'Where would he go?' Nando says.

She pulls a folded magazine out of her apron pocket and slaps it on his knees. It is the motoring magazine that Stefano subscribes to. Plenty of jobs in there, she says.

He glances at the circled advertisement on the open page. 'Cross the New Driving Frontier.' 'We don't want him going to Africa,' he says.

We don't want him dead either.

'I'll talk to him,' he says. 'Make him see sense.'

⁓

A few weeks after Stefano's sickness, Liliana was sitting on the bed with her legs stretched out, doing her homework. It was springtime, early evening and still light outside.

She heard Stefano come in and go straight through to the other room, and then voices. After a while he came in and sat on the end of the bed. He put his hand on top of her foot inside its white sock and he smiled at her, and then he looked down.

He was better. He was back at work. He had been sick for eight days and then he had recovered, but when he came out of it, it was as if he had travelled down a dark tunnel and had been changed. He was always arguing with their father, although she did not know what about because they stopped if she came into the room.

'I can't stay here any more, Lili,' he said. 'There is no place for me.'

She hesitated only for a second. Anything, she thought, to

make him happy. Anything to bring back the Stefano from before. She said, 'You can have the bedroom.' She thought that was what he meant, that he was fed up of sleeping in the living room, always being the last to bed and the first to rise and not having a proper place to put his things, having to use the sideboard to store his underwear and the back of the door to hang his shirt.

He moved his head around in a circle and mashed the back of his neck with his hand as if it were stiff. He wanted to say something but he didn't know how. It occurred to her that for ten years before she came along, this was his room, and then he had had to accommodate her, squeeze another bed in, cope first with a baby and then a little girl disturbing his sleep. By rights the room was his. He was the grown-up and the man who brought the money into the household. 'We can change places again,' she said. 'I don't mind. I don't mind sleeping on the daybed.'

'That's not it,' he said.

'What then?'

'I've got a new job and I'm leaving.'

'Are you going back to Milan?' she said. 'Don't go back to Milan. Stay here.'

'I'm not going to Milan.'

'Are you getting married?' she said. 'Are you marrying that Teresa?' She didn't much like Teresa, but at least that would mean he would be somewhere near by.

'Teresa isn't my girlfriend any more,' he said.

'She's a witch,' Liliana said. 'I never liked her.'

Stefano sighed heavily. 'Just be quiet and listen to me for a minute,' he said.

She stayed quiet, but he didn't say anything for a while, so she knew it was a difficult thing for him to say. Then he took a breath and told her that he had got a job in Tripoli, where they were about to build a brand-new race track, and he was going to be involved in it right from the start, the way he had been with the one here in Monza.

'Is Tripoli near Rome?' she said.

He gave a barking laugh. 'They don't teach you geography at that school then?' he said. 'No, it's in North Africa.'

'I was thinking of Tivoli,' she said, 'Tivoli is near Rome,' and then she realised what he had said. 'Africa! You can't go to Africa.'

When people emigrated, Liliana knew, they went and they didn't come back. In 1921, when she was ten and Stefano was twenty and still working in Milan, three girls left with their families all within the same month, including her best friend, Benedetta. That was a time when so many people left. The men had been laid off from their jobs and couldn't find any work. Some of them had work but didn't earn enough to feed their families. People were going hungry. They packed up their best possessions, sold what they couldn't carry and embarked on one of the big ships from Genoa. Benedetta's family went to Argentina. When she left, Liliana buried her doll, also called Benedetta, in the park, and wore her white communion gloves to wave goodbye. They promised to write letters to each other, but she had heard nothing since.

'Please don't go,' she said.

'I have to. There is no place for me here, Lili.'

'What do you mean?' she said.

He let go of her foot and slid up the bed to sit nearer. 'I can't really explain,' he said, 'but you'll understand more when you're older.'

She hated it when people said that.

'But listen,' he said, before she could object, 'it isn't the same as going to America or Argentina. It's just the other side of *Mare Nostrum*.'

'I don't know what you're talking about,' she said.

'It means "our sea" in Latin. It's what the Romans in the olden days called the Mediterranean.'

'I know what *Mare Nostrum* is,' she said, offended.

'All I'm saying,' he said, 'is that it isn't nearly so far away. Once I'm earning decent money, I'll come back and visit. I'm not going for ever.'

'But you've got a good job here.'

'This one is better. Better than I can get here,' he said.

'Are you following the gleam?' she said.

He smiled at her then. 'I suppose I am,' he said. 'It doesn't shine so bright here any more.'

She felt a sort of thud inside at these words, a pain behind her ribs, as if she had been punched from the inside. 'Take me with you,' she said.

'I can't, Lili. I don't properly know what I'm going to. For now, you have to stay here. You have to go to school and learn everything you can so that you can be a teacher or a secretary or whatever you want to be when you're older. You have to look after Mamma and Papà for me.'

'I don't want to,' she said.

'We all have to do things we don't want,' he said.

'Not you,' she said.

He turned his head to the side and scratched his neck. He drummed his fingers on his knee. She thought he was going to tell her more. 'Lili,' he said eventually. 'It's just how it is.'

'Can you leave me in peace? I have school work to do.'

'Don't be like that,' he said.

She lifted her book up so it covered her face.

He stood up and went to the door. 'If you come to the

Autodrome after school on Friday, I'll take you round the track on a Harley-Davidson,' he said and then he left.

Later, her father called all the family to the living room to announce the news of Stefano's new job. He called it a tremendous achievement, an opportunity not to be missed.

'A wonderful thing,' her mother said, trembling next to Liliana on the flowery sofa with the curly wooden arms.

'Has he lost his job at the Autodrome because he was off sick?' Liliana asked. It was easier to say it here with them all in the room, her father standing in front of the sideboard, she and her mother on the sofa facing him, Stefano sitting on the daybed, his back against the wall.

No one spoke for a moment. She glanced at Stefano. He was watching their father, and his eyebrows were raised as if he couldn't wait to hear what he was going to say.

'No, nothing like that,' her father said eventually in a shaky voice. He turned his head so that he was looking directly at her brother. He cleared his throat. 'I'm proud of you, son,' he said.

She looked between them, at the line of their gaze, but she couldn't fathom what was going on, what it was that no one was saying out loud.

Her father turned back to the middle. Africa was the land of opportunity, an exotic location where a young man could make his mark, he said. If he had been younger he would have gone himself. He talked about how the little-populated area of Italian North Africa was wide open to Italian civilisation and would also, he believed, solve Italy's labour problems. People would no longer have to travel across the Atlantic Ocean to find work or a piece of land to till. They would sail instead to a land in the making, a land of opportunity that would ultimately be a little piece of Italy on another shore of *Mare Nostrum*. As he spoke, his voice gathered strength and took on a more resonant timbre. He explained the concept of *Spazio Vitale* and how Italy was energetically stretching out, occupying the vital space she required to fill her expansive geographical lungs, to breathe in and out in amplitude and without restriction, to become mighty again.

Liliana kept looking across at Stefano, whose face was pale and grim.

Their father recited an Ungaretti poem, 'Girovago' – I wander. 'I seek an innocent country,' he said, explaining how the area of North Africa under Italy's control, where Stefano was going, was just such a place, primitive, empty and undeveloped.

Liliana wondered why Stefano didn't look more proud and excited about his noble adventure.

The conquest of this part of North Africa that had begun in 1911 and which had been put on hold by the war, was once again under way, their father said. The humiliation of the post-war period was coming to an end.

Stefano got to his feet. He stood in front of the daybed shaking his head.

Their father, oblivious, continued. But this time, with Mussolini at the helm spreading modern fascist ideals, progress would be speedy, he said. Italy would no longer be a bystander in world history, but a protagonist.

Stefano started to clap slowly. 'Bravo,' he said. 'Let's go and whip a few primitives and then we'll be glorious again. How wonderful. The Roman Empire reborn!' His voice dripped with contempt. 'The Duce should be paying you, Papà.'

'Stefano!' their mother said in a warning tone.

Stefano started to sing. 'The red flag will triumph,' he sang in a hoarse voice. Three times he repeated the line, punching the air with his clenched fist.

When he fell silent, no one spoke. He picked his jacket up and slung it over his shoulder. 'Sorry, Mamma,' he said and left the room. Soon after came the click of the front door.

As soon as Stefano had gone, her father took his cap from the back of the door and planted it on his head. 'I'm going out,' he said.

Liliana and her mother were left sitting on the flowery sofa. Liliana got up and went to the window. She opened it and stuck her head out. She watched her brother emerge two floors below. He crossed the road and hurried away towards the centre of town. Then her father appeared and set off in the opposite direction, towards the train station. She closed the window. 'What's going on?' she said as she turned back into the room, but her mother was no longer there.

For four days Liliana did not speak to Stefano. Every time she nearly relented she remembered that he was leaving her behind, that the gleam for him was elsewhere, somewhere that she was not. She half knew he hadn't meant it in that way, but she pretended to herself that was what he had said. It was easier to be angry with him than to think about what was really happening. The family splitting apart. Her father maimed and distant. Stefano always angry and silent and leaving for a foreign land for reasons that remained obscure. Her mother was always on her knees or grabbing Liliana by the hand and marching her to church for the afternoon rosary.

'Are we praying that he doesn't leave?' Liliana said one time when they were kneeling in the side chapel of Santa Maria in Strada.

Her mother gave an impatient little shake of the head. 'That he doesn't get eaten by lions,' she said.

Liliana was going to question whether they had lions in Tripolitania but thought better of it. 'Is Stefano one of those Bolsheviks?' she whispered.

'Of course not,' her mother said.

'Why did he sing that song?'

'To provoke your father.'

'Why did he want to provoke Papà?'

'Shush,' her mother said.

'I don't understand why he has to go,' Liliana said.

'It isn't our place to understand,' her mother replied, 'but to have faith.'

How great the hole her brother left. The stuff of Liliana's life changed. It lost its savour, like bread without oil, pasta without salt.

STRAY DOGS

Item: A cutting from La Repubblica *newspaper dated May 1980, of an article entitled 'Attempted Assassination of Libyan dissidents in Rome'.*

The sky was grey, but it was warm and the forecast said no rain. The sun was going to come out later and burn off all the cloud. It was early May and, for the first time in the year, it was proper sandal weather in London. Liliana pulled the canvas bag where she stored her summer shoes out from under the bed and there, lying across the top of them, was one of Alan's grey socks.

She sat back on her heels and looked at it.

Alan had died before Christmas and she had cleared all of his clothes away in February. Her friend Joan had told her it would be therapeutic and had come round to help. Joan was a longstanding friend from church, but they saw a lot more of each other now that Liliana was a widow too. Alan's shirts and his suits, ties, belts and brogues, his big overcoat and the best of his jumpers were packed into bags to go to the charity shop where Joan volunteered on Muswell Hill. His pyjamas, underwear and socks had gone in the rubbish. No one wanted to wear someone else's old socks, Joan said.

There was a pair of hiking socks he had only worn once. Alan had been a keen walker. Sometimes Liliana had gone with him, up to the Yorkshire Dales. Climbing in big boots and waterproofs to the top of hills in the drizzle and then peering out into the mist. Liliana had never quite got what the point of it was, but she didn't let on. It was one of those peculiar English things, like Yorkshire pudding with gravy, mugs of tea, vinegar on chips and sticking it out on the beach even when the weather was chilly. She had embraced all of them, because she had made England her home, especially so after her brother and his family had disappeared. She had had no other family but Alan since then.

She picked up the lone sock that had escaped Joan's cull. There was something stuffed in the toe. She put her hand in and pulled out a wad of cash, held together with an elastic band. Tucked into the very middle was a note in Alan's handwriting that said, 'Treat yourself, love.' She counted it. Five hundred pounds.

Fancy that, she thought. A gift from beyond the grave. Dear old Alan. She pushed her feet into her sandals, put the money and the note in the zipped inside pocket of her handbag, and set off out into her day.

The horse chestnut trees along Priory Road were laden with blossom, dark pink and white, hanging heavy amongst the fat green leaves. Generous, bountiful trees, Liliana thought as she walked beneath them, contemplating her windfall.

Treat yourself.

What did it mean? She stood in the bus shelter. Alan's instruction suddenly seemed momentous and powerful and obscurely challenging. She wasn't sure she knew how to go about treating herself, what it might involve. She was suddenly aware of the invisible forces that had directed her life and that had somehow, arbitrarily, brought her here, to this road in North London, and to now, May 1980. She had always reacted and coped and made do, rather than chosen, or sought out treats.

The W7 bus arrived and she climbed aboard.

She was meeting Joan for a sandwich after Joan finished her charity-shop shift, but she was going to the library first to read the Italian newspapers. It was a newish thing, catching up on the Italian news. A habit she had acquired over the last couple of months. On Tuesdays and Thursdays, the days that Joan volunteered at the shop, she would catch the bus up Muswell Hill and sit for an hour or so reading the previous day's *La Repubblica*. It was as if, after decades of being more English than the English, the land of her birth was calling to Liliana. Not shouting. Not gesticulating. Not with any urgency. But in a soft, un-Italian sort of way, it seemed to be suggesting that whatever she had turned her back on when she moved to London decades before was all a very long time ago. Water under the bridge, it murmured. Or rather, in its own words, water that no longer turns the mill. No, that wasn't right. *Acqua passata non macina più.*

Her Italian was so rusty. It was fine to read, but she didn't know what would come out of her mouth if she tried to speak it. She hadn't spoken her native tongue in years, not even to herself, not even when she stubbed her toe and cursed. Damn, she would say, or Flaming Nora, which was one of Alan's expressions. Sometimes, she dreamt in Italian. In her waking hours, never. She had tried to become English. To leave Italianness behind. That was the thing. It had seemed important. Necessary, even.

Water that has flowed past can no longer grind. That was an inelegant translation, but was what the saying meant, more or less.

She imagined a pebble, smoothed and softened and rounded by the flow of the tides.

When she got to the library, she took the copy of *La Repubblica* from the rack in the reading area and sat at a table near the window. The last time she came she had read about the mafia killing of a police captain who had been helping expose corruption. Not even forty years old. 'Nobbut a boy,' as Alan would have said.

In a detached, uninvolved sort of way, she was trying to work out if Italy now, in 1980, was a more or less violent place than the Italy she had left for good in 1938. You didn't have the *squadristi* smashing things up and swinging their 'holy' cudgels at people any more, but the mafia seemed to be a serious problem and there were the Red Brigade terrorists as well. The front page today was all about political wrangling between the Christian Democrat Party and the Republican Party, both members of the coalition government. That was the big change, of course. Democracy. And that Italy no longer had a monarchy. Impossible to imagine those two things back in 1938. Impossible for Liliana, anyway. Back in her day there was just the one party, the Fascist Party. By the time she left, the fascists had been in power for sixteen years and pretty much everyone who disagreed with them had been silenced in one way or another.

She flipped over to the next page and there on the reverse side, staring out at her, was the face of a man she had not seen for fifty years.

Ugo Montello.

At the sight of him the breath left her body as if she had been punched in the solar plexus. She slapped her hands over the picture and looked up. A turbulence invaded her. She thought she might be sick. Sit still, she told herself. This will pass. She closed her eyes and behind their lids, momentarily, she saw a little baby with black hair and sapphire-blue eyes. It was an image she has seen a thousand times before, but not for a long time. All around was darkness. She opened her eyes and met those of the old gentleman in a flat cap sitting opposite, who had lowered his copy of *The Times* to observe her. She was breathing heavily and noisily and her mouth was open. She shut it and swallowed.

She looked down, but without focusing on the newsprint visible in between her spread fingers. Around her the quiet business of the library continued. When she felt calmer, she lifted her hands.

It was an old picture that must have been taken back then, when she knew him: in his heyday, with all his swagger. He was wearing his air-force uniform, his peaked cap in his hands, and his wavy hair sprang up from the top of his head. The obituary described his distinguished career and how in the 1960s, when he was a police commissioner, he had led a high-profile campaign against criminal gangs. It stated that he served as an air-force pilot in the inter-war years, rising to the rank of Colonel, and played a significant role in the 'pacification of Libya' and, later, the Ethiopian campaign. He had died peacefully at his home in Via Nomentana in Rome. He was survived by his wife of fifty-five years, his three children and his seven grandchildren.

She refolded the newspaper and got to her feet. She stood for a moment with it in her hand. Ugo had been alive all of these years. Somewhere, elsewhere, until very recently, he had been breathing. And now his lungs had stopped, but hers were still working, sucking in the warm air in this North London library and letting it back out, in and out. She was breathing and Ugo was not.

Next to the newspaper rack there was a pile of old magazines. She lifted them and slid the copy of *La Repubblica* underneath, burying it at the bottom. She wiped her hands on her skirt and left.

She had half an hour before she was due to meet Joan. She could do some window-shopping. She might start planning how to spend the five hundred pounds. Or she could go to the post office and deposit it in her account, although neither of those options satisfied the notion of the extravagant treat that the note from Alan had inspired. As she walked down Queen's Avenue towards the roundabout, a vision came to her of Alan thrashing in pain in his hospital bed. 'Don't let me die in hospital,' he had pleaded, but how was she supposed to get him out once he was there, in the hands of the system? They wouldn't let her. And Ugo had 'died peacefully at home'. Tears sprang to her eyes. She fetched a tissue out of her handbag and dabbed them discreetly.

Ugo and Alan were in her head. They should not both be there, not at the same time. It made her head jangle.

There was a W7 bus sitting at the stop. She climbed aboard and went sailing down the hill. Her thoughts seemed to be ranging through the forest of her days, along the pathways of her existence, skimming the grey and muted expanses, flying over the impenetrable thorny part at the centre, circling and flapping like a weary bird that could not find its nest, not knowing where to land.

When she got home, she telephoned Joan's shop and left a message to say she wouldn't be able to meet her today. Something had come up.

That night, when she closed her eyes, Ugo was there. It was as if he were sleeping at her side. He used to sleep the way he did everything, with great energy, snoring and filling the room with his vibrations. In the darkness, she felt the texture of the air thicken. She seemed to be in Ugo's bedroom in Via Ovidio in Tripoli, lying on his big walnut bed under the slowly rotating wooden blades of the electric ceiling fan. She sat up and switched on the bedside light. There was the indigo counterpane and the blue damask curtains with the cream and pink motif, the bedside rug with her furry slippers. On the wall opposite was the print of Ingleborough Peak that she had bought Alan for his sixty-fifth birthday. All the familiar objects were in their usual places. She was at home in London and Ugo's remembered snores had not torn through the fabric of time. She went downstairs and made herself a cup of camomile tea. When she returned to bed, Ugo was still there, lying on his back, the great barrel of his chest rising and falling. She used to place her head there, the skin of her cheek on the skin of his chest, and she would listen to the beat of his heart, loud, strong and certain.

He had died two days ago. Peacefully at home. He must have been nearly ninety. He had never been called to account. Was there no justice in the world?

She kept turning over, trying to find a comfortable place to rest. She lay on her side and pressed her ear into the pillow. There was always a whispering sound in her right ear, an indecipherable murmuring. Tonight, accompanying it, was her own fast pulse, like a drumbeat in double time.

On Thursday morning she found herself back in the library. She had caught the bus up the hill because she was meeting Joan at lunchtime and needed to do some grocery shopping first. Muswell Hill Broadway was as good a place as any for that. She had had to pop in to Alexandra Motors too, because they had finally managed to sell Alan's old Ford Cortina and had a cheque for her. She used to work in their office part-time, keeping their books, and so knew that they were trustworthy. It was a shame she was past retirement age because she would have appreciated that little job again to fill the hours, now that she didn't have Alan to look after. She herself had never learned to drive, but she liked to be among people who cared about cars. She had also wanted to call in at the junk shop on Colney Hatch Lane to see if any new fabrics had come in, but it was shut. She was always on the lookout for silk scarves. She was making a silk patchwork bedspread for the spare room.

She hadn't really meant to come to the library today. She had thought she would give Italy and Italian news a miss for a while, but she had finished her errands and had five minutes to spare, and so here she was.

She saw that the pile of old magazines had gone. Better that way, or she might have been tempted to trawl through the obituary again, looking for facts that she had missed. Had it mentioned a funeral date, for example? The gap between death and funeral was much shorter in Italy; not as fast as in Muslim countries, but much more expeditious than in England, where it could take weeks. Ugo would almost certainly have been laid to rest by now and a stone placed on his grave. A cold feeling surged up her back. It felt like an icy hand. She shook it off.

She lifted the latest *La Repubblica* from the rack. 'Attempted Assassination of Libyan Dissidents in Rome' was the front-page headline. She had no actual connection with Libya any more, not since Stefano and his family had disappeared, but still she always read any news she came across about Italy's ex-colony, its former 'fourth shore'.

She settled herself at a table near the window. Two men had been shot in a café in Rome, near the railway station. They were probably victims of the 'physical liquidation of stray dogs' campaign announced by the Libyan dictator, Colonel Gaddafi. All opponents of the Libyan revolution living abroad were to be eliminated, he had declared. There was a photo of one of the victims, Khalid Al Mafoudi. He had fallen foul of the Libyan regime because he was allegedly a member of a political party, and political parties had been banned. The other man was thought to have been caught in the crossfire, rather than a target. The men were injured and in a critical state. Towards the end of the article, the other man was named too. Liliana's heart stopped for an instant and then straight afterwards beat so clamorously, her blood pulsing so hard, that she put her hands up to cover her ears. Abramo Cattaneo al-Arufi.

There was no mistaking it. The Italian surname might be buried in the middle, but this was her nephew, Stefano's son Abramo. He was in Rome. He had been shot.

She rocked in the chair, her hands clutched to the sides of her face. The Libyan desert blazed in her head. The intense heat and light outside and the stuffy claustrophobic darkness inside the tent, where the fabric itself seemed to sweat. The cries in the darkness. Newborn Abramo with his tuft of black hair and his dimples, his dark unfocused eyes and his helpless dainty-boned feet.

She had been there when he was born. She had been the first to hold him. She had handed him to his mother.

She stuffed the newspaper in her bag and fled the library.

Joan was already in the café, sitting at their usual table, when Liliana staggered in and flopped down on the chair opposite, panting. She was gasping for air, as if she had been held under water and had only just broken the surface.

'Lil, what's up?' Joan said in alarm. 'You look as though you've seen a ghost.'

Liliana drank a few sips of the water that Joan poured for her. She took some deep breaths as instructed. She collected herself while Joan ordered leek and potato soup for both of them.

'Tell me what's happened,' Joan said.

Liliana put the newspaper on the table and pointed to the article.

'It's in Italian,' Joan said. 'I don't know what it says.' She looked across the table and shook her head with a little shrug, as if she had been asked to translate.

'It's about two men who have been shot in Rome,' Liliana managed to say.

'Oh, right,' Joan said. 'I forget you're Italian! Your English is so fluent. I hardly even notice your accent.'

Liliana blinked, searching for words. Her fluency had deserted her. 'I gave them up for dead,' she said at last, 'years ago.' She tried to get a hold of herself. If Joan weren't looking at her in such a concerned way, she might be able to push the churning inside back down. 'I stopped looking for them,' she said in a wobbly voice.

Joan pulled a bunch of serviettes out of the holder and handed them to her. 'Who?' she said.

'I mourned them,' Liliana said. 'I sent so many letters to Tripoli and they never wrote back. At first I thought it was because of the war.'

'Who didn't write back? You're not making sense, Lil.'

'Because of Britain and Italy being on different sides in the war. Belligerents. Then afterwards . . . ' Liliana took another breath, '. . . I wrote again. I made enquiries. But there was no information.' She shook her head.

'Sorry, Lil. Who are we talking about?'

'My brother,' Liliana whispered.

'I didn't know you had a brother!' Joan said.

She had stopped talking about him years ago. There had been nothing new to say. Of course Joan wouldn't have known. A warning voice in her head was telling Liliana to be quiet, to slow down, but like a running tap with a faulty washer, she couldn't control the words spurting out. 'And his wife,' she said, 'and the children, Nadia and Abramo.'

'Your brother and his family lived in Tripoli?' Joan said. 'In Libya?'

Liliana nodded.

'I don't even know where Libya is! I don't think I could find it on a map,' Joan said. She raised her eyebrows and shook her head, wonderingly.

Liliana let out a sigh.

'Sorry,' Joan said. 'It doesn't matter whether I've got the story straight. What matters is what has happened now to send you into such a state.'

'I think one of those men who have been shot in Rome is my nephew,' Liliana said, tapping two fingers on the article laid out between them. Her voice wavered. 'And I don't know what to do.'

Joan blinked at Liliana, taking her words in. She took off her glasses and got to her feet. 'You have to go to him,' she said.

'Oh, I can't do that,' Liliana said.

Joan turned away to speak to the waitress. She was cancelling the soup.

The idea of getting on an aeroplane and flying to Rome, just like that: no, Liliana couldn't comprehend it. It would need planning and organisation and she didn't know what.

She didn't know Rome at all. She didn't know her way around. She'd only been there once, fleetingly, when she was a girl. And she couldn't just leave everything here. And then, there was another thing, another reason why she shouldn't be hasty. It was flickering in her head like a faulty torch, switching itself on and off, but it didn't stay on long enough for her to grasp.

'Do you agree?' Joan said.

She had missed whatever Joan had been saying.

'I said, don't worry about the cost of a plane ticket, if that's what's bothering you. I can lend you the money,' Joan said.

'No, that's not a problem,' Liliana said, and she told Joan about the cash from Alan.

'That's it then!' Joan said, clapping her hands together. 'The Lord works in mysterious ways. That is your guardian angel guiding you to your nephew.' She nodded. 'Come on. My car is round the corner. I'll drive you home.'

'I don't even know what hospital he's in,' Liliana said.

'You can telephone the likely hospitals in Rome and find out.'

Liliana was still sitting at the table, her heart pounding and a rushing sound filling her ears.

'Lil,' Joan said, 'this newspaper is from yesterday. The shooting happened the day before. You probably won't get there until tomorrow.' She looked at her watch and back at Liliana. 'There isn't a moment to lose.'

'Perhaps you're right,' Liliana said weakly.

'Let's go and book you a flight.'

〜

A thousand miles away, in Rome, Zaida was listening to the doctor who was telling her about her father's condition. Two days before, when he and her uncle were drinking coffee in a bar behind Termini station, gunmen ran in and shot them both. The men were from one of Gaddafi's hit squads. They were aiming for her father, but Khal Abramo was with him and he got hit too. The doctor was giving her important information and she needed to concentrate, but other things, things that didn't matter right then, were pulling at her attention. The window was open a notch, and a slight breeze blew the blinds, and the bobble on the end of the string that was used to open and close them pinged against the frame. She was trying to detect a rhythm in its knocking. And the notice on the board, about germ awareness and washing your hands, seemed to be shouting at her: *Look at me*, it was saying. *Read me again*.

She closed her eyes to shut out the distractions.

'Fetch a glass of water. She's fainting,' the nurse said. And another voice, the doctor's: 'Who is responsible for this girl? Isn't there an adult?'

Zaida opened her eyes again and blinked at them: at the doctor in his white coat, his stethoscope around his neck, his furrowed, sloping brow; the nurse with her black and silver striped hair. 'Occipital lobe,' she said, repeating the doctor. She nodded at him to show that she had understood. He was explaining how the bullet had entered her father's head. That fragments and debris had been removed, but that they would keep him in an induced coma to allow the swelling of his brain to come down.

Earlier, she had heard the nurses in their curtained alcove talking about her. They were saying that arrangements might have to be made because of her being a minor. She wasn't sure whether it would do any good to tell them she was capable of caring for herself. That in terms of shopping and cooking and cleaning, of laundry and ironing, she was the one who did the looking after, not her father. That in point of fact it was she who was trying to bring *him* up, drag his hidebound stuck-in-the-olden-days Libyan sensibility into the twentieth century, turn his face to the changing role of women. Khal Abramo at least had a few domestic skills and came round to prepare Libyan food for them once a week. *Bazeen* cooked with mutton and spicy tomato sauce; lamb soup that they called *sharba*; ground meat balls, *kufta*, spiced with coriander and garlic. Her father was useless, though. She had been trying to teach him to iron ever since they had come to Rome three years before. He seemed to think he was constitutionally incapable of doing it. It was almost a point of pride. He would come to her with his crumpled shirts. 'I will bring shame on the house, going out like this,' he would say, quoting her grandmother, his mother. And she would sigh and grumble and iron his shirt again, for the last time.

'Poor child. What a terrible thing,' she had heard the stripy-haired nurse say. 'I actually thought she was Italian,' the other one, the young one with glasses, had commented. 'I'd never have thought she was an Arab.' She sounded aggrieved, as if Zaida had played a trick on her. 'She is part Italian, wouldn't you think?' the older one had said, but the young one didn't want to be mollified. 'What was her mother thinking of, that's what I'd like to know,' she had said.

After the doctor and nurse had gone, Zaida sponged her father's poor swollen face. She didn't want to leave him alone, but she had to check on how her uncle was doing and then telephone her mother in Libya. She had booked a call. There was an armed guard sitting at the threshold to make sure no one intruded, so it would be all right for a few minutes.

The guard at the door was a different one from earlier. He slouched in the chair with his gun across his stomach. She introduced herself and shook his hand. 'I am going down to reception to use the telephone,' she said, 'to try and call my mother. I won't be long. Thank you for keeping a lookout while I'm away.'

He smiled at her and said he would be very alert. That no one would get past him. He sat up straighter.

She called in at the ward where her uncle lay. There was no armed guard on his door. It was her father who had been the target, they said. Khal Abramo wasn't political, or not in the way her father was. As a poet, it was his job to take the long view, to observe and to express the anguish of exile rather than to participate. And he had other battles to fight, or perhaps to dodge, personal ones. 'Raise your words, not your voice. It is rain that grows flowers, not thunder,' was his motto. That was Rumi.

There was no member of staff around for Zaida to ask how he was doing, but they probably wouldn't have told her anyway because they didn't know Abramo was her uncle. She had kept that information to herself. The less anybody knew, the better. That was her thinking. Always, too, she was fearful for the family back home.

Khal Abramo looked dreadful. Not as bad as her father, but still dreadful. She kissed his forehead and his eyelashes fluttered. 'Thank you,' he seemed to mutter. He smiled as if he could see her through his closed lids.

'I will come back and recite you a poem,' she said. And then she thought better of that idea. If he was semi-conscious now, then this was a good time. She had fifteen minutes before her telephone call. She settled on the seat. She consulted the small but ever-growing library in her head. With his help and encouragement, she had been learning a poem a week and had been translating them into Italian. 'I've become a sadness junkie,' she began, reciting Nizar Qabbani, one of her favourites. 'So now I fear not being sorrowed.' She hesitated. She sought something more cheerful, but nothing came to her. 'The depth of your love today is the depth of your wound tomorrow,' she whispered and she kissed his brow again.

'Thank you,' he mouthed.

'You don't have to thank me for my kiss, Khal Abramo. I give it freely,' she said and she laughed. Her laugh sounded like a sob in her own ears. 'I'll come back later, after I've talked to Mama and sat a while with Baba, and I will recite you the whole of "Night and Day".'

'Signorina,' the man in the next bed called out as she stood up to leave. He had knocked the chocolates to the floor and couldn't reach them. They had rolled under the bed and behind the bedside cabinet. There were all sorts of different ones wrapped in variously coloured tinfoil. She scooped them up and back into the box and put it on the bedside table. 'Has anyone ever told you that your eyes have flecks of gold in them?' he said. 'Never,' she said. 'Glints of sunshine,' he added. She smiled at him and opened her eyes wide to accept his admiration. 'Would you pass me a choc?' he said. He opened his mouth. He had three teeth on the top row and four in the middle on the bottom row and nothing either side. She unwrapped a sweet and popped it into his chocolatey mouth. 'Take some with you,' he said. 'Take more. Take a big handful. I've got too many.' And to oblige him, she filled her pockets.

'ARAB BEAUTY'

Item: A postcard from Tripoli depicting a local girl and captioned 'Arab Beauty'.

Stefano's monthly letter has arrived. Liliana and her mother are sitting side by side on the sofa. Her brother is due to come home for his first visit since he left three years earlier. He will be in Monza in time to attend the motor race in September and, for the first time, he will take Liliana with him. They will be going as bona-fide ticket holders, not just visiting the mechanics in the pits, but up in the grandstand with the other spectators. It is late August. Outside it is hot and dry, and the grass in the little park between their apartment and the railway line has turned yellow.

Liliana and her mother are waiting for Liliana's father to read the letter to them.

This is the high point of their month, the news of the young man at large in a world they can hardly imagine but which he has tried to describe for them. Their young man, out there in Africa, helping create the colony that will provide employment and a livelihood to hundreds and thousands of needy Italians. Sometimes, the way her mother talks about Stefano to the neighbours, you'd think he was singlehandedly bringing civilisation to Africa.

Her father always reads Stefano's letter through to himself first, standing in front of the sideboard where the fine china with a gold border is kept. His glasses are pushed down to the end of his nose because he can't read with them on. He holds the letter at arm's length, out on his left-hand side, to use his good eye. He moves his lips and mutters to get his mouth and his mind around the shape of the sentences and then he pushes his glasses back up, nods and looks at them, her mother and Liliana, to make sure they are paying attention. Then he slides the glasses back down and begins to read it out loud, the single sheet of thin paper covered on both sides in Stefano's cramped handwriting.

In this way, they have learned that the city of Tripoli has great white buildings and walls of stone. That when approached from the sea, it looks like a giant castle. That the bay in which it sits is guarded by rocky islands, and that at one end of that bay is the Kasbah, a fortified castle that now contains the government offices where he had to queue for hours to get his documents stamped. That it is a desert town, the end and beginning of many caravan routes across the Sahara. Stefano has told them how camels bring barrels filled with water into the city from the wells outside, and that the men in his boarding house named the camel that supplies their household Arturo because that is what the camel-driver's shout to urge his animals on sounds like to Italian ears. Liliana and her parents have heard too about the construction work going on across the city, all the beautiful new buildings, the Governor's Palace and the grand hotel, the cathedral and the theatre, and how water pipes have been laid. They have celebrated, belatedly, with him the moment when the pipes reached his street to the west of the city, rendering Arturo and his fellow camels obsolete.

They have heard something of the contrast between the new Italian section and the old town, its narrow streets covered with matting or built over so that they are like tunnels where the blinding sun and dazzling whiteness outside can penetrate only in beams that break through the gaps or the specially built shafts in the stone, chimneys of light. He has told them about the markets, jewellers, butchers and bakers, the weavers with their hand looms, the shoe-makers and the tanners, the candle-makers and the perfumers crowding these thoroughfares. Stefano has noted the absence of native women. How, if they come out at all, they are covered from head to toe in white cloth, with only their left eye showing. There has been some mention too of other women, of the *Ouled Nails* exotic dancing girls from Algeria, whom he has seen perform a belly dance in a café, gyrating their hips and swaying. His friend Alfonso, whom he met on the crossing, took him there. He saw some of the Italian men, army officers or the businessmen who frequent such establishments, sloppily kiss silver coins and press them, wet, onto the girls' foreheads.

Her mother was shocked to be told such a thing and, in her reply, Liliana told Stefano as much and asked if this Alfonso was a suitable companion. Liliana has struggled to think of things to narrate in her letters. Her life seems so humdrum and drab in comparison. Every week the same routine. Church on Sundays, rosary on Wednesday evenings, Saturday rallies with the fascist youth and only the occasional trip to the cinema to enliven it all. She is working now, in the office at the Hensemberger factory. There was a drama three months ago when a young woman in the assembly plant, Angela, was arrested for distributing seditious pamphlets, but that is a rare thing. There is a limit to how interesting she can make invoices for electrical storage batteries and letters about locomotive parts.

Stefano has told them that the streets of Tripoli's old town are too narrow for cars, and cannot even accommodate loaded camels or donkeys. Goods are carried by porters, their loads on their backs or their heads. Here, Stefano's interest wanes, and usually he moves on to preparations for the race, work on the track and the cars. Always the cars: the brand new two-litre Bugatti in which Materassi roared to victory in 1927 around the new circuit with banked curves. The Type 26 Maseratis, driven by Alfieri Maserati and Carlo Tonini that year, with an average speed of 113.37 kilometres per hour. The amazement in the pits when Borzacchini came in after driving on the rim for seventeen kilometres after a puncture. The drama this year when Materassi turned up at the starting line in his Talbot despite being disqualified. But the disqualification was applied anyway, which made for a boring race because Nuvolari was bound to win.

After the letter has been read and the three of them have commented, Liliana is allowed to take it away and pore over her brother's words.

But today is different. When her father takes the letter from the envelope, a smaller, tightly folded piece of paper falls out. Her father picks it up and examines it. 'For you,' he says. It is a sheet folded into three and then into three again, forming its own envelope and tucked into itself – something Liliana showed her big brother how to do years before, when he wanted to send a *billet doux* to a girl he admired. He has written Liliana's name on the front.

She clutches this special note just for her with excitement. He is coming home. Perhaps the letter will say that he has made his fortune sooner than he thought and he is going to stay; he will not be leaving again. Or perhaps that he is going to ask their parents to let him take Liliana back to Tripolitania with him this time when he leaves. Either of the scenarios would do. Marginally, she favours leaving, but would settle for having her brother back. She is lucky to have the job at Hensemberger, everyone tells her so, when so many men have been laid off and are desperate for work, but she would leave it at the drop of a hat. Perhaps Stefano will have made enough money to set up his own garage, and she can be his secretary and organiser. Then all the best bits of their old life will resume.

He will take her to the race track again. He will open up the engines and show her their insides and tell her things she doesn't understand or care about, saying words to which she can only fleetingly attach any meaning: carburettor, cylinder head, tyre gauge, spark plug. Sometimes these phrases he uses, the ones that have a ring to them, play in her head, but their only significance is a feeling of him, of her brother, his passion and his expertise. What she is really hoping is that he will introduce her to the dashing drivers, and now that she is older, perhaps one of them will notice her. Every week she hands over most of her wages to her mother but the little she is allowed to keep she has been saving for a dress to wear to the track. She has an idea of herself on a racing driver's arm. She knows she is not pretty, but she wonders whether, with a bit of money, she could be glamorous.

They are sitting on the sofa waiting for her father to finish his preparatory first reading. Liliana is itching to read her private message. She can hardly wait. At the same time, she is thinking about the race next month and wondering whether Tazio Nuvolari will be competing. He is so handsome and debonair. They call him the flying man from Mantova.

Unfortunately, he is married, but still thrilling to watch in the newsreels at the cinema, a daredevil. To see him in real life – that would be a thing.

Her father pauses in his reading. He is still on the first side of the sheet. He glances warily across at Liliana and her mother, shakes his head, sighs heavily and returns to the letter.

Something is wrong. Her mother reaches for Liliana's hand and grasps it.

Her father bites his top lip, sucks the end of his moustache and then puffs it back out. He clears his throat and begins to read.

Stefano says that he is very sorry, but he has to postpone his trip home. He has had unexpected expenses. He hopes that next year, perhaps, if things go well . . . He might get a bonus after the race, if it is successful, although at the moment even its continuation is in jeopardy because of a great hole in the funds. The race this year was disastrous, he says, and there is talk of the organisers abandoning it. He tells them too that he is well and that he has ridden a camel for the first time, and that the experience made him seasick. He does not explain what the unexpected expenses are. He says he can still get them two tickets for the Monza race. They can draw lots.

'What does it mean?' Liliana's mother asks.

'He's not coming,' her father says. 'He's not coming home next month.' He takes his glasses off and puts them on the sideboard, rubs his brow and strokes his fingers across the eyelid of his useless right eye. Liliana's mother lets go of her hand and stands up, undoes her pinny and drapes it over her arm. She takes a step towards her husband, and Liliana sees that her right hand is bunched into a fist, as if she might be about to punch him. Then she turns away and walks purposefully into the adjoining bedroom, shutting the door behind her. They hear one high-pitched, mournful cry that then settles into repetitive moans.

'She'll be all right,' her father says to Liliana. 'She'll grieve and then she'll get used to it.' He stands with his arms hanging by his side, shaking his head.

'But what about me?' Liliana mutters. The notion that it is just her now, here on her own with her mother and father until the end of time, is so dreadful that she has to put her hand to her mouth to stop herself screaming.

Her father turns his head to the side and fixes her with his good eye. He looks at her blankly for a moment. 'Keep an eye on your mother. I'm off to work,' he says. He means he is going to see if there is any day labour down at the railway yard. He'll stand up as straight as he can and try to look lively, but likely as not, he won't be picked. His partial blindness makes him a liability when cranes are swinging girders about in the air. And he's too old. He used to be a signalman, with his own wooden office warmed in the colder months by a paraffin heater, but he hasn't had a regular job for four years. Without the money Stefano sends home, the family would struggle even more than they do.

Liliana waits for her father to leave and then she pulls on her hat and jacket and goes out herself. A small part of her hopes that her own personal letter is going to explain things differently. Maybe Stefano has decided to save the money he would have spent coming home to pay for her passage to Tripolitania. As long as she doesn't read it, she can believe that this is a possibility. She can imagine that this delay is all about her. She walks quickly down the street and on into the centre of town, hardly aware of her surroundings, concentrating on this scenario. It will be hard for her parents if she leaves too, but it will have to be endured. A brief image of her weeping mother intrudes, and she pushes it away. What is there for her here, without her brother to introduce her into a more exciting world? To continue working at Hensemberger? To always scrape for the next lira? To marry one of the thuggish local boys and never amount to anything?

She has entered the great open space of Piazza Mercato and stops under the colonnade. She cannot wait any longer. She takes the note out of her pocket. On the other side of the square they are building a new cinema. The scaffolding is up, and a cluster of men are examining the work in progress. The hoarding that conceals the lower part of the construction site carries a poster announcing a rally to celebrate the sixth anniversary of the fascist march on Rome. There is an image of Mussolini with his fist raised and his mouth open, surrounded by a crowd of fervent young men. She looks down at the note in her hot hands. She has the sense that it carries her fate. She swallows. She unfolds it and reads it quickly.

She feels sick. Her brother, he tells her, has got married. 'Sort of married.' Whatever that might mean. He says he has been lonely. She stuffs the note back into her pocket and walks on, threading her way through the crowds and the white-tented stalls. Her mind is a jumble. Her brother. Married. She finds she is standing beside the usual vegetable stall. 'Signorina,' the stallholder, an old peasant with a dirty check headscarf, says. Her hands are streaked with the mud of the countryside. 'Lovely beans, fresh today,' she says, indicating a sackful of flat green Romano beans. She digs one muddy hand into the mound, picks up a handful and allows them to trickle back down so that Liliana catches their fresh, grassy scent. Liliana's mother loves this kind of bean cooked with tomatoes and garlic. But what is the point of green beans now? Liliana shakes her head and walks on. She passes the chicken man, the cake shop and the wine and oil stall, hardly noticing where she is going.

He has been lonely! He cannot know the meaning of the word.

She walks through the town, past the cathedral of San Giovanni, and then turns right towards the bridge and there, after nearly getting knocked down by a man driving a cart pulled by a donkey, she steps down onto the path beside the river. She sits on a bench beneath the oak trees, the leaves just starting to turn, the Lambro gurgling past. She reads the letter through again.

He has married a local girl. Her name is Farida. 'It's a bit of a shock,' he says, 'but you know I'm of an age, and there aren't any available Italian girls here; they're all married and they've come with their family. Or they're the flashy ones who like a man in uniform. They don't mean greasy overalls. Not that sort of uniform.'

That's not funny, and I'm not going to laugh, she thinks. She wants to be one of those flashy girls. He mentions again the pair of tickets he has arranged for the Monza race. But why would she want to go to watch the race without Stefano?

She looks at the patterns of light pooling onto the ground between the leaves, and she thinks that her life is in ruins. Her brother is not going to save her. There is no escape.

'Don't tell Mother and Father,' Stefano adds, 'not yet.'

Sometimes, in the gaps between Stefano's longer missives, a postcard arrives, and these Liliana has ranged along the back of the chest of drawers in her bedroom. She has pictures there of the new cathedral in Tripoli with its Romanesque bell tower, which is not quite finished yet, of the dockyard, and of a street corner with a bar called Bar Italia, a local woman in traditional dress, a castle beside the sea, a row of palm trees with sand dunes behind, a camel sticking out its huge tongue, and a picture of Emilio Materassi in his Bugatti when he won the Tripoli Grand Prix the previous year, in 1927. Among them is a photograph of a local girl. 'Arab beauty' is the caption. She has a dark cloth over her head, high arched eyebrows, sloping dark-rimmed eyes, silver hoops in her ears that look to be the size of bracelets, and a great quantity of other jewellery hanging round her neck and down her front, filigree pieces and something that looks like a scroll dangling from a chain. Fixed somehow to the left side of her head is a thin platelet of beaten metal, like a little cap. There is a mark down her chin below her bottom lip and another on her forehead. Her pale arms are bare and her expression difficult to decipher. It is not a defiant look, but it is not a welcoming one either. A kind of emptiness. As if she were allowing the photographer to do his business because she must, but was holding something back.

When she gets home, Liliana looks at the postcard again. Perhaps the girl her brother has married looks like this one. She stares at her with a new hostility. What she formerly interpreted as reluctance to be photographed she now sees as arrogance and disdain. This dreadful creature with her unexplained 'expenses'. What were they? Didn't she have enough bangles?

Liliana turns the card to face the wall. She cannot bear to look at the savage who has stolen her brother and her future away.

HABIBTI

Item: A squashed piece of chocolate wrapped in green foil.

Zaida had made three attempts to phone home to Tripoli but had not succeeded in getting through to her mother. Not even a dialling tone, just a high-pitched drone, the operator reported, suggesting that she should check the number and that it might be out of use. Zaida thought it was probably to do with whatever tapping device the authorities had put on the line. She was used to it crackling and to hearing a third person breathing or even talking sometimes, but to not get through at all was new. She was sure her mother must know about the shooting, but she might not know that both men were still alive.

The line didn't work this time either. She gave the operator the number of their neighbour, Abu Masoud, who lived opposite them on the sandy road on the west side of Tripoli. As the phone rang, she pictured her family home and the wild blue flowers that grew over the garden fence at the front and the Mediterranean glittering turquoise behind. She had been to the beach here in Ostia, the port of Rome, but the sea there didn't seem to sparkle the way it did back home. Abu Masoud answered. He said her mother had been phoning the flat in Rome. Zaida could tell from the echoey sound that his line was tapped. She wondered if he also knew this. 'There's no one there,' she said. 'We're all at the hospital. And anyway, we moved. We're not in that flat any more.'

She couldn't help it if her mother was going to get misinformation too.

'Give me the name and telephone number of the hospital and the ward, and I can tell her,' he said.

But she would be passing the information on to more than her mother. 'They are both critical,' she said. 'Very badly hurt. They might die.' She muttered to herself, 'But they might get better, God willing,' and touched her fingers to the silver Hand of Fatima that hung around her neck.

'I am so so sorry,' he said. 'May they recover, *Inshallah*. I have a pen. Give me the hospital details.'

'Abu Masoud,' she said, 'Abu Masoud can you speak up? I can't hear you.'

'I'm still here,' he said loudly.

She hung up.

On the way back to the ward, she passed the stripy-haired nurse from earlier going in the other direction. 'How are you doing?' the nurse said.

'Fine,' Zaida said.

'I'm sorry you don't have a relation around to look after you.'

'Me too.'

'Isn't there even a distant one?' the nurse said. 'We all have an auntie's second cousin we can dig up from somewhere, don't we?'

The nurse wasn't talking about people like Zaida. People in exile, whose relations were all on a different continent, apart from the brutally injured ones. She thought of her mother and her grandmothers and her big sisters, and how far away they were and how she couldn't even get through to them on the phone. She managed a smile because the nurse was trying to be kind. 'My other relations are all in Libya,' she said. 'They're not allowed to leave the country. No one is, without official permission, and they wouldn't get it because my father is an opponent of the regime.'

The nurse didn't say anything, but she was listening.

'My family in Libya has to be very careful. Hundreds of people have been arrested. You've probably seen that in the newspapers.' The nurse was affable and well intentioned but Zaida had to be careful about giving lectures. Her father had drummed it into her that they were guests in Italy, had found sanctuary here and must behave respectfully towards their hosts. She understood. She did. Up to a point. The thing was, though, that no one in Italy seemed to know about Libya. She could have understood it if they were talking about the Kazakh Republic or some other unheard-of part of the Soviet Union where Italians had probably never been, but this was Libya. The place where Italy had been the boss. Italy's fourth shore. Back home, none of it had been forgotten, and yet over here they didn't even teach it in history at school. Or not at her school anyway.

'But your family in Libya is safe?' the nurse said.

Zaida nodded. 'My father had to get out or he would have been put in prison. Not for doing anything bad.' She shook her head vehemently. 'For trying to do something good and brave. That's why Colonel Gaddafi wants him dead.'

She shouldn't have said the word 'dead'. As soon as it was out of her mouth she clapped her hand to her face to try to stop a horrible moan coming out. She had to be strong.

The nurse put a hand on Zaida's shoulder and gripped it. 'Your father's condition is stable,' she said. 'Don't worry. We are looking after him. And the police say that the attackers have left the country.'

'Yes,' Zaida said between her fingers.

'And we're protecting him.'

Zaida lowered her hand.

'He's terrible, that Gaddafi,' the nurse said. 'Sending assassins after peaceful people.'

'Yes,' Zaida said. 'He can't win the argument by reason and so he shuts them up another way.'

'Terrible,' the nurse said again.

'When I grow up, I'm going to be a lawyer,' Zaida announced. She had been thinking about it for a while. She wanted to be a dancer really, but perhaps a lawyer was more useful.

'Good for you,' the nurse said.

She was going to dedicate herself to the betterment of the human race, and fighting against ignorance.

'How come your father brought you here with him?' the nurse said. 'Wouldn't you have been better off at home with your mother?'

Her father had come into her room that night when she lay sleeping. It was his kiss that woke her. She had rolled out of bed after he had gone, and stood on the stairs listening to her parents making their hushed preparations, their fierce whispers, the argument about whether he should take her or not, what was best. He needed to leave immediately. The men from the revolutionary committee would be coming for him the next day, or the one after. He was going to try to get to Rome and to the sanctuary of their friend Madame Simone's home there. It was now or never. Her mother couldn't bear to part with Zaida, her baby, but she wanted a different life for her last child, a freer one. Her father didn't want to split a mother and her daughter apart, and he worried what would happen if they got caught at the border. Back and forth the conversation went. It could have gone either way. She had understood that they were thinking of her and that her days of living with both of her parents had come to an end. She had run upstairs and got dressed in the dark. She had packed a small bag. 'I'm coming,' she had announced. She was eleven years old. It was time for her to assume her destiny. 'You can't go on your own, Baba, you don't know how to cook.' There was sweat pouring down her father's face even though it was early morning and still cool, the sun not yet up. Her mother was crying.

'It's a long story,' she said to the nurse, 'but my parents wanted to give me an education and the chance for a better future.'

The nurse nodded.

'We ran away, my father and I. We sneaked across the border into Tunisia and then we came to Rome because we had a friend here, my sort of godmother, Madame Simone, and she helped us.' Khal Abramo had followed later. His reasons for fleeing were different from her father's. They were personal ones, he had said.

'And where is she now? Can't she look after you?'

Zaida shook her head. 'She was old,' she said in a low voice. She wasn't going to say that word again, not on purpose.

'Poor child.' The nurse gave Zaida's shoulder another squeeze and then let go. 'I thought you were part Italian.'

'I am. I'm half Italian. On my mother's side,' she said. Her grandparents were not married. The union that had produced her mother was not sanctioned by Church or state, but still.

59

'Not officially,' she said. She wanted to add something in case it sounded like she was boasting or thought that being Italian was innately better than being Libyan, which it was not, but she couldn't think what.

'Ah, there you are, then,' the nurse said. 'Something will turn up, you'll see.' She patted Zaida's arm again and moved on down the corridor.

There was a bench behind Zaida. The clock on the wall said it was 2 p.m. She decided she would give herself five minutes. She sat down. A conversation she had had with Khal Abramo came into her mind. She had asked him why people here didn't seem to know anything about Libya. In the thoughtful way he had, he looked at her before replying, as if measuring what level of answer to provide. 'There are two sides to that question,' he said. She could tell there were more, but he was simplifying it for her. 'There are those who know and choose not to speak of it, to hide it, even, and there are those who do not know because they have never been told and so do not realise that there is anything to know.' She thought about that for a while. 'So, if we don't know what we don't know,' she said, 'we don't know to ask the questions in the first place.' 'Exactly,' he said. He told her that people often hide what they can't bear to see or what shames them or what they fear would make their lives impossible. 'Like Baba,' she had said, 'having to hold his political meetings in secret.' Abramo nodded. 'Yes. People create and keep secrets for all sorts of reasons, good as well as bad, to protect themselves or others, as well as to conceal abuse, but whatever the reason, the effect is the same. To live with a secret is to be shackled.' Remembering how sad Abramo had looked when he said that made her want to run back to the ward where he lay, but she didn't move. She was conscious of her own secret. She had not revealed to the hospital authorities that Abramo was her uncle and a sort of shame, as if she had disowned him, came over her. But it was the opposite of that. She wanted only to keep him safe. 'Life's a compromise, *habibti*,' her uncle had told her. 'People lock their monsters away and they brick up the doorway so they can't hear the screams.' She thought the monsters he was talking about were all the bad things that Italy had done in Libya, like the concentration camps and the hangings, but at some point she realised that he wasn't talking about Italy and Libya any more, but about himself and about how his life had been in Tripoli, where men like him had to hide their true natures. 'The more you try to suppress a secret, the more your actions are bound by it,' he said. How lonely Abramo must have been, she thought.

She blinked and stared around her.

In the wall opposite was a long, low cupboard door. It had a round keyhole, but she knew it was the kind that she would be able to open with her fingernails. It probably contained electrical things. She looked up and saw a rectangular vent in the corridor ceiling. If she moved the bench along a metre and stood on its arm, she could press the vent open and pull herself up inside. She imagined crawling along the ventilation duct that must lie above, a secret passageway through the hospital.

Cubbyholes, broom cupboards, boiler rooms, cellars, out-buildings, doorways marked as being for the use of authorised staff only, anonymous urban shelters that occupied the in-between places and that other people might pass without seeing – they always shone out at Zaida as if they had a neon sign above. She had a mental map of them on all of her habitual routes through the city. She knew how big they were, how visible from the road, whether there was room to lie down, stand up, for two or three people. She considered ease of access, how overlooked the entrances were and whether there was a separate exit.

In their apartment block here in Rome, she had a secret underground hiding place. The building straddled two streets and had two separate entrances. One of them led to the flats on Stairway A, where they lived on the eighth floor in the apartment that had belonged to Madame Simone. The other led to those on Stairway B. Each flat had access to its own lockable storage area down in the basement, cell-like bunkers with metal doors off windowless corridors, which were lit by strip lights on a timer that crackled and whined when they were switched on.

At the end of the corridor on which their lock-up was housed, slotted in beyond the last of the metal doors, Zaida had discovered a different sort of door, a wooden one that was almost invisible because it was painted white like the concrete walls. It opened onto musty stairs that led even further down, to a passageway with a dirt floor that in turn led to a parallel set of stairs back up to another door and to the mirror set of storage cells that lay beneath Stairway B. There, going round pushing on all of the metal doors, she had found an unlocked one that was empty. The key had been left in the lock on the inside and she had pocketed it. The owner of the flat to which the storage space was attached might just have chosen not to use it. Or the flat itself might have been unoccupied. She had put some blankets and cushions from their own lock-up in it, and some tins of borlotti beans. She checked it regularly but was sure no one else ever went there.

Of all Zaida's hiding places, this was the best because it could be more than a temporary refuge. If they were being targeted or watched, or felt that they could not go home, she imagined that she would lead her father and perhaps Khal Abramo too down to this underground space. They might be seen going into their own building but then, once inside, they would disappear and wait it out.

But now here she was, on her own in the hospital, and her hiding-place planning was exposed as a silly, childish game.

If Madame Simone were still alive, she would be able to look after Zaida. Or if, as the nurse said, she had some distant relation. How lovely it would be if an auntie were coming. She imagined a big robust woman with an ample bosom and strong arms, like Madame Simone had been the first time they had come to Rome, when Zaida was six. She thought of how it would feel to be held, and even though she was a big girl now, probably not far off fully grown, even though all that was the case, she imagined this solid, fleshy aunt lifting her onto her lap and cradling her. She would smell of biscuits and eau de cologne. 'Darling,' the big aunt would say. '*Habibti*. Auntie's going to take care of everything.'

Zaida jerked awake when someone tapped her shoulder. 'What?' she said. 'What is it?' She was lying on her back on the bench.

The young nurse with the glasses and curly red hair, who put Zaida in mind of a squirrel, was leaning over her. 'You can't sleep in the corridor,' she said.

Zaida rubbed her bleary eyes to get them into focus, swung her legs down and sat up. The nurse seemed to be waiting for her to speak. 'Is there any news?' she said at last.

The nurse shook her head.

Zaida stood up. This nurse didn't like her and Zaida couldn't see what she could do about it because it was a problem in the way that the nurse saw things. Zaida looked down at their feet, hers and the nurse's, at her own red pumps and the nurse's regulation soft-soled white lace-ups, and waited for the nurse to leave.

When she had gone, Zaida took up her battle stance, spreading her arms, stretching out the index finger of her right hand to infinity. It was something Madame Simone had taught her when she was a little girl. 'I am a warrior,' she said under her breath, summoning the energy of the female ancestors who had helped form her and without whom she would not be here. Sometimes she chose Simone, who had lived a life without compromise but full of love. Other times she focused on her own mother, who had not wanted Zaida to leave, but had allowed it all the same. More often than not, she thought of her legendary grandmothers who, when they were very young women, fifty years before, had ridden across the desert carrying their babies while bombs rained down. Today, though, she thought of an old Bedouin woman from Cyrenaica, Zohra by name. When the grandmothers were on the verge of death, in an abandoned village in the desert wasteland, with neither food nor water and in mortal need, Zohra appeared as if by magic and saved their lives.

There was a commotion further up the corridor. A hospital bed was being pushed at speed by a porter, with the nice nurse, the one with the stripy hair, holding aloft a bottle of liquid attached by a tube to the patient as she trotted alongside. As it passed, Zaida saw it was her uncle in the fast-moving bed and her stomach turned over. 'Where are you taking that man?' she said.

'Theatre,' the nurse said.

'I thought he was out of danger,' Zaida called after them.

'I'll come and find you later,' the nurse said. 'Your father is stable. Try not to worry.'

Zaida hurried back to her father.

'All is well. No disturbances, Signorina,' the guard at the door said.

'I brought you some chocolates,' she said, fishing a couple out of her pockets and dropping them into his lap.

She seated herself at her father's side and resumed her vigil.

AN OASIS TOWN IN CYRENAICA

Item: A postcard depicting a camel and its rider silhouetted against a low red sun setting over the desert.

Stefano has acquired a wife. He didn't set off into the desert with that intention and it still isn't entirely clear to him how it happened, but it did. His life in Tripoli has changed.

By day, when he is at work, he almost forgets. He will look up from the car engine he is engrossed in and the fact of her will come to him, so extraordinary that he cannot take it in. He wants to run home to check whether he has dreamed her up, so impossible is it that such a thing could have happened to him, to an ordinary man like him. But he knows he lacks the imagination to invent such a creature as Farida.

He thinks, what have I done? And sometimes the question is full of wonderment and sometimes of dread, but mostly it swings wildly from one to the other like a needle on a barometer when a storm is coming. He has spent all of his savings, everything he had put aside for a trip home, on paying the bride-price and on an apartment for them in Tripoli's old town. He can't think how he will ever repay Alfonso all the money he owes him, but Alfonso will have to wait.

He is awed by her strange and foreign perfume, by her earthiness and her delicacy, by her presence. He sleeps with her in his arms and when he wakes in the night and feels her there, still enfolded, it seems to him that they are on a raft together, sailing the deep darkness of the Tripoli night.

It is early morning and she is not yet awake. He has opened the door of their cave-like room to let in some light and he has lain back down beside her. How did this happen, he thinks. You are going along in your little life, one thing seeming to lead to the next, thinking you know what is coming and then, wham, everything changes.

~

Back in April, after the Grand Prix was over, there was a slack period at work. Alfonso was in town for a few days. He was about to travel to the eastern colony of Cyrenaica and he invited Stefano along.

Alfonso painted a wonderful picture of the Cyrenaica desert. South of Benghazi and west of the Great Sand Sea, there was an oasis town where date palms swayed and a salt lake shimmered beneath a rose-pink moon. And that was where he was headed. 'It will be an adventure,' Alfonso said. 'We will sleep under the desert sky and drink camel milk by starlight.'

Stefano thought that he would prefer a glass of wine, but didn't say so.

'And you need a holiday. When did you last have a holiday?' Alfonso pressed him.

Stefano had never had a holiday, but it wasn't something he had hankered after either. Men like Alfonso, well-to-do businessmen, they took holidays, but not people like Stefano. And anyway, he was saving up for a trip back home. He hadn't been back to Italy once and he wanted to see his family. In particular, he wanted to see his little sister, not just because he missed her lively little face, but because something in the tone of her letters was making him uneasy.

But Alfonso said he would bear all the expenses, that he could really do with Stefano's company, that he would be a help. That was when Stefano had relented.

He had imagined that there might be some practical assistance he could offer. That he could at least look after the engine of the car they would be travelling in if it broke down. But they had discarded the vehicle where the road ended in a dusty town called Ajedabia and then had struck off into the desert with a pack of camels, of all things, and so what kind of help Alfonso had meant was not clear to him.

Stefano was a practical man and he liked having things to do, but when he adjusted the saddlebags on the camels, because he saw a smarter way of attaching the load, the camel-driver took offence and cursed him. Alfonso explained that the relationship with the natives was very different in the desert. You had to be careful because you needed them to lead you true, not to abandon you or hand you over to brigands.

As they plodded along interminably on their swaying beasts, Alfonso regaled him with tales of saboteurs who appeared and melted away again like mirages, so that you pinched yourself afterwards and wondered if it were a waking dream until you saw that the water-carriers had been slashed and the camels cut loose.

They didn't only talk about bandits. They talked about the state of their country too and Alfonso explained Carlo Rosselli's theory of liberal socialism and they both agreed that was what they were: liberal socialists. Carlo Rosselli had been given a five-year sentence and was on the prison island of Lipari. Alfonso had a way of putting things that helped clarify them in Stefano's head. It was as if he were saying what Stefano had already half-thought, but hadn't had the words to think properly, and to hear them expressed in this way, in whole sentences, sharpened his understanding. He was glad of this, despite the fact that what Alfonso told him was not hopeful. The voices of opposition in Italy were becoming increasingly rare, and because the news was censored, people were kept in ignorance. Fascist slogans were written in large letters in public places. The Duce is always right, was one of them. Many people believed it to be true. They wanted to believe. It made life simpler. And even those who retained some independence of thought, and who were not in prison or in exile, were becoming quieter. They were cowed. You didn't know who was an agent of the regime. OVRA, the secret police, had a surveillance network, with spies in every aspect of life. You didn't know who to trust. And now that the Church and the regime were talking and Mussolini, 'an avowed atheist until the day before yesterday,' Alfonso said, had suddenly become God-fearing and kept declaring new religious holidays, there would be no stopping him. It was easier to give in and believe, hand yourself over, Alfonso said. It all increased Stefano's concern for Liliana. It would not be surprising if she were sucked in to this way of thinking. To cheer them both up after these depressing conversations, Alfonso would sometimes sing. He had a fine tenor voice and knew the words of many popular songs. He had seen Puccini's last opera, *Turandot*, at the Teatro Costanzi and had learned a wonderful aria from it, called 'Nessun dorma'. '*Vincerò*,' he warbled into the desert air, 'I will win.'

Often, though, they plodded along without speaking because the desert lent itself to that. You were travelling in silence, the hooves of the camels soundless in the sand, but you still seemed to have to raise your voice to be heard, as if there were inaudible noises that you were having to speak over. It was an effort to converse, and they didn't always make it.

Stefano wished he were back in Tripoli where there were roads and paving beneath your feet and a cappuccino to be had in the piazza. There in the city, when he saw camels being herded in their hundreds through the streets, he didn't mind them. They were part of the exoticness of his new home. But close up he found he didn't like them. They were smelly and unpredictable, and their breath was foul. They moved at an agonisingly slow pace.

He preferred cars.

It was very generous of Alfonso to invite him along on this trip, but Stefano wished that he had said no. There was a horrible aching monotony to the days, a piercing cold at night, sand everywhere, and a constant nagging thirst. There was nothing to do but to endure.

In the evenings they watched Moussa, the camel-driver, and Hussein, their guide and interpreter, play draughts by firelight using white shells and camel dung for pieces.

After three days of travelling through a flat, colourless waste tufted with grey brushwood, they saw a row of dunes ahead with a faint blur of green around, a greenish mist. As their beasts trudged up the slope the mist evaporated without providing the cool freshness it promised, because it was nothing but a mirage. They dropped down over the ridge to the little white desert town nestled beside a lake so blue and translucent it seemed of another world. But the lake was an illusion too because it was saltwater and no fish could live in it.

The banner of the Senussi religious order, a silver crescent and star on a black background, flew above the *zawiya*, the

Islamic school, in the main street. The Bedouin people of Cyrenaica were all followers of the Senussi. The town was on a trading route. Caravans passing through carried ivory and ostrich feathers from the south, Hussein explained, and occasionally, still, they might bring a human cargo, smuggled African slaves for the markets in the north. When he heard that, Stefano's horror of the desert and its places intensified. They had only just arrived in this town and he could not wait to leave. Alfonso told him they would not stay long. A day or two and they would be on their way again.

On the second night, they were sitting around a cooking fire with some men from the town when Stefano felt a shortness of breath. He thought it was something to do with the fumes from the brushwood their hosts had thrown on the flames. He stepped away from the circle.

He walked soundlessly out of the courtyard that adjoined the low mud-brick house where they were staying, down a winding sandy track between windowless houses with low doorways, all shut, to the fringe of date palms that edged the lake. He stood under a tree and attempted to clear his throat with forced coughs, but it was not the sort of discomfort that coughing could dislodge. He wondered if he were ill. His eyes swept over the cluster of houses under the purplish rocky outcrop that rose up behind them, on over the eerie blue shimmer of the lake to the soft pale sand dunes on the other side. It was the last half hour of daylight, when the colours took on an extra intensity. The sky was bluer than seemed right, and the endless sand glowed pink. Soon, he knew, the sun would fall out of sight and all colour would be sucked from the landscape.

For the life of him he couldn't imagine what he was doing in some unpronounceable oasis town. Having now tasted the camel's milk, he stood by his assertion that he preferred wine. The milk was bitter in the mouth and heavy in the stomach. There was no quenching of thirst to be had here.

He stood beneath the tree and gazed across the salt marsh until his eye found the sharp line of the distant horizon, and an awful feeling crept up, from his soft red leather backless shoes that had been a purchase in Ajedabia, under his loose cotton trousers and up through the middle of him to his painful chest. He was not a man given to contemplating the infinite, but here it was all around him, undeniable, the great vastness of space and the hidden stars up there in the cold firmament, the huge expanse of featureless sand stretching behind and in front of him, on and on, remorseless.

Stefano had felt alone many times before. In 1924, when the political leader he most admired, Giacomo Matteotti, was assassinated. At work in Monza when he was ostracised for not joining in with the fascist fervour sweeping through Lombardy. When the *squadristi* caught him with clandestine leaflets and decided to teach him a lesson. When his fiancée Teresa dumped him and started cutting him dead in the street. He didn't want to be political, not really. He wanted not to be bothered with it, to save his radical thinking for the smooth running of an engine and the calibration of the tyres, but he didn't see how to avoid it. When his own father had forced him to choose – fit in or leave – that was a terribly hard and isolated time, and sometimes he hated his father for it. Kowtowing to the regime. Yes sir. No sir. He had been desperately lonely too, despite his bravado, when he had left the family home and set off for this new life, and there was a moment when that loneliness had reached a kind of crescendo on the turbulent sea crossing between Italy and North Africa. But then he had met Alfonso, and they had shared a rum, while all about them people spewed and turned green and wailed, and he had forgotten his dread. With Alfonso, the only other one to be standing upright on that little steamer, he had found cheer, not just in the grog, but in his own youth and physical strength and endurance, in the admiration the older man had for his spirit of adventure. Since then, too, he had experienced many a lonely time in Tripoli. Everyone else seemed to be married and had wives to return to after work, or fiancées back home who were going to join them before too long. But despite all that he had made a life for himself, and there were plenty of people in Tripoli to have a coffee with, or pass the time of day. Then there were a few of the lads who congregated to play cards on a Saturday evening in a café on Piazza Italia. And Alfonso, when he came over on one of his regular business trips, sometimes with his lady friend Simone and sometimes alone; then they would meet up, and Stefano would go to places that otherwise he never frequented: the cabaret club inside the Arch of Marcus Aurelius; a bar in the old town where they saw exotic dancing and smoked hubbly-bubbly pipes; the western beach.

So the loneliness, it came and then it went again. But here in the great lonely desert, there was no hiding from it.

He was a speck.

He counted for nothing.

He was lonely beyond endurance.

He raised his hands to his face and covered his eyes, pressing his fingers to his eyelids. He let out a groan. A sound off to his right made him drop his hands and swivel in that direction, horrified at the thought of being observed, but it was only a camel, moving slowly because its legs were hobbled, seeking fodder. He wiped his face with the backs of his hands. He took a cigarette out of his jacket pocket and lit it.

He didn't let his eyes stray to the awful vastness again but pulled his gaze in closer. He stared at the squat houses. There was no welcome for him in any of them. Their inhabitants probably hated him without even knowing him because he was one of the *nazrani* and an oppressor. Alfonso might be happily *fahdling* there, doing a deal with the village chiefs about the lease of hectares of land and irrigation from the wells and the planting of olive groves and all that, but Stefano knew, as Alfonso surely must, that these people, even when they seemed to smile and shake your hand, to listen and nod and agree, even then they wished you gone.

He turned away from the houses and blew his cigarette smoke towards the clump of trees to his right. He glanced up at the fronds of the palm leaves and their pattern against the sky, and down at the shadows they cast on the sandy ground, and as his eye roved up and down he noticed that there was a person, standing very still behind the tree.

Someone was watching him.

Although his heart was banging inside his chest, Stefano dropped his cigarette and ground it out as if he had noticed nothing. Looking down at the shadows, he could detect the shape of the person, the spy, against the tree trunk. He observed how motionless the stranger was. They stood there, two metres apart, neither of them moving. A thousand thoughts passed through Stefano's mind, of spies and saboteurs and men with long knives, but uppermost was the knowledge that this intruder had seen him unmanned. It filled him with rage, and his hands formed into fists. Then, as it did in that place, the sun dropped away, and it was night. In that blind moment when the only light was the dazzling afterglow of the sun behind his eyelids, which was not a light to see by, before the spy could escape in the darkness, Stefano leapt across the distance that separated them and grabbed hold. The other person, smaller than he had expected, gasped and tried to wriggle away, but did not shout or fight back. An outer garment – they wore so many – came off in Stefano's hands, and he clutched again and wrestled the squirming creature to the ground.

And only then, when he was lying on top of her, did he fully realise that the stranger was a woman. His ribcage was pressed against the softness of her breasts. His could feel her heart beating. He could smell her cinnamon breath.

He blinked to adjust his eyes. The cool lilac glow of the stars and moon behind and far above them took over from the vanished sun and illuminated her face. She was no longer struggling. He knew he should get up quickly, but he didn't. He gazed upon her.

Then he heard the sound of men's voices approaching. He rolled off and jumped to his feet. He held out his hand to help the young woman up, but she spurned it and rose unaided. He handed her the piece of cloth that had fallen, and she wrapped it around her head and over her shoulders. He expected her to run away, but she did not. She stared straight at him and she spoke, although he did not understand what she said, and then she stood there, and they both waited for the men to arrive.

He had been in the country for three years and he had never before seen the face of a native woman close up. In Tripoli, if they went out at all, they were fully covered from head to toe. Shapeless bundles with only one eye showing. Not really women to him. Out here in the villages and in the countryside, he had seen a few at a distance, waiting their turn at the well, peering down from flat rooftops, but not up close.

Men carrying lanterns arrived and surrounded him. The

young woman was taken away and Stefano was marched back to the courtyard.

'What has happened?' Alfonso said. 'What have you done?'

'Nothing,' he said.

But he was wrong. It could not be brushed off. It was not nothing.

Together with their guide Hussein, Stefano and Alfonso were taken to another house, through a maze of courtyards and rooms into a central but bare room, lit by candles, where red-dyed camel-hair rugs were laid out in a circle. They stood there waiting, surrounded by muttering townsmen.

'Let me do the talking,' Alfonso said to Stefano.

Another man strode in, a grey-bearded sheikh in a dark blue robe. His flowing white jerd was pinned back to show the scimitar hanging from his belt, and his hand was on the pommel. He eyed Stefano with a ferocious malevolence. The sheikh spoke and others joined in. Then Alfonso spoke, and Hussein helped clarify his words. Alfonso holding out his hands, palms up in supplication, touching his forehead and then his collarbone, bowing his head, strange movements that Stefano instinctively recognised as ritual gestures of appeasement. He too bowed his head. 'Tell him I thought it was a spy,' he muttered, 'an intruder like you were talking about earlier. I had no idea it was a girl.'

'The damage is done,' Alfonso said. His face was grey in the candle light.

The sheikh lifted his hand from the sword and gestured for them to sit. They arranged themselves in a circle on the rugs.

'All right,' Alfonso said, 'all right,' more to himself than to Stefano.

A brazier was carried in so that tea could be brewed in the

corner. Low wooden stools were set out and bowls of dates and almonds placed on them. When the first cup of tea had been poured, the sheikh spoke again. Hussein translated. 'Young man, you looked upon my daughter's face,' he said.

Stefano admitted that this was the case.

'And did her face please you?'

Stefano bowed his head and nodded. He had it there in his mind's eye. The thick black plaits framing it, the tattoo mark on her chin, the gleam of silver at her ears and around her neck, her eyes in the moonlight, dark pools outlined in black.

Then the sheikh clapped his hands, and the girl appeared, veiled this time. The sheikh stood up and made a speech, and other men joined in, having their say. The girl stood in the middle of the circle.

There was something in the way they spoke, these men, that, even without understanding the actual words, Stefano grasped that the girl was not really of importance to them. Her opinion was not to be sought. She was disposable. And it wounded him.

The sheikh finished speaking.

'Take her. She is yours,' Hussein said.

'What does he mean?'

'She is yours now. You must pay fifty silver pieces.'

Stefano, bewildered, turned to Alfonso. 'They are propos-ing *madamato*,' Alfonso said. 'They call it *mabrukah* here. It is a sort of marriage contract.'

'Marriage!' Stefano said. 'I don't even know her.'

'It's not a contract that would be recognised in Italy or sanctioned by the Church,' Alfonso said. 'But it happens in the colonies all the time. In Eritrea and in Italian Somalia, anyway. I haven't come across it here before, but that doesn't mean it isn't happening. I don't know everything.'

'I thought you did,' Stefano said, weakly trying to make a joke.

'It gives you rights but also responsibilities. Conjugal rights, I mean,' Alfonso continued seriously, as if Stefano had not even spoken. 'But you have to look after her and pay for her and maintain the household if there are children.'

'Conjugal rights,' Stefano repeated stupidly. 'She's only a girl.'

Alfonso turned to speak to Hussein, and there was a muttered exchange. Stefano had hardly learned a word of Arabic but he knew the numbers. He heard them say fifteen. 'Fifteen,' Alfonso confirmed, 'or she might be sixteen. Plenty old enough round these parts to be married.'

She was ten years younger than him. More or less the same age as his little sister. Stefano's thoughts flew to Liliana, far away in Monza, and he wondered if he would ever see her again.

Alfonso was still talking, telling him about soldiers he knew who had set up with local women, back when he used to trade in Eritrea. 'We can perhaps walk away from this,' Alfonso said, 'but we will have to pay the silver anyway. I can cover it. It will be a bit of a mess, but it doesn't look like they intend to kill us.'

'But what will happen to the girl?' Stefano asked.

'It is hard to know. There is such a gap between our understanding.'

Stefano's thoughts were in a fog. 'If we take her back to Tripoli with us,' he said, 'we could—'

'What? Send her to the nuns? Set her free? There is no such thing for women. They have no rights,' Alfonso said.

'But what does *she* want?' Stefano said.

'Oh, for goodness sake,' Alfonso said. 'How long have you been in this country?'

'I don't want to force myself on her,' Stefano said, conscious that he already had.

'I think,' Alfonso said, 'that it is too late for such niceties.'

'I must take her, then,' Stefano said.

'Let's not be hasty,' Alfonso said in his ear. 'Allow us to confer,' he said out loud to the assembled room, which Hussein translated. The sheikh, who had settled himself back down with his scimitar lying across his lap, wafted a hand at them, as if to say, take all the time you need. He spat a date stone daintily into a bowl and stroked the shaft of his weapon. He addressed the red-turbaned man sitting directly opposite him, the two of them leaning around the figure of the girl to see each other. The men drank their tea, cracked nuts, chomped dates. Some of them, unabashed, stared straight at Stefano and then muttered to each other. The girl stood in the middle like a statue, draped in cloth, ignored by all. He thought, if she can bear it, then so can I.

'Let me tell you something that no one else here in this country knows,' Alfonso said in a low voice, and he described his own marriage to a girl of sixteen whom he had not really known but who had captured his heart with her beauty. He revealed to Stefano that the French lady, Simone, who often accompanied him on his trips to North Africa was not his wife, but his mistress. That she was the one who made his marriage bearable and that, until he had met her, his life at home was a nightmare.

Stefano only half listened. He was too taken up with his own situation to be shocked by Alfonso's revelation or to see it as in any way relevant. He was mesmerised by the flickering shadows that the flames from the brazier cast along the far wall, and how they gave an impression of movement to the strange and motionless young woman. At the same time, his mind kept darting to Liliana. He was conscious of having abandoned her and that, if he borrowed all this money from Alfonso now, the abandonment would be prolonged. He feared for his sister without her big brother at her side. Then the doubts and the complications started to fade. His sister was far away, and he could do nothing for her if his throat were slit by a Bedouin tribesman. His thoughts came back to the girl standing in front of him. He was conscious that he had been trying to calculate something, a sort of sum going on underneath his other considerations, something about whether they could pay the money and leave without her and thus perhaps save her from social exclusion or worse, or they could pay the money and take her with them. He was starting to get a notion of which he would prefer. He was imagining lifting her veil and looking into her eyes, bowing his head, asking her forgiveness, claiming her. He was thinking that perhaps he did not have to be so lonely any more.

Alfonso tugged on his sleeve. 'I think this sheikh is a trickster. He seems like a cunning man to me, a fox. He is hoping to trick us into giving him money for this girl, but if we walk away what can he do? He might kick up a fuss, but then he'll forget about it.'

'But still, we cannot know what will happen to the girl.'

'Nothing will happen. She is his daughter.'

'I don't think that makes a difference,' he said.

'They want you to think that, Stefano. They can see that you are a soft-hearted man and they are making you feel responsible, but what happened? Nothing. You saw her face. It's not like in the city. Bedouin women only hide their faces before strange men. Within her tribe she probably mingles freely and without a veil.'

'But I *am* a strange man,' Stefano said.

Alfonso shook his head dismissively. 'You only saw her face. You didn't touch her.'

A pause.

'Oh, you did. You touched her?'

'I grabbed her. I thought she was a spy.'

Alfonso sighed. 'I suppose she *is* very pretty,' he said.

Stefano nodded.

'So what is your resolve?'

'To marry her,' Stefano said, getting to his feet.

'Ah well,' Alfonso said, offering his hand to be pulled up. 'You could probably do worse.'

The ceremony was simple and, apart from the handing over of the money, incomprehensible. The very next night, Stefano was given his own room and the girl, Farida, was brought to him, wrapped like a gift in many coloured garments of silk and wool, tied with gold and silver. She wore silk trousers under three tunics, each one a different shade of red; her chest was adorned with gold necklaces and brooches, and hooped earrings hung from her ears to her shoulders. Anklets banded her trousers and bracelets held her sleeves. On her feet she wore white leather slippers with gold tassels. Her hands were painted with intricate henna designs. When he lifted the many veils that covered her face, although her cheeks were marked with geometric patterns, her lips painted a glossy red, her plaits lengthened with twists of silver rope, he recognised the girl he had seen by starlight.

Somehow, as part of the bargain, Alfonso had acquired the sheikh's scimitar, with its curved blade and double-edged point, which he took back to Italy with him. He was immensely proud of it, as if he had won it in a duel.

Now here they are, Stefano and Farida, lying side by side, and if he waits quietly, watching, he will be there when she opens her eyes and he will be the first thing she sees.

'You have nothing to fear from me,' he said the first time that he lifted her veils. He did not expect that she would understand the words, but he hoped the sentiment would be clear.

'You have nothing to fear from me,' she responded.

He hid his astonishment. 'I will not harm you,' he continued.

'I will not harm you,' she repeated back to him.

She was just copying the sounds he made, but her ear was exceptional. She had caught his inflection exactly.

'I paid your father in silver pieces, but I don't own you,' he said. Above all, he needed her to know that she was not his chattel.

She gazed at him steadily, but didn't speak.

He could not be sure if he was making himself understood. He opened his arms to show his good intentions. She stepped forward and into them. He could hardly believe it, how she seemed to trust him so instantly. He felt that a solemn promise had been made. It went deeper than words.

All of that was three months ago. She has been studying Italian since, with the upstairs neighbour, and has made surprisingly fast progress.

Now, she opens her eyes and she looks at him.

'You are so beautiful,' he says, lifting her heavy hair away from her face.

'*You* are so beautiful,' she says. 'That is why I choose you.' And she laughs at his consternation.

A CRYING SHAME

Item: A boarding pass for a British Airways ticket from London Heathrow to Rome Fiumicino dated May 1980.

The hospital is enormous. Liliana arrives at its doors at 2 p.m., but they seem to be the wrong doors for the section she wants. She wanders about, trying to follow the signs, to find her own way, loath to ask directions. Each time she comes to a junction, she consults the map in the leaflet she picked up by the door, with its different colours to denote the different areas, but she can't relate it to where she is. Somewhere between London and Rome – cacophonous, intensely bright Rome, with its sky as blue as a child's colouring book version of a sky, a good fifteen degrees hotter than London, so that when she is not consulting the leaflet she is using it as a fan – somewhere in between the two cities her sense of purpose has deserted her. Her conviction, bolstered by Joan, urging her to go, not to waste this chance, has faltered.

'Keep calm,' Joan had advised but Liliana's heart is beating at twice its normal rate, there is a rushing in her head, her tinnitus is louder than usual, like a thousand urgent whispering voices. She is ludicrously overdressed for the weather in a long-sleeved blouse, trousers, cardigan and raincoat, with her voluminous silk scarf wound around her neck. Calm is not within her reach.

Everything is foreign. She has the feeling that if she speaks, no one will understand her.

She lugs her suitcase down an interminable corridor and climbs three flights of stairs because she can't find the lift. She emerges on a part of the third floor that does not connect with the section where her nephew is supposed to be. She follows a porter pushing a patient in a bed and thus discovers the lift. She gets out when he does, thinking it is the ground floor. The lift doors close behind her and she hears it whirr away. She watches the porter trundle down the dimly lit corridor and turn at a sign that says 'Morgue', and realises the person on the trolley is dead. A languor and an anguish grip her chest and she puts her fist against her breastbone to counter the pressure. She waits an age for the lift to return, and when it does she travels back up to the ground floor. She needs to start again. She goes back through the sliding doors and stands for a moment in the afternoon sunshine. There is a little stall selling drinks. She buys a bottle of cold lemonade from the man behind the counter. She is in a muddle. That much is clear. She is over-excited and trepidatious and muddled.

She did everything in such a rush. Cancelling appointments and the newspaper, paying bills, leaving a note for the milkman. All the little things that need doing before going away. While Joan was downstairs telephoning about flights, she had wrenched out the bottom drawer of her chest to reach the other, slimmer drawer that lay beneath. It is a sort of tray that used to slot into the top of her old travelling trunk. It has lain there hidden for years. She didn't open it. She barely looked at it. She placed it in the bottom of her suitcase, where it fitted snugly, and flung some clothes on top, and a random selection of scarves. She can't even remember what else she might have packed; hopefully some light summer frocks. It all happened so fast. There was no time to think.

She takes her raincoat off and hangs it over her arm. She unbuttons her cardigan. She has come rushing and racing and hurtling from London to Rome and now here she is, standing on a pavement in the shade of a roadside stall and she's not at all sure that coming was a good idea. She doesn't know this man in the hospital, and he doesn't know her. She shouldn't have let Joan persuade her.

A furled half-thought from yesterday suddenly flaps open like a banner in the wind: Abramo won't want to see her; she won't be welcome, because Stefano and his family don't want her. *Persona non grata*, she thinks. Periodically, over the years, this explanation for the unanswered letters, the silence from across the sea, has tormented her. Lord knows she didn't want her family in Libya to be dead, but if they hadn't all been killed in the war – and Abramo being alive enough to be shot two days ago proves that they hadn't – then might this other thing be true? She puts the empty lemonade bottle back on the counter.

'Come far?' the man in the stall says.

'From London,' she says.

'Visiting someone, are you?' he says.

She nods. She has come all this way, after all, and even if it were true that her brother dropped her, which it is not, Abramo is a different generation. And hasn't she done her penance now? All those years of living without them, of being denied any news, her pale London life. Let me back in now, she thinks.

'So nice to get visitors,' the stallholder says, 'it makes all the difference.'

'It's my nephew,' she says. Of course it isn't true that the family cut off ties. She just invented that notion in some paranoid moment when the much likelier explanation that they were all dead was more than she could bear. Her brother would never have turned against her. Unless. She pushes the thought back down. She's not going down that maudlin path. Not now. 'Thank you,' she says to the lemonade-seller.

As she goes back inside the hospital, she feels a surge of excitement. Abramo is alive. Others might be too. She sees a place where she can leave her suitcase. Unencumbered, she asks the way to the ward, putting on a slight English accent. It feels safer somehow. The directions are quite simple, and involve following the yellow route. When she gets there and hesitantly identifies herself as the person who called the previous day from London, she is taken into the ward manager's office and told to sit down.

She discovers that two hours earlier, when she was still up in the air, somewhere over the Alps, perhaps when she was looking out of the little window and wondering at herself, unable to swallow the food they brought, imagining all sorts of different futures, the things that she would tell him and the things that she would ask, Abramo Cattaneo had died.

'He never regained consciousness,' the nurse says, 'not properly. He looked as though he was recovering, but then there was a setback.' She talks about plummeting blood pressure and an internal haemorrhage. 'We took him back to theatre yesterday evening but we couldn't save him,' she says.

Alan's voice sounds in Liliana's head. What a shame, he says. What a crying shame. His phrases to articulate an event, stock phrases, truisms that are so much more muted than

Liliana's experience, sometimes help soften a blow, spread the sharpness of it into something more diffuse. Sometimes.

'I came as fast as I could,' she tells the nurse, as if her speed is relevant. She can't take the information in. She wants to ask if the nurse is sure.

'We did all we could,' the nurse says. She starts shuffling through the papers on her desk, arranging them in a different order, looking for something. They have very scant information on him, she explains, and are hoping that Liliana will be able to fill in some of the blanks.

'Oh dear,' Liliana says.

As far as they knew, he lived alone in Rome, the nurse tells her, but the police were still making enquiries. He had his identity card in his jacket pocket, but it was damaged in the shooting and is not entirely legible. She pauses, looking down at her hands holding one of the pieces of paper, a typed form. She looks up and across the desk at Liliana. 'I'm sorry,' she says, 'that was insensitive.'

Liliana isn't following. 'Pardon?' she says. There does not seem to be sufficient room in her head to grasp what she is hearing.

'No, no, never mind,' the nurse says, 'my mistake.' She looks at the paper in her hand.

There is a diagram of a human form on the sheet of paper now uppermost on the desk. Circles have been drawn on the stomach and the chest and the right thigh. 'Oh,' Liliana says again, understanding that it shows the places where the bullets entered Abramo's body. The identity card must have been in his breast pocket. Internal injuries, she reads upside down. Multiple organ failure.

'We managed to extract some information from the card. It gave his place of birth as Tripoli in 1931,' the nurse says.

'No,' Liliana says.

'Isn't that right?'

'No,' Liliana says again, and she leans forward in the chair and drops her head into her hands. 'Oh God,' she says, 'oh God,' and for a while that is the only coherent noise she makes. Garish images are flashing behind her eyes, one after the other in quick succession, senseless and sickening. There is a girl lying in a pool of blood. There is a baby, a newborn baby with tiny wrinkled feet, smeared still in vernix. There is an old woman, like a witch, bending over a body, wrenching and tearing at it.

It is as if someone with a sharp hook is fishing these images out of a place deep inside where they have lain hidden. They were dormant, they were under rocks, behind locked doors, bolted in, imprisoned, and now they are being dragged out and freed, all at the same time, whether they like it or not, and they are being shaken awake, and they are monstrous.

The lurid images subside. She sits up.

The nurse has poured her a glass of water and is holding it out. 'Take your time,' she says.

'Thank you,' Liliana says. She reaches down for her handbag, unclasps it and finds her pills. 'Headache,' she explains. She takes two out of the box and swills them down with the water. 'Sorry,' she says. 'Yes, he was born in 1931. That would be right.'

The nurse lays her form on top of the report. 'Do you know who his next of kin might be?' she asks.

Liliana shakes her head. What exactly was the crying shame, she wonders. Was it her nephew's solitary death? Or was it that she had come at all? That she had known to come? That she had opened the newspaper yesterday morning and seen the article.

The nurse puts a question mark next to the line that says next of kin.

Or was the crying shame that Liliana had come too late? 'I'm too late,' she says out loud.

'I am sorry,' the nurse says. 'It must be a terrible shock.' She tips her head on one side and looks at Liliana as if she hadn't properly taken her in before. 'And you've come all this way,' she says.

Liliana bites her lip, looks down at her lap. 'Too late,' she says again.

'There was nothing you could have done,' the nurse says. It was quite natural, she adds, people often felt that if they had only arrived earlier or done something differently then the outcome might have been other.

But Liliana doesn't only mean too late for Abramo. She means too late for herself.

'I tried to keep in touch,' she says, 'but after I moved to England I never heard from them again. From the family, I mean. The war came along and of course there was fighting there too – in North Africa, I mean. But then, after the war, when we were allowed to correspond again, there was still no reply. Never a reply. I contacted the authorities. The Italian side and the British too, because by then Libya was under British administration. But there were, you know ... there were lots of Italians still living there, apparently. I thought perhaps they'd moved. They could have gone to Benghazi. He had talked of that, my brother. Benghazi was very heavily bombed in 1942. He always used to write. Regularly. Letters and postcards. He always did. I still have them.' Liliana becomes aware that she is burbling. She lapses into silence and looks across at the nurse, who is nodding gravely. 'He always used to write,' she says.

She fishes out a handkerchief from her handbag and pats her forehead. It is stifling in this little room. Airless. The nurse is giving her information about the next steps, but she is only half listening. All she needs to do now is get up, shake the nurse's hand, thank her and be on her way. She is picturing the suitcase that she has left downstairs and, in particular, the shallow tray at the bottom, the one that used to fit across the top of her travelling trunk and was originally intended for gloves and jewellery and ribbons – accessories, they would call them now – but for many years has contained the documents and small items she chose to keep from her time in Libya. She is thinking how among those items are two locks of dark baby hair, one cut from Abramo's head and one from Nadia's. The knowledge of that tuft of his baby hair two floors below is so infinitely poignant that she can hardly hold herself together. She hitches her handbag over her arm.

A few days ago, in the library, she was thinking about water that had passed and how it was no longer capable of turning the wheel, of grinding the corn. And then *this* happened. Whatever this was.

This bereavement.

This grinding.

She will return immediately to the airport and she will board the next flight to London and she will shut this back down. Quickly, before any more of the past seeps into and poisons her present, such as it is. She should never have come.

There would have to be an autopsy because of his death being a crime, and it might be some time before his body could be released for burial, the nurse is saying.

Liliana gets to her feet. 'Thank you for all you have done,' she says.

She came to visit a living man, not to bury a dead one.

THE DOMAIN OF THE SENSES

Item: A handwritten note scribbled on a sheet of paper bearing the logo of the Ambassadors Hotel, Via Veneto, Rome. It says: 'Tripoli cathedral. Midday. 8/5/1929. Don't forget.'

Liliana is on her way to Tripolitania to visit Stefano. Tomorrow morning she is to travel by train to Naples to board the mail boat, but tonight she is staying at a hotel in Rome.

She can still hardly believe that this day has come, that she has been allowed to travel, that her mother has let her go, that Stefano has sent the money for her ticket, that she has left her job at Hensemberger. Everything. All the different things that needed to align for this journey to take place.

She is in Rome. She is going to a fancy-dress ball. She has dabbed French perfume behind her ears and on her wrists.

She stands at the little balcony in her high hotel room, gazing down at the comings and goings in the street below, her extraordinary and daring costume shimmering and jingling around her. She feels lucky and strange and disorientated. Her prayers have been answered.

First of all came the telegram from Stefano. He wanted her to come to Tripoli for an extended visit without delay. He had a job for her and was sending funds for her passage. His subsequent letter explained that the Governor of Tripolitania himself, Marshal Badoglio, had intervened to save the Tripoli Grand Prix. As usual, Liliana's fate was in the hands of others, and she did her best not to seem over-keen, to bide her time, to allow obstacles to be surmounted. Respectable chaperones for the journey had to be found and her mother's multiple, vehement objections had to be overcome.

Liliana started to pray. She went every evening after work to church, where she told God that His will, not hers, should prevail, but she hoped that their wills for once might coincide.

Her father found Liliana's travelling companions: General Todino, a much-decorated war veteran, now retired from the army, and his wife, the Contessa. The General had been on the board of the railway company where her father used to work and had business interests in Tripolitania. Her father had written to him and the General had agreed – graciously agreed, her mother said, the least he could do, her father said – that Liliana could travel with him and his wife all the way to Tripoli.

Persuading her mother to let her go was more problematic. 'It's because she will miss you so,' her father explained when her mother shut herself in the bedroom to weep and loudly pray. 'Go and talk to her,' he said, 'gently. Tell her it's not for ever.' Liliana knelt on the other side of the bedroom door and, as carefully as she knew how, unwrapped each of her mother's fears – that Liliana was abandoning them in their old age, that she would be kidnapped by savages and made into a slave, that she would catch some hideous tropical disease and die – and exposed them to the light of reason. But reason only made her mother more agitated.

'It is only a visit, Mamma. I will be coming back,' Liliana said.

At that, her mother wrenched open the door, purple-faced and wild-eyed. She looked down at Liliana kneeling on the edge of the rug. 'But *he* won't, will he?' she said. '*He* won't be coming back.'

And Liliana understood that her mother wept only because her daughter's departure made Stefano's return less likely. 'I'll try and get him to come home,' she said. 'And perhaps, if this temporary job he has found for me is lucrative, I will be able to send funds for you to come to Africa too.'

'You won't catch me going to the savage lands,' her mother said.

Now Liliana leans against the metal rail, breathes in the city air and catches the lily-of-the-valley scent of the perfume, warmed and released by contact with her skin.

The theme of the fancy-dress ball is *Spazio Vitale*. It is a celebration of a renewed vigour in building the Italian empire.

And Liliana Cattaneo, dressed in gold chiffon and pink satin, bejewelled and perfumed, is, in her own little way, also stretching out. She feels it as her ribcage pushes against the tight bodice. When her lungs contract, the chiffon of her tunic softly skims the skin around her arms and across her breastbone.

Down below in the street, fashionable ladies with their shopping bags board a tram, a pair of businessmen in dark suits stroll, a white-gloved traffic policeman at the junction directs the flow of motor cars. The street lamps have just been lit. She follows from lamp to lamp the progress of a man wearing a straw hat, swinging his cane. It is early in the year for straw hats, but then Rome is warmer than Monza.

Just like that she has become someone who knows, from personal experience, that Rome is warmer than Monza.

The man in the hat raises it gallantly as his path crosses

that of two elegant women in fur collars. Liliana switches her attention to the women. How she would love a fur collar. She puts her hand to her collarbone and fingers the three strings of beads that hang there. One of the women wears high heels and has a lovely sway as she walks. When the pair disappear around the curve of the street, Liliana moves her gaze to the boy in a cap on the pavement directly opposite who is selling newspapers to the passers-by. He is shouting out the headline to make people stop and pay attention, and waving a folded newspaper in the air. She cannot make out the words but it will undoubtedly be about the plebiscite that has just been held – the vote for the list of deputies put forward by the Grand Council of Fascism. Liliana isn't entirely sure what it means, but the Todinos think it is a thoroughly good thing.

'It will shut those whining liberals up,' the General commented over tea in the hotel lounge earlier. 'Give us a chance to get on with what needs to be done.' He has told Liliana much about what needs to be done in the country to which they are travelling and about the aircraft, motor transport and brilliant logistics that the Italians are using. Unruly tribes are being brought into the fold and disarmed, he says. Many have surrendered. He calls them the *sottomessi*, the submitted ones. His wife, who had been engrossed in the *Piccola* magazine that she had bought for Liliana, put it down. 'Hail the fascist revolution,' she said, and swung her right arm up in the Roman salute.

Liliana, after the briefest of hesitations, did the same.

Prior to her acquaintance with the Todinos, Liliana thought of salutes as reserved for ceremonial public occasions, for marches and rallies and of course, when she was younger, for school assemblies, when they honoured the national flag.

She had not come across them in private exchanges. There is something thrilling about joining in, as if she were more than her own little self, part of something noble and big.

From her balcony, she sees a white official car pull up at the kerb, and a man in uniform gets out. She can see straight down on to the top of his cap. She cannot see his face but she recognises the uniform of the *Regia Aeronautica Italiana*, the Royal Italian Air Force.

She is looking down on him, his body foreshortened, the white glow of him standing beneath the lamplight and, as she watches, he takes off his cap and runs his thumb around the rim of it and then he looks up. He might be looking at the evening sky, at the palm trees, tipping his head right back and craning upwards. He cannot possibly see her leaning against the metal rail in the gloaming, on the other side of the lamplight and the palm leaves, and yet he looks up as if at her and seems to stretch out his arms. And she has the strangest sensation that if she were to tumble and fall from this great height, he would catch her.

The man puts his cap back on his head, turns on his heel and enters the hotel.

General Todino has explained to her that while the women at the ball will, like her, be dressed in picturesque costumes, representing the people of the subjugated lands of Italian Africa – tribeswomen from Somalia, Eritrean ladies, slave girls from the Fezzan, possibly – the military men will be in uniform. They do not need to dress up because they are the ones out conquering the vital space for all to enjoy and are already suitably attired.

She is lucky to be with the Todinos, to have their protection and influence. Because she is with them, because they have taken her on, Liliana is travelling in style and comfort.

She is staying now in one of the best hotels in Rome. Her room attaches to the Todinos' suite via a connecting door.

Liliana has not been in the company of wealthy people before. Ease and comfort are a revelation to her. She is unfamiliar with a world in which the question of whether to wear the pearls or the diamonds is a legitimate concern. She wonders if she could get used to it.

She is on her way, and nothing is going to stop her. She is, as Contessa Todino likes to put it, an Italian woman of the new order, which seems to mean many sometimes contradictory things: bright and well-dressed and ambitious, bold but demure, pious but elegantly sceptical.

She thinks now about Contessa Todino and about their meeting at Monza station three days before. She remembers the walk with her father to the station, how she slowed to his pace instead of her usual stride, how he wheeled her trunk along on a trolley he had borrowed and told her about the Todinos and what an influential couple they were. She must be respectful, yes, but not over-deferential. She had her own reasons for travelling to Tripolitania, was not beholden to them for her fare or her lodgings en route, was not a charity case. Her father had never met the General's wife, but he knew that she was born rich so she could afford to be kind, not that that necessarily followed. She remembers her first sight of the fine lady, wreathed in steam from the locomotive engine, in her Persian lamb coat with her golden crimped hair, her diamond rings and her matching diamond hair clasp. She was like a movie star. Like Greta Garbo. She eclipsed her husband, standing to one side in his hat and dark coat. Liliana thinks of how, when her father pushed her forward, unsure of etiquette but thinking to strike a note of confidence and to show willing from the outset, she stuck out her hand to shake Contessa Todino's and of how the other woman looked her up and down as if she were a specimen not encountered before, or at least not close up. She relives the discomfort of seeing herself in the mirror of Contessa Todino's gaze. She lowered her eyes and stared at the lady's embossed leather suitcases on the porter's trolley, understanding with a sickening feeling that the travelling arrangement her father had made was reversible, and that it hung on the whim of this woman. Some instinct told her not to speak out or protest or plead or claim that she would be no trouble, not to explain that she had deliberately worn her second-best frock for travelling so her best would not get crumpled, but to keep her head lowered, to wait passively, to be humble. She was aware that General Todino was speaking to his wife, but his voice was a rumble and she couldn't make out the words. Her father stepped forward and said something too. Don't beg, Papà, she thought. And, beg, Papà.

And then her hand, that she had half lowered but that was still held out in front as if she were asking for alms, was caught up and enfolded in the two gloved hands of Contessa Todino. 'Poor little mite,' she said.

Liliana looked up.

'She's shaking,' the Contessa announced in an accusing tone to her husband, to Liliana's father, to the two porters and another young woman, laden with bags and packages, who had now appeared and who seemed to be attached to the party.

The Contessa smiled at Liliana as you might at a small child. 'So pale and thin. You have been ill, have you?' she said. And Liliana, who had been in good physical health throughout the dark winter months, heard herself confide in a delicate voice that she was much better now, thank you.

'I am going to take care of you,' Contessa Todino said. 'We will eat delicious food, and I will fatten you up and make you delicious too.' She let go of Liliana's hand and clapped hers together. 'What fun,' she said. She tucked Liliana's arm under hers and drew her in close. 'I am taking this young lady into my charge,' she said, as if no one else could be trusted.

Contessa Todino has indeed taken Liliana under her wing. Liliana is a quick student, understanding when to step forward, to ask bright questions, and when to quietly step back. She is allowed to shine, as long as Contessa Todino has applied the polish. Contessa Todino has given her magazines and fashion advice, lent her jewellery, shown her how to make the best of herself, taught her about the behaviour that is appropriate in a young lady of today, the new *Italiana*. It is Contessa Todino who has insisted that, if Liliana is to travel with them, then she must properly be with them, and not like some poor third-class relation. 'You don't have wealth or standing but you have youth. You must use it. Perhaps a bit china doll. A bit fragile. But some men like that,' Contessa Todino has pronounced.

Contessa Todino's ideas about women, what they could and couldn't, should and shouldn't, do, are difficult for Liliana to grasp. On women's suffrage, for example. Women had the same rights as men to vote in England, and had done since the previous year. 'You are a little goose,' Contessa Todino said when Liliana expressed surprise at this. 'A dear little goose. I shall call you gosling. What do they teach you on those summer camps?' There was no chance of women being given the vote here in Italy, it seemed, which was a good thing in Contessa Todino's opinion. 'Spinsters,' she said of the women who advocated such a move. 'Are they?

Liliana asked. 'Are they all spinsters then?' 'As good as,' Contessa Todino enigmatically replied. 'Our influence is other. It is more subtle,' she explained. 'Our domain is that of the senses.'

Liliana has been feeling her way into the role that Contessa Todino has assigned to her. It is as if she has been made to wear a costume that does not quite fit, but she must act as if it does. It is uncomfortable, but needs must. She is only seventeen, but she has worn many different costumes over the years: her school apron, her ONB Fascist Youth uniform, her mantilla and white gloves in church. Each has required some special behaviour and way of thinking, and she has dutifully espoused them all, studying her books, swinging her arms with the other marching girls at Saturday-morning rallies, fasting before communion, saying her nightly prayers. But this one is trickier because it shifts with Contessa Todino's mood and has not involved an actual outfit until now, this evening, for the fancy-dress ball.

'We must have you perfect for this evening,' Contessa Todino said. Liliana has not understood why. Or what perfection might mean. Or how it could possibly involve appearing in a public place half naked.

Liliana was not even going to the ball until Contessa Todino intervened. 'You can't sit up here in your room all alone while we're dancing under the chandeliers,' she exclaimed. 'Can she, treasure?' she said, appealing to her husband but not waiting for an answer. Contessa Todino negotiated with the woman in the costume shop on the telephone. Liliana heard herself described. 'Yes, yes that will do, she is quite thin,' Contessa Todino said, 'and small. What's that? Yes, *gamine*, that's what I mean.'

What Contessa Todino managed to obtain was a dancer's

costume from the Araby lands of the southern Sinai. 'Don't worry about the cost,' she whispered to Liliana, who hadn't until then, 'we have an account. The General will settle it.'

'Where is the Sinai? Is that one of ours?' Liliana asked.

'Not yet,' Contessa Todino replied. 'But I think it might be part of the longer-term plan.' She put her finger to her lips. 'Shh, don't tell the Brits!' she said. And when she laughed, Liliana warily joined in.

The Contessa came to Liliana's room when the costume was delivered. 'It is strange, this outfit,' she said, lifting bangles and bracelets, a glass jewel on a leather cord and an array of flimsy pink and golden garments out of their tissue wrappings. 'They mostly cover themselves up, these Arab womenfolk. Not the dancers though, obviously.'

'My brother has seen some dancers in a nightclub in Tripoli who dance with their stomachs,' Liliana said.

'Has he indeed?' Contessa Todino replied. 'Is that what Signor Cattaneo gets up to in his spare time?'

'Oh no. Just the once, I think,' Liliana said. 'Someone took him to a club in Tripoli.'

'Young bachelors, they need these outlets,' Contessa Todino commented.

'Do they?' Liliana said. She has kept quiet about her brother's so-called marriage.

'Oh yes, they're different from us. It is like a constant itch to them, and they need to scratch it. Like dogs,' she said.

'Oh,' Liliana said and blushed at the idea of 'it'. Stefano must have had these urges, and the Bedouin girl was what he had found to scratch his itch. It will be short-lived then, she thinks, comforting herself, like an itch is. Probably it is already over, and that is why he has sent for Liliana.

'I think you are right. This is a belly-dancer's outfit,'

Contessa Todino said, holding the various parts of it up to the electric light: the sequinned bodice, a length of golden chiffon cloth, a pair of pink pantaloons through which Liliana could see the painting on the opposite wall. 'Not everyone could carry it off. It might be deemed immodest, but because you're so . . . ' – she sought the word – '*gamine*, it will be fine. I couldn't wear it. I would look too provocative. Because of my curves.' She laid the costume on the bed, put her hands to her waist and smoothed them down over the swell of her hips. 'These damn curves.'

'I wish I had your curves,' Liliana said dutifully.

'Well, you're young. You might yet develop,' Contessa Todino said. 'Come on. Put the outfit on and let me see you, and then Marta will do me.'

The room that Liliana has been given rightfully belonged to Marta, the maid, so that she could be at the beck and call of the Contessa and General Todino at all hours. Liliana did not know to what distant chamber Marta had been banished, nor how she was now summoned. 'Oh, I am sorry, Marta,' she had said at the time. 'I don't like to put you out.'

'Don't fraternise,' the Signora said to her after Marta had gone. 'If you want to go back to your kind, just say the word, but if you're in my party stick to the rules and keep standards up.'

Liliana sees that the Todinos each have their own way of being chummy with maids, servants, porters, officials and domestic staff, but their dealings are conducted as if from a great height, from a certain elevated ledge of privilege and certainty.

Contessa Todino sat on the bed and directed operations as Liliana pulled on the pantaloons, then buttoned the tight little bodice that fits snugly over her breasts and clasps her ribcage.

Two of the larger bangles went around her ankles and the others around her wrists. Under Contessa Todino's scrutiny, she was conscious of her bare arms and the great naked expanse of her middle, her belly button on display in a way it never had been before. She picked up the length of golden cloth, thinking to wrap it around her middle section and reclaim some modesty.

'No, no, this next,' Contessa Todino exclaimed, getting up from the bed with the leather cord and the bright stone in her hands. 'Let me,' she said and, instead of tying it around Liliana's neck as she expected, the Signora spun Liliana so she was facing the mirror, reached forward so that her body pressed against Liliana's half-naked back, encircled Liliana's waist with the leather cord and, resting her chin on Liliana's bare shoulder to look at their conjoined image in the mirror, jiggled the cord so that the stone came to rest in the hollow of Liliana's belly button. When she had ascertained the right length, she fastened the cord behind. 'There,' she said.

Meeting her own eyes in the mirror, as Contessa Todino lifted her hair and stroked it back, she caught the light there, an almost feverish glow. Liliana's hair is, the Contessa said, 'like a bush that has never been pruned', but she brushed it and beat it into shape and plaited it so it hung smoothly down her back. Then she slid her hands down Liliana's arms to her wrists, took hold of the bigger bangles and pushed them up so that they encircled her upper arms. 'These are worn like this,' she said and then she lifted the heavy loop of Liliana's hair, bent down and kissed her so softly on the nape of her neck, such a slight brush of the lips that a tingle went down Liliana's spine. 'My little harem girl,' she whispered.

Liliana, standing on her balcony, does not know what to make of it, and she is trembling. She is wondering if she can feign a headache, stomach cramps, anything not to be made to parade in public dressed in this immodest fashion. She wanted to make an impression, but not like this.

Now there comes a tap on the door that connects Liliana's room with the Todinos' suite. 'Are you ready, gosling?' Contessa Todino calls.

Liliana turns to face into the room as the other woman comes gliding through. Contessa Todino is wearing the Arabian princess costume that was delivered from the theatrical costumier's that afternoon, a full-length striped silk gown in purple and gold, her feet encased in high-heeled golden slippers and her golden hair held in place with a jewelled tiara. She takes up position in front of the mirror, pausing there to allow Liliana to admire her. 'I know,' she says, 'that the tiara is not authentic but, really, have you seen what those savages wear on their heads? It's ridiculous. I wouldn't be able to lift my head up.'

'You look dreamy,' Liliana says.

'And you, gosling. Let me look at you again,' Contessa Todino says.

Her husband appears at the open door. 'Are we ready, ladies?' he says. 'What do you think, treasure?' Contessa Todino says, drawing Liliana forward. 'Delectable, isn't she? Good enough to eat.'

When the General looks at Liliana, she sees his eyes momentarily widen, as if in shock. His voice when he speaks is mild enough. 'I think she will catch cold,' he says. 'It's chilly in that ballroom. Don't you have a shawl you can lend her? The pink one, I think. The one I brought you back from the bazaar.' He doesn't look at his wife but turns back into their room. 'Marta,' he calls.

'It came with a sort of shawl,' Liliana says, snatching up the length of golden cloth and clutching it to her. Marta has appeared in the doorway. 'Help her, Marta,' the General says. The golden cloth is draped around Liliana's shoulders and pinned around her middle section, as if she is a parcel that needs an extra layer of wrapping. The seductive shape is gone. Modesty has prevailed.

'Spoilsport,' Contessa Todino says, but her husband merely shakes his head and tuts.

'Let's go and drink to the mighty fascist state,' he says. 'Death and destruction to its enemies.' He makes the fascist salute.

His wife and then Liliana join in.

'Let's drink champagne!' Contessa Todino says.

'Oh let's,' says Liliana, as if she drinks champagne every day, conscious now that she has lost her place in Contessa Todino's good books and will have to find a way back in.

Liliana descends the grand curving staircase on General Todino's arm. 'Let her fend for herself,' he says of his wife. 'She prefers it. She likes to make an entrance.' The General walks slowly because he is old, and, perhaps to make up for that and to entertain her during the sedate descent, he tells Liliana about the manufacture of the balustrade, and that the same density of iron is used for the edging on the railway line. 'Your father would be interested to know that,' he says. They pause at the turn of the stairs.

'I'll tell him,' she says, but she isn't thinking of her father. She's looking down through the wide-open mirrored glass doors to the crowd in the ballroom beyond. She sees that people are mostly clustered around the edges of the room, with only a few standing chatting in the middle. Huge candelabra are set at each end. At the far end of the room, on the edge of the mingling of people, a small orchestra is tuning up. Many of the women are dressed in exotic outfits, approximations of what might be native dress in the colonies, belts to gather in and give shape to voluminous robes, coloured cloths wrapped around their hair or twisted into it. It is all right, she thinks. She will pass unnoticed.

As they move on down, the General indicates the detail of the chandeliers to Liliana. Four hundred and thirty pieces of Venetian glass each, he says. She looks up and admires their sparkle. They are taken down once every two years to be cleaned, he adds.

At the bottom of the staircase they turn to watch Contessa Todino's stately descent, her princess dress swishing around her, the light from the chandeliers catching the gold of her hair and the shine of the tiara. She is breathtaking. Expensive. Chic. Sleek.

She strikes a pose halfway down. There is a flash of light and Liliana notices the photographer next to one of the columns.

Contessa Todino comes tripping lightly down the last stretch of the staircase to join them. The General directs Liliana's attention to the Brazilian marble columns and the Murano skylights.

'Stop boring the poor child with these pointless facts,' Contessa Todino drawls as they enter the ballroom. 'Find some handsome officer and introduce her.'

'Would you like that?' the General says, and he turns to cast a doubtful eye over Liliana.

'Is the Marshal here?' Liliana asks, for something to say.

'Goodness, you're setting your sights high,' Contessa Todino says.

'I only wanted to thank him,' Liliana says. 'You know, for saving the Tripoli motor race,' but Contessa Todino isn't listening. Someone more interesting has claimed her attention, and she wanders off.

'The Marshal obtained funding for the motor race to go ahead and that's how my brother got his bonus and so paid for me to come on this trip,' Liliana explains to the General.

'Let me see if I can spot him,' the General says, raising his monocle to his eye and scrutinising the guests.

Mirrored glass is interspersed with real glass in the floor-to-ceiling windows. Waiters bearing trays of drinks thread through the crowd. The General hands Liliana a glass and takes one for himself. 'I can't see the Marshal,' he says. There are many military men. They have their medals pinned to their chests, their brass buttons shine, their moustaches are waxed, their boots gleam. A few of the ladies have made only a token gesture to the theme in their choice of outfit. They wear evening gowns in silk and taffeta but with bright sashes bearing patriotic slogans – *Spazio Vitale*, *Mare Nostrum*, *Evviva il Duce* – across their breasts. The General points people out to Liliana, naming them, giving their rank or status, and she nods and sips her fruity drink, taking little of it in, feeling safe and anonymous at his side. And then her gaze, roaming the room, snags on a man opposite who seems to be watching her. For a moment they look at each other and then she looks away, takes a breath, feels her ribcage press against the chiffon binding. Her gaze creeps back. Someone tugs on his sleeve and he turns away to speak to them. The man is wearing an air force dress uniform: a short white jacket, dark trousers, gleaming shoes, a white cap with a gold band and a dark peak, a row of medals hanging from ribbons over his left breast pocket, a white shirt and black bow tie. The concession he has made to the theme of the evening is a dazzling piece of vermilion cloth worn across his body and pinned by a jewelled brooch to his shoulder. She is sure he is the same man she saw arriving in an official car, although she does not know why she thinks it. He is talking to the man at his side, but when the other person speaks he turns to look at her and she looks away again.

General Todino has found a young man to introduce to Liliana, an earnest young army major who tells them about a marvellous speech the Duce made, and how the last dregs of democracy have been drained from the Italian Parliamentary chamber. In celebration, Liliana drains the dregs of the punch she is holding, even the fruity pieces in the bottom of the glass, and accepts straight afterwards a flute of champagne.

The music starts up. The General hands her to the officer, and they dance a waltz in among the other couples. When that dance finishes, another young officer presents himself, and she moves straight into the next one, and then the third, pausing only long enough to drink more champagne. She has no shortage of partners, youngish and not-so-young men, some there with their wives. The waltz and the foxtrot are the only dances Liliana properly knows but she finds that her partners do not mind. They are keen to teach her, and in their arms she glides about the dance floor. All the time she dances, she is aware of the watching man and his whereabouts as he moves about the room, chatting with different guests. He has a solidity about him, a kind of density, as if the air is more concentrated where he stands, and wherever he is, he draws her eye. He is so smart and formal and proper, and yet there is a wild restlessness in his eyes as if, at any moment, he might do anything. At one point, clutched in the arms of an elderly colonel of the Alpini regiment who smells of lemon balm and whisky, looking beyond his shoulder, she sees the airman deep in conversation with Contessa Todino; they both look up at her at the same time, as if they felt her looking, as if they were talking about her, and the knowledge that she could never compete with the beauty, wealth, poise, charisma of Contessa Todino makes something slide uncomfortably inside her. Of course they wouldn't have been talking about her. She is hardly worthy of their consideration. The next time she sees the man, he is smoking a cigarette and in conference with the General and another man. She has these glimpses of him as she whirls about the dance floor and she knows that he is following her progress too.

She waits for him to ask her to dance, and while she waits she dances with the others, as if she is practising. Always, at all times, she is aware of him.

The watching man's gaze changes the way that she moves. It is as if he sees through the chiffon wrappings that bulk out her middle section, that make her into a column like one of the white marble ones that stand sentry at the bottom of the curved staircase. He sees through to her naked, undulating self beneath. She feels that every other man in the room has asked her to dance, except him. And yet it is for him that she dances.

The music stops and Liliana, who, with her latest partner, happens to have come to a standstill at the orchestra end of the room, watches as the musicians lay down their instruments and rest their bows across their knees. The cellist inserts his instrument into a black stand at his feet, then sits back in his chair, lifts and lets fall his shoulders three times, raises his hand to the back of his neck and kneads it.

A bell is rung. Silence gradually falls across the ballroom, the buzz of chatter, the clink of glasses fade, a rearrangement of the people takes place as all turn expectantly to face the end where the orchestra sits and where Liliana stands. They press forward; Liliana can feel the heat of the bodies behind. She finds herself surrounded by a gaggle of the stately women wearing patriotic slogans across their bodices.

A small wooden rostrum with two steps is placed on the marble floor in between Liliana and the orchestra and she realises that she is in the front row for whatever is to happen next. She glances around, seeking out the man, but he is nowhere to be seen. At the thought that he has gone and they have not danced, her heart sinks.

More drinks are brought, until everyone has a glass in hand. She becomes aware that she is gazing disconsolately at the cellist and that he has noticed. He raises an eyebrow at her, as if to say, 'Look at you all dressed up.' She has been recognised for what she is. An impostor. She raises an eyebrow back at him and tosses the drink down her throat, then looks at him scornfully. I do belong. I will belong. You are there working and I am a bona-fide guest. He shakes his head at her, almost a warning, and she sees that everyone else is holding their glass untouched, brimful of bubbles. She suddenly understands. There is to be a toast. She reaches out to a passing waiter, deftly places her glass down on his tray and picks up a full one. She looks at the cellist. He nods and smiles. He is like her father, she thinks, and has a sudden idea of herself stepping forward across the few metres between them and sitting on his lap because, even though she is standing still, Liliana feels unsteady and friendless. She closes her eyes a moment to dispel the feeling and staggers as if the floor has tilted. She quickly opens them. She wants to leave, but the throng are between her and the door. She must stay. She steadies herself by fixing her eyes on the little rostrum, the steps leading nowhere.

A door she has not previously noticed swings open, and in strides the air force man. How can that be when he was in the room already? She sees now that it is an emerald scarab brooch that holds his red sash in place.

He steps onto the rostrum and from this elevated stance he regards the people in the room. He does not look at Liliana, despite their proximity. He waits, his hands held in front of him, palms outward, like a preacher. The crowd thought they were already quiet, hushed and attentive, but he wants more. He is silently calling for an even greater level of silence, a greater level of attention. It must be absolute. Once this is achieved, he addresses the crowd. Liliana hears the commanding tone more than the words. His voice reverberates in her stomach. She stands on the edge of the circle of women. *Mare Nostrum*, the man booms, echoing the slogan on the woman's chest next to her. Liliana feels like she is swimming in it. *Spazio Vitale*. She feels her lungs compress and tries to suck air in. When her lungs expand she feels her sides push up against the thick golden cummerbund of chiffon that encircles her waist. And when they contract, the piece of chiffon pinned around her shoulders softly skims the skin around her armpits and across her breastbone. *Pax romana*. She is churned up. She is at sea. There will be no peace.

When she first saw this man from her balcony, Liliana's view was a bird's-eye one of the top of his head and, briefly, the blur of his upturned face. Now she is looking upwards at the jut of his jaw, at the swell of his chest, as if he were a monument on a plinth. She feels nervous, on the edge of something as if, after all, she might jump.

The man explains that the Marshal is not coming to the ball because he has flown straight to Tripoli to watch the motor race there, but that he is here in his stead. Liliana watches him in wonder, her head awhirl. He talks about the plebiscite and how there will be no stopping the fascist revolution now. She hears phrases that she stores in her fuzzy champagne head, thinking she will ask the General what they mean later. As Italy expands further into its vital space, the injustice of the mutilated victory will become a thing of the past. The man proposes a toast to the fascist revolution, and the crowd responds with a cheer. They all raise their glasses. Liliana takes a sip of champagne and puts the nearly full glass back down on the tray of a passing waiter rather more vehemently than she intended. The back of her neck aches from tipping her head upwards. She would like to sit down, but there is no chance of that, pressed as she is at the front of the crowd.

She watches the cellist again as, along with the other members of the small orchestra, he takes up his instrument. Poised, his bow at the ready, he glances at his fellow musicians, a look of bemused resignation on his face, raises one eyebrow and nods and, as one, they launch into 'Giovinezza'. All the uniformed men bare their heads and the whole room sings with gusto of the new borders, of youth triumphant, of redemptive fascism.

The woman next to Liliana sings an octave higher than everyone else, a piercing soprano that threatens to shatter the glasses some people still hold in their hands. The cellist is sawing away at his instrument, that lugubrious expression still on his face. Liliana joins in the singing. She feels something give as she takes in a breath, a sense of release. For a moment she doesn't understand and then she realises that the pin holding her cummerbund in place has come undone. She holds the cloth, clutching it to her side so that she doesn't unravel. She can hear her own voice, high and warbly and tuneless, and a sort of snort comes out of her mouth, as if she might be about to collapse in laughter. Or in tears. She has difficulty suppressing it. How ridiculous we all are, she thinks. We are all playing a game. This is a piece of theatre and we all have our parts. She suddenly understands why the air-force officer left the room. He went out in order to be seen coming in. This is a show, and he is the chief showman.

She looks up at him again. She can see his jaw working, his lips moving, but she can't distinguish his voice. He has a stentorian speaking voice but a very soft singing one. Perhaps he can't hold the tune and knows it. In the hush when the anthem finishes, he steps down from the rostrum, bows to the crowd and leaves the room. Exit, stage left, Liliana thinks.

But still she wishes he had taken her with him.

As the dance music starts up again, a lively polka, she makes her way along the length of the room, holding her chiffon cummerbund in place. She needs to get out, breathe some air, tie herself back into the costume. She is coming undone. She is only halfway down the hall when another man claims her and ignores or doesn't hear her protestations and nervous giggles, or takes them as encouragement. She cannot resist him gathering her up and galloping her around the room. She keeps one hand to her ribcage, clutching the cloth and so has only a tenuous hold on her partner, an enthusiastic, rumbustious fellow, spinning her round with more vigour than the tempo of the dance warrants. When, at the height of a turn, her one-armed grip on him loosens, she spins out of control, staggers, but is caught from behind, landing in another man's arms.

'I've got you,' the scarab man's voice says and she sinks back against him, allowing herself to be held for a moment before she straightens up.

She turns to him; her face feels hot and sticky. With what dignity she can muster, she says, 'Thank you.'

He takes hold of her hand as if he is going to lead her back onto the dance floor but instead they go out through the double doors, across a hallway and through another door onto a terrace where people are standing about in clusters, smoking, admiring the night sky and the lights of the city. At a word from him they disappear, until there are only the two of them. A very important man, she thinks, who must not be disobeyed, and she giggles.

He takes a step away from her and looks her up and down, his face a serious mask.

'I wasn't laughing at you,' she says and sees from the expression on his face that the idea had not occurred to him. 'I nearly made an awful fool of myself in there. My outfit is coming undone.' She indicates with a movement of her hand the loose end of her cummerbund.

'I saw you were in some difficulty,' he says.

He takes the end of the cloth she is holding out of her hand. He is standing very close. She can smell his cologne, an astringent pine scent.

'The dancing girls don't wear these around their waists,' he says, his voice teasing and low. He lowers his head, looks up at her from a lowered stance, like a bull about to charge, and he tugs on the cloth. At the same time, with his other hand, he reaches for her shoulder and pushes against it, so he is pushing and pulling at the same time and she understands the movement required. Slowly, inexorably, she starts to turn on the spot, allows him to unravel her until she is standing with her bare middle on display, the jewel in her belly button. 'Yes,' he says.

'Excuse me, Colonel,' a man who has appeared at the glass door says. 'Sorry to disturb you. Your car is waiting.'

He is a colonel.

'I have to leave now,' he says. He hands the bunched golden cloth back to her. 'When can we meet?'

'I'm going to Tripoli tomorrow,' she says.

'And I the following day!' He is going to fly on a sea plane. He will be there first. He will be waiting for her, he says. He takes a little black diary from his pocket and flicks through it. 'Let us meet at the cathedral at midday, a week on Wednesday,' he says. 'That's a good central location. Easy for you to find. We can go to my hotel.' He has his pen poised. 'Lunch. Would you like that?' he asks.

She nods.

He writes the date in his diary and replaces it in his pocket. He takes her hand in his and walks her inside, to one of the little writing desks that are dotted here and there about the hotel. He leans down, jots the date and time of their meeting on the pad of hotel writing paper, tears off the sheet and hands it to her. He pulls her closer. 'Don't forget,' he whispers in her ear.

'I won't,' she says.

He lets go and steps back. 'I will send a car for you,' he says. And then he is gone.

She already has an assignation in Tripoli, and she has not yet left Italian shores.

I AM MINE

Item: A lock of baby hair wrapped in tissue.

The small white room where they had put Abramo Cattaneo smelt of disinfectant. He had been washed and laid out on a trolley bed like the one Liliana had seen earlier. The sheet that covered him was folded over and tucked in as if he were just having a nap. There was a high window with no curtain on the far side of the bed, and a wooden chair on the near side. A white plastic crucifix hanging on the wall was the only decoration.

They stood at the foot of the bed, Liliana and the nurse. Abramo had close-cropped thick dark hair, greying at the temples, and a short beard that was almost white. Of course, everyone looks grim when dead, she thought. Even when they tidied you, touched you up with a bit of make-up, arranged your features to make you look peaceful, aimed for that 'gone to a better place' look, even then you looked grim. And dead. That was the main thing. There was a sameness about death. When the life had gone, Alan had looked like a generic old man. And at least he'd lived out his three score years and ten, and a few more. But this man, who used to be her nephew, he had been blasted out of his life.

'He had a load of hair as a baby,' she said, for something to say, thinking again of the little lock wrapped in yellowing tissue paper in the tray inside her suitcase. 'Tight curls all over his head like a Roman emperor.' There was a high-pitched quality to her voice. She didn't understand what she was doing in this bare, white-walled room. Surely, she had been going to depart. She had been bidding the nurse goodbye.

The nurse said she would leave her alone with him for ten minutes, and Liliana thought she would make her escape as soon as the door closed.

But instead her grief burst forth. The power of it shocked her. At first she sat on the chair at his bedside, doubled over with dry sobs, but then she had to stand, pace up and down at the foot of the bed and howl into her handkerchief.

She kept telling herself that she had not known him, Abramo, and so couldn't mourn him. That there could not be a gap where there had not previously been a presence. But still, to have him there and then snatched away. Not to have known him in life again, even for five minutes.

She paced and she wailed, but no tears came. Everything in her rejected this as an ending.

And suddenly there she was at the other end of his life again, at his coming into the world. The images flew up at her like a flock of startled sparrows. Farida in the sweaty darkness of the camel-hair tent that smelled of blood and animal fat from the lamp, of woodsmoke and of the incense they burned in the village to keep the flies away. The milky muffled warmth and blood. Farida's eyes rolling back in her head, and how Liliana took hold of him, slippery little thing, and slid him onto Farida's belly. From outside, in the horrible unforgiving light, the relentless sun, came the thrum of an

116

engine, a noise like thunder. And the blood, so much blood. The bleeding wouldn't stop.

What village was that? Whose blood was it? Did she, Liliana, have blood on her hands? Please God, no. Always she has been haunted by this fear and there was no one to ask.

She blinked, and the vision vanished. She sat back down heavily by Abramo's side.

She observed him more closely. She took in the detail of him. His jawline beneath the beard, a streak of whiter skin on his right temple that must be an old scar, his full lips and the dark moustache above, the spray of tiny lines around his eyes that comes from squinting against the brightness of the sun, and the furrow between them. The features were regular. The nose straight. In life, he would have been a handsome man.

She lifted the corner of the sheet and felt beneath for his hand. She caught a faint and fleeting scent, something peppery, with a trace of ginger. The picture it conjured of Abramo patting cologne into his shaved cheeks and neck, the reality of how recently he had been alive, made her gasp. His hand was rubbery, but she held it anyway. He wore a thick silver bangle around his wrist, and she wondered if that were odd, for a Libyan man. She ran her thumb along the smooth metal. She and Farida had had matching silver bracelets. Liliana had bought them from Yaacov's silversmith in Tripoli with her first pay packet. She had had them engraved with the image of a bird. Her own with a closed beak and wings slightly raised, and the other, Farida's, with an open beak, as if chirruping, because Farida used to sing and chatter and hum all the time. She knew the words to dozens of old Italian songs that she had learned from the gramophone. There was one about fireflies. How did it go? 'We shine in the shadows,

117

slaves of a brutal world.' Liliana tapped the beat on her knee with her free hand. Oh Farida, your son is dead, she thought, and she quickly pushed the thought back down, unable to bear it. She didn't know what had become of her own bracelet. She must have lost it in Libya. 'Not long now, love,' she said out loud in English. It was something Alan used to say to her when he lay dying. She didn't like to think too hard about what it might mean, and today the phrase did not provide its usual meagre comfort.

She would leave now, collect her bag and head back to the airport. Or she might just find a quiet little hotel for the night because she was very tired and shaky. She had never stayed in a hotel on her own. She didn't quite know how to go about it, but she could ask the taxi driver for advice. Perhaps there was a bland sort of hotel near the airport. She didn't even need to look at Rome. She would shut her eyes. There was nothing for her here. She hadn't been any good to this man all the years of his life, and now it was too late. If she stayed she might find herself caught up in the police inquiry. In the absence of a known next of kin or any other contacts for him, she might even be inveigled into taking responsibility for whatever happened next. The thought of having to organise another funeral made her feel sick.

She let go of Abramo's hand and covered it with the sheet again. She got to her feet. She placed her palm on his cheek and held it there. She could feel his stubble beneath her fingers. She bent and brushed her lips against his cold forehead.

From beyond the grave, Alan, her dear, quaint Alan, had allowed her to lever open a door she had closed long before. She saw it as a trapdoor, beneath her feet, as if she had inhabited the top floor of a house with all sorts of unopened, unvisited rooms below. She had lived up in that attic with

Alan for forty-one years. But now she had lifted that half-concealed trapdoor and then precipitately, unthinkingly, she had dropped down and landed here, where there was nothing but a dead man and a dead end.

She lifted her hand from Abramo's face, picked up her handbag, draped her raincoat over her arm and stepped out into the corridor. She set off in the direction of the lifts at the far end. Her heart was beating fast in its alarming new way, but her body had slowed down. All her speed was concentrated in her thumping heart. It had gone into overdrive. She was creeping along, as if she had become one of the infirm and sick, her legs moving at a snail's pace while her blouse quivered at her heart's furious pulsing.

When she was nearly there, the lift doors opened. A slight figure shot out as if catapulted and stood staring wildly about. A teenage girl in baggy jeans and bright red shoes with her black hair in a long plait. Liliana noticed the logo on the girl's T-shirt – 'I am mine' – and wondered what it was supposed to signify. The girl started to move in Liliana's direction, her plait swinging from side to side as she turned her head to read the numbers on the doors. As their paths crossed, Liliana had a sensation of slippage. It was fleeting, like one of those dream episodes where you seem to trip and then quickly right yourself.

The girl's bracelets and necklaces jingled as she passed.

Liliana kept walking. The girl must have had some terrible news. Her hazel eyes were wide with shock and grief. Poor child, Liliana thought as she stepped into the lift. Poor little thing.

A SECRET MISSION

Item: A third-class ticket for the steamer Elettrico *for the voyage from Naples to Tripoli, calling at Catania, Siracusa and Malta, dated May 1929.*

The passengers come up on deck to watch as the ship enters the port.

There on the jetty is the stripy pillar of the new lighthouse. Along the seafront, among modern buildings, sits the rose-coloured castle, and behind that, stretching away into the distance, an endless array of flat roofs, the domes of mosques, the slim spires of minarets, a brick tower that might belong to the new cathedral. Liliana recognises the landmarks from Stefano's postcards, but she is unprepared for the clear etched outline of the city, its white towers hanging between blue water and bluer sky, the intense shimmer.

As the boat manoeuvres up to the wharf, men on board wearing green overalls throw fat mooring ropes to other men on the land, who catch them and hang their looped ends over bollards. Voices, Italian ones calling instructions and native ones replying in strange accents and in another language with a lower, more guttural register, a language that must be Arabic but which to Liliana sounds like a series of throat clearings in which she can discern no individual words.

There is a clanking noise, the repeated clink of metal against metal, the distant sound of an engine starting up, the murmuring of the passengers waiting to disembark.

Looking at the scene, Liliana feels as if her eyes have been cleaned of a dust she did not know was there, so that colours and contrasts, light and shade, blast at her just as the heat does now that the sea breeze has gone. They blast at and through her, and a smudgy fog that has hung around her the way the ship's steam hangs around the funnel, fattening and blurring its outline, lifts and dissipates.

Down below, porters, dark-faced men in baggy white and grey trousers with white skull caps, stand in a row with their wooden trolleys, ready to load the passengers' trunks and wheel them to the waiting vehicles: three black motor cars and a long line of horse-drawn cabs with native cabbies in long pale robes sitting at the reins. And in a separate space in the middle of it all sits a sleek black racing car. Leaning with his back against the side of it, smoking a cigarette, is Stefano.

He is wearing a white shirt, open at the neck, and belted dark trousers. He has pushed his black floppy hair back from his face and is scanning the line of passengers, but has not yet seen her among the crowd on the deck.

Apart from the movement of his hand as he raises the cigarette to his mouth, Stefano is still. Her brother, unmistakably her brother, but somehow altered and different and at ease amid the strange and foreign bustle.

At the sight of him, something inside Liliana quietens, a furrowed-brow agitation that has been with her for days and she has not known how to quell. She is so glad that he has come alone. It confirms what she has suspected – that it must be over with his so-called wife. It was a temporary arrange-ment that has come to an end. The itch has been scratched. That is why he wants his sister here, because he is lonely. A seemingly unconnected thought pops into her head: she might not go and meet the airman, Colonel Ugo Montello, the day after tomorrow. She doesn't have to. Their paths need never cross again.

The intimate unravelling on the hotel terrace can be con-signed to the past. The thought of her near-nakedness suffuses her with shame and desire. That man and the champagne cast a spell on her, but look, here is her brother, wholesome and present.

She calls out Stefano's name and waves furiously. He con-tinues to squint up, his gaze raking the row of passengers, but still does not see her nor shift his easy leaning stance.

'Is that your brother?' says Contessa Todino, who has appeared at Liliana's side.

'Yes,' says Liliana, glad that he is looking so dashing.

She has hardly seen the Contessa on the journey. The Todinos were on the upper deck in first class, and she was on the lowest passenger deck, sharing a tiny cabin with, as it turned out, Marta, their maid. The berth was booked in advance by Liliana's father, and perhaps could not have been changed at short notice by the Todinos, had they wanted to keep Liliana close. Her glimpses of the Contessa – reclin-ing on a deckchair with her husband in the sun, drinking cocktails in the starboard bar, promenading with other fine ladies or on some gallant's arm – have been from a distance. Sometimes the Contessa has actually seemed not to see her. Liliana has adopted a jolly all-encompassing wave as she walks briskly past. She has understood that, unless she struggles against it, her place, the one to which she will be consigned, is down below with the servants, or at best one floor higher. Balls and luncheons and excursions in charabancs to the oases and the Roman ruins are not going to be on offer. She has clung to the Contessa's promise that they will see each other on the other side. Now here is the great lady and it is as if they have never been apart. 'Handsome chap,' she exclaims.

Just at that moment, Stefano catches sight of Liliana and waves cheerily. He leans back into the car and without turning round, reaching behind him, he hoots the horn three times.

'And what a gorgeous car!' the Contessa says.

'He works at the race track,' Liliana says.

'What a bore that we have missed the race,' the Contessa says. 'Some of the drivers might still be at the hotel, I suppose. They won't all have packed up and gone home yet. Let's go and get all the gossip from your brother. And hand you into his care.'

Stefano is waiting at the foot of the gangway. He only has eyes for Liliana, and she can't help herself; she forgets decorum and runs ahead into his waiting arms, leaving the Todinos behind. She is lifted into the air and swung around in a great circle so that her hat goes flying off onto the cobbles. Stefano puts her down, laughing, retrieves her hat, draws her into his side and drapes his arm over her shoulders.

It must be some special Fascist Party ceremonial day, because for his arrival in Tripoli the General is wearing his centurion uniform, with an ornamental dagger at his belt. He makes the fascist salute to Stefano, who inclines his head slightly in return, a gesture that could be interpreted as a sort of bow. The Contessa takes Stefano's hand and kisses him on both cheeks.

Stefano is not dazzled by Contessa Todino. He is polite

but formal. He thanks the Todinos for looking after his little sister. He lifts Liliana's heavy trunk, swings it onto his shoulders, and apologises that he is in a hurry. He is due back at work.

The Contessa and the General walk with them to the car, plying Stefano with questions about the race. The winner was Gastone Brilli Peri, he says.

'Conte Brilli Peri?' the Contessa says. 'From Florence? We know his family. His father owns the estate next to my brother-in-law's.'

'Yes, that'll be him,' Stefano says as he straps Liliana's trunk to the back of the car. 'People love him here. The Arabs as well as the Italians. They call him Gastone the African.'

'Good work, young man,' the General says. He nods at Stefano, clicks his heels and goes off to supervise the loading of their own bags into one of the black motor cars.

'There was no beating Brilli Peri this time,' Stefano says. '*Maktub*, as they say in these parts.'

'Oh yes, *maktub*,' Contessa Todino agrees.

'Margharita,' her husband calls from their waiting car, and with a flurry of kisses and *arrivederci gosling*s and *come and see me at the hotel*s, she is gone. The Contessa has left, and there is no concrete arrangement to meet again. Still, Liliana has her appointment with the airman, although she might not go. And Stefano has made a wonderful impression, and so an invitation will surely follow.

'She fancies herself, doesn't she?' Stefano comments as they watch the Todinos depart.

'What's *maktub*?'

'It means, "thus it is written". They're a fatalistic lot over here.'

'Like Mamma?' she says.

'Let God's will be done,' he mumbles in a fake meek voice, and she recognises their mother in his tone.

She looks at him uncertainly. Is he mocking Mamma? At her glance he drops his head and starts muttering, passing imaginary prayer beads through his hands as if he is saying the rosary.

He raises his eyes to hers, his bright lively gaze, and he laughs.

And she, uncertainly, laughs too. They are so far from home, she thinks. No one is watching them. They are so deliciously far from home. A whole sea and the length of the land separates them.

'No, not like Mamma, because the people don't complain about their fate. They submit. Or fight,' he says.

'Do they fight? I thought we had conquered all resistance,' Liliana says, thinking of the General and his endless statistics.

'So they say,' Stefano says, without much interest. 'But that out there,' – he nods at a big ship at anchor in the bay – 'is a troop carrier.'

All the other passengers have gone. The cars and carts have departed. The only people left, apart from Liliana and her brother, are the working men, unloading the mail now and some crates that are being pushed on trolleys to the warehouses. Only them and the blue lapping sea and the brighter blue sky where seabirds wheel and squawk.

Stefano turns to her. 'I am so happy to see you, little sister. You are the answer to my prayers. Now you are here, things are going to get better.'

'I hope so,' she says, touched by his trust, and a part of her, a new uncomfortable part that makes her a stranger to herself, is thinking of the airman and her arrangement with him, which sometimes she characterises as a tryst and other times as just a friendly lunch.

'Let's get going,' Stefano says. 'It'll be a bit of a squeeze because this car's only designed for one.' He laughs.

He helps her clamber in and then vaults in the other side. They are both narrow of hip, and there is enough room on the seat for them, but they have to do some jostling to accommodate their shoulders.

'I don't think I allowed for the fact that you'd have grown,' he says. The arrangement they come to involves Liliana leaning forward and twisting towards him, lifting her shoulders free so that his can be square against the seat back. He cranks up the motor and, with a roar, they are off.

The position the cramped arrangement demands means that her face is in close proximity to his and for the whole journey his profile, his straight nose and the lick of black hair that flops forward is in the forefront of what she sees.

Once they are off the wharf they swing left onto the seafront road. The thought that she is on the other side of that sea, away from it all, everything reversed, a new start, reverberates through her.

Stefano takes his hand off the wheel and lightly taps her knee. 'How do you fancy taking this for a spin?' he says. 'We could drive out to the oasis before I take you to the apartment. Or are you too tired? I've got all morning.'

'I thought you had to go to work!'

'That's just what I told your snobby fascist friends,' he says.

She raises her eyebrows at him, but he doesn't notice. He's got his eyes on the road. She's not used to anyone talking about fascists as if they are a separate breed. She doesn't know what he means. 'Well, we're all fascists now, aren't we?' she says after a while.

'Huh,' he says. 'I suppose we are. Or act as if we are. Some of us are more fascist than others. You should see the poor people here, Lili, the natives I mean, when the cannon goes off. Jumping to attention, right arm swinging up as if it's pulled on a string. Long live *Il Duce*, they all shout, even though half of them probably don't even know what that means.'

She doesn't understand what point he's making. 'Perhaps they want him to have a long life,' she says.

'Or they want to have one themselves!' Stefano says.

Liliana stays quiet.

'But you,' he says. 'To put up with that terrible man for a week. Hats off to you, Lili.'

'What do you mean?' she says. 'What's General Todino done?'

'Don't you remember?'

'What?' she says.

'Oh,' he says, disconcerted. He shakes his head. 'Of course, you didn't know. You look so grown-up now. I forget you're only a girl. General Todino was on the board of the railway when Papà used to work there. He might still be, for all I know. He's definitely involved in the project to expand the rail line here.' He nods, as if he's checking the information with himself, that he is being accurate and fair. 'General Todino chaired the panel which decided the accident that cost our father his right eye was not the company's fault.'

Stefano glances sideways at her to make sure she is grasping this. 'It was, somehow, his own fault that a crane hook swung into his face. It's because of that man that Papà receives only a third of his pension.'

A shiver runs through Liliana. 'Oh,' is all that she says.

'I remember Papà coming home. He told me that it was General Todino himself who broke the news of the company's decision to him. "Todino's going to see me right," Papà said. "He's going to look out for a suitable role for me.'"

'He didn't, though, did he?' Liliana says in a small voice. What a fool she has been to think these people cared for her at all.

'Sorry,' Stefano says after a while. 'Did you think he was a nice old gentleman?'

'Why do people never tell me anything?' Liliana says. 'How am I supposed to manage if I'm kept in the dark?'

'Papà probably just wanted to make your trip easier,' Stefano says.

'Perhaps General Todino felt guilty,' she says. 'He wanted to make amends and so he agreed to accompany me here.'

'Doubt it,' Stefano said. 'Perhaps he wanted your company. Or his wife did. I don't think men like him have a conscience. They have to keep it simple. Black and white and no shades in between. They're the ones in charge.'

They are driving slowly along the seafront, stuck behind an overladen truck.

'And he didn't exactly do you a big favour did he? They were coming here anyway. It's not like they paid for you, is it?' Stefano says.

The room in the Rome hotel, the hiring of the costume, the pile of nearly new clothes that the Contessa has given her flash through Liliana's mind. Perhaps she will think about these things later, when she is alone.

The truck that has been wobbling slowly along in front of them turns off, and a great long stretch of empty sea road opens out ahead. 'Hold on to your hat,' Stefano shouts above the engine noise, 'we're going to the oasis!' With a great roar, the car accelerates.

*

128

On the way back into town after their walk in the oasis, Stefano regales her with tales about the infamous Gastone the African and the other racing drivers. How, the night before the race, there was a major problem with Gastone's Talbot because it was running on a special fuel called Elcosine, which had altered in composition, perhaps because of the heat. They discovered, don't ask him how, that pure alcohol worked just as well. So they spent the evening going round all the chemist's shops in Tripoli buying up bottles, flasks and tins of raw alcohol to scrape together the three hundred litres they needed.

'We were here, on this road, on Lungomare Volpi. We filled her up, back there beside the castle,' – he jabs his thumb in the air behind him – 'and he came thundering down here. It was night, about nine. He came down this road like blue lightning. Hitting full speed, flat out, blasting along. I watched him from that jetty,' he says. He laughs at the memory.

He has changed, her brother. He is thinner than he was but at the same time seems more solid. He is enjoying his life.

'Blue lightning,' she says.

'Really. There were blue flames coming out of the exhaust. And the thing is, I think that weird mixture helped him win,' Stefano says. He nods in a satisfied way. 'It was a good race,' he says.

He tells her too about the car they are in, which is a Salmson, but not one of those supercharged four-cylinder ones, he says as if she might be familiar with such a thing. It was in the small-car category in the race. A chap called Mario Moradei drove it in his first race ever, but he had to pull out after only one lap.

She is thinking again about the airman, Ugo Mantello. It

would be a shame not to go and meet him, just to see, because it is only a lunch after all, and she has altered one of the dresses from the Contessa – the pink silk one with the lace overlay and it fits her so beautifully.

'Did a bit of work on the carburettor jet for Moradei and so he said I could take it out, come and pick my little sister up in style,' Stefano is saying. He turns and grins at her. The flash of his teeth.

It is so nice to hear him chattering about cars and drivers and steering columns and gearboxes again.

'That's the theatre there,' he says, waving his arm.

She twists to see a substantial two-tiered building in white stone with long arched windows and crenellations. 'Miramare', the lettering on the top says.

'Not that I've been. Ha ha,' Stefano says.

'Grand Hotel,' he says, and she sees another big white building, like a castle, with scaffolding in front of the right-hand side of its façade. That is where the Todinos are staying. Stefano swings the car right, away from the sea. She turns back to face him and sees beyond, down a big thoroughfare, the cathedral. Her stomach flips, whether at Stefano's swerve to the left or at the sudden memory that this is where she has the appointment in two days' time. She is to be at the entrance to the cathedral at noon. The airman will send a car to collect her. She has it all written on the card. She shakes her head. Nothing will happen if she doesn't go. Ugo Montello doesn't know her address in Tripoli. She might not go.

'I didn't know the cathedral was pink,' she says.

'Pinkish,' her brother says.

He pulls up beside the kerb in a broad commercial street, outside a café. If it weren't for the palm trees along one pavement it would look like a street in the middle of an Italian town. 'Is this where you live?' she asks as he wriggles his hips free and hauls himself out of the vehicle.

'That would be nice, to live on Corso Vittorio Emanuele,' he says, standing on the pavement under the café awning and smiling down at her.

'Well I don't know, do I?' she says. She is conscious that she is sitting in a pool of sweat, that her dress has fused with the back of her legs. She is going to look a sight.

'Sorry,' he says. He gestures about him. 'This is one of the main streets in the new Italian part of the city. The municipal buildings are up that end and over there is the main post office, and after that the castle that we passed on the seafront because we've looped round, and back the other way, where we came in, the cathedral, as you saw. I thought we could go and have a coffee before I take you home.'

He looks at her again. 'We don't live anywhere like this, Lili. We're in the old town. It's not far from here but it's like another planet. You'll see. I think you'll like it. It's got character.' He hums a snatch of dirge-like melody that she doesn't recognise and moves his fingers as if he's playing an instrument.

It is nice to be so comprehensively included. That he is saying 'we' and talking as if she is more than just a visitor, as if she is going to live here with him in his exotic foreign home.

She is here. She is finally here and she is with Stefano, and the African sun is shining down and sticking her to the car seat; she is about to drink her first cappuccino in Tripolitania and she has an assignation that she might or might not keep and something else, something sliding through her, like a glimpsed reflection in a mirror, a concentrated shining feeling. She smiles up at her brother standing on the pavement.

It seems to her that the feeling is contained in the trembling line of sunlight on the pavement between the two patches of shade cast by the awning.

'Before,' Stefano says, 'I was in the government lodgings, but that was when I was a bachelor.' He grins at her. 'Not suitable for a married man.'

The shiny feeling slides away.

'What?' he says. His grin fades.

'Nothing,' she replies. She flaps her hand in front of her face, fanning herself. 'It's so hot.'

'Well we *are* in Africa,' he says. He reaches both hands down and half heaves, half lifts her out of the car. 'Designed for speed,' he says, 'not for passengers, especially not girls in frocks.'

She follows him into the café, discreetly unsticking the back of her dress from her legs. It is empty apart from a man in uniform seated with his back to them on one of the high stools at the chrome counter. He turns, but it is not Ugo Montello, nothing like.

She has got it all wrong. Stefano has not separated from the native girl. All this time he has been with her. When did he send that little note, folded inside his monthly letter? It was August last year. They have been together for at least ten months.

Liliana and Stefano sit at a round chrome table away from the window, in the relative shade at the back of the café, where an electric ceiling fan stirs the sludgy air. Liliana takes her hat off and pats her hair into shape.

'What I want you to do,' Stefano says, when their cappuccinos are in front of them, 'it's sort of a secret mission. I want you to teach her – Farida, my wife – Italian ways.'

'Pardon?' she says.

There are so many expectations that she didn't quite fully know that she had. Balls and soirées and admiring young officers. An interesting job in the office at the race track. Trips to the local markets with elegant young women, friends of the Contessa. She can feel them abandoning her and fragmenting, being chopped up and dispersed as if by the whirling blades of the fan above.

'I want Farida to learn Italian ways,' he says again. He speaks in a low and conspiratorial voice. His face is shiny and nervous and boyish. She thinks that of course the girl won't resemble the strange creature on that postcard, with tattoos and oversized dangling jewellery like silver plates, but what is it her brother is asking of her?

'So, this girl lives with you here in Tripoli?' she says.

He scrutinises her. A wave of irritation crosses his face. 'Where else would she live?'

'And you want me to teach her Italian ways.'

He nods, slightly impatiently, as if to say *are we still only at this stage of the conversation?* He explains his plan. He speaks in a low voice so that the bartender won't hear. He wants her, Liliana, to 'Italianise' the girl, Farida. To teach her their customs, to bring her out of herself. To practise the language with her. She already speaks it quite well, but it needs to become more fluent. Help her to read and write. But most of all, the main thing, is that he wants her to dress like a European and come out of the house with him. 'I want her on my arm,' he says. 'But she'll only go out if she's covered in a barracan, one of these big white blanket things they wrap round themselves.'

'She can't read?' Liliana says.

'No, they don't teach girls here. Well, most of them can't read or write, not just the girls.' He nods to himself. 'She can write her name and a few other words in Arabic, but she doesn't know our letters at all.'

Liliana doesn't know what to say.

'She comes out wrapped in that bloody blanket and she walks three paces behind me as if she is my servant,' he says.

While Liliana is trying to come up with a response other than 'well, at least one of you knows her place', he launches into the tale of how the two of them met. He tells her about the desert. Sand everywhere, he says. It gets in your teeth. He doesn't like it, but he has respect for the Bedouins. 'They live out in that God-awful desolation and they produced Farida,' he says. 'There's two impressive things they've done. Some of them, they've seen our inventions and they just don't care for them. They're not duped by our gadgets and our machinery, the stuff we call civilisation.' He shakes his head at the wonder of this. 'Not like me,' he says. 'I'm a dupe. A total dupe.'

In more ways than one, she thinks.

'I didn't think it would happen overnight,' he says, 'of course I didn't. But I thought by now ...' He bites his lip, looks woefully at Liliana.

Her big brother.

'She is covered from head to toe in that stupid barracan like a blinkered camel, so she can't even see where she is going properly. It took her an age to find her way to the fish market and the vegetable market. I'm stuck, Liliana. *We're* stuck. I don't know what to do.'

'And you can't, you wouldn't think of ...' She looks at him, testing the ground.

'What?'

'Sending her back?' she blurts.

His face falls. He takes a breath and lets it slowly out. 'Oh, Lili,' he says.

134

He scrapes the chair back and gets to his feet, stands for a moment leaning on the chair, closes his eyes and squeezes them as if he is in pain, as if he is trying not to cry or is about to burst with rage. But is it so unreasonable, what she has said? This girl is not his proper wife, not really. He's not thinking straight.

He looks blankly over her head in the direction of the window onto the street. He shakes his head slowly from side to side. After a while he takes a packet of cigarettes out of his pocket, taps one out and sticks it between his lips. He lights it, and only then does he look at her. 'I've arranged for you to come here to do this job. I'm not sending her back. There isn't anywhere to send her.'

He goes to the counter and pays, swings out of the café door and stands outside, smoking.

She gets up and follows him. 'I'm sorry,' she says. She inserts her arm through his. 'I will try,' she says. 'Explain to me again. I'm tired from the voyage. I'm being dense.'

'If anyone can do this, you can,' he says. 'I'm not saying convert her, make a Catholic of her. Nothing like that. I don't mind much about the reading either. Lots of Italians get by without being able to read anything other than their own names.'

The girl is not even a Christian! And she is illiterate.

'Let's give it three months. And if you can't make it happen, then I will have to think again. And you will have to go home.'

$\sim$

He didn't handle that well, Stefano thinks as they set off again in the car. He was clumsy and insensitive, just coming out with his plan like that and expecting her to go along with it straight away. He has been thinking about his Italianisation scheme so much that he hadn't allowed for how outlandish it would seem. And of course Liliana hadn't had a sniff of it beforehand. He hadn't allowed for that either.

He couldn't tell her about it in advance. He was wary of the censors. A guy he knew who worked at the air base at Mellaha told him a letter of his home had so many black lines through it that all his wife could read was 'give my love to little Pino'. He was a military man and that might have been why they were down on him. But anyway, Stefano is careful in his letters and he makes sure always to mention something good about what Italy is doing here in Tripoli. Building churches and hotels and beautiful piazzas, laying sewage pipes, opening new Italian bakeries where you can buy cornetti, using the grapes from vineyards in the Jebel Nafusa in western Tripolitania to make home-grown wine. That sort of thing. He never mentions the poverty, the naked children with flies sticking to their snotty faces, the shanty town with open sewers running through, the squalid shacks with tin roofs. He never mentions the treatment of local people he has witnessed, the kickings and the whippings. Nor the stories he has heard of bodies hanging from gibbets, of summary executions. Stefano doubts he is of sufficient interest to the authorities for anyone to read his letters home, but he isn't going to risk it.

The last time he saw her she was a gawky kid with her hair in pigtails. Now look at her. Her hair brushed as smooth as it will go and pinned up under her hat. She's wearing lipstick and heels. She looks like one of the girls that parade along the seafront with their parasols.

But it was something else that had made him say it all so baldly. Something in the way she had said 'Well, we're all fascists now, aren't we?' As if it was entirely normal and incontrovertible. A fact of life. A mark of civilisation, even.

And the way she had looked at him when he'd said whatever it was he'd said about not being a bachelor any more. The way her face fell.

He has feared this. The relentless propaganda back in Italy poisons impressionable young minds like hers. It reduces the world to extremes.

And no one has offered her an alternative viewpoint. Their father, who used to be a thinker, a man who asked questions, has capitulated so utterly that it makes Stefano ashamed. He should at least have told Liliana about General Todino. What was the point of babying her?

Stefano had had the best of their parents, that was certain. And he at least had known a time when there was some middle ground in Italy. But Liliana has known no different.

It took him a long time to be in a financial position to lift her out of it, to bring her here. He thought he was never going to manage it, but then two things happened to change the situation. First, he was paid a bonus after the race; and second, Alfonso, passing through town on another of his business trips, announced that he was writing off the bride-price debt. The sheikh's scimitar that he had acquired during their adventure in the desert was recompense enough. He had hung it in his hallway and liked to tell his daughters that he had won it from bandits.

Alfonso had brought gifts for Stefano and Farida on that visit, wedding gifts: a gramophone and several records of popular music. He had wanted to bring the whole of *Turandot* for Stefano, but the opera had not been recorded. He had, however, found a disc with Beniamino Gigli singing 'Nessun dorma'. You wound up the mechanism with the handle, placed the steel-tipped needle on the outer edge of the record and the tunes played out through the speaker. 'I know you love machines,' Alfonso said to him. But Farida is the one who loves it most. She listens to the songs while he is out at work and sings along in her husky voice. The records have been a help in improving her fluency in Italian and she is a quick learner. For nine months, too, the youngest daughter of Signor Yaacov, their landlord, came and gave Farida daily lessons in Italian. But Esther left a month ago to get married. Esther, being Jewish, went out unveiled and he had hoped that would encourage Farida to do the same, but it had not. When he is at home he talks to Farida all the time. He reads to her. He tells her about his day, but really, now, she needs another teacher and a companion, someone to bring her out of herself. That is where Liliana comes in.

It's not Liliana's fault, not really, that she has become a proper little fascist in his absence. He could tell it from her letters, that disconcerting blend of religion and the cult of *Il Duce*. Somehow God was called in to do Mussolini's dirty work. How had that happened, for goodness sake? And the way she talked about Angela, the girl at her work who was arrested for distributing anti-fascist leaflets. 'One of those clandestines,' she wrote, as if Angela deserved her fate. He wanted to tell her that Angela and people like her were brave. That when Angela rose at dawn to get to work first and place the forbidden leaflets and the newspapers next to people's lockers or on their machines, fear would have dogged her. That she would have had her heart in her mouth. But he couldn't write that in a letter.

He hopes it's not too late. He glances sideways at her as he pulls up outside the Tobacco Factory on Via Gioia. He catches her eye and she smiles at him. How endearing she was when they were at the oasis, curious about everything. Of course it isn't too late. He has given her a shock. His dear little sister. She and Farida will be so good for each other. He climbs out of the car and bends to lift her. He says, 'I am so glad that you are here.'

WHERE THE LIGHT ENTERS

Item: A fold-out map of a hospital.

There are two rows of benches set back to back in the reception area. One set faces outward, to the hospital's double doors, and the other inward. Liliana is facing inward.

On the way down in the lift, she felt faint. When she arrived on the ground floor, she spotted the benches and thought she would have a little sit down. It has been half an hour and she is still here.

Her careering heart has slowed and the dizziness has passed. In theory, she could get up and go, but she has come to a halt. It is not just the heavy weariness and sadness that have descended on her. It is the realisation that, once she leaves, this interlude, this moment of possibility when doors might have been opening instead of closing, when her lost family might have been found, comes to an end. She will have to go and try to resume her life in London. She tries to imagine unpacking her suitcase at home in Crouch End and replacing that tray of memorabilia underneath the bottom drawer in her bedroom chest. She wonders how she will find the strength, and what the point would be.

The noises of the hospital surround her: the swish of the

sliding doors behind, the clank and bleep of the lifts, the occasional blare of an ambulance siren, the jingle of the coins dropping into the public payphones, the buzz of voices. There is a constant movement of people, on foot or in wheelchairs, sick people, old people, people carrying children, doctors, nurses, orderlies, visitors.

The notion that she will never now know what became of Stefano and Farida is unutterably sad. But almost worse than that is the not knowing what happened in the dark place to which she, Liliana, descended when her life in Tripoli went wrong. The thing that she used to try to piece together from disparate fragments, but has never been able to assemble into a coherent whole because something vital is missing. The tent and the blood and the witchy woman with her torturing hands. Liliana knows that she was not well back then, in the last few months before she left Libya. She was sick in body and in mind. Stefano called it the weeping sickness. She became unmoored and Farida took her away from Tripoli to recover. She remembers the boat trip and snatches of their time in Benghazi, and then nothing except those garish fragments until they were back in Tripoli in the new apartment Stefano had found near the sea. She wasn't yet well. Her mind was still confused and her body weak. Even when she returned to Monza her head continued to be fuzzy, and by the time she might have wanted to make sense of things she didn't know how to go about it. There were questions that scared her so much she had difficulty allowing them to formulate in her mind. She never quite has. It is as if they are on a high shelf, just out of her reach, and sometimes she stretches for them, but she never manages to get a grip. Her mind seems to slide away. Perhaps, if she had ever been in Farida's presence again, things would have become clear without her having to ask the impossible questions. But that hadn't happened. And then the letters stopped and the years went by in silence and the chance of it ever being known disappeared and, as best she could, she stopped thinking about it.

The special little girl, who looked at her once with sapphire eyes when everything else was darkness. Was she too good for this world, was that what it was?

How can she bear to live without knowing? A phrase Farida used to use is playing in her head. 'The wound is the place where the light enters you.' Farida had many sayings to help make sense of suffering. Liliana can feel the wound as she sits here on her own in the hospital, but there is no light.

In coming here so unprepared, she has thrown caution to the winds. As if, at her advanced age, there might be some different future awaiting. What a fool she is. She closes her eyes for an instant and lets tears trickle from inside her closed lids down her cheeks. All these years, she thinks, all these uncounted years. The unanswered letters. The pitiless surge of hope she experienced with each new major event in Libya – the ending of the war, Italy relinquishing sovereignty in 1947, the proclamation of the United Kingdom of Libya in 1951, the 1969 coup overthrowing King Idris – as if the country's history were a tablecloth that was periodically lifted and shaken and they, the members of her family who resided there, the crumbs, the unwanted crumbs, might be thrown up by these ructions. She thought she had finally given up on them when Gaddafi had evicted the remaining Italians in 1970 and they were not among the shocked twenty thousand shipped with one suitcase apiece home to a land they didn't know. But she hadn't, not really. Somewhere within she had held on to a pathetic scrappy rag of hope.

And now it is time to let it go. Here in this hospital foyer.

People come to use the telephones hanging from the wall in front of her and snatches of their conversations intrude on her thoughts. 'You're right,' a man says, 'where there's life there's hope.' 'I told you to buy chicken,' a woman says, 'not lamb. What am I going to do with lamb?' It is strange to be surrounded by people who are all speaking Italian.

She hears a young female voice speaking in Arabic. She looks up. Even though the girl's back is turned, she recognises her, the girl she saw in the upstairs corridor. The scarlet shoes, the thick black plait hanging down between her shoulder blades. She sees that the blue thread tying the plait-end has come partially undone and is trailing. The girl is on the last phone in the line, the one reserved for international calls.

The girl replaces the receiver and leans forward, her body weight slumping, her shoulders rising and falling, weeping into the hospital wall.

Liliana is on her feet. She has forgotten what little Arabic she once knew. 'Are you all right?' she says in Italian.

The girl swivels round and her plait swings over her shoulder. She wipes her nose with the back of her hand.

Liliana feels it again. That sensation of losing her footing. Something about this girl is so achingly familiar. She unclips her handbag, finds a clean tissue and offers it. 'Is there anything I can do?' she says.

The girl looks at her with a fiery intensity, examining her. Instead of resenting the scrutiny, Liliana finds she wants to pass the test, whatever it is.

'Signora, do you know me?' the girl says.

Liliana looks at the girl's bleary frightened face and, even though she knows that they cannot possibly have ever met, she wants to say yes.

'Perhaps I was very small at the time,' the girl continues, and she indicates with her hand the height of a small child.

Somewhere in the dim recesses of Liliana's brain, a little voice, Alan's voice perhaps, is saying *careful, love, watch how you go, take a moment*. She shakes her head. 'I knew Abramo Cattaneo,' she says. Is that careful enough, she wonders.

The girl's eyes widen. She lets out a faint cry, but doesn't speak. She stands with the tissue crumpled in her hand, tears running down her face, staring at Liliana as if she were an apparition.

'I knew him when he was a child,' Liliana says. 'I read about the shooting in the newspaper and so I came here to visit him at the hospital and I've just found out that he's . . . ' She shakes her head.

The girl speaks so quietly that Liliana doesn't quite catch it. She thought the girl said Abramo was her uncle, but that couldn't be right. The nurse would have told her if Abramo had a niece here.

'I haven't told them,' the girl whispers, 'the people here. I haven't told them that Abramo is my uncle.'

'Why not?' Liliana says. She is whispering too.

'Because I was frightened,' the girl says, and she starts to cry again.

Liliana can't take in what any of it means, but her poor tired old heart leaps. 'You poor darling,' she says. 'I'm here now.'

THE DESERT GIRL

Item: A postcard of Tripoli showing the Jewish quarter of the old town.

Stefano parks in front of a big building called the Tobacco Factory. He has not spoken at all since they climbed back into the car outside the café. He has been lost in his own thoughts, but now he lifts Liliana out, plants her on the pavement and tells her how happy he is that she is finally here. They are to walk the last part of the journey because the streets of the old town are too narrow for motor cars, he tells her now. The doorman will keep an eye on the car for half an hour, and then Stefano will have to get going or Moradei will think he's stolen it.

He unstraps Liliana's trunk, heaves it onto his shoulder and holds it in place with both arms up above his head. As they walk, through a crumbling archway and into an ancient street, Stefano keeps up a stream of talk.

Liliana walks quietly beside and sometimes behind him. She is conscious of a blinding whiteness and a crumbling filth, and mostly keeps her eyes down to avoid stepping in one of the piles of rubbish or donkey dung. Occasionally, when she is behind, she looks up at the patch of sweat on the back of Stefano's shirt and the way the muscles of his arms strain against his sleeves.

Her brother's home is just down here, round this corner with the studded doorway and along this walkway beneath the three white archways, round two more corners, the second with three distinctive square apertures high in the wall, and past this pale orange-coloured building with ancient inscriptions that is the Dar al-Bishi synagogue and here in this street which is a dead end, like a little square really, their own square. He has rented the apartment from a Jewish merchant, a Signor Yaacov who lives above them with his wife in a large apartment with a roof terrace. He has three daughters, all married. The youngest, Esther, used to come downstairs to teach Farida Italian, but she has moved away now with her new husband. This neighbourhood, the Jewish quarter, is known as Harar al-Yahoud. It might feel as if it is deep inside the Medina, but in five minutes, once she has learned the way, she can be in a place from where she can see the ocean. These old buildings have thick walls and few windows, which keeps the interior cool in the heat of summer. Later Stefano plans to move to a house by the sea where the air is fresh and clean, and the sea breeze cools it all, but for now this is a good place, a bit out of the way, a bit hidden.

All of this Liliana learns during the walk from the Tobacco Factory.

They have arrived. The cul-de-sac, an ancient tree twisting up in the centre, is surrounded by white-painted windowless buildings. This is the place.

'You'll like it,' Stefano says again with an embarrassed laugh. 'You can imagine you are living in ancient times. Biblical. Yes, very Old Testament.' He pushes against a battered-looking wooden door into a corridor, a blind sort of dark tiled corridor, calling the girl's name, Farida, that it is only him, that he is back, that their guest has arrived, his little sister is here. They turn a sharp corner and suddenly are in a bright open space. 'I so hope the pair of you are going to be great friends,' he says over his shoulder to Liliana. He steps aside.

And there she is, his sort of wife. She is both like and unlike the Arab beauty in Liliana's postcard back home. Her hair hangs in long black plaits. Her black and bronze striped dress is voluminous and seems to flow about her body. Her chin and forehead are tattooed. She has a small oval face and big topaz-coloured eyes, outlined in black. Silver jewellery hangs around her throat and ankles and wrists, and from her ears. She is small and delicately made and looks ready to take flight at the first surprising noise or sudden movement. The word ethereal comes to Liliana, and with it the notion that the girl needs all those metal objects hanging about her small person to weigh her down and keep her earthbound.

They eye each other warily. The girl glances up at Liliana's hat and then down to her stockinged legs and the straps on her shoes. Her eyes stray to Liliana's neck, where she wears a tiny gold crucifix on a chain. It had not occurred to Liliana to think about the desert girl's opinion, to think of her having an opinion. But the sizing-up is mutual and the awareness of that makes her skin tingle. Please accept me, she surprises herself by thinking, and then, at sight of the girl's bare feet painted with intricate patterns, she really is a little savage, and then, I would like to kiss her.

Liliana can smell rosewater and spice and something unrecognisable but earthy, like upturned roots. There is the tinkling sound of water somewhere near by. They are in an atrium open to the sky, an internal courtyard, an unexpect-edly bright space full of sunshine and shadows. What hidden loveliness! Who would ever have thought?

She smiles uncertainly at the strange desert girl and the girl smiles back. For another moment they continue to stand there looking at each other, and in that moment Liliana has the sensation of something hard and stony in the middle of her chest, a sort of pain in and behind her sternum, throbbing as if it is about to disintegrate. When they do step towards each other and take each other's hands and lean in to kiss cheeks and murmur words of greeting, there is a sort of familiarity mixed in with the strangeness, as if some part of each of them had gone before and had already met.

Standing like that, with clasped hands as if they are about to play a game of ring-a-ring-o'-roses and dance in a circle in the courtyard, they both turn to look at Stefano.

'Tea for the traveller!' he exclaims.

And soon Liliana is seated on a cushion and drinking her first cup of frothing mint tea, poured from an orange enamel pot.

GUARDIAN ANGELS

Item: A fraying strand of blue woollen thread.

Zaida stirred into semi-wakefulness and for a fraction of a second, before sliding her hand out from under her head and turning to face the other way, placing her cheek down on a damp patch of dribble, she thought she was home in bed and that the alarm had not yet gone off. Then she remembered.

From under her eyelashes, she watched the elderly lady sitting at the other side of the bed. When she had had the impossible idea of conjuring up a distant family member, she had imagined one of the women of her home town who would wrap her in their embrace and confound the Italian authorities with their otherness, their stubbornness, their alternative rules. Or, even better in the circumstances, some-one like Madame Simone, a big-boned, cushiony woman who had a gift for hugs but who also would have known the system and would have argued or charmed, depending on what was needed. Best of all, although it galled Zaida to admit it, would have been a man. Because here, as at home in Libya, men could cut through it all if they were on your side. She was going to change that one day, but she had to bide her time. She was fourteen. She was the daughter of a political exile who had been hunted down. Her beloved uncle was dead.

The dread was clutching at her. She must not let it take hold. Later, there would be time to weep.

The person who had turned up as if in answer to her plea was scarily frail herself. The only bold things about her were her wild white curly hair and her emerald green scarf. Otherwise, this elderly, apologetic and strained-looking lady who spoke a soft and halting Italian and occasionally twitched as if someone had crept up behind her and tapped her shoulder, seemed at least as bewildered as Zaida herself about how things worked. She was the unlikeliest of saviours, but there she was and she wanted to help.

Zaida was mystified by Signora Jones from London. She could hardly begin to know what to think of her. She knew only that Signora Jones, like her, was grieving, and that their sadness was the place where they had met. She didn't understand why Signora Jones had come to visit her Uncle Abramo when she seemed to have known him only as a baby and not seen him since, but it didn't matter. Signora Jones must have known her mother too. She would have time later to discover these things.

To have Signora Jones there made Zaida feel less alone.

Signora Jones was moving her lips, muttering under her breath and looking down at her hands, which were twisting in her lap. Zaida, watching, saw the effect of the invisible tap on the shoulder, the shudder that suddenly ran through the older lady. It gave her goosebumps to see it. Signora Jones raised her eyes, glanced towards Zaida's father and then across at Zaida. She could not know that, beneath the mass of her hair, Zaida's eyes were open, but Zaida closed them anyway and feigned sleep. She didn't want to pry.

'Your beautiful daughter,' Signora Jones said out loud. 'She asked me to talk to you and tell you a story, and here I am lost in my own thoughts.'

Signora Jones was talking to her father.

'Sorry,' she said, 'I promised her that I would keep guard.' Signora Jones gave one of her funny little laughs that indicated embarrassment rather than amusement.

It was true, Zaida had asked the lady to swear she would not leave the room and would wake her if there was any change. In response, the old lady had crossed her hands on her breast and then pointed her right hand up at the ceiling. Zaida had not understood, but Signora Jones explained that it was a thing that some people in England, mostly children, might do to make a promise, and that they also said 'Cross my heart and hope to die.'

Half-listening to the lady's soft voice and soothed by it, Zaida fell back asleep.

∼

The nurse had said that the man in the bed, with tubes connecting him to a bleeping machine, might be able to hear, even if he didn't respond. Liliana picked up the newspaper. The front-page news was another killing. A journalist in Milan gunned down by suspected left-wing terrorists. On the second page was the same photograph of the man that she had seen in the newspaper in Muswell Hill library. 'Would-be Assassins Get Clear Away' was the headline. A speedboat had been waiting for them at Fiumicino. It wasn't the first such attack in Rome, and there had been others in LA and Athens, as well as in London. The article said that Gaddafi, who liked to be called the Brotherly Leader, wanted to show how long was his reach, how impossible sanctuary. One by one, he was picking his opponents off. In London too, masked SAS troops had stormed the Iranian Embassy, throwing stun grenades through the window and putting an end to the siege there.

None of it seemed appropriate to read aloud to a man with a bullet in his brain.

Liliana took off her reading glasses and put the paper down. She didn't look at the man's face. She had caught a glimpse of his blackened eye sockets and awful pallor when she first came into the room, and once was enough. They said he was fighting for his life, but it was a very quiet fight, going on deep inside.

'I was at home in London,' she said, 'when I read about you in the newspaper.' Hard to believe it was only yesterday. 'My friend Joan urged me to come. She said finding the money showed it was meant to be. It was my guardian angel guiding me, but then when I got here . . . '

She stopped. Telling this man that his fellow victim was dead wasn't going to help. Not just his fellow victim but his – what? His brother-in-law, yes. To reach this man in that dark recess to which his self must have retreated, her words needed to present beauty and light.

'Joan believes in guardian angels,' she said. 'She doesn't think they are an abstract concept. She thinks they are actually there, wings and all. Invisible but present.'

Liliana thought about the hidden cache of money from Alan and how she had sat on the indigo counterpane in the bedroom counting it. She pictured her home in London, the curtains and cushions in gorgeous old fabrics discovered in junk shops and at auctions and that she had made herself, the long narrow garden with the pond at the end, the gnarled apple tree, the garden furniture on the patio, the tipped-up plastic chairs. She remembered the spade she had noticed lying near the vegetable patch, which she must have abandoned during a half-hearted attempt to dig the bed over, to keep things the way that Alan would have done. How temporary it seemed. How arbitrary. She had lived in England for forty years, and now it seemed like an interlude, time out from the stuff of reality. Blood and violent death.

Treat yourself, love.

Liliana had accompanied the girl, Zaida, up here to the room where her injured father lay. They had followed the yellow line. Purple for oncology, green for maternity, yellow for head trauma. It reminded Liliana of the line along the platform in London Underground stations, demarcating the safe place to stand and wait for the train. Liliana had the feeling that her four decades of staying behind the line, of keeping a distance between herself and the danger, might be coming to an end.

In a minute she was going to get a taxi to Zaida's apartment to collect some clothes for her. She had the keys in her handbag and Zaida had written out the address. She has even agreed to stay the night. She doesn't know what has come over her.

She gazed at the sleeping girl on the opposite side of the bed. Zaida had made a pillow of one folded arm next to the lump formed by her father's right knee, and had laid her head there, her long hair tumbling about on the hospital sheets, black electric filaments against the white, the gorgeous, careless profusion of youth.

The girl turned her face to one side. Her mouth was ajar, her cheek puffy and tear-stained. The hand that wasn't serving as a pillow gripped the sheet. She had created a handhold in the cloth and, even in sleep, she was hanging on, as if to a cliff face, dangling by one clenched hand. Around her wrist were five silver bangles, and trailing alongside her arm was the blue thread she had used to tie her plait. There were patches of purple nail varnish on her short nails. Asleep, the wariness gone, she looked even younger. Liliana reached across and picked up the blue thread, idly winding it round her finger, staring at the girl.

It was as if she were looking through the window of time. She had barely been fourteen when her brother left Italy. By then, the fascists had been in power for three years.

Such different times they had been born into, and yet, perhaps, what this girl had experienced in Libya, before she and her father had fled, had much in common with Liliana's early years in Monza. Clearly they were both brought up in tyrannical, oppressive systems where freedom and individuality were crushed. Libya was a secretive regime, but Liliana knew, because that was why Zaida's father had fled into exile, that political parties were banned, as they had been in Italy in her youth. Dissent was not tolerated. In fascist Italy it was often punished with beatings by the *squadristi*, or by internal exile. Thousands were transported to the prison islands and other remote locations so that their voices would not be heard. In Gaddafi's Libya they were locked up or hanged. Both states used assassination as a weapon. They sent out killers to gun down their opponents wherever they had fled. Stefano's hero Carlo Rosselli, who had escaped from his prison on Lipari, was assassinated by hired killers in France. And now Gaddafi's agents were travelling to foreign countries to gun down the so-called stray dogs as the fate of this comatose man and of Abramo testified.

And the question that was playing in Liliana's mind was: how come Zaida had not been moulded and squashed by her background in the way that Liliana had?

She tried to picture Zaida in the white shirt, black tie, black pleated skirt and white ankle socks that were the uniform of the Opera Nazionale Balilla, the Italian fascist youth organisation, swinging her arms and doing regimented star jumps with hundreds of others, but she couldn't. She couldn't press this girl who, even when slumbering and grieving, seemed to burst with vitality and curiosity, into that restricted shape. Zaida simply wouldn't fit.

She pondered this, looking at the sleeping, tear-stained girl. How different things were if one were taught to ask questions, to argue, to look at all facets of an idea from a range of angles. A girl she had known back then, Angela, appeared in her mind. She felt ashamed now at how she had gone along with the others and condemned her for handing out anti-fascist leaflets. So facile and glib, she had been.

She unwound the thread from her finger and dropped it into her handbag.

Liliana had not even been aware that she was growing up in what a friend of Alan's described as a 'blighted time'. But Zaida knew where she came from. She was as innocent as Liliana had been, more so, if innocence means purity of heart, but she was not blinkered. That was the difference. But this freedom of thinking came at a price. If you speak out against a regime that brooks no dissent, then you live a life of danger, always looking over your shoulder, and you might be forced into exile and separation, or even death. Is it worse to be free on the inside and have to meet the punishment of the outside, as Zaida was doing, or to have your inside scooped out and live with the anguish of being a half person or less, as Liliana had? Trying to conform to a set of second-hand beliefs that strike no chord of truth within you?

Poor little thing, she thought, and she wasn't sure which

one of them it was that she felt more sorry for, her own young self, or Zaida.

She unwrapped one of the chocolates Zaida had given her and put it in her mouth.

ASIDA AND RUB

Item: A postcard of a typical Tripolitanian house showing the tiled internal courtyard and fountain.

The desert girl, Farida, is preparing breakfast for them both in the sunlit central space. She is like a little bird, a shy little bird landing momentarily in a patch of sunshine and then hopping into the shade. She moves quickly about, gathering what she needs: a pot of salt from the shelf, the sack of flour, a cloth that she drapes over her shoulder, a big yellow plate, a jar of oil and a tub containing a dark paste.

Stefano has long since gone to work, and they are just the two of them at home, Liliana and the strange bejewelled girl with the painted eyes and patterned feet. Liliana is mesmerised by her.

The atrium is half open to the sky two floors up and half covered by the overhang of the floor above, which is held up by slim columns of pink marble. There is a high veranda on the north side of the wall, with a carved fretwork screen, a *masharabia*, enclosing it. Once it would have been accessed by the ladies upstairs and would have allowed them to peer down on this central space and watch the goings on below. It belongs to their landlord, is in Signor Yaacov's section of the building, but he has told Stefano that the door to the veranda has been boarded up on the other side and no one can now spy on this household. Three rooms open off the atrium – Stefano and Farida's sleeping room, a narrower one that is Liliana's and a store room. At the end of each there is a raised platform called a *sedda*, which can be used as a bed and for storage. The bedrooms have no windows. Heavy wooden doors adorned with old brass nails shut them off from the atrium. Liliana left her door half open during the night. It is not so much the darkness that bothers her as the feeling of there being no way out, the sensation of imprisonment.

She has unpacked her trunk and placed it at the end of her *sedda*. She has hung her dresses on a rail attached to the wall.

Down the corridor that leads to the outside there is a white-tiled washroom, in which there is a high, glassless aperture, the only window in their part of the building. They cannot see out from here, and nobody can see in. This is how the women live, Stefano has told her, here in the town, although some have *masharabias* on their outward-facing balconies, through which they can glimpse the outside world, or rooftop terraces from which they might peer down. Signor Yaacov's household apparently has a roof terrace that connects via a second-storey bridge to a larger one from whence the city's rooftops and minarets can be seen. She can hear the women now, somewhere up above, their high voices and laughter. Signor Yaacov's wife has visitors.

Their communal life is conducted here in the courtyard, with its white and green tiled walls and floor. The kitchen stuff is stored on a shelf on the covered side. All the cooking is done on a small terracotta stove that they call a *kanoon*. The furniture is minimal. The long, low bench on which Liliana is sitting also serves as the table. To eat, the night before, they sat around it on big colourful cushions on the floor. Stefano said he was getting used to this way of sitting. He likes it. It's more convivial, he said. 'You're going native!' Liliana said and felt the girl's eyes on her, but when she turned to meet them she could not read her expression.

Farida served meat stew and couscous, and afterwards they drank cups of bitter tea. 'What happens when it rains?' Liliana asked. 'It doesn't much,' Stefano said. 'All the things dry so quickly you forget they were ever wet. The rain isn't a problem. It's the *ghibli* you have to watch out for.' He nodded and rolled his eyes. 'What's a *ghibli*?' she asked, seeing that he was dying to tell. 'It's when the desert comes to town,' he said. He described the sand-laden wind that came sweeping in from the Sahara and covered everything in yellow dust.

From the low bench she watches the girl flitting about the room, her bare feet making only the faintest of slapping noises on the tiled floor. She is wearing the black dress with bronze vertical stripes that swishes about her as she moves. She takes no notice of Liliana and seems to mutter to herself under her breath. It might be a prayer or invocation, or it might be instructions to herself, or a commentary, but she seems unaware that she is doing it. Or unaware that it is not the done thing to talk to yourself in company. Or perhaps it *is* done where she comes from, perhaps the men talk to each other and the women talk to themselves.

Liliana watches and does not know what to make of her. She fears she has offended her. She cannot tell.

Earlier, Liliana laid out on the bed in her room one of her own frocks that she thought would do well for Farida. It has long sleeves and a high, buttoned neck with a white collar, and comes down to her calves. Very modest and demure. She had the door propped wide open and when she saw the girl out in the central space she called her in to show her. Farida came across to the threshold but didn't enter. 'I thought this would fit you,' Liliana said, picking the dress up and shaking it out to its full length. The girl seemed not to understand. Liliana held it out towardss her, but the girl took a step backwards. 'For you,' Liliana said, walking towards her with the dress in her hands.

'Thank you,' Farida said and stood half in and half out of the room in a shaft of morning light with the dress draped over one arm as if she didn't know what to do with it. Visible on the uppermost fold was a place where Liliana had darned a little tear. She had sewn it carefully, but the mismatched thread was very obvious in the daylight.

'To wear,' Liliana said.

Farida kept her eyes on the dress

'Until we can get you some clothes of your own.'

'I have clothes,' Farida said.

'Yes, but this is for when we go out,' Liliana said. She indicated the girl and herself, arm-in-arm, and mimed the action of walking with her fingers.

The girl looked at Liliana's little finger legs strolling and then up at Liliana's face with horror. It was if Liliana had asked her to strip naked and parade like that through the streets. She uttered a stream of unknown words, put her free hand to her throat and then to her brow. Then she seemed to collect herself. 'No,' she said. 'I cannot.'

'Later,' Liliana said quickly. She scooped up the dress from Farida's hands. 'Not now. Another time. Later, later.' She waved her hand in the air as if she were wafting the very notion away.

The girl bowed her head. As she glided away, Liliana wondered if Stefano had even told her about the task he had entrusted to his sister, the Italianisation project, as he calls it. She had been sure that the idea of going out demurely dressed, two young women together, would not be as problematic as her brother had implied. She had been fretting instead about what to do about the tattoos on the girl's chin. Stefano had not mentioned them, as if they would disappear when Farida was wearing Italian clothes, as if just putting a dress on would somehow suffice, but they are not henna and will not fade. They are inked into her skin, like a little railway track running down beneath her lower lip. Anyway, she sees now that the tattoo dilemma is not of immediate concern. There is something much more fundamental to overcome first, and she cannot imagine how to go about it.

When Farida has assembled all she needs for her cooking, she squats by the *kanoon* and fans the coals with a palm leaf, bringing a pan of water she has set there to the boil. She sings softly as she works.

Liliana looks on from the bench.

The girl takes up a fistful of flour and drops it into the liquid, stirring it in with a wooden spoon. Her bare feet are planted flat, heels together, and her knees are apart with the folds of her dark dress flowing down between and around them to the floor. Suspended thus, close above the floor but on a level with the little clay oven, she is able to rock to one side to take another handful of flour from the sack and back to the middle to let it fall from her fist into the stiffening mixture while she stirs ever more vigorously with the other hand.

'What are you making?' Liliana asks.

The girl looks up at her and smiles. 'This is *asida*,' she says. 'We eat it with *rub*.' She lifts the tub of paste up from the floor and holds it out. 'This is *rub*. It is made from dates. The fruit of the palm. Very sweet and good.'

Liliana rises up and comes across to the stove, takes the tub and sniffs. She does not recognise the smell but it is sweet and fruity. 'Lovely smell,' she says. She fetches a cushion from beside the bench and sits on the other side of the oven to watch more closely. Some instinct tells her to be companionable, to emulate the girl's stance, but her skirt is too tight to allow such a movement, and she is not sure that she wouldn't topple over, so she sits with her legs sticking out in front and her back propped against the bench.

Farida repeats the flour-trickling until the contents of the pan become too hard to stir one-handed. She flips the thick cloth from her shoulder, wraps it around the hot pan and, at the same time as lifting it off the heat, she settles her weight back onto the floor. Everything about her is foreign. Even the motions of her body. She makes movements that Liliana would never make, that are not called for or considered decorous in her world. Now, sitting on the floor, her knees wide, she places the cloth-wrapped pan between the soles of her feet, curving them round the arc of the bowl, clasping it with them. How on earth can Stefano expect Liliana to civilise this primitive creature who uses her feet as an extra pair of hands? Now Farida has both hands free, she uses them to wield the wooden spoon, to force it through the thick and resistant dough, lifting it from the sides and then pushing it back against them and pressing with all her strength.

Inside her slippers, Liliana arches and straightens her feet.

Farida has now taken up the plate and placed it in her lap. She pours some oil from the jar onto it and spreads it across with her fingers, coating the plate. She lifts the stiff dough out of the pan with the wooden spoon and dollops it into the middle of the plate, shapes and forms it into a mound with her hands and creates a hollow in the middle. She sprinkles it with more oil and spoons some of the paste from the tub into the middle.

Liliana swivels round as Farida lays the plate on the bench and puts two spoons in the dough. She would have thought it needed more cooking, baking perhaps, but no, they are going to eat it like this, semi-raw dough. 'This looks delicious,' she says. They are to share it, to eat from the same plate, Liliana understands.

'Shall we go to one of the markets?' she asks. She hears the softness in her own voice. She modulates it as if she were coaxing a little bird. 'I'd love to see the artisans market. Will you show me the way?'

'You can wear your barracan,' she adds.

SHIFTING AND SPLICING

Item: A scrap of paper on which is scribbled a Rome address, Piazza Armenia. On the back is a list of clothing and other items, including pyjamas and a toothbrush.

Standing on the eighth floor of Zaida's apartment block, Liliana kept very still. She heard voices somewhere from the stairwell, the slam of a door and the clatter of feet, the distant thrum of the traffic far below. But closer in, nothing. It was so quiet in her immediate surroundings that the murmur in her own right ear, the constant whispering companion of tinnitus that she was aware of only when sounds outside abated, seemed loud.

She had come in a taxi from the hospital. She had spent ten minutes in a bar across the road watching the big green-painted metal and glass front door of the apartment block for any suspicious activity, but there had been none. She had had time to examine the curved façade, the four square marble steps leading up to the door, the symmetry of the small balconies to either side, the pinkish brickwork and the uniform brown slatted shutters at all the windows. The building must date from the early 1930s, she thought. It had probably not even been built the only other time she had come to Rome. The seeming familiarity of the address when she read it out to the taxi driver must have been an illusion. Her tired, over-emotional mind was playing tricks.

Eventually, carrying her suitcase and a small bag of provisions she had purchased at the nearest grocer's, she had crossed the road, let herself in to the vestibule and travelled up in the lift. She had wedged her suitcase in the lift door so that no one else could summon it away. It was her getaway route. Now she pushed the key into the lock and turned it. The three bolts slid sideways into their casings. It wasn't the sort of door you could unlock soundlessly. She nudged it half open with her knee and waited. Nothing. She pushed it wider but did not cross the threshold. She caught sight of her own pale face in an ornate gold-framed mirror directly opposite and looked quickly away. There was a curved hall table beneath the mirror and next to it an umbrella stand and a hooked pole for opening high windows.

She took a step in, placed the bag of shopping down on the polished parquet floor, glanced quickly to the left to a half-open door from beyond which the last light of the day streamed in, and to the right towards closed doors and back at the mirror. She put a hand to her heart, took a deep breath and sighed it out. Her heart was beating like crazy again. It might be the unaccustomed espresso she had drunk while keeping watch, or it might be terror.

She blinked at herself. She felt that no one was here. The air had a staleness, but still she needed to be careful. It wasn't a game. One man was dead and another in a coma.

She switched on the light, selected an umbrella from the stand, one with a metal tip, and set off to reconnoitre, leaving the door ajar. On tiptoe, she moved to the right, swinging the umbrella in front of her like a metal detector. Or a mine sweeper. At the end of the corridor was a tiled bathroom with a shower cubicle in the corner. There were magazines in Arabic on a little white table next to the loo. The window that gave on to the service shaft was open a slit. As she crossed the room to close it, a flicker of movement rooted her to the spot for a second, but it was only her own reflection in the mirror above the wash basin. She moved on.

She worked her way back along the hallway. She came to a kitchen with fitted cabinets and a built-in cooker. A dirty cup stood next to a radio on the table. The blind at the window was half down, as if it had been arranged to stop the morning sun slanting into someone's eyes. She opened the corner cupboard warily. The shelves were stacked with tins of tomatoes and beans, bags of rice and pasta, an open packet of coffee.

She moved out into the hall again, waving the umbrella in front of her. The next door opened into a large bedroom containing a double bed and a single one, both neatly made. A mirrored wardrobe stretched most of the width of the far wall and colourful cloths hung from the ceiling. She made her way around the double bed, past a painted chest of drawers, and slid the nearest door of the wardrobe open with one hand, the umbrella ready in the other. Why an assassin should be hiding in the wardrobe, she did not know. She saw some tops and jeans, a pair of dungarees and a couple of dresses. They must belong to Zaida. Next to them, a shabby jacket with patched elbows, four men's shirts and several pairs of trousers. Her father's. Both sets of clothes were squashed into the right-hand section of the wardrobe. On the floor of the wardrobe lay two pairs of pink ballet shoes, one of soft leather and the other of pink satin with ribbons. She hesitated before opening the other door. She bent and waggled the umbrella along

166

to the left and met resistance. She froze and held her breath. Nothing happened. Nothing moved. The tinnitus rustled in her ear like a thousand indecipherable voices. She leaned in and tapped the umbrella against the obstruction. Wood, she deduced from the sound it made. She withdrew the umbrella and slid the door shut. Her eyes briefly encountered her own reflection, only lingering long enough to note how ridiculous she appeared, standing there in her raincoat, her silk scarf wound around her neck, armed with an umbrella. She slid open the left-hand door. There was a row of shimmering dresses, arranged by colour. They filled half of the wardrobe but were still pressed into a smaller place than they needed. Some were wrapped in polythene. Underneath them was a shelved box containing dozens of pairs of women's shoes. That was the obstruction the umbrella had met. She felt as if she had stepped onto a film set. A sheen of unreality overlaid everything.

She pulled the door shut and moved on through the flat. In the final room, a sofa bed was folded out, with untidy sheets. Otherwise it was an elegantly appointed room. A television set stood on a low table and a shelving unit full of books covered the wall behind. In the corner was a round dining table with a red damask cloth and four dining chairs around. Paintings hung on the walls, and above the sofa a display of black and white photographs and an ornately framed clock. Two floor-to-ceiling glass doors opened onto a terrace. One was slightly ajar.

What if an assassin, Gaddafi's man, was outside, pressed against the strip of wall in between? She had read in the newspaper that the men responsible had escaped and left the country. The police had assured the girl, Zaida, that they were gone. But could there have been another one? She stepped out brandishing her weapon. The terrace was empty. There were some pots containing herbs, a small metal table, two spindly metal chairs and against the wall a collapsed apparatus for hanging out washing. The traffic moved dizzyingly far below.

There was no one in the apartment. She was 100 per cent certain of that. She stepped inside again, shut the glass door and drew the curtains. She went out to the lift and freed her suitcase, dragged it inside and closed the front door. She locked herself in.

She again met her reflection in the gold-framed mirror. There were too many mirrors, catching her unawares all over the place. Her eyes were wide and staring, her forehead furrowed in a worried frown, her hair a wild mess and her shoulders hunched, like a fugitive. She dropped the umbrella back into the stand. She took off her coat, undid her scarf and hung them both on the rail beside the door. She turned back to the mirror and ran her hands over her hair, patting it into shape. Even now that it had gone completely white, it was still thick and the curls were unruly. There was nothing she could do about her furrowed brow and the frightened-rabbit look. Her face seemed to be stuck. 'If the wind changes, your face will stay that way,' Alan used to say if ever she scowled at him. The wind must have changed.

She would be better after a nice cup of tea.

She unpacked her small bag of shopping in the kitchen. She had bought tea, milk, bread, butter and eggs, not knowing what might be needed. She looked for the kettle. There was no sign of it. Then she remembered that Italians didn't go in for kettles. She fetched a pan, filled it with water and set it on the stove. While it was coming to the boil she went back into the big bedroom. She looked up at the fabrics draped from the ceiling, at the woven patterns of geometric shapes, black triangles and diamonds and dots on a white background, interspersed with broad bands of red and ochre. Many years ago, she had sold textiles like this for a living and she traced her love of fabrics back to that time. Strange to see them here, draped and swathed and festooned, in imitation of a Bedouin tent. She went to the wardrobe and opened the side containing the shimmering clothes again. She lifted out a burnt orange kaftan such as people wore in the early seventies. Ethnic style. It was made for a large woman. She had thought that they lived alone, Zaida and her father. Obviously someone had stayed very recently in the television room, but that would have been a temporary guest. Here, though, was evidence of a large, dressy woman with an individual style. She put the kaftan back and took down another outfit. A calf-length white silk tunic with see-through sleeves and baggy silver trousers to go beneath, a European version of a North African party outfit. She held it against her body and a sudden memory of herself in diaphanous pink pantaloons and a sequinned bodice ignited in her like a firework and sent its sparkles coursing down her arms and into her fingers. She hung the outfit back in the wardrobe with tremulous hands. Mind your own business, she told herself.

Back in the kitchen, she found a squat china jug that would serve as a teapot, and a small plate to balance on top for a lid. She stood staring out of the window while it brewed. Her gaze travelled out over the dome and spire of a nearby church, over the roofs of the apartment blocks with their television aerials piercing the pinkish-orange sky, to a darkening line of distant hills.

She had come to Rome and she had encountered death and a dead end, but instead of stopping, as one should when the road is impassable, turning round and retracing her steps, she had leapt to her feet when she heard Zaida's voice and saw her dangling plait. She hadn't been able to help herself. There was that sensation of recognition, that this girl was family. But now, standing in a stranger's kitchen on the eighth floor of an apartment block in the San Giovanni area of Rome, she wondered if she had come too far. What was she doing here?

She gazed at the last red rim of sun and saw how the black and undulating line of the distant hills stood out against its glow.

She drank her tea and put the cup in the sink. Well then, she thought. Here she was and best get on with it. It was almost six o'clock. She was dead on her feet. She went back into the bedroom, to the painted chest of drawers, and chose a pair of cotton pyjamas, some clean underwear and a purple T-shirt for Zaida. She packed it all into a shopping bag she found hanging on the back of the kitchen door, along with both of the toothbrushes from the bathroom and a tube of toothpaste, a towel and a flannel. She locked the door carefully and went down in the lift.

She called at a tavola calda and bought a mixture of hot food: rice *supplì*, a slab of lasagna and some *mozzarella in carozza*, which they packed into two boxes for her to take away, and then she got a taxi back to the hospital.

The armed guard seemed to be asleep. His cap was tilted forward to shade his eyes. 'Excuse me,' she said to alert him to her presence and he straightened with a snort, pushed his cap up and examined her suspiciously. He was quite an elderly man, she saw. The danger level must have been downgraded. He waved her wordlessly past with a small shake of his head and a sigh to express his displeasure at being disturbed.

Zaida was sitting reading to her father. 'Oh, Signora Jones,' she said. 'How lovely of you!' There was no change. The doctor had been round. '*Supplì!*' she exclaimed when she opened her box of food. 'If anything will wake him, this will.' She spoke to her father in a low tone, wafting the little rice ball under his nose tantalisingly. Then she snatched it away and took a bite. She beamed up at Liliana. 'The smell of that *supplì* will call him back to the world,' she said. 'He loves his food.'

She didn't want to go back to the apartment with Liliana. The nurse said they would let her stay by her father's side one more night. She was going to hop into the camp bed the porter had brought as soon as she had eaten. And brushed her teeth, she added, as if Liliana had reminded her to do so, and Liliana, suddenly delighting in the role, did. 'Yes,' she said, 'clean your teeth, get your pyjamas on and get tucked up. Everything is fine at the flat.'

Liliana left the child there with her comatose father, the bleeping machines that gave off a greenish glow, the somnolent guard at the door, the darkened corridors where the lights hummed.

Back at the apartment, she ate her own now-cold food quickly at the kitchen table. Then she got ready for bed. As she stripped the sofa bed, she caught a whiff of an aromatic scent that she couldn't place, but which brought tears to her eyes. She stuffed the sheets into the linen basket in the bathroom, found clean ones and made the bed up again fresh, weeping all the while. Then she blew her nose, wiped her face, switched on the television and climbed into bed. There was a game show on, with incomprehensible rules. The commercials were all about ready-made frozen dinners. Surely that would never catch on in Italy, where cooking from scratch with good ingredients was so important. She was keen on the ready-made stuff herself, never having been much of a cook, and Alan didn't complain as long as it wasn't every day. The fact that she could understand every single word they were saying on the television made her aware that even after all these decades some words or turns of phrase in English still eluded her. She switched the TV off.

She lay there running through some of her favourite English idioms as an alternative to counting sheep. They're barking up the wrong tree if they think Italians will take to ready meals, she thought. Barking up the wrong tree, that was a good one. Water off a duck's back, that was another. In the sense of not easily taking offence, of consciously resisting the impact of an insult, she couldn't find an Italian equivalent. Perhaps the concept itself was alien. Throwing caution to the wind. That was another one she had thought of earlier to describe what she was doing right now. In Italian you threw caution into the nettles.

Into her mind came Peter, a work friend of Alan's, who discovered only on his fourth or fifth time of meeting her that she was Italian. She had said 'in this wood of the neck' instead of 'in this neck of the woods', which had never made sense to her anyway. Woods don't have necks. She would have made out it was a slip of the tongue, but Alan jumped in and explained her Italian origins. She couldn't stop him. He found her mistakes endearing. They infuriated her.

'It's as if you had excised your Italian self,' Peter had said.

'It's just that I am sort of English now,' she had replied, disingenuously.

Peter was being critical, but she took it as a compliment. And then, later, listening to her more attentively, he had said, 'You can hear it in your "r"s and your "th" and in the lilt.'

She had worked on both her 'r's and her 'th' afterwards, but she couldn't do much about the lilt.

People said that Italians couldn't lose their accent in English unless they had been brought up bilingual, but Liliana had given it a go. The hardest thing had been cutting off that sound, that extra vowel sound Italians like to add to the end of a word. Severing it. And then adding in an extra vowel sound inside the word, cutting it off the end and putting in the middle or at the beginning. Shifting and splicing.

THE SWIVEL POINT

*Item: The cover of a tourist brochure for Italian
North Africa, featuring Tripoli's Grand Hotel.*

From the relative shade and cool of the cathedral entrance,
Liliana peers out into the square. She has come by horse-
drawn cab all the way from the el Gedid gateway, which is
near their apartment, around the perimeter of the old town,
along some bigger roads. She feels that she has used up a day's
worth of boldness in the walk out through the archway, in
daring to approach one of the wizened and brown-faced men
in their robes like rags, who sit in a line, occasionally flicking
a whip at the smelly old horses with their bony haunches, in
navigating a way through the horse dung, ignoring the stares,
climbing aboard without anyone to help her up in her pink
silk dress and then sitting there by herself for all to see. She
has worn herself out. Completely worn herself out.

The cathedral square is spacious and empty. It is so clean
and new that it hardly seems real. Even the cathedral itself
feels unreal. It is too unused. It lacks the indentations and the
accumulated pleas for intercession of centuries of kneeling
penitents, the ingrained scent of incense and candle wax,
the generations of women muttering their rosaries. It has

no history. It is all like a stage set; she, in her unaccustomed outfit that seems now like a costume, is waiting to make her entrance, and she is quaking, as if with stage fright. The costume is of someone playing the part of a sophisticated young lady about town, who is used to meeting high-ranking fascist officials in the colonies.

It is hard to believe the airman will come. Or, rather, that he will send a car for her. He probably will not. It is ten days since she met him in Rome. He might have forgotten her.

It is only a lunch, she tells herself, a lunch at his hotel is what he said. It will be in a public place, she reasons, a restaurant, and there will be other people, and she does not know what to make of anything but she is wearing one of the dresses that the Contessa passed on to her, the pink silk one that she altered to fit while she was on the boat, and her straw hat that is her only hat and so will have to do. She has trimmed it with a matching silk ribbon and is wearing it pinned at an angle in imitation of the way the Contessa wears hers, although it seems not to be the right sort of hat and keeps wanting to sit more squarely on the top of her head. She has never owned anything like this beautiful dress. It gives her, she hopes, a touch of class. She clutches a pair of white gloves that her mother gave her as a going-away present. They seemed elegant when she received them, a token of the life to come, but with her new outfit she is not sure that they pass muster. Her standards have changed since she spent time in the company of the Todinos. It is too bad that Stefano has forbidden her from looking them up.

Oh, she needs the airman to come. Otherwise what will her life in Tripoli be? Stuck in that little apartment with the strange girl who speaks more to herself than she does to Liliana and sometimes, incongruously, bursts into song.

She has put the gloves on and taken them off so many times that they have a crumpled, forlorn look.

The airman might be away on urgent colonial business. He might be out flying his plane over the dunes. Or have been recalled to Rome for a briefing.

If no car comes to collect her, she won't go straight back to the apartment. No. She will walk down to the seafront. She can't be far away because she can smell the sea. She will go for a stroll. She will pass in front of the Grand Hotel and perhaps she might bump into the Todinos. She will not actively seek them out, but if their paths cross by chance, she can hardly snub them. A sudden vision of the Contessa looking straight through her on the promenade deck comes to her. She wishes she did not have to put up with such behaviour, and one day she will not, but for now needs must. Her father knew that too or he wouldn't have sent her with the Todinos in the first place. Her heart aches at the thought of the wrong that the General did to her father.

Please send the car, she thinks, but some consciousness stops her from adding the word God and turning her plea into a proper prayer. Because if it doesn't come, how will she manage? Would she even have come all this way from Monza if she had known that the job Stefano had lined up for her was as his housekeeper, a savage-tamer? What a horrible thing to think. Farida is Stefano's wife, his sort-of wife, and she can't be blamed for not being Italian.

She needn't have worried, because here it is, an official-looking car with an African driver wearing a uniform and a scarlet fez with tassels. A black Fiat 525. It pulls up at the bottom of the steps. And now she finds herself shrinking back. Perhaps she will not go, after all. She retreats further into the vestibule. She has a sensation of imminent danger, as if she is about to be kidnapped. She will go into the cathedral and pray for guidance, and when she comes out the car will most probably have gone. And that will be it.

The back door of the car pushes open, a pair of male legs swing down and the airman steps out, planting himself solidly on the pavement in the bright sun. He is not in uniform. He is casually dressed, in a light-coloured suit with a white hand-kerchief in his breast pocket. He has come in person. The man himself. The force of him, the pure life force he ema-nates, hits Liliana like a shockwave. She feels the magnetic pull. The part of her that thought any of this was optional is silenced, forgotten, left behind there in the cathedral doorway along with her grubby gloves as she trips lightly and irresisti-bly down the steps towards him. He looks older in the harsh light of the high sun. 'My dear,' he says, and he takes her hand, bends and kisses the back of it, turns it over in his and keeps hold, claiming her. She has been claimed.

The relief of it.

He hands her into the back of the car.

He does not ask her how she is finding Tripoli or how her voyage was. He does not really speak at all, but murmurs endearments. He sits very close in the back of the car and keeps hold of her hand, turning it over in his. She wants to be amusing and witty, but her mind is a blank, and she cannot think of anything to say. Pull-down paper shades cover the glass in the side windows.

He pushes his fingers in between hers. His hand is chunky, strong-boned and broad, and his fingers prise hers apart. She wonders where her gloves can be. She was too anxious this morning to have breakfast, and her stomach is rumbling, but thankfully it is not audible above the sound of the car.

'I'm so glad you came,' he says. 'I wasn't sure.' He is looking at her as if he already loves her, and she has the feeling that he might have mistaken her for someone else.

She is not sure how to address him, what she should call him, what form to use. He is older than she is. And he is a colonel or a lieutenant-colonel. And they don't really know each other. So she just smiles.

'You have a dimple when you smile,' he says, 'just here,' and he traces the curve in her left cheek with the nail of his little finger, their hands still conjoined. He leans forward to say something to the driver, some instruction in a language that she doesn't understand. The imprint of his finger in her cheek, as if he were drawing her smile. She wonders where they are going and finds she doesn't much care so long as he doesn't let go of her hand.

They turn onto the sea road again now, one of the stretches she drove along with her brother. The colours, seen through the window shades, are muted.

'I've booked a room at the Grand,' he says.

The Grand. That is where the Todinos are staying. Perhaps she will have lobster. The Contessa has told her the lobster they serve at the Grand is simply divine. Or perhaps she will choose something that she knows how to eat, something without claws, which doesn't require special implements and skills she doesn't yet possess.

The car comes to a halt in a parking area behind the building. Without preamble, he turns to her, takes hold of her chin, tilts her face to his and kisses her on the mouth, pressing his fleshy lips over hers and gnawing her as if he intends to eat her face. He smells of leather and lemon balm.

She doesn't know what to do. She lets it happen.

He detaches himself. His face is a centimetre from hers. He licks his full lips. 'Fresh,' he says, as if to himself.

He keeps a firm hold of her hand as he leads her up the outside stairs and into the back of the hotel. 'Wait here,' he says, 'I'll get the key.' He leaves her in the corridor beside a shut door that must lead to the hotel kitchens, because she can hear the clatter and sizzle of cooking and smell garlic, olive oil, butter and fresh basil. 'Excuse me, Signorina,' a man says. She half turns and steps back into the alcove formed by the stairwell to let him pass. He is carrying a crate full of lobsters. The uppermost ones are waving their pincers in the air. A small one in the corner of the crate has attached itself to the rim and is trying to lever itself up, making a last doomed bid to escape its fate.

The man disappears inside the kitchen, and she hears a roar of approval, as if the cooks have been waiting for this delivery. Then a waiter emerges, clad in a striped uniform with a white cap, bearing a tray with a silver salver set in the middle, and two white bowls containing a creamy yellow substance, gleaming silver cutlery, folded white napkins. He is going the other way, towards the front of the building, and does not need to get past Liliana, has not even seen her although he is only two paces away. She steps out into the corridor again and watches him go. He pushes through a distant door and she has a brief glimpse of a sunlit dining room, tables with white cloths, glassware sparkling, and out through an arched window, the glittering blue sea, before the door swings shut behind him. A minute later another waiter emerges from the kitchen and follows, and no sooner has he pushed through the faraway door than the first one returns, his empty tray dangling from his fingers.

Liliana stands in the corridor, her stomach rumbling, absorbed in the to and fro of the waiters, the way they turn away from the restaurant door at the last moment, lean against it, pushing with their backs and then, at a certain point, swivel into the room beyond, their trays balanced. She sees how they must wait until the exact moment when their weight against the door, the pressure they apply, has set the swing of it in motion, and then must straighten and turn and be poised, ready to face what lies beyond. It is too far for her to be able to see their faces, but she imagines that they compose their expressions too, and perhaps there is a point, the swivel point, in which all the little changes – the release of the spine from the door, the rebalancing of the tray, the adoption of a neutral but accommodating facial expression – are concentrated. The feeling of unreality that she had in the cathedral vestibule strengthens. The waiters are actors in a show, and she is seeing them as they prepare to go on. There's something else too, something more than what she is just observing, and it is to do with turning, balancing, looking back at where you've come from – she glances briefly behind her and out through the open doorway by which they entered to the car park, where a donkey and cart now sit next to the black Fiat – something else that she needs to understand. And it is to do as well with the occasional glimpses of the sunlit restaurant as the door swings open and shut again with each coming and going of the waiters. The restaurant is starting to fill up. Those people must have entered from the front of the building, from some unseen door. Unlike Liliana and the airman, these luncheon guests have not come in through the trade entrance. It strikes her that she has assumed that the airman brought her in the back way because the scaffolding at the front of the building prevented access, but that is obviously not the case.

And why does he need a key?

Understanding seesaws in her head and tips over to near-certainty. Explicit words might not have been spoken, but by allowing the unravelling in Rome, by turning up today, by letting him claim her, kiss and manhandle her in the back of the car, she has agreed to something. She feels it now as a sort of urgent whisper telling her to take action.

She looks back again at the doorway through which they entered, and she turns and walks resolutely out of it. The driver is squatting next to the bottom step, smoking a cigarette, his cap balanced on his knees. She hesitates a fraction and starts down the steps. Once she is past him, she will run. The driver stands as she approaches and says something that she doesn't understand. 'I have to leave,' she says. He indicates that she should go back the way she has come. He speaks again and points. He is barring her way. She retreats back into the building.

She sets off in the direction the waiters have taken towards the front of the building. She will find the front door. She will go down the steps. She will cross the road and walk beside the sea where people might be promenading. Or she will turn the corner that her brother drove down. It is the next street along, or the one after, and there were shops. Ordinary-looking, Italian shops. She will go there and she will be lost in the crowd, and then later she will find a gharry to take her back to the Tobacco Factory.

She takes a few uncertain steps forward and comes to a place where the corridor opens out to the reception area. There is a lift to one side, and in front, down another corridor, she can see the main entrance. The airman is there at the desk, his back to her. He is talking to someone on the hotel telephone. His tone is argumentative. She will have to pass behind him to get to the front door, and what if he were to turn? She withdraws. She takes up her place beside the kitchen door. 'I fancy the lobster,' she will say when he returns. She will say it in an easy, light way, and he will understand that she is not the sort of girl to take up to a private room. She will speak as if she has no idea of his intentions, but she can't pretend that she doesn't, not really, not to herself at least, not after that kiss. Voracious, it was. Animal. What did he mean, 'fresh', she wonders. She wanders to the back door again, thinking that the driver can't have meant to bar her way and that he might have moved on by now, but he is still there, and he is no longer alone. A small group of men have joined him, squatting in a circle or sitting on low stools. They have lit a little brazier and seem to be brewing tea, but none of them are speaking. There are no Europeans in sight. It is more than she can manage to walk past them.

She knows so little about Ugo Montello. Except that he is an important man and that she is both dying for him to return and dreading it. She returns to her spot, and a moment later so does he. The brief interlude is over. His face is flushed. 'Sorry,' he says. 'Some confusion.' He takes hold of her hand again, leads her up a wooden staircase, which she knows must be the service stairs used by the domestic staff, and now his grip is even tighter, as if the confusion, whatever it was, has made him more determined to get his way. Or perhaps he knows she thought of fleeing.

There is still a tiny strand of belief within her that sees them sitting at a little table on the balcony. It is, after all, only lunchtime.

He unlocks the door of the room without letting go of her, leads her in and takes her with him across to the window where, with his free hand, he reaches for the blind. 'Seafood do for you?' he says. 'I've asked them to bring something up.' A barking laugh bursts forth from her mouth, a mixture of relief and embarrassment at what she had been thinking, at her unwarranted suspicions. 'What's so funny, you funny little thing?' he says. 'Don't you like seafood?' He lets down the blind and shuts out the sun and the sea and the sky. And without waiting for a reply he is upon her, and she is laughing into his mouth. He puts his hands on her shoulders and grips them; she can feel the urgency of his fingers on the skin of her upper arms and he presses his fleshy mouth over hers again. One of his hands slides down her back and clasps the small of it. He presses her, pushing at her, not just with his hands, but with his whole body, and she reverses a few steps until the backs of her knees encounter the bed and then she topples softly backwards with him on top of her. He lifts his mouth from hers and nuzzles her neck, bending so that he can pull the skirt of her dress up and hook down her drawers and all the time with one hand flat against her middle pinning her down, keeping her in place, and his hand roams up over her stomach, pinches at the flesh of her waist. His fingers poke at her, his hard fingers and her softness, and he is talking all the time, fiddling with his own clothes and she feels something give and it is all so fast. 'My little belly dancer,' he says. 'No,' she says, but he doesn't hear her because he's telling her what he wanted to do to her when he saw her on the dance floor in Rome, that he knew what she was like, he knew they would fit.

But they don't, not at first. She cries out from the pain. It is excruciating.

'I didn't know,' he says. 'I didn't know,' looking at her in wonder. 'Thank you,' he says. 'I'll be gentle,' he says, 'and careful.'

She does not really know what he means. There is nothing gentle going on. It is hot and wet and bloody and it burns like hellfire. 'No,' she says but more weakly now, because it is too late to make him stop.

GIFA

Item: A photograph cut out of a newspaper of Colonel Ugo Montello sitting in the open cockpit of a Caproni Ca.73.

In the first blush of dawn, when the stars have not yet entirely faded and before the glare of the sun becomes blinding, the pilot pulls his goggles down over his eyes, adjusts the leather strap to tighten them and then lifts his machine up into the brightening air. As his engine quietens to a buzz, he hears the others spreading out behind him. The eight of them flying in a wide-angled triangle formation, each bird a part of a bigger bird and he, at the front, the tip: he is the sharp beak.

At first they hug the coast, keeping the glitter of the Mediterranean and the Gulf of Sidra on their left-hand side. When he sees the turret of the fort at en-Nofilia up ahead, he veers to the right and inland, swooping south. The army down on the ground is squeezing the troublesome Magharba tribe from their oases and their encampments. It is the aviators' job to track down those who have fled.

The lead pilot has no proper printed map. Where they are going is uncharted territory. Once this job is done, this land subdued, men will come, experts, topographers,

184

cartographers, quiet specialists who will mark things out, draw lines and measure, name each runnel where a stream sometimes flows, each rubble-strewn plain and scrubby hill. They will make the maps for the more civilised times that are to come.

But not now. Not yet.

Anyway, he thinks, as he glances at the hand-drawn sketch spread out on the dashboard, he prefers it this way, and he prefers it now. This is his time and his place at the sharp, raw end of the civilising force, without a map, but with his weapons and his wits. This is when and where he wants to be.

They fly out over the desert, the great faceless desert. He looks again at the piece of paper, compares the pencil marks with what he can see below, the colourless waste tufted with grey brushwood. You have to keep it in your head, the memory of the coastal line behind, the sweep of the land in front, the way the tribesman who described the location to him spoke and moved his bony long-fingered hands to show how one thing followed another, the gravel plateau, the *erg* that must be crossed and then the dried-up river bed, the *wadi*, whose course he must follow. There is a trick to holding them together in your mind, the detail and the huge arc. The curve of the earth and the footprint of a child.

The place they seek is not a settlement. There are no buildings or permanent encampments there. It matters, though, even if it isn't shown on the maps, because it has plentiful water, grazing for the livestock, relief for the thirsty enemy and their families fleeing towards the oasis of Zella further south, trusting in the desert and in distance.

Down below him now are scattered rocks and boulders, some of them bigger than houses. The surface of the moon might look like this close up. This is not a place to crash-land, no smooth stretch anywhere in sight. He spots the *wadi*, no more than an indentation. He drops lower, wipes sweat from his brow with the back of his hand. Sometimes, when you're flying low like this, you see little creatures scattering, jerboas scuttling into holes at your approach. Better than those are the great herds of gazelles that roam across the Sirtico hinterland. It is hard to see how they survive on the meagre rations on offer, the sparse clumps of vegetation, but they do.

Round here, mostly, you don't get so many gazelles. You're just watching your own shadow, darkening the land below.

He is seeking a place where the earth dips into a vast hollow, his eyes attuned to the idea of pasture, but there is nothing green as far as he can see. He banks higher, circles, and the others follow.

If he keeps going he will get to the bony protrusions of basalt and lava in the volcanic field of Harugi, and then he will know he has gone too far. They will have to turn back because there is no fort or refuelling station there.

But there is not enough here to draw the eye, no distinguishable landmark in the monotonous terrain. The telling detail eludes him. There is only the sad greyness of the steppe and the desolation.

Then he sees it: not green, but silver. A flash of silver and white movement in the corner of his left eye. He turns the plane towards it and drops lower over a clump of grey-brown shrub. He is only a few metres above the ground; the silver thing has vanished, but there is something else.

Tracks in the sand. He follows them and the other seven planes fan out behind.

Then, in a delicious moment of discovery, they are upon them, a seething ants' nest of people and animals. Women and children, cowering, huddled together, stray infants being pulled into their mothers' sides. Dirty snot-nosed children with flies in their eyes, camels munching dusty tufts of grass, the odd goat grazing. Most of the goats and sheep were wiped out by the army at Nofilia. Without their herds, the Magharba aren't worth much.

There are few men. Old men, by the way they stand. The fighters must have gone ahead. The way they look up and shake their fists is a sight. Pointlessly, stupidly shaking their fists. The pilot pulls back, higher into the sky, the great silent blueness of sky, uninterrupted, no sound except the whirr of the engines. He holds it all in, and then he gives the signal. One after the other they skim over the gathering and drop their loads. Boom. He circles, waits for the air to clear, wheeling high above with the hawks and the other birds, and then passes back over again and again until there is a crater where before there was only a dip. A rag and bone-filled crater.

When there are no living creatures left, they blast holes in the dirt, sending dust clouds up and making the still air swirl. They are a force of nature. They create sandstorms.

As they turn away, their job done, he sees the flash of silvery light again, the sun glinting off metal. He makes another circle, but only the dust plumes move. It might have been a trick of the light, but still he signals to his fellow pilots to set off while he drops lower. His eyes scan featureless, barren sand.

A lone horseman suddenly appears, breaking cover, where there was no discernible cover to be had, only the scraggy scrub they passed before. They are sneaky, these desert rebels. They hide where there are no hiding places.

The horseman must just now have sheathed his useless sword. He must have watched the devastation. Now he gallops.

He should have waited.

The pilot has no bombs left. He is all emptied out. Sated and empty. He reaches with his left hand for the machine gun. The man is riding like fury, his white robes billowing around him. *Look up. Look up at me. See my face.* The pilot wants the man to know that without the silver glint of his sword, they might not have found the gathering. *Thank you,* the pilot mouths before he shoots. *Shukran.*

MARY AND THE ANGELS

Item: A blue beaded rosary with a silver cross.

The driver drops Liliana where she was first picked up, outside the cathedral, as if that is where she lives and, not knowing what else to do, she totters weakly up the steps and enters.

She stands at the back, in the middle of the aisle of the vast, empty church. She closes her eyes and waits to be struck down. 'Take me, Lord,' she whispers. After a while in which nothing happens, perhaps it is a long time, perhaps it is only a second, she opens her eyes again and stares about, at the distant altar, at the solid fluted columns, the rows of empty seats, the dark wood kneelers. Her gaze alights on her own crumpled white gloves lying on a seat in the back row. She snatches them up and presses them to her nose, catching the residual scent of the lavender from the sprigs that her mother folded in among her clothes when she packed them. A scream rises in her throat and she clamps the gloves over her mouth and holds them there, gagging herself. The sound that comes from her, drawn from deep down in her gut, is like that of a wounded cow.

No one comes to see what is the matter, to reprimand or comfort or cajole her, or tell her that church is not the place for such behaviour. There is no priest or nun or flower arranger or aisle sweeper to shake her back to decorum and seemliness, to a time when she had no knowledge of the carnal beast that resided within. She puts her other hand to her stomach, low down, in the place where, earlier, the colonel's hand pressed and where now, on the inside, there is a heaviness, a pulsing ache that drags at her. It folds her forward and she wraps her body over her source of pain. The keening noise spills out around her.

After a while the dreadful noise abates, and no one has heard. Liliana straightens up.

She has not been struck down. She has not even been heard or noticed. There is neither solace nor reproach to be found in this church. It occurs to her that the church is very new, perhaps it has not yet been consecrated, is not yet a proper church. She wipes her wet eyes and streaming nose on the gloves, ruined now beyond any remedy.

She adjusts her hat, pulling it forward so that it partially obscures her face, turns and walks slowly out of the cathedral and down the steps, as if in a dream. A covered horse-drawn cab pulls up for her. She has forgotten what the old city gateway near to Stefano's apartment is called, and anyway she does not want to go there, because how will she face the girl? Farida? Farida will take one look at her with her clear topaz eyes and she will know. Liliana can remember only the famous monuments. She names one. The arch of Marcus Aurelius, she says to the driver, and she clambers inside. She knows it is on the northern edge of the old city.

She gazes blankly out as they pass through the Italian thoroughfares, behind the castle, past the clock tower, briefly along beside the sea and then, just before they come to the customs house, sharp left into a narrow street and there she is, next to the ancient Roman arch that is in the process of being restored. She climbs down and pays the driver. There are people strolling about and, not wanting to draw attention to herself by seeming uncertain, she plunges down an alleyway to the side of a huge mosque with a green-topped minaret. The notion of losing herself in the maze of narrow streets of the old city appeals to her. She will go deeper and deeper into the labyrinth until it swallows her up because she is an adulterer, a fallen woman, a sinner, and there is no going back. She is not dead, but she has killed her own life. She has turned on her best thing, whatever that was, and she has stabbed it dead. She hurries blindly along, following the twists and turns of the little streets, passing another mosque that pale-robed men are entering, turning unerringly at corners as if she knows the way, but keeping her head down. She enters a tunnelled lane where the buildings to either side send out struts that meet above, and she welcomes the blotting-out of the sun and the great blue sky. She is heading towards obscurity.

But then, suddenly, the street opens out into a square, and the harsh light pours down again, and there in front of her, unexpectedly, is another church.

She takes it in. A homely sort of whitewashed church with a bell tower and a clock that shows the time as half past four. There is a noticeboard to the right of the entrance. She steps forward to read it. Santa Maria degli Angeli, the church is called. There is to be a mass at 5.30 p.m.

Not away from, but towards, she thinks. It might be a sign.

She steps inside, into the closeted dark warmth, and is greeted by the scent of incense, the hardness of wood and stone, the murmur of prayerful voices. This is a proper church, not a stage-set like the cathedral, and so a more likely setting for God to strike her down, and yet now she feels that He will not. His purpose must be other. She dips her hand in the holy water, blesses herself, moves quietly forward up the central aisle. A scattering of women are kneeling in a side chapel, reciting the rosary together, one of them calling out the first half and the others picking it up and intoning the second half.

Liliana kneels in the nave in front of the high altar and closes her eyes. She joins in with the rosary prayers. *Holy Mary, Mother of God, pray for us sinners now and at the hour of our death*, she mutters along with the others. The words were imprinted in her consciousness from such a tender age that no thought is required. They flow out of her and around her, and she is subsumed in the chant, a soothing, babbling stream. Thoughts bob up to the surface and float past. She is an adulterer. She is kneeling in the church of the Virgin Mary, but she herself is no longer a virgin. She has not been struck down. Someone comes and kneels in the same row, and she glances up to see a matronly figure who nods at her in greeting and she thinks, what, doesn't it show on my face? Can't you tell?

She picks up the chant again. Ugo Montello is a married man. His wife, who lives with the children back in Rome, is probably old like him, and he will find some reason to put her aside in favour of Liliana. Until then, she will be his lover, his mistress, his concubine. She is a sinner. She should not even think these thoughts. To think them in church is worse. *Forgive me my trespasses*, she says, *deliver me from evil*. No one else will have her now. But that is all right, because she doesn't want anyone else. Only him. She adores him. He tricked her. He deflowered her. She went with him of her own free will. Did she? Was there force? There was no force. No one else will have her now, that is a fact. If her brother

192

knew, if her parents knew, would they cast her aside? She wanted to cast herself aside half an hour ago, but instead her feet brought her here, to this church. Not her brother, surely, her beloved brother who looks at the savage girl the way the airman looked at Liliana. He is old enough to be her father, although much younger than her actual father. *Blessed is the fruit of thy womb*, she mumbles. There will be no fruit of her womb, the airman assured her. He took precautions. The first time, he pulled out. *Coitus interruptus*, the method was called. The second time he wore a sheath made of animal skin. She saw it afterwards, glistening with her blood. She can hardly believe it. If the evidence were not there in her own body, her sore body, her aching legs, her fast-beating heart, in the memory of that blood, his endearments: my darling dancing girl he called her, my morsel.

Contraception is forbidden both by the Church and by the state. He who is not a father is not a man, the Duce has said. But Ugo is already a father. His three children are with his wife in Rome.

Still chanting the rosary, Liliana lifts her gaze and looks up at the painting that hangs above the high altar. It depicts Mary, dressed in dark blue and red, holding the infant Jesus and surrounded by angels playing musical instruments, a sort of fiery light emanating from her. In the background is Tripoli as it must have been in the previous century.

The Virgin Mary is here with Liliana in Tripoli. She was here already, waiting, and Liliana has found her, or she has been found.

When the rosary is finished, Liliana bows her head again as if deep in prayer, until the other women disperse. Then she gets up, moves to the back of the church and waits for mass to begin.

Instead of a sermon, the priest reads out a letter that has been sent to all churches by the Holy Father, Pius XI, to notify them of the Lateran accords signed between the Church and the fascist government back in February. The priest explains that under the accords, Catholicism has been recognised as the only religion of the State of Italy, and that the Vatican City is now a sovereign territory with the pope as its supreme ruler. The priest has a breathy way of talking, and sometimes a little whistling noise, which might be coming from his bulbous nose, accompanies the words. The Church and the fascist state are now working hand in hand, he says, and share many of the same goals – to fight communism and godlessness, to inculcate a sense of duty, patriotism and self-sacrifice in the bodies, hearts and souls of the noble Italian nation. The priest asks the congregation to consider what this might mean for them here in the colonies.

He speaks of belief, obedience and enthusiasm, of how the spiritual values of fascism are superior to the self-interested individualism of liberal cultures. He speaks of taking the leap of faith.

All the contradictory thoughts that Liliana has had reassemble themselves into a different order, like cards being shuffled and dealt.

Ugo Montello is an important and senior official in the fascist regime. He has chosen her. So she is a chosen one. To serve the nation and the Church calls for self-sacrifice. She has sacrificed her innocence and her virginity. She, Liliana Cattaneo, is important not as an individual but as part of a greater whole. What comes after does not matter. Ugo Montello is a man far from home, carrying out the civilising task of the nation, and her role is to help him. She has been chosen as his helpmate. The practicalities of it might be shocking, bestial and profane, but the end justifies the means.

Her reasoning is so convoluted that she has difficulty in holding on to it, but it all boils down to a set of certain precepts. The Catholic Church and the Fascist Party have issued a declaration, a covenant. They are inextricably linked, there is a mystic communion between them, so that to all intents and purposes to serve one is to serve the other. Her destiny is that of her country; she is an agent of its campaign and she has been chosen. This is no time for her faith to waver. She has been called upon to sacrifice herself for the greater good, to offer herself up.

It is her fate. She must embrace it.

At the end of mass, the priest waits at the doorway to speak to parishioners. A part of her wants to skulk past with her head down, but instead she looks him in the eye. Thank you, Father, she says. That was a very illuminating sermon. She has never spoken to a priest like that, like a grown-up, before.

He smiles at her in his priestly way. He looks at her and he does not see that she is a Jezebel. He is Padre Francesco and he welcomes her to the parish.

Emboldened, she gets an urchin to show her back to the cul-de-sac near the synagogue where her brother's lodgings are. She is conscious that she has left Farida alone all day, but the girl does not reproach her, in word or glance. 'Go and wash the city dirt off your skin,' she says, 'and I will make you tea.' She is preparing food for their dinner. Couscous and spiced lamb.

Liliana goes and washes herself. She fills the hip bath with water and plunges into it, sits there and watches a trickle of red blood dilute to pink, like ink dispersing. She puts on a plainer dress and hangs the silk one on her rail. Then she comes into the courtyard and helps Farida with dinner, checking she knows the words for the ingredients, getting her to repeat descriptions of the processes.

Stirring, chopping, beating.

A SLEEP AS SWEET AS DEATH

Item: A small and well-thumbed copy of Les Fleurs du mal *by Charles Baudelaire. An inscription in green ink on the first recto states that the book was awarded as a prize for 'oratorical skills' to Ferdinando Cattaneo in 1884.*

Liliana cannot sleep. She keeps thinking of the girl, Zaida, on her own in the hospital with her unconscious father. The look on Zaida's face when Liliana arrived with the *supplì*. That was delight. Zaida was delighted to see her. Real, genuine, you've-made-my-day delight. She doesn't know the last time someone looked at her like that. She is wrapped in the feeling it has evoked, like a warm blanket.

But then, too, she can't get Abramo out of her mind. A newborn baby she helped bring into the world, a middle-aged man lying cold and stiff. To have attended both his birth and his death but not to have known the decades in between, as if his life had been snuffed out almost as soon as it had begun.

But he lived for forty-nine years. It is just that she didn't know him.

She sees again his slippery newborn body, the inside of that tent, the sweat and the blood and the stifling heat.

She sits up in bed and switches the lamp on. This memory, if it is a memory, fills her with dread. It has no context. It answers no questions. Why was there only one baby? Where was Nadia? Whose blood was it? Did someone die?

Liliana has a recurring dream that she is a killer. That she committed a murder and buried the body or hid it beneath the sand, and that she has gone on living when she should have been punished. Sometimes the detail of the dream is very convincing. It is not just anyone that she killed. It is her own baby. When she has that dream, she wakes in a panic, full of horror at herself, and it takes a long time to dissipate. She's not sure that it ever really does. She feels that she carries its residue, the knowledge of her own true nature, within her.

Sometimes she wonders if the baby with the sapphire eyes could have been Nadia, because Nadia had blue eyes. They weren't as startlingly blue as the baby in the vision, although eye colour fades. But the sapphire one, whatever she was, was Liliana's baby and Nadia was not. Liliana didn't have a baby. She couldn't have babies.

For goodness sake, she thinks, and swings her legs down. She sits on the edge of the bed with her toes brushing the floor.

She remembers arriving back in Tripoli, she and Farida, when they returned with the babies from Farida's home region, Cyrenaica. Nadia has appeared in the picture by then, lying top to tail with Abramo under a white blanket in a basket made of woven palm leaves. She and Farida held a handle each and carried the basket between them. Liliana had been ill and was still weak, but much better than before they went away. Stefano had rented an apartment, west of the city centre and close to the sea, for his new family. You could always smell the sea from that apartment, and if you went up onto the roof you could see it. They used to sit up there in the evenings and look at the stars.

When she wrote to Stefano and the family, in the years after she left Libya, before she went to live in England, before they disappeared, before they stopped answering, she would picture them in that apartment by the sea, sitting on the roof in the evenings, watching the sun go down, the children playing around them. Sometimes Liliana thought it wasn't fair that Farida had two babies when she didn't even have one, but then she remembered that she didn't deserve a child, and she put her head down and got on with the life that she did have.

She couldn't get her job back at Hensemberger, not just because she had been away a long time but because there were tighter restrictions on certain businesses, particularly strategic businesses manufacturing machine parts, employing females. All of the women she used to work with, bar the war widows, had been dismissed. She found work, though, in the office of the hat factory. The girls she had grown up with were married now and had children. She had little in common with them and preferred to keep herself apart. The age and infirmity of her parents meant that she was exempt from the *dopolavoro*, the after-work activities in which all citizens had to participate, and so she was able to live a quiet and retiring life and, really, she asked for no more. She was failing as a good *Italiana* because she was not marrying and bearing children as was her patriotic duty; she seemed to have become one of those spinsters of whom the Contessa used to speak so scathingly.

Every month a letter from Tripoli would arrive in Monza. She would go and sit on the bench beside the river, read it through and absorb its impact. Then she would go home and stand in front of the sideboard and read it out loud. Her parents would sit together on the flowery sofa that had seen better days, and she would recount the exploits of the grand-children that they would never meet – their first words and steps, their first day at school, how Nadia had performed in a dance at the Monument for the Fallen, what a fast reader Abramo was, how both of them loved going to the beach and had learned to swim by the time they were five. Whatever difficulties the family might have had were rarely mentioned. Sometimes there was a separate note for Liliana, written in a cryptic style, without giving people's real names. From these she learned that Farida's brother, Sadiq, had been killed in the fighting on the Jebel Akhdar. But, on the whole, the picture Stefano presented in the family letter was that life was rosy. The children thrived. Their new home suited them well. Farida – or Rosita, as Stefano called her in these letters – was well and sent her best wishes. The race track went from strength to strength after the introduction of the lottery to fund it in 1933. By the mid-1930s it was the richest and fastest track in the world, and people travelled to it from all over. So high had her brother's star risen that in 1935, when Italo Balbo, the governor of the now united colony of Libya, held a gala reception in the palace in Tripoli, Stefano was one of the guests. Later on that same year, she heard that Ugo had gone to Abyssinia to fight in the new war there, strafe a few thousand more innocents no doubt, and take part in the next chapter of Italy's brave colonial adventure, and her fear that he would exact some terrible retribution on Stefano faded.

When she read those letters, with their depiction of a happy family life, she knew that she had been right to leave. They were all better off without her.

She felt the pain of the separation most in a place in her core, behind her ribs, as if she had been kicked by a horse or a camel and there was long-term damage, but that it could be accommodated if she held herself carefully and did nothing to exacerbate it. It had the purple-black of a bruise and it coloured her insides. At least for those seven years in Monza she had the letters. It was the silence after the letters stopped coming that finished her off. Whatever she may have looked like on the outside, inside she was a bruise.

Come on, bruise, she says to herself. She gets to her feet and wanders around the flat, putting her head into the rooms, opening and shutting cupboards as if she has misplaced something. She looks into the big bedroom, where she can see by the bluish glow of a light outside reflected in the mirrored wardrobe that everything is neat and in its place. She goes to the bathroom and switches on the light, opens the cabinet and looks at the shaving soap and brush, the tube of toothpaste, closes it again and watches a spider cross the tiles, then turns the light back off, exits. In the kitchen she gets down a glass from the cupboard and fills it from the bottle of chilled water in the fridge.

Her bare feet slap on the parquet floor in the hallway and halfway along she pauses, standing between the front door and the table. She listens, but can hear nothing untoward. It is not that she is frightened as she was earlier. She is quite sure that there is no one else present, but still she cocks her head to one side and concentrates, listening for something she cannot hear, that is perhaps pitched too high, beyond her range.

It occurs to her that this is the first night she has spent in Italy since 1938. What would Alan think of her here? Flaming Nora, love, he might have said. What are you getting yourself into?

The day she met him is etched in her mind. After her

mother's funeral, she had gone to talk to Sister Maddalena at the convent of the Poor Clares because she had thought perhaps, after all, it was not too late to become a nun. She had been casting about for someone to dedicate her life to now that her parents were gone, she can see that now. Poor lost soul that she was. She had thought perhaps God would do. Until that conversation with Sister Maddalena, she had not really acknowledged her loss of faith. Not properly. She still went to mass every Sunday. She came away from the convent in a black cloud of despair and on the way home she stopped in Piazza Trento Trieste and walked up the steps of the great bronze war memorial that had been built while she was away in Tripoli, and which was officially dedicated in 1932, the year after she came back. In her pocket she had the latest letter from Stefano, but she hadn't opened it yet. Without the incentive of reading it to her parents, without the buffer they provided, she couldn't face it. Instead she stood in front of the monument and read the names of the people of Monza who had sacrificed their lives and she wondered what she was going to do with her own life now.

Standing in her nightdress in the warm darkness of a May night in Rome, her thin bare feet planted on the wooden floor, a tenderness for her own younger self touches Liliana. She had only been twenty-seven. She had thought she was washed up and that her life was over.

She had walked down to the river with the intention of sitting under the trees. There was a man there already, sitting right in the middle of her bench. The bench of her sorrows. The man had his elbows on his knees and his chin cupped in his hands and seemed lost in contemplation of the flowing water. He had hair the colour of sand and a woollen jumper to match. She was going to walk on by but he looked up at her from behind round-rimmed glasses and, without saying anything, he shifted along the seat and patted the space next to him. It wasn't so much the kindliness of the gesture, although it was kindly, but the request she saw in those blue-grey eyes. It was as if he had said 'please'. She sat down. He resumed his contemplation of the river. She fished out the letter from Stefano. As usual, it was mostly about cars. Preparations for the Grand Prix were under way. German drivers and the Mercedes-Benz were likely to dominate, he thought. German engineering was second to none. Abramo had won a prize at school for a story he had written. He takes after Papà, Lili, he's good with words, Stefano wrote. Nadia spent hours skipping in the lane outside the house and could do tricks. He mentioned that he was thinking about leaving the race track and moving to Benghazi and setting up his own business there. There were good opportunities in Cyrenaica, he said. Farida was well and sent her love. She had a small loom now and had taken up weaving.

At some point while she was reading the man next to her had got up and left, and Liliana felt the weeping coming on. The previous seven years had been dedicated to not allowing it to start. Weeping in small ways over the little things was allowed, but the bigger things had to be kept under lock and key, down in their dank cellar. So she put her head in her hands and rocked to and fro, trying to clamp down on it because the wail that wanted to find its way out of her mouth would be huge and deafening. She feared it because it was going to knock her off the little ledge she had found to perch on, and her grip was already loosened, and it was coming now and it was going to be a landslide. And then a voice with a strange, foreign accent said, 'The railway station?' She looked up and there was the sandy-haired man. He said some more things that she didn't understand because he was speaking English and, strange though it seems to her now, she could not yet speak English. She didn't understand the words but she understood the gestures. He was miming confusion and even miming being a bit of a fool for having lost his way, and there was something so ingenuous and kind and different in his grey eyes that she jumped up and said, 'I'm going that way. I'll show you.'

This man, who turned out to be Alan, had little idea either then or afterwards that not only had he saved Liliana from descending to that dark place from where she might never have emerged, but that he kept her afloat for the next forty-one years. He was a British engineer, part of a small team working with a local company on a project to develop the railway. He was in Italy for five months, at the end of which time he asked her to marry him, and she pretended to think about it for about five minutes and then she said yes.

In 1938, the Italian state outlawed *madamato*, the practice of taking a native bride in the colonies. It was considered detrimental to the purity of the Italian race. It meant that Stefano couldn't have brought Farida and the children to Italy, even if he had wanted to.

Dear old Alan. She wonders how their lives together would have been if they had been able to have children. Another memory surges up. The night she became a seductress for him. He was back after the war and they were rubbing along again nicely, but she wanted a child and she had started to think that their dutiful lovemaking once a week with the lights off somehow wasn't enough to make that happen. A more intense and vigorous and prolonged sexual encounter was required. She had never been forward with Alan, never instigated anything, but she didn't know what she would do with herself without a baby. And she was thirty-five, so it was now or never. She timed the seduction to coincide with when she should be most fertile. He was shocked, she thought, because she'd never shown that side, always been modest, but he responded. She used to think about how their child would look. How it might have pale skin like his rather than olive skin like hers, whether it would inherit her curls or Alan's straight sandy hair. After that, every month when she was ovulating she repeated the seduction, with subtle variations. She kept it up for a few years. It was, for that period, a feature of their life together. After one of those unbridled nights she would catch Alan looking at her warily, as if he didn't actually know her, which was true in a way. She often wondered what Alan found to love in her when, to her mind, there was so little on offer, such a reduced and dilute thing she felt herself to be.

Poor old Alan, coaxed and teased and lasciviously tugged out of his rectitude, fondled and licked into ardour. But it didn't work. Eventually, she gave up trying. It was too much to bear, having her hopes dashed every month. She had a feeling it was a relief to Alan, but they didn't discuss it. They still made love. They never stopped doing that, but it reverted to a cosier and sweeter sort of coupling.

She would have so loved to have a baby.

The little special one with dark hair and bright blue eyes appears in her mind's eye, and the grief that suffuses her is total. She stands in the hallway and lets it pass through. Slowly, she becomes conscious of her own physical presence and of the shape of the place around her, its boundaries, the small space that she occupies and all the space she doesn't. Her bare feet and the feel of the wood under her soles, the cool curve of the glass in her hands, the whispering of the tinnitus in her right ear, the familiar ache in her left hip, the warmth of the air around her face.

She wanders back into the living room and to her bed. There is a large bookcase above the television. She has glanced at it before, seen that nearly all of the books, strangely, are in French and so dismissed it. She looks more carefully now, but there are only a few history books in Italian. She picks up a magazine from the paraphernalia on the television table. Beneath is a slim volume with a familiar cover.

Les Fleurs du mal.

There are dozens of French-language books in this apartment and its presence is not strange at all, but still she feels a sort of muffled shock of recognition, as if this might have been what she was looking for when she was opening all the cupboard doors. It has that same old photograph of the author on the cover that her father's edition had. She remembers saying to her father once, thinking he would be flattered, that he resembled Baudelaire. His high, noble brow, his intense gaze. 'Look like that debauched opium eater?' her father said, outraged. 'Thank you very much!'

She carries the book across to the bed and climbs in. She holds it in her right hand and flicks through it from back to front with her thumb, noticing that someone has annotated it in pencil, in Arabic, and that these marks are made next to and around earlier pencil notes in Italian. She holds the book open halfway through and looks at the two sets of notes. It seems to her, from their placing, that the later marks, the ones in Arabic that she cannot decipher, are both a commentary on the poems and on the earlier comments that are faint now and all but illegible.

She turns to the title page and sees that it is her father's copy. It was a school prize. There is the green-ink dedication to Ferdinando Cattaneo and, on the opposite page, in Stefano's handwriting: 'For Abramo, in memory of your grandfather. November 1938.'

She holds it tight. Her father's book that she sent from Monza to Stefano in Tripoli and that has now returned to her in Rome. She thinks of the last time she had this book in her hands.

~

In the autumn of 1938, on the morning of the day she was to leave for England, when her trunk was already packed, bills settled and the apartment cleared, the doorbell rang. Liliana clattered down the stairs expecting that it would be the neighbour come to collect the key but found instead a delivery man with a parcel.

The stamps commemorating the Tripoli international trade fair showed where the parcel had come from, and she recognised her brother's handwriting on the label. Yet she wanted to refuse it. She wanted to say no, sorry, Liliana Cattaneo has gone, you had better take it back.

The impulse was fleeting, and she didn't act on it.

She carried the parcel upstairs as if it were immensely fragile, although she could feel that the contents were soft, not breakable at all. Once inside, she placed it under the window in the living room. She took a step back and looked at it.

Everything was done, all the arrangements had been made, and all she had to do was lock up, leave the key with the neighbour and make her way by whatever meandering route she chose to the railway station, where she was to board the night train. She was still here, physically still in Monza. Her old life was over, her new life had not yet begun, and she had entered an in-between zone, a dreamy association-free place that was neither here nor there.

She was unprepared for this interruption. She had not braced herself.

She contemplated the parcel. It must be a gift from her brother, she thought. He had never sent her a gift before. Letters, postcards, the occasional photograph. How cruel to send a gift now, when in her mind she had already gone and could not bear to be called back.

She wondered if she could just leave the parcel here, unopened, as if it had arrived too late.

Don't be silly, she told herself.

She knelt down, sat on her heels, undid the string and opened the wrapping. The softness inside was a dark blue shawl in fine silk. She lifted it up with both hands and let it trickle through her fingers like water. The parcel also contained a letter, drawings and a formal photograph of the whole family, taken – she saw from the address printed on the back – at the studio on Via Manzoni in Tripoli. Nadia had drawn a picture of their apartment building and the sea beyond, herself skipping on the flat roof 'for Auntie Lili'. Abramo had made a paper aeroplane with coloured wings. *Romeo type C4*, he had written in black ink on the fuselage, unaware that his aunt, of all people, would recognise the markings without explanation. At the end of her brother's letter, partly devoted to a description of the new Maserati three-litre fixed head eight-cylinder engine, he asked if Liliana would pick out something of their parents' for him. 'Something special, that Papà and Mamma held dear.'

Beneath the window, where the pooled cloth of the shawl lay, a rectangular patch of darker wood showed where the sideboard once stood. Along with the sofa, the best linen, the matrimonial bed and the day bed, the table and chairs, the 'Persian' rug and the crockery, it had been sold at auction. The gold-rimmed china had fetched quite a good price, as had some of her father's books at the antiquarian bookshop, which had taken the lot. Her father's one-time favourite poet, the man he called 'the prophet', Gabriele D'Annunzio, was enjoying a resurgence apparently, since his death earlier in the year. Her parents' good clothes and personal items she had given to the nuns at the convent of the Poor Clares, who distributed them to the needy. Everything that could not be sold or donated or passed on had been thrown away.

There was nothing left.

Liliana let her head drop forward to the floor and buried her face in the cloth of the shawl. It carried a faint scent of rosewater and cinnamon, and an image of Farida's fingers working the loom came to her. She lifted her head a fraction, eased herself sideways and then let her head fall back down to the bare floorboards, her forehead hitting the wood with a satisfying bang. She raised it and banged it down twice more. Then she rested there and focused on her throbbing temples and waited for the pain to subside.

When it was manageable, she got to her feet, gathering up the contents of the parcel and the packaging, and went to the hallway where her trunk and day bag sat ready for departure. The day bag contained all that she would need for the journey: her nightdress, her wash things, including a bar of lavender-scented soap she had bought at the chemist's, a change of underwear and a new blue-black crêpe dress she planned to wear for her arrival in London. She folded the shawl and placed it in the bag. Then she opened the trunk and lifted out the drawer compartment inside and removed the one book of her father's she had kept, the Baudelaire, and her mother's mantilla. In their place she put Stefano's letter, the drawings and the new photograph. Then she re-fastened the trunk and sat on it, the book and the wrapping paper on her lap.

Stefano would not be able to read the Baudelaire because he did not speak French, and in any case he was not much of a reader, except for motor-car magazines. She didn't know what he might do with the mantilla. But there was nothing else for her to send.

The Baudelaire was the first book of poems her father had ever owned and the one that ignited his love of poetry. In his middle years he liked to declaim D'Annunzio's obscure and mystical phrases. A 'fistful of incense over ember, the scent of a pure soul', was the measure of a man, he mysteriously claimed. But he gave up on all that, part of a bigger disillusionment as his old convictions deserted him one by one. He had lost faith in fascism and in Mussolini. The decline might have begun with Stefano's departure for Tripoli back in 1925, and with the events that precipitated it. It must have accelerated in Liliana's absence, because when she came home in 1931 she was shocked by how thin and out of sorts he was. She came to see that he had stopped believing he had any capacity to change anything. That any of it was up to him. He had even stopped countering his wife's fatalistic pronouncements. When she said it was never the place of little people like them to change anything, theirs was to endure and to submit, he would nod and say, 'You're right' which wasn't intended to take the wind out of her mother's sails, but invariably did.

Baudelaire, long neglected for being French – her father held the French responsible for the unfair division of territories after the war – had come back into favour because her father had long since lost interest in the notion that Italy deserved the restitution of its 'unredeemed' lands. What little French Liliana had, she had acquired through the recitation of her father's favourite poems from *Les Fleurs du mal*. She even knew some verses off by heart. If she were ever to go to France, she would be able to make cryptic pronouncements on beauty and melancholy, but ordering a cup of coffee or asking the way to the nearest grocer's would be beyond her.

When she used to read out loud, her father would join in and, as often as not, take over. He would correct her pronunciation and repeat the phrases that most closely touched him. 'My youth was nothing but a dark storm' was one of these, and 'I want to sleep! To sleep rather than live! In a sleep as sweet as death.' When he remembered, he would smile at her to make out he wasn't really as sad as he seemed, although they both knew that he was.

In his final days, his voice was no more than a sigh, an intention rather than a sound, and she would falter on alone. 'Be patient, oh pain of mine,' she had read many times, 'you pleaded for twilight and here it now comes.'

For a long time before he died, her father was ailing, and it looked as though his end would be the culmination of this slow petering out, that he would fade and fade until there wasn't quite enough of him to go on any more.

But it didn't happen like that.

On 9 May 1936 the fascist empire was officially declared. It seemed that fascism reigned supreme. The Ethiopian campaign was hailed as a tremendous success. The Duce could do no wrong. The following day her father set off for a walk, saying he didn't want company. He took the black umbrella that he sometimes used as a walking stick.

He went to the railway yard where he used to work and

somehow contrived to fall in front of a slow-moving goods train. How this could have happened was a mystery, and there were no witnesses other than the driver, who hadn't seen him but had felt the bump. People pointed out that her father was blind in one eye, increasingly deaf and unsteady on his feet. It was an unfortunate accident, they concluded.

Certain words and phrases in the book had been underlined, and notes made in the margins. These pencil marks were old and faint, but it was because of these near-illegible comments and explanations written by the boy that her father once was that Liliana had chosen to take this book with her to England. This book was proof that, before he was their father, before he met their mother, before life and war and mutilation ground him down, Ferdinando Cattaneo was *that* sort of boy – a bright one who won school prizes, who read in French, who annotated the text with comments like 'symbolism = clothe the ideal in a perceptible form' and 'the poet's vocation is to express beauty and, thereby, to touch on the infinite'. It testified to its owner's particular ambition – for debate and mental stimulus and intellectual reward. And even when that other future it hinted at turned out to be beyond his grasp, the arrangement of these words and the ideas behind them, about how beauty and meaning might lie beyond, about what he described in one scribble as 'the necessity for the poet's unflinching gaze', still constituted a bright thread running through his reduced life, like a creek in an arid plain.

Liliana sat on her trunk just inside the front door and leafed through the book, trying to find an imperfectly remembered phrase, something about dancing being poetry with arms and legs. She couldn't find it and wondered if perhaps it was not Baudelaire at all. Never mind, she thought, these

212

phrases were in her head. These lovely pitiful French words that seemed to act on her father the way that religion acts on believers.

She closed the book and gazed first at the porter's trolley she had borrowed from the station propped against the wall and then at the hooks on the back of the door where their coats used to hang. She thought about her mother and how religion never seemed to offer her much solace, despite her piety and her dedication. Her mother claimed the stiffness and pain in her knees was to do with how much kneeling she had done. She died a year and a half after her husband, just because she now could, or so it seemed. There was no one to hold her back. She lacked the stomach for life once she didn't have Liliana's father to contradict. Even if Liliana had said, 'I have won the lottery, Mamma, and I am flying us both on the sea plane from Ostia to Tripoli to meet Stefano's family there and make the acquaintance of this famous Rosita (aka Farida), about whom you have heard so much but know so little,' her mother would have replied that she was too tired and that she looked forward to hearing about it when Liliana got back. If such a trip had come about, on Liliana's return her mother would have told her all the rosary group gossip and how delicious the custard inside the filled panettone that the baker made was, and she would have cast about for what other news to impart, but she would have forgotten to ask any questions. For the eighteen months between the deaths of her parents, Liliana's mother's curiosity was largely confined to the workings of her own bowels and where the next piece of cake might be coming from.

Liliana took a piece of paper and a pen from her bag and wrote a note, which she placed in the front of the book. She turned the wrapping paper inside out so that the stamps and address label were hidden on the inside and parcelled it up. She printed Stefano's address on the front and tied the string.

She didn't much mind letting it go, not really. She found Baudelaire's predilection for bitter gulfs and endless agony depressing. She didn't think he was looking for the beauty in evil. She thought he was addicted to misery. He liked having a pained soul. If he had had some real bitter gulfs to endure, if he had been dropped into the abyss like she had, perhaps he would have had more of an eye for the sunshine.

French was of no use to her now anyhow. She was going to England.

Afterwards, after she had been to the post office and sent the parcel off, she came back and collected her bags, shut the door for the last time, dropped the key in with the neighbour and walked slowly to the railway station, dragging the trunk on its trolley behind her.

Her train was not for three hours yet, but there was nowhere else she particularly wanted to be. She had said goodbye to it all already: the hat-factory office, the cinema, the market, the park, the bench beside the river, the race track. She wanted none of it any more. She sat on the platform and she waited, trying not to think too much. After a while, she fished out the English grammar and phrase book she had bought when she took in her father's books to the antiquarian bookshop. It had phonetic transcriptions next to the phrases. 'How do you do?' she muttered. 'Do you mind if I close the window?'

∽

So Abramo had kept their father's book all these years. Kept it and loved it and leafed through it often and thought about what the grandfather he never met had to say about it. Stefano must have passed it straight on to his son as soon as it arrived in Tripoli. Perhaps Nadia received the mantilla.

Those were Abramo's sheets she stripped earlier and stuffed in the linen basket. He must have slept right here, the night before he was shot. For a moment she imagines running to the basket and pulling the sheets out to catch another trace of him, as if that might bring her brother closer.

It is a balmy night, but Liliana lies shivering. Questions and possible explanations form and fizzle out in her confused mind. Zaida is Abramo's niece. Abramo stayed here. Therefore, what? She starts to think about it and then finds that she has veered off somewhere else, the train of thought unfinished, abandoned on some forgotten pathway. Perhaps Zaida hadn't meant that Abramo was her real uncle. Perhaps she called all Libyan men here in Rome uncle, or what was the word she had used? *Khal.* Liliana's confused mind is like a dense forest through which she is trying to find a way. If Abramo was indeed the girl's uncle, he was either married to the sister of the man in the coma – which he can't have been, because they told her he was a bachelor, although you didn't need to be married to father a child of course – or the man in the coma was married to Abramo's sister. This was clear to her at the same time as being opaque. Her thoughts keep breaking off and then she starts again, taking a different tack. Whose are the clothes in the wardrobe? What is she to deduce from them? She is poking around in the tangled forest and stepping on thorns, tripping over roots, getting nowhere.

GHIBLI

Item: A postcard tinted in shades of yellow, showing a storm rising over the desert.

The *ghibli* is coming.

It is the fishmonger at the next stall who alerts the Friday morning market shoppers. He points to the sky above the sea where a great murmuration of starlings is swarming into strange shapes and squiggles, painting black signs across the cloudless blue. The *ghibli* is coming, he shouts, and he starts to pack up his stall, waving away the customers, slotting the crates on top of each other, tugging out the tarpaulin he stores beneath the table. The warning is passed along the row of stalls, and suddenly everything is in commotion.

'What? What is going on?' Liliana asks. She is waiting to buy some mullet. She is going to make a fish soup following a recipe given to her by the wife of their landlord, Signor Yaacov.

'Serve us my fish first, Mohammed,' the woman next to her says. 'Go on. It's the *ghibli*,' she says, rolling her eyes at Liliana.

The word is vaguely familiar, but Liliana has forgotten what it means.

'The *sirocco*,' the woman explains, packing her fish into her basket. 'It comes up from the desert and it blows over there' – she makes a gesture of picking up and flinging something across the Mediterranean. 'And then it falls on my family in Siracusa and they call it blood rain.' She rolls her eyes again. 'As if they've got it bad,' she says.

'Oh, it's the desert wind, you mean,' Liliana says.

'Go home and batten down the hatches,' the Sicilian woman says.

'I haven't got my fish yet.'

'You won't get any now,' the woman says and scurries away.

Liliana hurries home by the most direct route, down Sciara Hara Kebira where the traders are dragging their trays of sweetmeats inside and pulling down the shutters, counting the turnings so that she does not make a mistake. If she gets as far as Sciara Hosc Angelo, she will have gone too far.

'Farida,' she calls as she comes in by the green door.

Farida is sitting on the floor in the courtyard, grinding spices in a bowl.

'The *ghibli* is coming,' Liliana says.

Farida looks at her wide-eyed and then she is on her feet. 'Get the covers from the beds,' she says. Quickly she unties the pieces of camel meat hanging from a line on the sunny side of the patio. She has been drying them for a great delicacy she intends to make next week.

Together they use the covers to wrap the food and kitchen stores, tucking them in tight beneath, weighting them down. The cold box containing the fresh vegetables for tonight's fish stew, the tomatoes and onions, garlic and coriander, they drag into the store room and cover with another cloth.

They fill a jug with water and take it into the bigger bedroom. And then they retreat there and shut the door, plunging the room into darkness. Farida lights the lamp and sets it on the chest at the end of the bed. She rolls a towel into a cylinder and packs it along the bottom of the door. Liliana sits on the bed.

Farida is standing just inside the door, very still, waiting, listening. There comes a sound as of water boiling inside a lidded pan. 'There it is,' she says.

She lifts her barracan down from the back of the door and sweeps it around her. 'In the desert, when the *ghibli* comes, we do this,' she says. And she pulls the cover up over herself and sinks to the floor. She pops her head out of the opening and sees Liliana's surprised face, and they both laugh. She rises up with the cloth flowing around her and twirls about making strange little sounds and then melts back down into the cover, disappears inside and becomes still and silent. An unlikely desert boulder on the bedroom floor.

Liliana bends down and lifts up an edge of the cloth. 'Can I come in?' she says. She crawls inside and sits on her heels facing Farida, their heads the poles of the little twin-peaked tent. Out in the streets of Tripoli, the harsh sand- and grit-laden wind might be clogging the air, coating everything with yellow dust, silting up cracks and passageways. It might be howling and whistling down the alleys, gusting in through the arches of the minarets, flying out over the sea to meet the humidity and hanging there, a sulphurous cloud. But here, in their temporary tent, it is quiet. There is no sound except their breath, no scent except their breath. In the dim and diffuse light of the lamp, Liliana can make out only the silver gleam of one of Farida's earrings and the whites of her eyes.

'How long might you stay here?' she says. 'When you're in the desert and the *ghibli* comes. I mean, how long does it last?'

'It can be a long time,' Farida says.

Apart from when they are shopping for food, Liliana has never heard Farida use a precise number. 'A whole morning?'

'A day. Days.'

'And what do you do?'

Liliana can tell from the ripple of the cloth that Farida has dipped and raised her head. It is the gesture she makes when she doesn't understand and wants clarification. No change in her expression accompanies it. No sign of bafflement such as a shrug or a frown or a questioning look. It took Liliana a while to decipher, because it is not dissimilar to a nod. She knows that there is no point repeating what she has said, that the failure to communicate is not down to Farida misunderstanding the words. 'What do you do to while away the time?' she says eventually. 'To keep yourself occupied?'

Farida repeats the gesture of incomprehension and clicks her tongue against her teeth for emphasis. She can click from different parts of her mouth, and each sound has a distinct meaning. If she lifts her head, rolls her eyes upwards and makes a single click, it means *no*. A double click against the palate, accompanied by a little backward movement of the head, means *I think you are joking. Really? Are you sure about that?* She uses it a lot with Stefano, who likes to tell tall tales and see how they are received. A wetter sound, when she puts her tongue behind her bottom teeth, seems to have a wider and more abstract application. Liliana thinks of it as denoting something about what a never-ending and wondrous mystery the world is.

She has another gesture that involves the thumb – she flicks her thumb under her top teeth – and it means *no way, nothing, this is a dead end*. There is something slightly vulgar and street urchin about it, and Liliana finds it thrilling. She imagines it might be something that the women do when they are on their own, but not in the presence of men.

219

Liliana casts about for an activity that might be conducted by a person alone inside their barracan in a desert storm. 'Do you sing, perhaps?' she says. Farida likes singing. They put the gramophone on sometimes and sing along.

'We go inside,' Farida replies.

'Oh,' Liliana says, and she thinks about this conundrum for a minute. 'Where inside?' she says.

The cloth momentarily billows around her as Farida leans forward. Liliana feels Farida's hand on her brow, the print of her thumb in the space between and above the eyebrows. 'There inside,' she says. She mutters some words in her own language, seeming to be seeking a clearer way of explaining herself. She keeps her thumb where it is, pressed into that place in the middle of Liliana's forehead as if she is anointing her. It is the same spot where the priest dabs the ashes on Ash Wednesday.

'Inside there,' Farida says after much thought. She holds her thumb pressed into the spot, her fingers fanning out above Liliana's eye like the splayed feathers on a bird's wing, latticing the lamp's soft light so that it stripes the edge of her vision.

'And then what?' Liliana says.

'We wait.'

'What happens if you get hungry and thirsty?'

'Nothing.'

Farida is still so close. Her face is just inches away. Liliana lifts her hand and presses her thumb into the same place on Farida's forehead. 'Inside there,' she says. Liliana wants to tell her. She wants to say, Farida, when I get the note delivered by that boy and then I go out to meet the people from the boat that I have told you about, my Italian friends, really I am going to meet my lover. He makes me do such things. I don't know myself when I am with him. I am frightened of him. I adore him. Will I go to hell?

'How do you say "hell" in your religion?' she says, but Farida speaks at the same time. 'Pardon?' Liliana says. 'What?'

'Inside here,' Farida says, pressing once more and then lifting her hand away, 'and inside here.' And she places the palm of her hand over Liliana's left breast.

No one but Ugo has ever touched Liliana's breasts. She holds her breath.

Farida lets go and rocks back to her previous position, but Liliana knows that she is still being observed.

'You are like your brother,' Farida says, 'and not like him at the same time.' She stands, and as she does so lifts the barracan off them both and hangs it back on the hook. She sits on the bed and swings her legs up.

Liliana is still on the floor. She does not know what just happened, but she is tingling from head to toe. She gets to her feet. 'Were you very frightened when they took you to my brother? The first time?' she asks.

In the dim light from the lamp, she watches Farida shift over to the far side of the bed. She sits in the space beside her. 'I saw him come to my town,' Farida says, 'I watched him. I followed him to the shore of the lake. I hid behind the trees.' She rests her head against Liliana's shoulder. 'I wanted him,' she says. Liliana thinks about this. Stefano has told her the story of their meeting, but this is a new perspective. 'And were you happy to leave your home?' she says after a while, but Farida has fallen asleep. Liliana lies beside her, listening to the little particles of desert grit pinging against the other side of the door. And, just before she drops off, an idea about a deal she might strike with Farida comes to her. 'I will go out wearing your clothes, if you go out wearing mine,' she will say.

'What on earth are you two doing?' Stefano's voice wakes them.

While Liliana is still blinking her eyes open and trying to remember where she is, Farida has rolled from the bed ledge to the floor. She is quick to fall asleep and quick to wake. She greets Stefano. 'Is the *ghibli* finished already?' she says, and she moves past him and out of the door into the courtyard.

'We fell asleep,' Liliana says unnecessarily, sitting up.

'What are you doing just lying there in the daytime like a great lazy Arab?' Stefano says.

'Someone's in a bad mood,' Liliana says mildly.

The courtyard is covered in a layer of yellowish dust. They shake out the covers and sweep everything clean while Stefano has his bath.

Farida lights the *kanoon* and prepares mint tea scented with geranium leaves.

'What have you learned today?' Stefano says as she fills his glass and hands him it on a round tray with a bowl of salted almonds.

Liliana comes to her rescue. 'The *ghibli* got in the way today,' she says. 'We had to stay mostly at home. But I learned a new word. *Haraimi*. It means fish stew. Or is it fish soup?' She looks across at Farida.

'Yes,' Farida says.

'You're meant to be teaching *her*. Not the other way round, Lili,' Stefano says. 'That's the way it works.'

'Yes,' she says. 'I know.' But as he launches into the story of his day, about clogged carburettors and nearly skidding into the barrier when he was road-testing the revamped Bugatti, and, in the telling, forgets that he was cross with them and thought them indolent, she thinks that actually it has to work both ways in order to work at all.

THE TURKISH MARKET

Item: A picture of the long street known as Souk el-Turk, the Turkish market, with the clock tower in the distance.

Yaacov comes out of his shop on Souk el-Turk and looks up and down the street.

The merchant on the other side sits with his feet in his hands on a little mat on his doorstep as he always does, motionless. Yaacov is not one for sitting with his feet in his hands. He has a bench, a chair and a ledger inside his shop, where he does his accounts and sometimes reads or entertains his customers. Now and then he comes out onto the street to have a look at what is going on and he paces up and down in front of his shop. When his assistant is present, he sometimes visits the silversmith he owns in a different quarter of the old town to check on work there, but today his assistant is out collecting the rents on Yaacov's properties.

There is a wide assortment of merchandise, a little bit of everything on Souk el-Turk. In the markets of Tripoli, if you know what you want and you only want one thing, silver or gold, leatherwork or cloth, slippers or incense, you will go to one of the specialist areas. If you wanted a decorated brass dish or vase, you would go to the bronze and iron workers near the clock tower where the rat–tat–tat of the artisans' hammers can be heard from morning through to night.

But if you want to browse, then Souk el–Turk – the Turkish Market – is the place. It thrums with life and business and variety. This section, where Yaacov has his shop, is quieter, and there are shops of all shapes and sizes, from alcoves in the wall like the one opposite, where a few dusty jalabiyas and some grubby-looking burnouses hang, to vast emporia containing ancient weapons – rifles with long barrels, scimitars, powder flasks, embroidered straps for rifles or sabres, travelling bags, harnesses for horses and for camels, incense and carpets, china and herbs. And the traders come in all shapes and nationalities too. The Jewish merchants like himself, specialists in precious metals; the Arab and the Italian shops and grocers' neighbouring each other; even an occasional display of goods from the Far East. There are traders too from the Eastern Mediterranean. The Armenians are experts in copper, the Greeks and Maltese in products from the sea – coral, shells and sponges. Ben Gema's perfume shop can be found at one end of the street, not far from the Alhambra theatre, which shows films but also sometimes opera. There is a place where you can taste desserts and fritters, almond macaroons and coconut ice.

It is the best area for a tourist looking for gifts to take back to Europe or America, as Yaacov does not tire of pointing out. The tourists, in fact, need go no further than his store, because what he doesn't stock he can acquire for them quickly and at a good price while they sit and drink mint tea and munch on salted almonds, or study his exquisite collection of ancient tapestries and silks.

This is the coolest and shadiest part of the street, three

metres wide with a roof formed of a wooden trellis with an ancient vine trained across. The twisted trunk and intertwined lower branches of the vine have eaten into the pockmarked wall of the building. It is hard to tell if the vine is holding the wall up or if the reverse is true. Shafts of diffuse pearly light fall between the trellis onto the paving.

Yaacov claps his hands, and one of the barefoot boys who crouch in doorways springs to his feet and comes lolloping over to him. He gives him a coin and while he waits for the boy to return with a cup of steaming coffee – he fancies coffee this morning, not tea – he takes up his favourite position against the gnarled branches, part man, part tree, part wall, and lights his cigarette. The tobacco factory has brought out a new brand called Leptis, and he finds it very good: aromatic, but mild.

People come and go. Peoples come and go. His people were here first, or so his father told him, before the Phoenicians and the Turks and the Arabs. Not before the Romans, of course, of whom these Italians claim to be the second wave, their noble ancestors, their first coming. But not long after that. The difference was that his people did not retreat and abandon this land. They stayed. They may not be many, they may not be conquerors, but they are necessary and they are still here.

The child brings his coffee. He takes a sip and perches the cup on a ledge in the wall. From his position, enfolded in the shade of the tree, he watches a young European woman wearing a straw hat and sunglasses come wandering down the street, looking around at all the goods hanging outside the shops. He can tell that she has a purpose. She is not just idly looking. She has not noticed him, half hidden there.

She pauses at Moustafa's stall. She seems to be enquiring

about the price of the barracans hanging there. She must have passed a thousand barracans already. These are not the finest. Yaacov watches Moustafa get to his feet. He has a way of standing up from sitting that Yaacov envies. A fluid hands-free motion for someone who is no longer young. Still, Yaacov has his bench, and what were seats and cushions, sofas and divans, invented for if we were all to sit on the floor? Moustafa unhooks a barracan and lays it in the girl's hands. Yaacov can hear their voices but not their words. He thinks he could step in and help the young woman negotiate a good price, but then reconsiders. Why should he have any more loyalty to the Italians than to the Arabs? This is an interesting question and one that, now he considers it, makes him step out from his place and introduce himself.

It is only then that he realises he has met the girl before. She is the sister of the young man who rents his apartment near the synagogue.

Why does an Italian girl want a grubby barracan, he wonders. He introduces himself, reminds her that they have met, that he is her landlord. He offers to negotiate on her behalf. Moustafa eyes him suspiciously.

'I was just looking,' she says. 'Just wandering and looking.'

He invites her to take a rest in his store, to tell him what in particular she is seeking in case he can advise her, and she accepts.

'There is a strange smell round here,' she says.

He sniffs. He can detect nothing. This is his air. He shakes his head.

'I can pick out some things,' she says. 'Oil of cloves, amber-gris, benzoin.' She nods at him as if he should be impressed by her discerning nose and he nods back. 'But there's something else here too that I can't make out.'

He glances round at the heaps of things that may be emitting an odour that his own atrophied senses cannot detect.

'Perhaps it's just the smell of old things,' she says, 'mysterious old things.'

'I think you might be right,' he says.

'I didn't expect to see Christian things here in the souk,' she says, 'but just the other side of that jewellery shop back there is a little shrine to the Madonna on the wall.'

She smiles at him, and he smiles back and doesn't disabuse her. He doesn't tell her that it is not a shrine but a plaque to indicate the entrance to a brothel.

It turns out he can be of help to her. She wants to know of a good tailor to alter some clothes. She is carrying a bag of hand-me-downs, given to her by a Contessa no less, over her arm. She pulls them out to show him. Silks and satins, lace and taffeta.

'And where will you wear this finery?' he asks. She blushes. Aha, he thinks. She has an admirer. That is what has changed since he first met her.

She tells him that a businessman friend of her brother's is coming to visit next month, and they are going to be dining out at a seafood restaurant.

He points her in the direction of a good tailor. He gives her an address and presses his card into her hand. He explains how to get there. He would take her himself, he says, but he cannot leave the shop.

VIA OVIDIO

Item: A postcard showing the Governor's Palace in Tripoli.

Their meeting place has shifted to Ugo's lodgings, a modern apartment on Via Ovidio not far from the Governor's Palace, where he stays when he has business in town. He is always saying that they will go back to the Grand Hotel one day, that they will have supper there, but that hasn't happened yet. It is more convenient for them to meet at the apartment, he says. It makes sense. They can be comfortable, away from prying eyes, they don't have to pretend, they can just be themselves.

It is all right with Liliana, because whatever Ugo wants is what she wants too. Yes, much more convenient, she agrees, to give the impression that she has a say in the matter.

It happens like this. A note is delivered, usually by Ali, a scarecrow of a boy who works for Ugo. Ali, by some arcane network whose structure and workings she cannot even guess at, can find Liliana even if she is out shopping or at church or taking a solitary walk along the seafront. Sometimes she emerges from Santa Maria degli Angeli to find him squatting in the square outside, a note for her clasped in his hand. When she exclaimed at this mysterious ability of the boy's, Ugo said only that Ali had been a porter before, one of the ragged bare-foot boys she has seen carrying parcels and packages around the old town, loading the carts after the Tuesday market and steering them through the streets, and then running with the parcel to its final destination down the narrowest lanes, where not even a donkey could fit, and so Ali knows his way everywhere. That was why he took him on, Ugo says, which doesn't explain how Ali can find her when she has told no one where she is going. The note specifies a time and place – next to the fountain in Piazza Italia or outside the municipal offices on Corso Vittorio Emanuele or in front of the post office on Via Emilio de Bono – always public spaces in the new part of town where Italians congregate and where she might have legitimate business. Liliana presents herself at the location in good time and loiters until, at the allotted hour, the car with the blinds in the rear windows glides to a halt near by. She slips into the back seat. No words are spoken. The first time she made the mistake of waiting on the pavement for the driver to get out and open the door for her, but she knows better now.

The driver does not even turn his head. In silence, he drives the few blocks to the apartment. There is nothing self-effacing in his silence. The opposite, in fact. The inside of that car throbs with his taciturn presence, and Liliana can hardly wait to get out, but more often than not she is there for longer than she wants.

The driver usually pulls up at the end of a side road opposite the apartment and holds up his hand, as he did the time he barred her from leaving the Grand Hotel, indicating that it is not yet time. Ugo receives other people at the apartment, and Liliana must wait her turn. When this is the case, the driver hunches forward over the steering wheel and twists his head to the left so that he can peer up at the window. As if it is a point of pride, he keeps his right arm rigid in that gesture of warning that tells her not to move, not even to think about moving, until he gets the signal to proceed. Liliana tries not to fidget, staring at the purple tassels that hang down at the side of the driver's high red fez, their ends brushing against the thick silvery line of a scar that forms a ring around his long black neck. Most often she finds herself staring at the back of his hand, waiting for the snap of his finger and thumb that will indicate it is time to move. His fingernails are always very clean, filed into elegant arcs with a pinkish sheen. A part of her wants to protest at a servant treating her in this peremptory manner, but another, much larger, part fears him. He gives her the creeps. His carved ebony stillness is like that of a crocodile before it strikes, and she always fears that, instead of snapping his fingers, he might suddenly swivel with ferocious speed and bare his terrible sharpened teeth.

Ugo calls him Muntaz — a reference to the rank the man holds. It means corporal. The African troops serving in the Italian army here are mostly, like Muntaz, from Eritrea. They are known as the Ascari troops and have their own infantry battalions and camel cavalry called *meharisti*. They are fierce and merciless in battle, Ugo says.

When Ugo said that they could be alone at his apartment, he meant away from other Italians. As well as Muntaz and Ali there is Ibrahim, a young Tripolitanian man whom Ugo inherited from the previous occupant of the apartment. He keeps the place clean and tidy, cooks meals and makes tea, deals with the laundry and sleeps in a sort of cupboard off the living room. He is a very respectful young man, who wears a clean white jalabiya and a knitted white cap. When he goes out he throws on a black cloak that he ties at his right shoulder. He keeps his leather sandals near the front door and goes barefoot inside. He speaks quite good Italian. Others come and go, but these three, Ali, Ibrahim and Muntaz, are constants. Muntaz almost never speaks. Sometimes he and Ugo converse in Tigrayan.

The men who come and go, whose departure is what keeps Liliana waiting in the car with Muntaz, are a mystery, but Liliana, impatient for the signal that the tense, silent waiting ordeal is at an end, is not particularly interested in them. She sometimes sees them leaving the building. They are local, of various ages and social standing, it seems. More than once she has seen the same man, a black-haired and -bearded local leader, a sheikh. On one occasion, Ugo accompanied one of them to the end of the street, and she entered the apartment before he was back. Ibrahim was still clearing away dishes, stacking cushions and opening the windows to let out the smoke, and she saw that several people had been there, but usually the men come singly. Another time Ugo called out of the window instead of signalling and Muntaz hurried off, making the gesture that told Liliana to stay where she was. Five minutes later she saw Ibrahim and Muntaz staggering down the road with a man propped between them. He must have been taken ill, she thought. Ibrahim reappeared shortly afterwards and re-entered the building, but Muntaz did not come back. She thought she had been forgotten, but then Ugo himself came to fetch her and, unusually, they went for an iced coffee before going back to the apartment together.

Ugo never refers to these visitors, and neither does she, but from what always happens next she understands that the meetings are challenging for him and that afterwards he needs to release pent-up energy. That is where she comes in.

When the signal comes, followed by the swift snap of

Muntaz's fingers, Liliana is out of the car, across the road and up the flight of stairs to the first floor in a flash. Ugo lets her in. Before anything else, before any refreshment or conversation, he is at her, pulling at her clothes, tugging at reluctant buttons and belts, hoisting her skirts up, hooking her drawers down, lifting and twisting her, propelling her into the bedroom, pushing her onto the bed or up against the wall. It is as if they have choreographed it, this strange and inelegant dance, although, at the beginning, it was more a question of Liliana, the novice, following Ugo's lead, because she has handed herself over to him entirely and there is no room for demurral. To demur would mean forfeiture of the complicated equation she has formulated to justify her actions.

The equation plays in her head in the awful emptiness that follows these assignations. It goes like this: Ugo is an important, upstanding man and he knows best. He is a dedicated servant of the fascist regime, which is the secular arm of the Church. Therefore, whatever her qualms, however sinful her actions, their seeming depravity, they serve a hidden but noble cause, and she is doing the right thing. Anyway, she is powerless to resist. She is utterly in his thrall.

He has chosen me, and I adore him, she thinks.

The apartment, in an ultra-modern block, consists of a large living space with a small kitchen at one end and Ibrahim's sleeping cupboard at the other, as well as a bedroom and a bathroom. The furniture in Ugo's bedroom, the big bed and the oval free-standing mirror, the tall chest of drawers and the rail where his clothes hang, is made of dark polished walnut. The slatted blinds are saffron yellow and the walls white. It is one of the first apartment blocks in the city to have hot water and electricity. There is even a dedicated underground garage in the building opposite.

She hates it when Ugo leaves. She knows the moment is coming and is inevitable, but she always feels it as a shock, a bleakness, a creeping coldness and darkness in her spirits. Terrible doubts assail her. She wants to cling to him, to say take me with you, put me in your pocket, please don't go. But she knows she must not. He is an important man with weighty responsibilities and he hates to be importuned. Instead, she puts on a bright demeanour. She murmurs endearments and encouragement to him as he dresses, or she preens herself in the other mirror in the hope of drawing his attention. He likes it when she watches herself in the mirror. She would have polished his shoes and made him coffee, but Ibrahim takes care of all those things. Sometimes, though, Ugo lets her knot his tie for him.

When she is apart from him, she imagines sometimes that she will turn the tables and invent a pressing appointment of her own, and she will be the one who has to hurry away, but then when she is with him it becomes unthinkable.

If no one else is coming he lets her linger in his apartment after he has gone, so that she can have a bath before she returns to Stefano's. She does not feel so alone when that happens because she is there with his things and she can pick them up and turn them over, feel them and sniff them. The jar of sticky pomade that he rubs into his scalp, which smells of rosemary and pine. The oval ivory-backed hair-brush and the matching smaller one for his moustache. The cream linen suits and the dress suit and the row of pressed shirts hanging on the rail below a shelf of stiff collars. She is alone there, while elsewhere in the apartment Ibrahim is busy with his chores. She fills the white porcelain tub with the clawed feet that stands in the middle of the bathroom. She adds rose oil to scent it. She lowers herself into the hot water and bathes herself free of the smell of Ugo. She dresses. Muntaz always brings her to Ugo's apartment, but she makes her own way back.

She likes it best on the rare occasions when he is not in a rush to leave. When, after they have made love, they go in their dressing gowns – he has one for her too, which he keeps hanging on the back of the bedroom door, made of dark yellow silk – and they sit in the living area, and Ibrahim brings them tea. And then she reads out loud to him, or sits on his lap in the wicker chair by the window.

He likes to talk about his planes. He loves them with as great a passion as Stefano loves his cars. But where Stefano likes to explain the workings of the machines themselves, the engine parts and the adjustments that make them more efficient, faster, safer, that reduce friction and ramp up the speed, for Ugo, all that is other people's job. His is to pilot the machine, to fly it low and high, to swoop with it over the earth. It is like a dragon, breathing fire.

He tells her about the different aeroplanes they have at the base. The Capronis and the Romeos and the Mechili. How the bigger ones can carry heavier loads and are used to re-equip the people stationed at outposts in the deep south. Some require a crew of four and others a crew of two, the pilot and the engineer or gunner. He knows how to fly them all.

But he prefers to fly solo. He prefers not to be accountable. Just him and his mighty steed.

Liliana is jealous of his plane.

COMPARTMENTS

Items: The removable tray from an old travel trunk containing postcards, photographs, letters, tickets, pressed flowers, a rosary, tufts of baby hair, a book of poetry, some newspaper and magazine articles, a length of blue thread and other memorabilia.

Liliana is up, washed, dressed and ready, waiting for it to be time to go to the hospital. It feels as if she has hardly slept, but she supposes she must have done. She is sitting at the dining table, drinking a last cup of tea before she sets off.

Intermittently throughout the night her mind has continued with its convoluted wanderings and they have not stopped with the daylight. She keeps coming up against a kind of reluctance, a dark, tangled patch that defeats her. Then, after a moment of blankness, she starts up again. If the man in the hospital is Abramo's brother-in-law, does that therefore mean that Zaida's mother is Nadia? Or not? She is bleary with it, but seems unable to stop.

She has leafed through *Les Fleurs du mal* a dozen times. Twice she has gone to put it in her suitcase and then reconsidered.

For the umpteenth time she tries to follow a line of

reasoning through. If Abramo is the girl's uncle and she is Abramo's aunt, then surely she must be the girl's great-aunt. But something prevents her from celebrating this conclusion. Its logic seems faulty. Uncomfortable thoughts of what she does and doesn't know jiggle inside her head, and one of them relates to the possibility that Abramo was not her brother's son. Even to think it for a second seems like a betrayal. There is a darkness on the edge of her perception. It is like looking at a bright light, squinting into the sun; the dancing spots around the edges are opaque and prevent her from seeing clearly. What was it Farida used to say? Something about trying to cover the eye of the sun with a sieve. She shakes her head, abandoning that line of thinking.

She starts again. If Abramo is the girl's uncle and if Abramo is Nadia's brother, that must mean that Nadia is Zaida's mother.

It is impossible for Liliana to sit still and entertain that thought. It hoists her up to her feet and across the room and out of the glass door onto the terrace, where she puts her hands on the rail and breathes the morning air. Zaida must be Nadia's daughter, but she has not inherited her mother's blue eyes. Liliana's father's brigand-blue eyes skipped a generation. Neither Liliana nor Stefano had them. Nor did Abramo. Nadia did, but her daughter does not.

The other one, the baby with the sapphire eyes that Liliana only saw the once, but that she loved more than her own life, she is there in Liliana's head too. It all sends her into a spin and she cannot catch hold of it.

She takes a step back from the terrace edge. She remembers standing on a high balcony when she first saw Ugo and having the feeling that if she fell he would catch her. How wrong a person can be, she thinks.

She can't know any more unless she speaks to Zaida. She is terrified of talking to Zaida.

Back in the living room, she glances up to check the time on the wall clock and the framed photographs catch her eye. She squeezes herself in behind the sofa to examine them. The first is an oasis with leaning palm trees framing a couple who wear wide-brimmed hats; the upper half of their faces is obscured and only their wide, laughing mouths can be seen. They are standing, hand in hand, at the foot of a steeply sloping dune and the woman is as tall as the man. In the second one the woman is on her own, posing among Roman ruins. The distinctive pair of very tall columns at one end tell Liliana that this picture was taken at the Severan Basilica at the Leptis Magna ruins on the Libyan coast. The photograph is black and white, but she remembers that the columns were made of pink granite. The final picture shows the man standing on the bend of a race track that she knows is the Tripoli Grand Prix circuit at Mellaha. He has on a light-coloured suit and his hand is held over his eyes against the sun, but his face is more visible in this one. A thickset, middle-aged man. She thinks she knows who it is, but she needs proof.

She scoops her clothes out of her suitcase and dumps them on the bed. Underneath is the tray compartment. She lifts off the lid.

Inside lie all the little bits and pieces she has kept: letters, photographs, postcards, brochures, articles cut from magazines, pressed flowers from her notebook, little notes, bills and ticket stubs. She has taken the things out many a time to look at them over the years, but nothing new has gone in since 1938. She rifles through the contents, seeking out a particular photograph.

She finds it. Stefano in his engineer's overalls standing next to that same man in that exact same spot. Stefano had written on the back: 'Me and Alfonso at the track, 6 May 1934'.

The letters are organised in date order, and each year is held together with a clip. She quickly locates the batch from 1934. She had been back in Italy for three years by then. The letter that accompanied the photograph was all about the race. Achille Varzi won it in an Alfa Romeo. Piero Taruffi's front wheels jammed and his car came flying off the track. He was flung out, broke his arm and took the skin off his leg. The car only stopped when it hit a hoarding advertising Poretti beer. 'Did I tell you we've got a brewery in Tripoli now?' Stefano has added in brackets. Simone had taken the photograph and had given it to him as a parting gift, but he thought it would be nice for Liliana to have it, for her collection. Simone and Alfonso had been on a tour, visiting Sabratha and Leptis Magna, but got back to town in time for the race. She flicks through the other letters from that year until she finds the one she wants. Here it is, in a postscript. Alfonso had bought a new apartment in Rome, where Simone was going to live. The address, in case she ever needed it, was Piazza Armenia 10, Stairway A.

There it was, written out in a letter from all those years ago, the address of the flat she was sitting in now, Simone's flat.

That was why it seemed familiar when she gave it to the taxi driver. She had sent a letter here a year or so after she went to England, before the war, to ask if Alfonso had any news of Stefano. Simone had replied, telling her that Alfonso had died of a heart attack the year before and that she had written to Stefano to tell him but had never heard back. She had no other address for him, and was sorry she couldn't help. Alfonso died in her arms, she said.

What Liliana is thinking now, as she clips the letters back

in place, is that it cannot have been true that Simone had lost touch with Stefano. How would Zaida and her father be living here if that were the case? So Simone must have been in on it. 'If she gets in touch, say you don't know where we are,' they must have said. Farida must have told Stefano what Liliana did and he must have decided he no longer wanted to include her in his life. This is not a new fear. It has flared up and faded away many times over the years, like an old wound affected by the weather. Sometimes it hurts more than at other times but never quite as much as now, because there has never been any hard evidence for it before.

She can't stay where she's not wanted. She packs her father's old copy of *Les Fleurs du mal* into the tray compartment. She takes out from her handbag the blue woollen thread from Zaida's hair, the boarding pass and the green foil chocolate wrapper, the fold-out map of the hospital, the scrap of paper with this address written in pencil in Zaida's hand, and even the original newspaper article about the Libyan dissidents shot in Rome that she finds crumpled at the bottom of her bag. She drops them all into the compartment, consigning them. She replaces the lid and piles her clothes on top. Despite her hasty packing before she left London, she somehow managed to bring the five most lovely of her scarves. She had picked out a red satin-silk square with flame-orange flowers, found in a box of bric-à-brac at St Joseph's jumble sale last year, to wear today, but it is no longer appropriate. She chooses instead the shawl that Farida made for her, that she has kept all these years.

She fastens the suitcase and puts it beside the front door. She strips the bed, makes it back into a sofa and puts her bed linen in the basket in the bathroom. She takes Abramo's sheets out of the washing machine and carries them to the terrace, where she pegs them onto the drying rack, keeping as far away as she can from the edge, which has a vertiginous pull. She feels that her movements are stiff, as if her joints are seizing up. It is similar to what people mean when they say that it is too cold to snow. She is too sad to cry. She is frozen with sadness.

She checks that everything is in order in the flat and that she has got all of her belongings. She looks one last time in the mirrored wardrobe. Simone's clothes, she thinks. She only met Simone twice. She remembers an extravagantly dressed, big-hearted woman. An older woman, she thought at the time, but actually Simone would have been youngish, perhaps ten years older than Liliana herself, in her late twenties when they met in Tripoli, much younger than Alfonso anyway, who died in her arms of a heart attack in 1938.

She sets off for the hospital in a taxi. She will hand the keys back to the girl, tell her she has to leave and say goodbye. Thank goodness that she did not reveal her connection to Abramo. It means she can fade away again. It will be a relief to leave all this disturbing stuff behind. Get back to her life.

At the hospital, she decides it is not worth leaving her case in the cloakroom. It won't take long. She takes it with her in the lift and lugs it along the corridor. The armed guard nods her in.

At first she thinks the man is alone, because the chair is empty. Then she takes a step towards the bed and sees that on the other side of it, the girl is still fast asleep on the camp bed. Liliana puts the case down and stands looking at her, her black hair spread over the pillow, her hand holding the sheet, her chipped nail varnish and the sweet curve of her cheek.

How can she leave this child? What was she even thinking? No arguments. No more contorted thinking. No more scrabbling for understanding where there is none. Liliana is going nowhere. She pushes her suitcase out of the way, into the corner of the room.

She sits down on the other side of the bed, waiting for Zaida to wake. It doesn't matter what has happened in the past or whether she has been spurned. She is staying until this child no longer needs her.

Liliana's mind calms.

TWO BARRACANS

Item: A copied-out recipe for haraimi, *fish soup.*

Wearing their barracans over their indoor clothes, they slip out into the little dead-end square with the ebony tree and its white-painted lower trunk and the solid windowless buildings. The square is empty, as it usually is at this early hour. The children who use it for their ball games come later in the day. It is not a thoroughfare and there are no shops, and so no wanderers pass by.

The two young women move quickly, as quickly as their cumbersome garb allows, out of the square, past the bathhouse and around the corner where, outside the entrance to the Jewish school, Signor Yaacov is talking to a bearded man dressed all in black, with a black skullcap. He glances up but seems not to see them. They glide past.

The smells of donkey manure and unwashed people and eucalyptus and dirt and another scent, like a kind of pungent incense, or an animal smell, musk perhaps, imbue the air that they breathe, filtered by the wool and moistened by their own enclosed exhalations.

Farida leads, and Liliana follows. They cross into another street, a narrow twisting one where the houses are joined at the level of the first floor, forming a canopy beneath. Here there are other women like them, silent, shuffling creatures, clad from head to toe in white.

Liliana has practised at home. She has swished around the courtyard while Farida watches, shaking her head and making her do it again. She has a tendency, it appears, to stride and to bob her head and to bounce when she walks. These previously unknown aspects of her deportment have been revealed by Farida's imitations. She must curb her natural pace and she must keep her head steady and level, as if she is carrying a pot. She must not clutch the cloth too tightly to her body – her form must not be evident – nor too loosely lest it flap open. But the courtyard is very different from the streets. She concentrates on keeping up. She is fearful of being stranded and alone somewhere in the medina, and of having to try to find her way back, one-eyed, parcelled from head to toe in wool and unable to ask for directions, because to speak would be to betray herself.

She holds her barracan in place with one hand. The art of it, she has learned, lies in wrapping the cloth correctly, in the positioning of the folds around head and shoulders, in the angle of overlap, the way it is held closed from the inside with the right hand, ensuring it crosses sufficiently in front and that the face, the entirety of the face apart from the left eye, remains hidden at all times. The arrangement of the cloth must ensure that it is not too long, or you might trip. Nor must it be too short, as a dangerous amount of ankle might show. If you need both hands free, you grip the cloth in your mouth and hold it there with your teeth.

They turn into an uncovered alley that is the street of tailors and where she has been only once before, two days earlier, when she took the Contessa's dresses to be altered.

She went to the third tailor on the right, as recommended by Signor Yaacov. Al-Sharif, the one with the sign hanging above his shop saying 'Italian spoken here' in Italian and 'English spoken here' in English, neither of which assertions are true but which testify to the man's accommodating spirit and entrepreneurship, according to Yaacov; traits sadly lacking, he told her, in most of the local population. As far as she could tell, Al-Sharif's knowledge of Italian is confined to '*Sì Signora, no Signora*' and the days of the week. But he understands sign language. She mimed making the dresses fit her. '*Sì Signora*,' he said eagerly. He bowed to the ground when she left. She is to collect the dresses tomorrow evening.

Some of the tailors use hand sewing machines placed on little tables at their sides and work cross-legged on the floor of their cubbyhole stores. Others, like Al-Sharif, have full-size machines and sit on stools in their doorways to operate the treadles. Liliana glides between the rows of men sewing, through the whirring sound. She comes to Al-Sharif's store and there he sits, a white cloth wound around his head, and when she sees that he is working on the Contessa's turquoise taffeta tunic with the jet beading, she comes to a halt. He must already have cut the garment down to its new size because the surplus beads glisten blackly in a little pot. Good, she is glad he isn't wasting them. She will use them to decorate a choker. She is planning to wear it for dinner when Alfonso and his lady friend Simone come to Tripoli. The tailor is sewing the new side seam and, because it is a fabric that rumples easily, he is proceeding slowly but steadily, feeding it in and smoothing it with the flat of his hand as he goes. She watches his technique with curiosity. He glances up, sees her there and a sneer crosses his face. He growls something that she doesn't understand but that might be a way of telling her to get out of the light, because then he lifts his hand and waves her away dismissively. When she doesn't immediately move, he snarls at her.

For the briefest of moments Liliana stands there stunned. Two days ago this man bowed low to her. '*Sì Signora, sì*,' he said unctuously. 'Wednesday, *Signora, sì*.' She imagines throwing off her wrapping and confronting him, snatching up the precious garment that he has beneath his palm, telling him that she will take her business elsewhere, that she will report his insolence to Signor Yaacov.

But, under the terms of the deal with Farida, the most important of the three tasks that she must successfully accomplish on this outing is not to be discovered. And so, along with the spurt of rage, there is a satisfaction in having duped him, in having become, with the mere application of a white blanket and a bit of kohl around her eyes, unrecognisable.

So she swallows her anger, turns away and moves on.

The other two tasks are that she must speak in Arabic to someone, elicit a response and reply to that, and finally that she must notice one new thing about the city that she has never noticed before. But, above all, she must not be found out.

'It's not the same,' Farida said when first Liliana made the proposal – that she would go out in the streets disguised as an Arab woman if then Farida would come out disguised as a European. She has presented it as a sort of game. It is not serious, it changes nothing in their essential identity. It is an acting role and no more. She does not know what part of her argument has swayed Farida, or whether it is only that Farida, like her, wants to show Stefano some progress. Still, she didn't concede immediately. She held her hands in front of her, palms up, fingers curled, and moved them up and down as if each contained a melon and she were comparing their weights. 'It's not equal. It's not fair,' she said.

It is true, of course, that it is much easier to throw on a cloak and cover yourself up than it is to take that cloak off and expose yourself. 'Nothing is fair,' Liliana said. She lifted her own hands up and held them out, threw back her head as if she were seeking fairness and equality somewhere up there in the heavens, spread out her hands to take in the whole of society around them. She looked at Farida and shook her head.

Farida took a step towards her. She reached her hand up and pressed her thumb into Liliana's forehead. 'But between us,' she said.

Liliana trembled at her touch. 'Make it equal, then. Make it harder for me,' she said eventually.

Walking, she absorbs Al-Sharif's behaviour and what it tells her about the position she now occupies in the hierarchy. She absorbs it into her body and she feels her gait alter, a kind of moving stillness inhabiting her, a self-effacement of which the apparel is only the outward sign. Farida has given her an Arabic name for when she wears the barracan. She is no longer Liliana. She is Salwa.

The next street is wider, with a different sort of bustle and a more varied traffic: street-sellers pushing barrows and shouting their wares, donkeys pulling carts laden with barrels and boxes, a barefoot nomad leading a camel with baskets of esparto grass hanging from its flanks. A cart passes, pulled by a particularly miserable donkey. The animal is covered in sores and has an open wound behind its ear. The child on the cart shouts at it and uses his whip. At least she is still a notch higher than a donkey.

They turn again, into another of the vaulted walkways, more residential and with fewer distractions. She is starting to get used to her skewed vision and the different perception of space and edges it affords. She thinks of her father and the funny way he holds his head since his accident, and with what apparent stoicism he has borne the loss of sight in one eye and the diminution that has ensued. She hopes that she has been kind to him, and that the pair of them, her father and her mother, are managing in her absence. She suddenly remembers, as she shuffles along with all the other white-robed women, her head slightly bowed as if in prayer, that when she was a child and thought she would be a nun when she grew up, she would wear her mother's long apron that trailed down to the ground, and her mother's mantilla on her head to serve as a veil. She would contemplatively pace the hallway, muttering blessings. Now here she is, seemingly enacting that distant fancy, dressed in quasi-religious robes, one of the many in this great silent sisterhood, following the unspoken, unbreakable rules.

She tries to believe that she is accommodating herself to the feel of the garment around her. That is not as suffocating as she feared, because the fine wool mesh flows and moves and so creates its own small currents of air. But she wants to throw it off.

And now Farida has led her to a new place, somewhere she hasn't been before, the street of the weavers where big looms and frames are worked by teams of men. She wants to watch but knows better than to stop and stare now. She flows on by in the quiet and endless procession.

One moment she thinks she cannot breathe and the next that she is breathing more easily than usual. They alternate in her, these irreconcilable states, as if, like a piston in an engine, she is being compressed and released. It seems to her that this is the way of things here. Everything is a dance of opposites, of contradictions.

With her one eye she suddenly notices where they are: they are approaching Santa Maria degli Angeli, where the road widens into a square. Ahead of them, standing in front of the main doorway of the church, she spies Padre Francesco talking to a parishioner. She catches up with Farida and tugs at her arm, pulling her into the shelter of one of the side doorways. They are so close to Padre Francesco that she can see the white hairs growing out of his ears and the lone black one sprouting from a mole on his bald patch. She can hear the rasp in his breath at the end of his inhalation, as if he sucks in air through crumpled paper, and the whistle at the end of his exhalation. Then the parishioner departs, and the priest is alone. The church bells start to ring, and he looks up at them and then at the clock, checking the time and comparing it with his watch. Then he looks around the square. His eyes pass over Liliana without pause. It is not that he does not recognise her, or is ignoring her. He simply doesn't see her. She has become part of the fabric of the place.

They are again in a narrow twisty street with the arches overhead, slats of blinding light and shadow, in single file because there is no room to walk abreast, and she keeps Farida in sight. Even when someone comes in from a side alley and joins the procession, she can tell which one is Farida by the set of her shoulders.

She might only have one eye with which to look, but she has the sensation of seeing familiar things anew. The women whose paths she crosses, for example. She notices that some have a dark patch of damp in the mouth area. And as she passes them, these other women who look just like her, the silent throng, she starts to notice other tiny distinctions. All signs of femininity are hidden, apart from the eye, but much can be told from and through an eye – is it made-up or unadorned, are there crows' feet or is the surrounding skin smooth, is the brow above arched or straight, plucked or left natural? She sees that the women notice her too. She is not invisible to them.

Something happens as she walks with the other veiled women. There is an easing of her spirit.

Farida stops at a fruit and vegetable stall. They are on their roundabout way to the fish market to buy tonight's dinner, having a second go at the *haraimi* dish that Liliana has copied down on instruction from Yaacov's wife, but they need lemons. Farida withdraws to one side. Liliana presses forward.

This is the second of her tasks. '*Limoon*,' she says, indicating the lemons, but with her hand still tucked inside the barracan it is unclear what she is pointing at. She needs to get the hand holding the basket out from under her barracan both to point and to have her basket filled. She is not sure how to get round this problem. The stallholder says something that might mean 'what' or might mean 'how many?' '*Tlata*,' she says. Three. He shakes his head at her and turns to the next customer. He isn't going to waste time on a stupid creature who can't say what she wants. The woman beside her, of whom she can see nothing, not even her eye, says something in a soft voice, wanting to help her out. Liliana is conscious of Farida, standing quietly under an archway, observing. She has to complete the transaction without coming out of character. She has to convince. '*Tlata limoon*,' she whispers to the woman, who relays her order to the greengrocer. She fetches out her arm and the basket with the tiniest flick of the cloth. '*Shukran*,' she says, thank you. She hands over the coins and rejoins Farida with a small feeling of triumph.

It is at the fish market that she notices that some women are accompanied by a black servant girl with a handkerchief or coloured scarf covering her hair but leaving her face exposed. The girl carries the palm-leaf basket and walks behind her veiled mistress. So it is not only donkeys who are lower in the hierarchy.

When they get back home, Farida throws off her barracan as she always does and immediately starts unpacking the shopping. Liliana, following behind, copies Farida's action, unpeeling the barracan as she enters but walking on, with it held in her hands, continuing through the courtyard and into her little room, where she sits on her bed and bursts into tears, the barracan on her lap and the basket of lemons on the bed beside her.

Farida comes and kneels at Liliana's feet and holds her hands. She looks up into her face and murmurs soothing words. 'What is it?' she asks. But Liliana cannot say. How to explain that for a while, when she was enveloped in the barracan, all her anxieties and dreads seemed to float away? And now they have come back down on her shoulders and taken up residence again behind her temples and in the place where the back of her skull joins her neck, and she is heavy with them. Her constant nagging anxiety about Ugo: her place in his heart, if she even has one; their future; her sense of sin and guilt; her yearning for him and her revulsion; how she wonders what he is doing and with whom, all the time that they are apart; how debased and empty she feels at the end of their encounters. The relief she feels when he is away on a mission, and she knows she will not be summoned. Her concern that Stefano will send her back to Monza and she will never see her beloved Farida again.

All of this anguish lifted away from her for the length of a covered street, and it felt like freedom.

After a while, she wipes her face on the handkerchief that

Farida is holding out to her, and they go into the kitchen. Liliana consults the recipe and assembles all of the ingredients she needs for the *kamoon hoot* spice paste.

Farida lights the *kanoon*, puts water on for tea and starts to prepare the fish. 'Next time, before we go out, I will paint your feet with henna. Shall I?'

Liliana sits on a cushion with the mortar between her feet, as she has seen Farida do, and starts to prepare the marinade, grinding the chillies and caraway seeds, coriander and cumin, the garlic and the dried mint with the pestle. 'People will see,' she says.

'I will paint only the bottom of your feet, where no one looks.'

'But if no one can see, what is the point?'

'That is the point. That no one can see. What is hidden is more beautiful for not being on display.'

She, Liliana, would know, and it would help her transform into Salwa. 'Yes, then,' she says. 'Let's do that.' She transfers the ground spices to an earthenware bowl, slides it between her feet and adds lemon juice and water. She stirs the mixture, pressing her soles against the sides of the bowl.

'What new thing did you see today?' Farida asks.

Liliana mentions the black girls that she saw.

'*Abid*,' Farida says. Slaves.

'But we don't have slavery any more,' Liliana protests.

Farida clicks her tongue twice and throws her head back, her chin up.

'No!' Liliana says.

'Same as slaves,' Farida says. She carries the pieces of fish across and drops them into the bowl.

When the tea is ready, she places the tray on the floor between them and sinks down onto the cushion opposite.

251

She pours the first frothing glass and, as they drink, they start to plan future outings, and the time when Farida will become Rosita.

They hear the click of the door and Stefano's shout of greeting. Farida gets up to put more water on to boil. Liliana lifts the bowl from between her feet and puts it on the low table.

DIRT

Item: The pressed flower heads of a cluster of creamy yellow buds from Lawsonia inermis, *commonly known as henna, labelled by hand in black ink. Beneath the flower name, a note in different ink says: 'The prophet Mohammed's favourite scent!!!'*

'Wash it off,' Ugo said. 'It looks like dirt.'

She has not told him that the henna tattoo does not wash off, that no amount of scrubbing will remove the designs from the soles of her feet and that only over time will they fade and disappear. That the skin on the sole of the foot is thick and absorbs the henna pigment deeply, giving it a rich dark colour and ensuring that it lasts a long time. You would have to remove the upper layers of skin to get rid of it quickly. She is sitting in his bath in deep, soapy water where, one sole at a time, she has scrubbed them until they are red, but the pattern that Farida painted there can still be seen. She has scrubbed them so much and so hard she does not know if she will be able to walk.

She can hear Ugo on the other side of the door, talking to Ibrahim. He will soon be leaving for the air base. She will stay in here soaking until then. Her fingers are crinkled already.

When he is gone, she will get out and she will ask Ibrahim to call her a taxi. She will not walk at all. Not even as far as Via Orazio, where the gharries congregate. She will go home as quickly as possible. If she had her barracan with her, she would slip it on and disappear. But no, that wouldn't work. A woman in a barracan would be noticed in these Italian streets. She would be shouted at, shooed away.

She thinks of Farida, and her heart, already beating too fast, speeds up. Her overloaded heart. She puts her hand to her chest, holds it there.

Farida had bought the henna leaves at the spice and herb market and then ground them in the big mortar. She sifted some of the crushed henna through a fine cloth and mixed the green powder with water and cold tea and lemon juice. She left it to rest in a bowl on the floor in a corner of the courtyard.

The paste let off a pungent earthy smell, like wet hay. It was very different from the fragrance emitted by the little flowers that Liliana had picked at the oasis and pressed between two sheets of paper inside a book. Farida had told her that the scent of the henna blossoms was the Prophet Mohammed's favourite, and Liliana had wondered how she knew, and what Jesus' favourite flower scent might have been, and how she had never thought about such a thing.

Liliana had lain on her stomach on the cushions in the courtyard with her feet in Farida's lap while Farida painted her soles with henna. At first Liliana had wriggled and giggled because of how much the brushes and little sticks tickled. The big toe of her right foot twitched uncontrollably. Farida had put a hand on Liliana's calf to still her, and told her not to move or it would smudge. Liliana had settled into a sort of quivering stillness in which the sensation in her feet, the tickle and the touch and the tingle, came to fill her consciousness, as if her essence resided down there, in her heels and arches, in the balls of her feet and in her toes. Her feet were receptors, feeling even the lightest of strokes, and her toes were lightning conductors sending the feeling onward through her body and that was why she quivered, but the quiver was infinitesimal and did not deter Farida. When she had finished, Farida had come and lain alongside her on the cushions while the henna dried, and told Liliana about the night before a wedding, when the women come to decorate the bride-to-be, and how they incorporate the name of the groom into their design as well as marks that signify the tribe.

'Did you have a henna night?' Liliana had asked, although she knew already that she had, because Stefano had related how Farida was attired when she was brought to him, how decorated and adorned.

'Yes,' Farida had said.

Liliana wanted to be able to picture the ceremony. 'Did your mother paint your hands?' she had asked.

'No, the lady of the village did.'

'The lady of the village?'

'Yes.'

Often after these exchanges Liliana felt no wiser than she had been at the beginning. Farida proffered pieces of information in a way that seemed arbitrary but might be governed by some arcane logic. Liliana had the sense too that the more she heard about Farida's origins and thinking, the less she knew. The only facts she could own to were that in Farida's desert home the women mostly went about unveiled, that the tents were made of camel hair, that of all her siblings, she and her brother Sadiq are the only two to survive, that she does not know where Sadiq is now, or if he is alive, that it was not Farida's job to fetch the water from the well because the slaves did that, and that there was a lady there who special-ised in painting with henna. They were not so much insights into that other life as pictures that floated in Liliana's mind, luminous and disconnected.

Afterwards, Liliana had admired the soles of her feet in the mirror. She had sat propped against the bench with her legs out straight so that she could see them both at once. The curls and squiggles and dots outlining their contours and filling in their internal plains, the hinterland of her heel, were beautiful and mysterious. They made the soles of her own feet, that she did not remember ever examining before, her previously neglected soles, lovely in her own eyes. Later, Liliana had prepared Farida for her first outing in European clothes. Using theatrical make-up that she had bought from a stall in the herb market, she covered Farida's face tattoo. Three layers were needed to mask it entirely. Then she patted powder over the top to seal it. They are the same size, more or less, Farida perhaps a centimetre taller, and are both able to wear the altered hand-me-downs from the Contessa, but for the first few excursions, no more than short walks around their neighbourhood, Farida wore the old high-collared loose frock of Liliana's that she had first picked out for her. Once Farida had got the hang of it, Liliana picked out a jade green cotton voile dress for her foray as Rosita into the wider world. She painted Farida's lips with rose pink lipstick and twisted her long hair into a low chignon. They went to the artisan market and looked at woven baskets.

There was no harm in any of it.

In a moment, Ugo will be gone and she will heave her sore, raw body from the water that is starting to cool, and she will hurry home to Farida and she will think of a plan to protect her and to protect Stefano.

And she doesn't now know why she didn't think to lie and say she had had her feet done at the beauty parlour, that it was the new fashion among the Italian girls here. But he seemed intrigued rather than angry, and she didn't really have time to think.

No one else was supposed to see them.

But Ugo, he looks at every part of her body. He likes to look at her body more than at her face. At different times he will bestow his attention on her bottom or her armpit or the inside of her thighs or the backs of her knees. And so he saw her painted feet. It was her own fault. She shouldn't have put them on the footstool.

Today he was fast and rough. She kept her eyes shut throughout and made herself as pliant as she knew how, and when it was finished they lay for a while, she with her head on his chest, and he briefly dozed. He had a languid, satisfied air, lying there on his back.

She hears the click of the front door and sits up in the water. Has he gone?

Earlier, while Ugo was taking *his* bath, she went and sat in the living room. Ibrahim was still clearing up. She watched him as he emptied ashtrays and replaced them on the coffee table and on the arm of the sofa, swept the floor, righted the portrait of Mussolini that had somehow slipped to one side. 'Ibrahim,' she said after a while and he straightened, bowed his head, 'I haven't seen Ali for a while. Do you know where he is?'

Ibrahim's eyes flicked to the side, as if Ugo might be able to see them through the bathroom wall. He shook his head.

'A different boy brought me the note yesterday, and the last time I came here,' she said. 'I hope he's not ill.'

'Not ill,' Ibrahim said.

'What then?' she said.

His eyes veered sideways again.

'I'm just worried about him,' she said. 'He's only a little boy.' Twice when she was wandering about the streets in her barracan, although not for a few weeks now, she had seen Ali and she wondered if he were looking for her. She had seen Ali, and he had not seen her, and although she had not been hiding from him, there was a satisfaction in knowing that she could.

'The master sent him away,' Ibrahim said.

'Oh no! Why?' she said.

'He was not so good at his job,' Ibrahim said. 'He takes a long time and sometimes it is too late. So he's gone.' He made a motion with his hand as if he were swatting a fly. He picked up the tray of cups and bowls and went into the kitchen.

She had the sensation of Ali's absence, of missing him, although she only ever saw him for an instant.

She got up and went to the kitchen door. Ibrahim was washing the dishes. He looked up. She wanted to ask him if it could have been because of her that Ali was banished. Was it that he was unable to find her to deliver a note? She did not know how to phrase this. 'Does the master treat you well?' she said instead. He lowered his head so that he was staring into the bowl of washing-up.

She retreated quickly to her seat by the window.

Ugo came into the room, bathed and pomaded and already in his uniform. He declared himself a new man. He kissed her. 'You do restore me,' he said. He sat in the big wicker chair at the window and she opposite him, with the little footstool and the coffee table between them. Ibrahim brought them a tumbler of whisky and soda each, the ice clinking, and

Ugo tossed his straight down his throat and had his glass re-filled immediately. He swilled the whisky around in his glass.

At the thought of what happened next, she hugs her knees to her chest and she listens not just with her ears but with the whole of her – her submerged skin that has wrinkled and puckered in the bathwater, her exposed skin where the hairs are standing on end, the tips of her shoulder blades.

She felt relaxed and confident, and she put her feet up on the footstool as she sipped her drink.

'What's that on your feet?' Ugo said. He got up and he came and knelt to look more closely. 'Henna tattoos,' he said in a soft voice. He seemed entranced. 'How come?' and he smiled and stroked her feet. 'My little belly dancer.'

He wasn't supposed to see them. They were a secret. Her secret. Hers and Farida's. She could not think of anything to say.

'And these,' he said, tracing the lines with his finger, 'these are words in the centre, aren't they? What do they say?'

'They're just patterns,' she said.

'No,' he corrected her. 'They are words. There is writing here.'

'Oh,' she said. 'I thought they were just patterns.'

'Ibrahim,' he called. 'Come here. What does this word mean?'

سَلْوَى

Ibrahim read it out. 'Salwa,' he said. 'It is a little bird that we eat. I don't know the word in Italian.'

'And this,' Ugo said.

فريدة

'Farida,' Ibrahim said. 'It is a name. A woman's name.'

259

That was when Liliana learned that Farida had painted her own name, which meant unique and lovely pearl, on the bottom of her right foot and Salwa, which meant solace or consolation, but was also, apparently, a little bird that people like to eat, on the bottom of her left.

'You can leave now,' Ugo told Ibrahim. 'They're splendid,' he said to her. 'Very beautifully executed.' He knelt there with her feet in his hands. 'And who is this Farida?' he said in a light, conversational tone.

Sometimes she would imagine that Ugo asked her to stay in the flat and be his sort-of wife the way that Farida was Stefano's sort-of wife. His *madama*. A man could have a *madama* even if he had a proper wife back home. 'She's my brother's wife,' she told him. 'Sort-of wife.'

She didn't see the harm in it.

'Really?' he said, and his eyes were alight with interest and amusement. 'Tell me more,' and he started to massage her feet.

He knelt there, all sleek and groomed in his uniform, stroking her feet while he plied her with questions. Where was the girl from? How had Liliana's brother found her? Nothing Liliana had ever said had captured his interest like this.

'Is she beautiful?' he asked.

'Yes,' she said.

'As beautiful as you?' His hands had strayed up as far as her knees.

'More beautiful,' she said.

'I doubt it,' he said. 'Women are not necessarily the best judges of such things. And he wants to keep her, your brother?'

She is shivering in the bathwater. She doesn't know for sure Ugo has left, if it's safe to come out. That was the moment when she should have lied. When Ugo said, 'And he wants to keep her, your brother?' she could have said, 'No, he's sending her back home next month,' or something. She understands that now. But she was talking to her lover, in private. He was fascinated by her every word. She didn't see the harm.

'Yes, very much so. He wants her to learn Italian ways,' she said.

'To pass her off as an Italian?'

'Not exactly,' she said. 'Just to dress in a European style, cook more familiar food, venture out with him. That sort of thing.'

'Because even if they learn our language and dress in our clothes, that doesn't make them Italian.'

'Of course not,' she said.

Ugo smiled and nodded. 'She cannot become Italian, or European. It isn't in her. She cannot be part of our history. She is not of our race.'

'No,' Liliana agreed.

'She can only, at best, become an imitation. Inside, she would still be inferior.'

Farida can speak three languages, can feed a household on a tiny budget, can sing a whole repertoire of Italian songs, can retreat into the wonderland that is herself and find comfort there, can survive. She is unschooled but learned, capable of holding contradictory thoughts in her head at the same time. She is a woman of complex allegiances. She is intelligent and gentle and devoted and fierce.

'Is she loyal?' he asked.

'To Stefano, do you mean?' she asked.

'To her people,' he said.

'I don't think she has any contact with them,' she said.

'They've probably cut her off because she's a whore. Pity.

Find out, though – she may be contacting them in secret. Find out who her father is and whether he commands any men.'

'Why?' she said in a little wavering voice.

Ugo rested back on his heels and looked straight at her. 'Does your brother's employer know that he harbours one of our enemies in his home? In his bed?'

'Farida's not our enemy,' she said.

'They're all our enemies,' he said, getting to his feet and standing over her.

'They are treacherous. They say one thing and mean another.' His gaze left hers and he looked to the side, out of the window, thinking. He nodded to himself and turned back, looking down on her. 'I will tell you something that shows what they are like and then you will understand. The ones who have joined us, who fight on our side, the so-called submitted ones. We discovered that on the battlefield they were not using the ammunition but dropping it on the ground for their compatriots to find afterwards and use against us.' He blinked down at her. A slow blink over his big peeled eyes, waiting for a reaction.

'What happens to those people?' she asked.

He put his hands around his neck, encircled it like a noose, pressing his thumbs into his Adam's apple and letting his head loll to one side, his eyes opening and staring, rolling them up into his head. It was momentary. Fleeting. An unthinking pose held for a few seconds before he removed his hands and leaned down towards her, smiling.

It was all she could do not to flinch. He put his hands, his hangman's hands, on her shoulders and bent his head to one side to kiss her neck. He scooped her up and carried her back to the bedroom.

'Tell me more about her,' he said, 'your brother's Bedouin

whore.' He undid his trousers and lay down on the bed. 'Come here,' he said and he sat her across him. She was only wearing her silk gown. 'Turn round,' he said. He lifted her so she was facing away from him. 'Don't stop telling me about the girl. How tall is she? Have you seen her naked? What is her body like? What colour is her skin?' He pulled up Liliana's feet so her legs were bent and he put his hand between them and he lifted her buttocks and spread them, held her there hovering in the air, moved his hand so she was sitting on it and the warmth in her almost falling out, the weight of her and then he guided her onto him. 'Keep talking,' he said. He flipped the cloth of her gown up and over her head so that her upper half was wrapped in it and her lower half exposed. With his knees he pushed her legs further apart.

It was then, belatedly, that she started to describe a different girl. She invented details that were not Farida's. A mole on her breastbone. A wide bottom. Curly hair. A ring through her belly button. A jewel in her nose.

'Your brother should tread very carefully,' he said afterwards. 'He isn't a member of the party and so he doesn't have our protection.'

She swallowed. There was a sick taste in her throat. 'He was talking of joining,' she lied.

'Too late,' Ugo said. He swung his legs off the bed, buttoned his trousers and stood in front of the mirror, smoothing his hair. 'He should have joined before he left Italy. We wouldn't have him now.'

Then he told her to wash the henna off.

Someone is moving about in the kitchen. A drawer opens and then shuts. She hears the clatter of cutlery. That must be Ibrahim. Ugo must have gone.

She lets out a pent-up breath. She slides her hand behind her head and lifts her unbound hair away from her neck, drapes it over the rim of the bath so that it won't get wet and slides her sore body down one last time into the tepid water.

The bathroom door opens and Ugo walks in. He stands at the end of the bath and he smiles down at her. She shrivels. He is still here. It must have been Ibrahim who went out. He takes off his jacket and hangs it on the back of the door, and rolls up the sleeves of his shirt. He reaches down into the water and hoicks out one of her feet. 'The water is cold,' he says. He examines the sole of her foot and shakes his head. He drapes that leg over the side of the bath. 'Show me the other one,' he says and obediently she lifts her other leg. 'They're still dirty,' he says. She has her elbows braced against the sides not to slide under. He drapes that leg over the other side of the bath and then moves closer in so that he is standing between her knees at the end of the bath. He hooks his hands underneath the back of her thighs. 'Take a deep breath,' he says and speedily, unceremoniously, he lifts the lower part of her naked body out so that her head is dragged along the bottom of the bath, beneath the water. Her weight is on the back of her neck and her hands reach up and clutch the sides of the bath and she opens her eyes, watches the bubbles of air rise as she expels her breath, looks up through the water at his staring face. She is empty. There is no air in her.

But it's over in a moment. He fishes her out and wraps her in a towel and she gasps and he sits on the edge of the tub with her on his lap and says, 'There, there, I've got you, little bird. Did you think I'd let you drown?'

And she thinks, confusedly, that it is funny that Farida has named her after a bird when it is the other way round. A long time before, when she first knew her, she watched

Farida hopping about in the courtyard and she wondered, can I make this little bird sing? She thinks of a bird in a cage, clutching its swinging perch with its talons, chirruping a tune as if the bars weren't there.

'There, there,' Ugo says. 'I've got you,' and he rocks her on his lap. 'I'm sorry I was angry.'

She nestles shivering in his arms. He loves her really. She knows he does.

A WHITED SEPULCHRE

Item: A magazine article from May 1980 telling of the accidental discovery of a hidden underground chamber in the catacomb of Priscilla in northern Rome.

Liliana has flicked through the magazine that came with the newspaper in search of a suitable and interesting article to read to the comatose man. Entitled 'A Whited Sepulchre?', the one she has chosen tells of the recent accidental discovery of a hidden chamber in the catacomb of Priscilla in northern Rome.

She begins to read it out loud. It narrates how a group of tourists were on a guided visit to the catacomb when one of their party, a child, somehow fell through a crumbly section of wall into the chamber, fortunately suffering only bruises and shock, no serious injury. Subsequently, a bigger incision has been carefully made so that further investigations can take place. It seems that the flattened earth walls of the chamber had been whitewashed many centuries before but, on one wall, fragments of colour show through. The newly discovered chamber is situated close to the Greek Chapel, which contains third-century frescoes depicting biblical scenes, and it was thought that the whitewash concealed another fresco of this type.

The article described the child as having 'literally tumbled through the levels of time'. Liliana's concentration snags on the phrase. It jolts her, as if she too is tumbling. She looks across at the girl, Zaida, curled there on the little camp bed, fast asleep although it is gone nine in the morning, and the hospital has been awake and busy for hours. When the medical staff come in, they tiptoe around her and talk in whispers. The child has been awake most of the night, they say, and didn't lie down until the early hours. Liliana is unsure whether to wake her and send her home to get some rest, if she will go, or to let her sleep on. She can see it is an inconvenience to the staff to have this second recumbent body in the small room.

The article says that the underground chamber must also have served at some time as a crypt because it contained several skeletons. It points out that the Priscilla catacomb is known as the Queen of Catacombs because it houses the remains of many martyrs and more than one pope.

In the centre of the wall, emerging from under the top layer of whitewash, the faded image of a mother and baby can be seen. The article considers what might be depicted in the fresco, why and by whom it might have been obliterated, what secrets might be revealed when and if it is fully uncovered. There has been some suggestion, it claims, that the mother and baby might not portray the Madonna with the baby Jesus, but a priestess of a primitive cult that practised human sacrifice.

Liliana pauses again as another jolt runs through her, causing her shoulders to hunch. Goodness, she thinks, what a bag of nerves. She shrugs off the feeling and resumes her reading. When she has finished, she tears the article out of the magazine, folds it into quarters and puts it in her handbag.

The girl sleeps.

The man lies unconscious and unmoving.

It is warm in the room, but Liliana has started to shiver. Water off a duck's back, she tells herself and she tries to draw on the feathery solace of those waxy wings that have guided her comportment through these many years. Instead, she is visited by a different bird, a Libyan one called the desert grey shrike, also known as the butcher bird. She can picture it sitting atop a flagpole, airing its wings. She remembers her brother telling her how it killed its prey by impaling them on a spike of some kind and allowing them to bleed to death. It seems important to remember the detail, because while she is thinking of the desert shrike, what is also coming to her is the idea of a man whose nickname was the Butcher. The people of Libya called him that, and he had earned the title in Fezzan before he ever came to Cyrenaica. The Butcher of Fezzan. To think of that bird and that man at the same time is to see the victims not as small mammals and fledglings, but as human beings. Men caught on spikes, thrashing to get free and only getting further entangled on the barbed-wire fence the Butcher had had erected the length of the border with Egypt. She is certain she never saw such a thing and yet she can picture the men trying to find a way through the fence, getting caught on its steel barbs, piercing themselves, and dying slowly. Who told her such a thing? Was it one of the dreams?

For the first time, Liliana turns her head to look properly at Zaida's father's face. The shivering gets worse. She is able to confirm what struck her the first time she entered this room. Although this man, Khalid Al Mafoudi, this particular individual man, is a stranger, there is something in his battered face, his puffy blackened eyes, his bloodied skull, that is known to her.

If she had ever seen such a thing, would she not remember? Can a memory be buried beyond possibility of access?

Or was it in a dream?

She has had such terrible dreams.

LEPTIS MAGNA

Item: a photograph and an article from a 1931 tourist brochure. The photo is dated January 1930. It shows a group of people, mostly men in suits, a couple of them in army uniform, women with parasols and hats standing among the ruins of Leptis Magna in northern Libya.

She is going to the ruins at Leptis Magna with Ugo. Finally, it is their special day, the outing she has been clamouring for and he has promised. She arrives at dawn at the downtown address given in the note that Ali's replacement, Hamid, brought. She expects Muntaz to turn up and whisk her to a meeting place. Muntaz, never late, is the necessary evil to be endured before the glory thereafter, but he does not come. 'My Muntaz', Ugo calls him. Ugo trusts the driver. It is something to do with the fact that he is Eritrean rather than Libyan, and that they were 'on the same side', by which Ugo means that they had fought alongside each other, and the other man had proved himself in battle. And he is a Catholic. All Africans are curs, Ugo says, especially these North Africans, but Muntaz is a faithful cur. She thinks about that while she waits, and about how Ugo would probably never have done anything to harm

Stefano but that she is glad she put him off the scent. She lied to him so fluently she almost thought it was true herself. 'The Bedouin whore has gone,' she told him. She didn't wait for him to ask. She volunteered the information. She whispered it at an intimate moment. 'I don't even know if she left or if Stefano threw her out, but she's gone.'

She stands on the pavement on Via Piemonte for twenty minutes while the street awakens.

She is there even before the shoe-shine boys set up shop. She sees them arrive, a ragged barefoot bunch coming from the direction of the port. She watches them laying out their boxes along the length of the Banco di Roma wall, with their cloths and their polish.

Perhaps no one will come for her.

The thought comes rushing up like a bubble rising.

It rushes up and it seems to pop in her skull as if she has stood up too quickly, and for a moment her vision dims and she sees stars.

This is how it will happen. One day no one will come for her, and she will be nothing. Or she will be a pile of dust on the pavement, and the street sweeper will sweep her up. People will say, where has she gone, that young woman that stood there waiting so long? What people? Who will say it? Stefano will say it. But if Stefano knew, would he not cast her out of his home? Farida, she thinks. Farida will say it. And she has a sudden vision of Farida coming and with her bare hands scooping up the dust that was Liliana, tipping her into a soft little drawstring bag and tightening it at the top so that not a speck is lost, and carrying her carefully home. I should tell Farida about Ugo, she thinks. She will not judge me. And the truth of that fills her with wonder and gratitude, as if she has been given a gift she wasn't expecting.

'Signorina Cattaneo?' a male voice says, and she starts in surprise. She turns to see a bespectacled man in a suit and fedora who has popped his head out of the doorway behind. 'Yes,' she says uncertainly.

He doffs his hat. 'We've been waiting for you,' he says.

'I'm sorry. I didn't know,' she says, following him through the door. At least it is not yet, not now. Today is not the day when no one comes.

It wouldn't do to tell Farida about Ugo. This part of her life, the Ugo part, is separate and secret and must be kept so.

A sign above the counter announces that this is the tourist office. They exit by another door, into a back street, a goods delivery area, where three open-topped Saharan motor cars await, two of them already with their quota of passengers. 'You probably weren't told to come around the back,' the man says deferentially. He is Signor Pario from the Ministry of the Colonies. He will be leading the tour. He lifts a megaphone to his lips. 'I've found her,' he announces in a loud, tinny voice that echoes off the sides of the buildings, 'our missing group member.' And the rest of the party, assembled in the waiting vehicles, cheers.

And so she discovers that a ticket in her name has been purchased to join a bespoke tour to the ruins, a party made up of a group of Italian agriculturalists, potential investors in the region, an American family – middle-aged parents, their grown-up daughter and a teenage son – and a photographer.

'Our first stop is Mellaha,' the Ministry man booms, and she smiles to herself as she takes a seat, as directed, in the fore-most car. Mellaha is where the air force base is. Ugo must be joining them there. She was right to wear her silk stockings.

She arranges the skirt of her dress carefully so that it doesn't crumple. She has on one of the Contessa's cast-offs – a soft blue crêpe with a dropped waist and a full skirt. It is a different thing, she tells herself, to know for certain that she will not see Ugo on a particular day. Then she doesn't set store by it and she gets on with her lessons with Farida, their explorations of the city, their shopping and their cooking and, best of all, their disguises; their alter egos, as she has taken to calling them. And always, whatever she is doing, she carries within her body the memory of him, his imprint, their last encounter, the throb of him. The knowledge of being desired and of desiring, of not ever getting enough, of always wanting more, and she knows he feels it too and so she is able to live her Tripoli life. But if she were to think she was going to see him, like today, and then that hope were to be dashed, that would be terrible. But it is all right. She doesn't know why she's even giving it any thought. She shifts sideways to make room for the photographer, who wanted to stow his tripod and other equipment in the boot but has been told there is no room because of the picnic hampers. Ugo will come on board at Mellaha, which can't be far because it's where Stefano goes to work every day too – the race track is in the same vicinity as the air base, on the perimeter of a salt lake. It's not what she had in mind and she cannot quite see how any privacy will be managed, but it's still going to be their special day and something Ugo has arranged, and so a sign that he does care for her a little bit at least, and a way of being out together rather than cooped up in his flat. It shows something, some progress, a development in their relationship. She is not just his part-time mistress, hidden away. They will be out together in public. She sets her mind to liking it all.

The photographer clambers in beside her with all of his paraphernalia, the folded tripod, his bag and lens case and light meters. He looks hot and flustered and she is moved to be kind to him, thinking that sooner than he knows he will have to give up his place to Ugo and probably squash in with the Americans. He has come from Italy to take pictures for a holiday brochure. As they set off he confides to her that soon, once the brochure is out and the beauties of the colony are more widely broadcast, there will be regular autobuses plying this route. He asks if she will pose for a photograph when they arrive at their destination. 'I didn't expect to be travelling in such charming company,' he says. He has shiny brown hair and a neat golden-brown moustache, and his name is Aldo. Once upon a time she might have looked twice at a handsome young man like this, but Ugo has spoiled her for anyone else.

He has spoiled her.

The first part of the drive, east past the city's oasis, is on a smooth, shiny asphalt road. 'As good a road as you will find anywhere in Italy,' Aldo tells her. As they drive along, the Ministry official gets to his feet and turns so he is facing backwards, gripping the door frame to steady himself and shouting information about the landscape they are passing through, the range of crops, how grasses have been planted on the dunes to prevent erosion. He sits back down and wipes his brow with the back of his sleeve. They pass through a vast empty square and he is on his feet again. This is the region's commercial centre, he shouts, Souk el-Giuma, the market, where shepherds from all around and merchants from the city converge to trade on a Friday. 'When you tuck into your cumin-spiced meat balls or your *shorba arabiya* at the Oriental Café on a Saturday evening, you can be sure this is where your meat will have come from,' he says.

Soon after, they come to the Mellaha air base. The cars pull up at an entrance arch where the Italian flag hangs limply from a metal flagpole and two Ascari soldiers in scarlet jackets

274

and fezzes with blue and red tassels, rifles at their shoulders and cutlasses hanging from their belts, stand guard. The official tells the group that the planes are kept in hangars on the other side of the buildings visible through the gates. Liliana peers down the drive to where long, low, white rectangular buildings are set among eucalpytus trees and she thinks about this being the place he lives when he is not in town. She is expecting him to come striding down the drive.

'There is a library, cinema and gym for the use of the men and the officers. The airmen all live there like one big family,' the ministry official explains and then he nods at the driver and at the two in the cars behind, and the engines start up. 'Next stop, Homs,' he shouts. He maintains his position so that he can point out a lump of rock off to the left that conceals the tomb of a holy man, a fourteenth-century marabout. Liliana swivels her head around to look beyond the clouds of dust sent up by the vehicles at the air base receding in the distance. When the official resumes his seat, she taps his shoulder. 'Excuse me, sorry,' she says, 'but why did we stop at Mellaha?'

She doesn't know what she is expecting. That he will clap his hand to his forehead in horror and order the cars to turn back, exclaiming, 'Oh God, I've forgotten the Colonel!'

'We're showing our guests from overseas how safe and well defended our colony is,' he says.

The pointless, useless oaf of a photographer is leaning in too close and regaling her with snippets of information about future tourist itineraries, and the Ministry official is up and down like a bouncing ball to make sure they do not miss a single ruin or mulberry plantation or rock formation or line of camels carrying loads or farmer tilling his arid land with an ancient hand-drawn plough, so that between them her head is a jangle. 'I'm sorry,' she says to Aldo, 'I have a headache coming on.'

She closes her eyes. It sinks in. He is not coming. Ugo is not coming, and the longed-for day stretches out in front of her, empty and monotonous, all life and joy sucked out of it, a day that she wants to be over rather than to live through.

Ugo cannot conceivably have thought she wanted to go on an excursion with a bunch of strangers. Ugo doesn't care.

～

After a while she opens her eyes again. The road has become more of a track. Sometimes it veers to the left and runs along beside the sea and sometimes it curves inland through scrubby plains where the occasional solitary shepherd with his flock can be seen wandering in the distance.

The cars rattle on. The journey is bumpy and interminable. Her head is banging.

When the sun is blindingly high in the sky, they stop at the side of the road under the thorny shade of some acacia trees. They drink coffee from a flask while Signor Pario lectures them about Homs, which the Arabs call Al Khums and which was the site of two major battles early on in the colonisation period, in 1911 and 1912, known as the Battles of Murqub after the castle there. Major victories for our brave Italian troops of the time, he says, very important in subjugating this coastal region. 'Did they have guns?' the American man calls out from the second car and everyone turns to look at him. 'Or were they fighting you with . . .' He mimes the action of shooting an arrow from a bow.

Signor Pario looks coldly at the man. Perhaps he does not like to be interrupted. 'They had guns. They were supplied with firearms by the Turks, who were their masters

276

before. There is still an army garrison here, but the fighting is long since over. The indigenous people are at peace with the Italian authorities now.' While Signor Pario continues extolling the virtues of the civilisation that has been brought to these people, Liliana remembers some pictures in a book Ugo showed her. There was one that he was interested in talking about – of the first aviator ever to use a plane as a weapon, back in 1911 when they were still trying to oust the Turks. He flew over the Gefara plain and tossed hand grenades onto the enemy below, the North Africans and the Ottoman Turks. Lieutenant Giulio Gavotti was his name. It had stuck in her memory because of Ugo's pride in the idea of a plane as a killing machine. But the picture on the facing page was even clearer in her mind. A circle of Italian soldiers, two or three deep in places, some standing with their hands in their pockets, some facing into the centre of the gathering, some looking outward or leaving the perimeter to wander away. A casual, purposeless grouping of soldiers at ease, milling about, and in the middle of the circle some piles of old cloth and rags. It was only after she had been looking at the photograph for a while that she saw that the rags were tattered clothes worn by dead rebels and that the ground was littered with them, these wretched, emaciated corpses. And she thinks now about how Ugo did not seem to notice them.

'But are they happy?' the American man calls out.

Signor Pario's brow furrows. Perhaps it is not a question he has considered. He seems to think about it. His eyes stray sideways, as if the answer might lie out in the desert wastes. 'They have sanitation now,' he says eventually, 'where before they lived in filth.' He nods at the man, as if to tell him that the question is now closed. Homs, he says, is the gateway to Leptis Magna, the most potent symbol of Rome's abiding presence in this land. He gives the signal to the drivers that it is time to depart and turns and faces forward, pointing with his free hand in their direction of travel, as if leading a charge. After a while he slides awkwardly back into his seat and dabs his sweaty brow.

Finally, they are on the last stretch, and there is the ancient city in front of them, its columns and temples shimmering in the heat. Signor Pario cannot resist getting to his feet again, balancing there for the last time and bellowing about how there, off to the left, is where Emperor Septimius Severus was born, telling them how this was the site of a Roman colony thousands of years ago, and now they have returned and how work is being done, important archeological work, to recover it from the desert sands that have protected it, that have kept Rome's historical patrimony safe. He shouts at the top of his voice because an ever-louder rumbling noise threatens to drown him out. Basilica and thermal baths, he cries. Mosaics untouched by human hand for centuries. But no one is listening to him any more, not in this car anyway, because the rumbling is almost upon them, and they are screwing up their eyes and shielding them with their hands to look into the sky. A black dot has appeared from nowhere against the sheer uninterrupted blue. It comes closer and closer and then it flies right over them, a small military plane, and they are in its shadow, looking up at its undercarriage and at its two wheels dangling down, so low that they instinctively duck. Then it flies on ahead and they see it land in the distance ahead of them in a swirl of dust. When they arrive, he is standing there.

How he loves to make an entrance.

He is wearing his desert uniform, his khaki trousers tucked into brown leather boots, and he holds his cap in his hand and bows.

She wants to see it as a wonderful surprise. But it has come too late. The headache is real. She can't quite pull herself back. And no one knows that he is here for her, and from the way he talks to Signor Pario in low tones, she understands that this was a long-standing plan about impressing the investors and the rich tourists.

They walk around the baths and the amphitheatre and they see a newly uncovered and restored mosaic depicting a goddess and her slaves. They eat their picnic in the shady northern apse of the Severan Basilica, where the columns are of pink granite, and Ugo pays attention to everyone else, at one point walking closely beside the American girl, and takes no notice of Liliana whatsoever. If she could leave them all and go off on her own, she would. There is a museum that houses the statues found during the recent excavations, and in there he draws her behind a pillar and presses himself briefly against her. His breath smells of the sardines he ate at the picnic.

At the end he gathers them together and announces that one lucky person will fly with him back to Tripoli. There is a terrible moment when she thinks he is going to pick the American girl. His eyes rest on her a moment, and if he did that would be it, but he doesn't; his eyes pass over her. 'Is there anyone here travelling alone?' he asks. The photographer and Liliana both raise their hands. 'Sir,' the photographer calls out, 'you should take me because I will take some aerial photographs for my brochure.' Ugo looks at the young man and he nods, and then he says, 'Excellent idea, young man,' and Aldo starts to gather his equipment. 'I will ask back at the base for one of my men to take you up for that purpose,' Ugo continues, 'but not now. Because this isn't about business, it is about pleasure.'

And he looks directly at Liliana for the first time. 'Are you travelling alone, young lady?' he asks, and if the photographer had not put himself forward in that way, she might have said 'No, I'm with him,' but instead, of course, she nods. 'Would you like to ride in my chariot?' Ugo says.

Up in the air he laughs, and she joins in, and he has no idea that she doesn't feel it. He has a way of throwing his head back when he laughs, showing his even white teeth and his big pink tongue. 'You're so good at surprises,' she says.

They swoop out over the sea. It glitters below them and she can see from the different colours where it is shallower and where it is deeper, and where there are rocks below the surface. It is turquoise and cobalt and aquamarine and it is thrilling to see from above; it would be, if only her head weren't aching so and if she hadn't thought he wasn't coming. And if she hadn't seen the way he looked at the American girl. She can't think of anything to say. '*Mare Nostrum*,' she manages eventually.

'Yes,' he says, 'all ours, and what isn't yet soon will be.'

They turn inland, and she sees how the desert plain begins just south of the coast, and how narrow is the cultivated strip.

There is a stick thing, a sort of lever poking out from beside the dashboard and Ugo moves it about sometimes, but mostly his hand just rests on it. He has its pommel in his cupped palm and he caresses it, his fingers still, and then moving again, rubbing its smooth surface, fondling it with his big clean fingers, stroking it with his thumb.

They pass over a native encampment near Tagiura, tents dotted about in the dirt. They come back around a second time so that she can look down on them more clearly, a circle of conical tents in the centre, more rectangular ones grouped around the perimeter like the suburbs of an impoverished little town, people moving about on the tracks between the tents, a line of camels tethered at the edge, a flock of sheep and their shepherds near by. They all look so small and vulnerable from up here. Like ants that a giant's foot could crush without even noticing. 'They look so tiny,' she says.

'We come down lower than this when we're bombing,' he says, 'so we can target more clearly.'

A nauseating image comes into her head of the sole of a giant's shoe, encrusted with crushed people and flattened animals. But he doesn't mean villages of defenceless people and livestock. Of course he doesn't.

He swoops still lower and she can see a woman carrying a bucket trudging to the well. The woman does not look up but pulls her shawl over to cover both her head and the child she is carrying.

'That bundle on her back,' he says, 'might be a stash of rifles. She might be carrying them to the rebels, hiding out in the desert.'

'I think it was a child,' Liliana says, suddenly fearful.

He laughs. 'I know,' he says. He takes his hand from his beloved lever and briefly squeezes her knee.

And she laughs too, wanting to be reassured. Up here, in the great luminous softness of the air, her headache starts to fade. She thinks how, with this different perspective, to be able to look down on people and on human habitation is to understand how little and how futile it all is, how petty small human concerns and jealousies. She is struggling to express the feeling of wonder and awe that has come to her. 'All laid out beneath you,' she says, 'and you up here, Godlike.'

'The way I like it,' he says. He lifts the plane higher, and they fly over the desert, a monotonous ochre landscape unfolding beneath, broken up only by patches of scrub and brownish scatterings of rocks, so that she can appreciate the vastness of the desert, he says and just as he turns to go back she spots a lone building, an unlikely protuberance on the desert floor, and points it out. It's a fort, he tells her, an Italian-built fort. He doesn't want the occupants to spot the plane because they'll think he's bringing fresh supplies and he wouldn't like to disappoint them. 'You should see their faces when we land with fresh fruit!' he says. 'Quickest way to a man's heart.' She turns in her seat to see, but already she cannot pick it out in the great scrubby sameness of the plain. 'I didn't know we had forts,' she says.

'It's not your job to know,' he says.

They sit in silence. This must be the longest time they have spent in each other's company without making love. As if Ugo is thinking the same thing, he reaches across at that very moment and squeezes her greedily between the legs. He keeps his hand there, palpating her in the same way he did the gearstick or whatever the lever is, while he tells her about the forts that dot the desert. They are milestones and surveillance posts for the traffic routes, places of support and re-supply for mobile troops, he says. Sometimes the men live in them for months on end and they become *insabbiati*, silted up, unable to adapt back to life in civilisation.

She looks at him. Just for a moment, she does not see her handsome, dashing, powerful lover. Her hero. He is just a man, and a smelly one at that. She can detect the odour of his fishy breath and the oily pomade. She pictures him at the mirror, smoothing his hair back from his brow with his ivory-backed brush, worshipping at the altar of himself. She looks away and out of the window. She wonders what Farida is doing today.

She turns back to him when he tells her to hang on to her

282

seat and he is grinning in that way he has, and there he is in all his glory, and she wonders how she doubted him. He makes the plane somersault in the air and she shrieks with fear and excitement.

They land back at the air base where Muntaz is waiting with the car, and like the first time they were together in Tripoli, they sit in the back together, Ugo idly fondling her while leaning forward to talk to Muntaz. When they pass through the Tripoli oasis, he orders Muntaz to stop so he can show her something and then he leads her up a little path into the mulberry orchard where the dangling fruit have ripened and are starting to drop, and crushed berries have split and spilt their red juice on the ground. She was here with her brother. They walked down this path and they were laughing.

Ugo leads her towards a little hut, where he shouts a local man away. He pulls her inside and turns her round to face the wall and hitches up her dress and takes her quickly and urgently from behind, sighing in the way that people do when a bodily function has been relieved.

Then they go back to the car, where Muntaz waits like a statue. They drop her off at the cathedral.

DUTY

Item: A business card in Italian and in Arabic, advertising the Libyan artefact export enterprise of Signor Yaacov Djebali of Souk el-Turk, Tripoli.

It was one of those days when Liliana had to sit in the car on the side road, staring at Muntaz's scar. After an unusually long period of time, ten minutes or more, Muntaz raised the hand commanding her to stay put while he leapt out to help with whatever needed doing.

She sat in the back seat for what seemed like another age, conscious mainly that she needed the toilet. When she couldn't wait any longer she got out and walked the few paces to the junction where something told her to pause, to check first. It was always a very quiet street in the early afternoon, Via Ovidio. The few shops, apart from the café at the far end, were closed for lunch and wouldn't re-open until four. As she stood at the corner, wondering if it was all right to go and ring the bell, the door to Ugo's building opened and Muntaz came backing out, carrying one end of something heavy, wrapped in cloth, taking small steps backwards, negotiating the doorway, and Liliana drew right back behind the corner because she could tell that he was about to look up and down the street. When she dared to peek again, he was out of sight. She stuck her head out further. He had completely disappeared. Muntaz, his burden and the person carrying its other end were nowhere to be seen. The only place they could have gone was the garage opposite.

She ran across the road, through the main door, which had been left ajar, and up the stairs, and rang the bell, but it was Ibrahim who answered, not Ugo. He shook his head at her and said, no, not yet Signorina, we are not ready, but she pushed past because she was desperate now for the toilet and ran straight into the bathroom, without looking to left or right. Only once she was in there did she register how dishevelled Ibrahim had appeared, how unkempt, with bloodshot eyes and his hair standing up and a rusty mark down the front of his usually pristine jalabiya. And the chaos she had glimpsed through the open door of the living room, the overturned coffee table and a spreading stain on the pale rug. And that Ibrahim answering the door meant it must have been Ugo himself carrying the other end of whatever had been taken to the garage. And that it wasn't a thing, but a person. But before she could even begin to ponder that, she heard the door slamming and Ugo's voice bellowing and a thwacking noise as of a slap, flat palm on flesh and bone. She glanced at herself in the mirror. She met her wild wide eyes. She looked and she started to see, but she pushed the seeing back down, out of her own sight. There was nothing to be done right now. Quickly she fluffed her hair and then stepped out of the bathroom into the hallway, where Ibrahim cowered with his hands to his head, and Ugo stood over him, fist raised.

'Darling,' she said.

In the frozen moment, before Ugo straightened and let

fall his hand, her gaze met Ibrahim's and all sorts of things became clear.

She struggled not to show any of them in her manner. 'Darling,' she said again, her voice catching. 'What's going on?' She reached out and touched Ugo's arm, but he shook her off. He had hold of the back of Ibrahim's jalabiya, and the hand he had lowered was still bunched in a fist. He swivelled, tugging Ibrahim with him. He eyed her suspiciously. She could see the great muscles of his shoulders tensed. He put her in mind of a bull, readying to charge.

He didn't know what she had seen, but he suspected. 'It's not Ibrahim's fault he let me in early. I pushed past him. I'm sorry.'

'See this man here,' Ugo said. 'He looks like us, does he not? His skin is not much darker, his arms are not put on in a different way, his arse shits the way ours does,' and with that he whacked Ibrahim's behind with such force that the young man toppled forward and had to do a skip to keep his balance, but Ugo still had hold of his jalabiya and dragged him upright again. 'This arse of a boy looks the same but the difference is all on the inside, and if we turned him inside out we'd see it. Shall we?' he said, and he unsheathed his knife from his belt. 'Shall we turn him inside out and show that the shit isn't just in his arse, but that he is riddled with it?'

'What has he done, Ugo? Why are you treating him like this?'

'Because he's full of shit and he deserves it. Because he thinks he knows better.'

'Darling,' she said again.

'And you. Why weren't you in the car?' Ugo said. His face was contorted with rage. A vein next to his left eye was pulsing. 'You're supposed to wait in the car.'

'I'm sorry. I couldn't wait,' she said, rolling her eyes towards the bathroom door. 'Forgive me.'

He looked her up and down. There was a coldness in his gaze. 'I thought you had run away,' he said.

'As if,' she said, and she took a step towards him and held out her arms.

'Clear up the mess,' Ugo said to Ibrahim, releasing him and picking Liliana up to bundle her into the bedroom.

As soon as the door was shut he went at her like a frenzied bull.

Afterwards they put on their dressing gowns and he sat in the big wicker chair at the window and she opposite him, with the little footstool and the coffee table between them. Ibrahim brought them drinks. He had on a fresh white jalabiya, and his hair was neatly combed. She made sure not to meet his eye. The room was clean and tidy. The rug had been removed.

She held her glass with both hands to disguise her trembling. She put her bare feet on the footstool to give an impression of being at ease.

Ugo looked at her bare feet. 'Tell me again what happened to the Bedouin whore,' he said.

'She left,' Liliana said.

'How come?'

'I don't know,' Liliana said. 'She just disappeared.' She managed a careless shrug.

'And what does your brother say about that?'

'Nothing,' she said. 'He never mentions her. He has his eye on a nice Italian girl who works in the office. Teresa.' She hadn't missed a beat. She was sure of it.

'Pity,' Ugo said. 'I'd have liked to meet her.'

He was looking at her again. He wanted to know what she

had seen, if anything. He was waiting for her to say something, to give herself away, to ask him a question. 'How come poor old Ibrahim has got on your wrong side?' she asked. She said it lightly, as if it were quite normal to threaten to slice a man open and turn him inside out.

He sat back in his chair. His shoulders relaxed. 'Ibrahim didn't do what he was told,' he said. 'He's a servant. He's supposed to do what he's told.'

That was a good question to ask, she told herself. It made Ugo think that was all she had noticed. Not the body, if it was a body. Not the blood, if it definitely was blood. What dreadful thing had he told Ibrahim to do?

'You're right,' she said. 'That's his job.'

'Don't worry your pretty little head about Ibrahim,' he said. 'I'm going to make sure it doesn't happen again.' His eyes half closed and he jutted out his lower lip, nodding to himself as if formulating a plan. Then he opened his eyes fully. 'Any other concerns?' he said.

She was struggling to stave off the full impact of what she had half witnessed. She could feel it on the edge of her consciousness: the truth. It was like a misshapen beast and it was starting now to lumber from its hiding place where it had lain neglected and ignored for so long. She couldn't allow it out now. She had to survive these few minutes. She still sat, her legs crossed at the ankles, her bare legs, her yellow silk gown, her face flushed and hair tousled from lovemaking. She ran her hand through her hair. She made herself smile across at him. She made her voice playful. 'When I'm sitting waiting for you,' she said, 'I have time to observe Muntaz's neck.'

He looked at her quizzically. He didn't know where this was going.

'It looks like someone tried to chop his head off.'

Ugo guffawed. 'Ha ha,' he said. 'You're right. They did. I saved him, though. Ha ha.' He threw back his head and laughed and she laughed with him.

When he went to bathe, she crept to the kitchen to speak to Ibrahim, but before she got there she heard Ugo calling her from the bathroom.

'Come and wash my hair one last time,' he said, when she opened the door.

His belly curved out of the scummy bathwater. The dark hair on his chest and head was all flattened down and wet.

She took the shampoo from the shelf and poured some into her hands. She started to lather it into his scalp. She could push him under. She wouldn't be strong enough to hold him there. 'Are you sending me packing?' she said after a while.

'Didn't I tell you?' he said. 'I'm being sent to Cyrenaica. I leave tomorrow.'

She filled a jug with clean water from the tap to rinse his hair and tested that it was neither too hot nor too cold. She could run and get a sharp knife from the kitchen and pierce him through. She would be doing the world a favour. 'Tip your head back so I don't get soap in your eyes,' she said. She poured the water over his head, smoothing it back from his forehead so that none ran down his face. She put the jug back on the shelf. Her voice cracked as she spoke. 'Leaving for good?' she said.

He looked up at her. 'I'm afraid so, little bird,' he said.

'Oh,' she said, and sat down in a heap on the bathroom floor.

He climbed out of the tub and started vigorously towelling himself. She watched him. He dropped the wet towel to the floor, wrapped another one around his head, put his robe back on and left the room.

She was vaguely aware of Ibrahim coming in, probably to empty the tub and clean up, and then withdrawing when he noticed her on the floor. She heard Ugo whistling, which meant he was pomading his hair. Then there was a period of quiet. She didn't know how long she sat there. She thought she heard the click of the front door. Eventually, she got up. She held on to the rim of the bath to get to her feet, like an old woman. She emptied out the water and swilled the bath clean. While it was filling she went out into the flat. 'Ugo,' she called, but she could tell that he had gone.

She filled the bath deep and added scented oil. She felt strangely calm. Soon the monster would have free rein, but not yet. She was holding him at bay.

Once she was dressed again, she went to the kitchen. Ibrahim was not there. She went back into the living room and knocked on his door. 'Ibrahim,' she called. He didn't answer. She opened the door. There was barely space for him to lie down. His sleeping mat was rolled up at one end and he was kneeling with his head on the floor, praying. 'Ibrahim,' she said. He looked up and she saw that his face was full of fear and incomprehension. 'I think you should leave before the master comes back.'

'Signorina?' he said.

'Run away,' she said. 'Leave.'

'I can't,' he said. 'Muntaz is waiting.'

'Muntaz will have taken the master to the base,' she said.

Ibrahim shook his head. He peeled back on to the balls of his feet and stood up. He came through into the living room and went over to the window but made a gesture for her to stay back so that she couldn't be seen from outside. He stood to one side behind the blind and pointed. Muntaz was sitting in the car where he had parked it earlier, his head angled

290

so that he could see the front door and the sweep of street to either side. Ugo must have taken a taxi and left Muntaz behind to clear up.

'He is waiting for you to leave,' Ibrahim said and then he sat down abruptly on Ugo's wicker chair and dropped his face into his hands.

It was shocking to see him like that. 'Pack your bag,' she said. 'Be very quick. We will go down together.'

He jumped back up. He unhooked a small bag from the back of his cupboard door and slung it over his shoulder. 'I am ready,' he said.

At the bottom of the stairs, she told him to wait. She would go across and speak to Muntaz, and while she was blocking his view of the doorway Ibrahim was to come out, close the door after him and hurry away. She took out her purse and emptied its contents into his hands. He must get into a carriage as soon as he could and get as far away as possible before Muntaz realised he had gone, she said. Then he must disappear. 'Give me time to get across the road,' she said.

She took her clasp out of her hair and held it in her fist. She looked at Ibrahim one last time. She wanted to ask him about the body, if it was a body. She wanted to know what he had refused to do. There was no time. If she delayed further, Muntaz would come looking. She didn't have any advice to give him. What did she know after all? '*Shukran*,' he said. Thank you. There was a phrase that Farida had taught her, but because of her fear she couldn't remember it. She pressed his hand instead. 'Be careful,' she said, 'and go quickly.'

She stepped out into the street and closed the door behind her. She walked across the road to the car and Muntaz watched her coming without moving his big impassive head and with no discernible change in expression on his crocodile face. She positioned herself so that she was blocking his view and tapped on the car window. He narrowed his eyes as if, despite being less than a metre away, separated only by the glass, he was having difficulty focusing on her. She rapped again on the window and started speaking. Her mouth was dry and she struggled to form the words. It didn't matter. He couldn't hear her. 'Excuse me, Muntaz,' she said. 'Excuse me, but I think I dropped my hair-clasp in the car. I think it must be on the floor at the back. Do you mind if I look?'

He wound down the window and she said it all again. A streaming prattle of nonsense about how it was the one that his master had given her, so special and precious. As if Ugo had ever given her anything.

'The door is open,' Muntaz said. His voice rumbled. She had heard him speak so rarely that it sounded portentous. She didn't want to move aside yet. She didn't know if she had given Ibrahim enough time. She couldn't think of anything to say and so she stood there, without any excuse, a twisted little smile on her face, playing for time. 'Muntaz,' she said eventually. 'I want to thank you for all the times you have picked me up so punctually and driven so smoothly.' She found she couldn't look at him any longer. She had not heard any sound from behind. She had to hope. 'Thank you,' she said. She stepped to the side and opened the back door of the car. As she bent down, she twisted her head. The door across the road was shut. There was no sign of anyone. He must have gone. Please let him have gone. 'Here it is,' she exclaimed and stood up, fastening the clip back in her hair. 'Goodbye, Muntaz,' she said. She felt his eyes on her back as she walked away.

She had given all her money to Ibrahim and would have to go home on foot. She went behind the Governor's Palace and turned right up Corso Vittorio Emanuele and walked the whole length of it, past the cathedral and the Palace of Justice and the town council building and the shops and the cafés and the posters on the walls advertising the show at the Miramare and a new brand of cigarettes and another hoarding about the boat race in the harbour and the new film at the Alhambra, and all the way she felt that the monster of realisation was stalking her but that she was outpacing it. She crossed Piazza Italia and stood for a while beside the fountain, where stone seahorses with wings held a giant overflowing bowl aloft, and she paused there a moment to catch her breath and listened to the water in the hope that it would soothe her, but it did not. She set off again at a good pace even though she was deadly tired and her legs felt weak and she badly needed to cry.

She went past the Mosque of Sidi Hamuda and then the Caramanli Mosque where men sat outside on stone benches passing the time and down the road that ran alongside the castle that glowed faint coral pink in the low sun. The loudspeaker hanging from the side of the clock tower was blasting out some news in Arabic. She carried on, and entered the old town via Souk el-Turk, which was where the monster, with no regard for the fact that she was in a public place, caught up with her.

It caught her in the backs of her knees as if she would fall, and the hand she reached out to steady herself came into contact with the branch of a vine that twisted up the wall and she held on and pulled herself into its cover. This monstrous truth had been lurking on the edge of her consciousness and now it stepped forward, this half-glimpsed thing, the dark and ugly beast, its blackened eyeless and misshapen head, as if it were standing in front of her, full frontal and naked, in all its unashamed ugliness. It was familiar to her. She could not pretend otherwise. How very known it had always been.

Sheltering under the branches, squeezing herself in among them, all the bad sad things forced themselves upon her.

~

Yaacov has recently had a telephone installed in his shop, the first enterprise in Souk el-Turk to do so, and he has a mock-up of his new business card in front of him, ready to go to the printers. He is looking to increase his exports to Italy. These Italians obviously intend to stay. Shantytowns have been razed to make way for gleaming new buildings and palaces. Apartment blocks and offices and hospitals are going up everywhere. The railway line is being expanded beyond Tagiura in the east as well as further south and west. The coastal highway is to be extended too, he has heard, so that it will be possible to get all the way from Tripoli to Benghazi by road and then, eventually, beyond, meaning that new land routes to Egypt, another vast market, might soon open up. There are ever more ships plying the various shipping lanes between Italian North Africa and the Italian mainland. Now is the time. He is seizing the day. The business card is in Arabic on one side and Italian on the other. But he is not sure, although he has read it a dozen times, that it is error-free. He will have to ask an Italian to check it through. He needs to deliver the cards to the printers today.

He gets up and goes out of the shop, and lights a cigarette standing on his threshold. He looks up the street to the left. The nearest Italian business is the sweet shop four doors up, but he is pretty sure that Sandro can't read and, worse, that he will pretend he can. He looks to the right and sees that his favourite smoking place under the twisted vine is occupied. A young woman has squeezed under its branches and is standing there, hunched as if sheltering from a rainstorm.

He takes a few strolling steps in her direction to take a closer look. He recognises Signorina Cattaneo and sees that she is weeping. 'Signorina,' he says. He has made his voice soft and gentle, but still she jumps and looks at him as if she has never seen him before. 'Signorina Cattaneo. It is me. Yaacov. Come into my shop,' he says. He offers her his arm, and she takes it and allows herself to be led inside. He sits her on the bench. 'Cry to your heart's content, Signorina,' he says. 'Take no notice of me. I will order tea.' He looks back at her from the doorway. She has wasted no time at all in following his advice. She has laid her head on her knees and is clutching her own shins and her shoulders are heaving. 'I am going to shut the door and put the "back in five minutes" sign up,' he says in a loud voice, although he is not sure she is listening. 'I will be back in five minutes.' He sends a boy to find a tea-seller and smokes another cigarette under the vine. When the tea-seller comes, he goes back in to find her in the same position. 'Time to dry your eyes now,' he says and gives her his own pocket handkerchief.

She sits up straight and wipes her eyes. 'Sorry, Signor Yaacov.'

'No,' he says gallantly. 'I am sorry. I am sorry you are sad. Tell me who has made you cry, and I will run him through with my rapier.' He points to the place on the wall where the rapier used to hang in among all the other antique weaponry and then sees the empty spot and remembers that an American tourist bought it the previous week. 'Or sabre,' he says, moving his pointing finger sideways.

She smiles at him then.

Good, he thinks. He may be old, but he hasn't lost his touch.

The tea-seller pours the first frothing sweet cup and Yaacov brings it to her.

'Tea is good for everything,' he says. 'You don't have to say a thing. If you need to unburden yourself, I am here. Remember, I am a father and grandfather and husband and so can be trusted.'

He can see she is not going to speak. Never mind. It is not his concern. It is probably some foolish affair of the heart.

She sips the hot tea. The colour is coming back into her cheeks.

'Can you help me, Signorina?' he says. He shows her the words he has written out for the business card. 'Is this correct Italian?'

She reads it through and she finds one tiny mistake. He has left the 'e' off the beginning of export. 'If you don't mind, I can think of a neater way of expressing this,' she says.

'Go ahead,' he says. 'Make it sound properly Italian.'

Now that she is not sobbing, it is nice having her sit there, improving his business card. She is always so well turned out. If that pink dress is one she had altered to fit at Al-Sharif's a year ago, it has worn well.

She reads out the new version. She has a lovely way of speaking, he thinks.

'Do you want a part-time job?' he hears himself saying. 'Making telephone calls to Italian clients and suppliers. Dealing with the correspondence with Italian traders?'

She is looking at him in surprise. He has surprised himself, but it is a good idea. It will enhance the prestige of his business. It is the way forward. 'Three afternoons a week?' he says. 'I will pay you cash.'

'Yes,' she says.

And that is it. They arrange for her to start on the following Tuesday.

'Thank you so much for rescuing me,' she says as she is leaving.

'*La shukran alla wajib.*' Don't thank me, it's my duty, he says.

~

As Liliana wandered away from Signor Yaacov's shop and on homeward down Souk el-Turk, that phrase floated in her mind. That was the one that Farida had taught her and that she had wanted to say to Ibrahim – that he shouldn't thank her because she was only doing her duty. It had seemed extraordinarily clear to her that she should use what little power she had to help this fellow human being in distress. That she and Ibrahim, in their different ways, were both victims and that Ugo, with Muntaz as his henchman, was the enemy.

She stopped so suddenly in her tracks that a woman in a barracan walking close behind had to take a quick dancing sidestep to avoid a collision. 'Sorry,' she said to the woman, who hurried soundlessly on. How could it be that she and Ibrahim were on one side and Ugo on the other? To think like that was to turn the world on its head. She was standing in the middle of the narrow thoroughfare obliging people to squeeze past on either side. She took a few more uncertain steps and turned the corner past the Othman Pasha mosque. The sound of chanting came from the other side of the turquoise-painted doors. She had never wondered what they were saying before, but now she paused on the side of the road to listen. It was meaningless to her. Utterly foreign and unknown and unknowable. A droning babble. But there were words in there and invocations and, she supposed, holy mysteries. She walked on.

If there was a body in a garage on Via Ovidio, oughtn't she to tell someone in authority?

But Ugo *was* the authority.

She came now to the square where Santa Maria degli Angeli stood and she paused again. She wondered about asking to see Padre Francesco, but she knew already that there was nothing to be expected from the priest. Padre Francesco represented the other arm of the same authority. He had announced it to the congregation himself.

She found that she was looking at the church, her eyes ranging over it, taking in the pattern above the main front door, the noticeboard to the left announcing mass and confession times, the white walls and the golden yellow porticoes, the cross on top of the bell tower, as if it were a despicable heinous creature, as if the building itself were to blame. Wicked, she thought. Wicked. She felt so sick and weak and bereft. Two women from the rosary group came into the square. They pushed open the central door and disappeared into the dark interior of the church. Liliana followed them. She dipped her fingers in the holy water and blessed herself and went to the front to kneel beneath the painting of the Virgin Mary with the angels.

There was nothing to be done. There was no one she could usefully tell about what she had witnessed. What she thought she had witnessed, she corrected herself. There was no earthly authority that might step in. She could keep her mouth shut and pretend she didn't know what she knew. Her punishment was to know how complicit she was, how ruined, to carry these horrible secrets within, to know what she knew and to bear it all silently, to offer it up.

She left the church and continued on her way along Sciara Mahmud. Her duty lay in caring for Stefano and Farida, easing their lives and now bringing in a bit of money to the household. What else could she do? Nothing.

She hoped she had helped Ibrahim and that he had found sanctuary somewhere. She didn't expect that anyone would connect her with his disappearance. She hoped too that she had lied convincingly enough for Ugo to have lost interest in Stefano and Farida. She felt that she had, and that anyway the fact that Ugo was leaving, had in effect dismissed her, cared for her no longer, meant that his mind had turned elsewhere and none of them were of any interest to him any more.

No more Ugo. No more Muntaz.

And already, before she had reached home, even as the grief and the shame made her feet drag and weighed her down, another tiny part that she didn't yet believe in started to feel a sort of relief.

AN EMPTY HOUSE

Item: A postcard showing a traditional medicine man with jackal tails hanging from his hat, a drum and a bone to beat it with.

While the girl still sleeps, Liliana sits thinking. When Zaida awakens, she will buy them both some breakfast and she will endeavour, discreetly, to discover the connection with Simone and more about Zaida's family. But her decision to stay and look after this child for as long as she needs her, whatever the conversation reveals, still stands.

There is no going back for Liliana. She won't leave the child and, therefore, the choice of squashing the past back down into its compartment is no longer there. She has lifted the lid. So now she is using this moment to push her mind back to the dark place, where the hidden thing lies, to see what fragments she can find. She is trying to isolate the unremembered part, to assemble all that she does know and see what can be made of it.

She draws her shawl more tightly around her shoulders, and closes her eyes to concentrate, because when her mind slides away and gets lost in the forest she intends to pull it back onto the path and keep inching forward.

There are the actual memories and then there are the disconnected images that are more like dreams than memories, and that assail her and are beyond her control and never add up to anything of substance. She wants to do her best to assemble them. She needs courage.

She remembers being ill in Tripoli. She doesn't remember falling ill. It wasn't that one day she was well and the next day she had a temperature. But she would find herself crying all the time and her mind was fuzzy and that went on for who knows how long. And she was physically sick. She thought she had been poisoned, but that was nonsense, presumably. Sometimes, she would have the sensation of standing, glassily, just outside of herself, and watching herself go through the motions of an activity. Eating, or washing her face, combing her hair, unbuttoning her dress, being sick. And when she was watching herself, she was troubled to see her automaton self, the shell, going about uninhabited in this way. As if she were a village and the people had fled. Or an empty house that looked sound enough but had had to be evacuated because of some structural defect, creeping damp or dry rot or subsidence. And at other times, even more disconcertingly, she found that the watching part went elsewhere: it just left or shut down, and so the empty house went unobserved and anything might happen, and possibly did because there was no witness. Then she would return and resume occupancy and she would have no idea of what had been going on, what she had been up to, but there was always a strange scent when she returned, like mushrooms. Hours went by like that. Sometimes, she could tell from her aching feet that she had walked miles, but she never remembered where she had been. She seemed to go on functioning at some level but the knot in the thread that tied experience to recollection had come undone.

Sometimes it was a physical sensation that brought her back. Her sense of smell was horribly acute. Smells accosted her, caught her unawares and made her gag. She had always loved mint tea, but the smell of it disgusted her. She can't abide mint to this day.

She can see now, with the benefit of hindsight, that her fragile sense of self shattered in the aftermath of Ugo. The realisation that she had failed to protect Farida was not something that she could accommodate and stay whole. At some point she stopped going to work at Yaacov's shop because she wasn't well enough. People were talking to her and about her, but she couldn't hear them properly. It was as if she were under water and she could see their lips moving, but their words failed to reach her. There was a scene in the courtyard when Farida announced that she was pregnant, and it should have been joyous, but it was not. It was dreadful. It was the worst.

It was the end, for Liliana, of any pretence, any ability to pretend that she could hold herself together.

This is one of the places where memory falters and reason comes in to fill the gap, but reason is inadequate. Reason is a fool. It throws up a dozen questions and no answers.

They left Tripoli, she and Farida. They went on the steamer to Benghazi, and they were going to visit Farida's family in Cyrenaica so that the baby could be born there. She knows that much. And that they were going to get treatment for Liliana's illness. At the time she thought that she was being taken to a witch doctor, one of the men with masks and drums and fetishes and necklaces of bones hanging around their necks.

She opens her eyes and looks around, at her suitcase parked in the corner, the crucifix on the wall, the comatose man and his bleeping machine, the girl still slumbering on the other side. It is warm in the small hospital room, and she is wrapped in her lovely old blue shawl, but still, she has the sensation of being horribly exposed. She wants to be able to tell herself that it is all right to ask the questions whose answers she dreads. In a minute, she thinks. She will get to the questions in a minute. She closes her eyes again.

On the boat trip, which took four days, she remembers that the little rug nailed to the floorboards between their beds in the cabin stank of mouldering old wool, like a rotting sheep. And one day a shoal of flying fish rose up in an arc and then plunged back down into the water, without making a splash.

In Benghazi, Farida left her alone in the hotel room while she went to make arrangements. She remembers looking out of the window onto the main square, Piazza del Ré, watching the smartly dressed Italians sitting at pavement cafés, drinking and chatting and smoking, watching them as if they belonged to a race from which she was now excluded. Italian officers in shining boots with badges gleaming on their lapels and Ascari soldiers like Muntaz in their scarlet fezzes and swinging capes with silver crosses hanging round their necks. She watched them all through the window and then she went down and walked about among them and no one took any notice of her. In the afternoon an orchestra played in the palm garden. The men tapped their toes in time to the music or dallied with the elegant Italian ladies and sipped wine out of long-stemmed glasses. She saw the silhouette of Mussolini built into the wall of the white municipal palace. She remembers returning to their room and waiting for Farida to return, and that Farida was gone a long time and she didn't know what she would do without her.

Liliana opens her eyes and takes a breath. A shudder ripples

303

through her and goosebumps prickle her arms. Someone must be walking over her grave. She waits for the feeling to subside. She stands up, takes off her shawl, shakes it out to its full size and then puts it back on differently, pulling it up so it covers her head, and wrapping it more tightly around her shoulders, across her chest and over her hips. Thus swaddled, she sits back down.

She remembers Farida coming back and saying to get some rest because they would be leaving before dawn. They were going into the desert together, to Farida's home town, where they would be safe. 'Don't cry, *habibti*, I'm going to look after you,' Farida said.

She doesn't know what came next. She can assemble her fragments, but whatever had happened did so in a place beyond thought and so cannot be salvaged via thinking.

THE LOST SOULS

Item: A postcard showing the wide curve of Lungomare Belvedere, lined with palm trees.

Liliana and Rosita are in their finery, sitting on two high stools at a round chrome table eating coconut ice cream out of blue china bowls. Liliana is wearing the navy blue serge with the dropped waist and the pleated skirt. Rosita is sleek and groomed in the jade voile cotton with her hair pinned up and, on her feet, Liliana's best pair of shoes, with heels and a T-bar strap.

Their initial outing in European clothes was a walk around the block, which lasted less than five minutes. They returned to the apartment straight away because Farida became breathless and disorientated. They were both giddy with it, but once Farida had recovered she wanted to try again. Since then, though, they have been on many outings. They have been to the artisan market, on a tour of the museum inside the castle, and have climbed the cathedral tower to look down on the city from above. When Alfonso was over from Italy on a business trip they visited his lady friend Simone for afternoon tea and cakes at the Vittoria Hotel. It was the first time Simone had met Rosita/Farida and she was entranced by her. Alfonso couldn't believe she was the same girl he had met in the desert.

The next outing they have planned is to the Tripoli International Trade Fair on Corso Sicilia, where Yaacov intends to have a stall, which Liliana will run for him. And when Simone is back in Tripoli with Alfonso, they are all going to go to the Miramare to see a show.

Stefano is delighted with their progress. One evening, the three of them went to the Alhambra to see a magnificent film called *Sole* and the newsreel from back home; the Duce in Rome with his great jaw working away so you knew he was shouting and the people cheering and bellowing his name. Farida's face in the flickering light from the screen, her mouth and eyes open in wonder.

This time they have ventured deep into the Italian quarter, to a fashionable ice cream parlour on Lungomare Belvedere. They have stopped being tentative. It is Ugo's absence that allows this expansiveness.

Liliana carries awful half-realised secrets about with her, and yet she is still alive, she is still here, and the dread has diminished. She lives with two people she loves and who love her. Her life in Tripoli has an everyday sort of quality that was lacking before. It is duller and safer than it used to be, and she does not ask for more. Sometimes, like now, she is surprised by glee.

An affable young Italian man sitting at the next table has been chatting to them. He works at the Agrarian Fund office around the corner and is on his break. Liliana has told him about her job in Yaacov's shop and how the trade in Libyan artefacts to the European mainland is prospering.

'Your sister doesn't talk much,' he says.

It is not the first time they have been taken for sisters.

'She's shy,' Liliana replies, and she looks at Farida who looks back at her and wiggles her eyebrows and they both burst into laughter.

'What's your name?' he says, and Farida momentarily drops her head and looks down, because she still isn't used to men looking her in the face, and then quickly remembers that her alter ego doesn't mind so much. 'Rosita,' she says.

'That's a pretty name.'

Farida is a wonderful mimic. She can do accents and impressions. She can copy mannerisms. Liliana is proud of the Italian version of Farida that she has helped bring into being. She particularly likes watching Farida when she encounters something beyond her previous experience, how she feels her way, how she accesses a kind of stasis, biding her time, seeing how others behave and react and then emulating them.

Stefano is going to start looking for a house for them to rent beside the sea, once things pick up at work. There was a fatal accident, and it has had a damaging effect on the Tripoli Grand Prix. Gastone the African, of all people. He crashed during the pre-race practice at the Souk-el-Juma bend, and the tragedy has cast a terrible pall over the event. Stefano is on a committee that is seeking new patronage and other forms of financing to ensure the race's survival. He is very distracted and working long hours.

Ugo has been gone for five months, and Liliana has had time to get used to his absence. She has heard that he is now stationed permanently in Cyrenaica. She knows too that he has been back to Tripoli more than once, but there have been no more notes. She enjoys working at Yaacov's shop. On top of her wages, which she contributes to the household, Yaacov pays her commission if she secures a big deal. With her first such fee she purchased silver bangles for herself and for Farida and had little birds engraved on them. She is able to pay for these excursions too. What is left of the commission money she puts to one side.

'Can I buy you a drink?' the man says.

'We're both spoken for,' Liliana replies.

'Even little Rosita?' he says and he leans across the gap between their tables.

'Especially little Rosita,' Liliana says.

'Oh, well. You can't blame a man for trying,' he says and he slides from the stool, pays his bill and goes on his way.

'We should be going now too,' Liliana says and just then, as she is picking up her bag, she glances out of the window and sees Ugo in his white uniform, the one he wears for parades, and his white peaked cap with the gold braid. On his arm is Contessa Todino. The beat of her heart quickens. She realises she has been thinking of him as a monster, in every way a monster, and yet there he is, urbane, smart, handsome.

He hasn't seen her. They are going past. Liliana has reached under the table and she is feeling for Farida's hand. Now they are lost to sight and Liliana lets out her pent-up breath. Her vision is misty, as if she might faint. It is all right. They have gone. No, they are back, the Contessa tugging playfully at Ugo's arm and bending to examine the different flavours of ice cream displayed in refrigerated tubs and turning coquettishly to look up at him and show him the one she wants, but he is shaking his head, saying something, he has somewhere to be, he is in a hurry. It is all right, the Contessa's focus is on the ice cream, she has not looked through the window into the interior of the café.

She is fabulous today, the Contessa. She is wearing pearls and a wide-collared coffee-coloured satin dress. Her hat has a floppy brim. She is charm itself. She will prevail, she always does, but no, he is refusing, shaking his head, tapping his watch, his eyes crinkling. He is softening his refusal with a smile, and a strand of Liliana's thought forms a question: did he soften his refusals to me? Did he ever? When she tentatively asked if he would take her with him to the Miramare, for example, did he bother? What did he say? He said no. Apart from Leptis Magna, which hardly counted, she never went out in public with him. The same strand is thinking this in a familiar petulant way and is noticing how handsome he looks and wondering how long he has been back in town and telling herself for the *nth* time that there will be, there must be, some honest explanation for that body, if it *was* a body. And for the blood on the rug and on Ibrahim's clothes that day. And Ugo's treatment of him. Perhaps he deserved it. Perhaps Ibrahim had done something very reprehensible. But then surely Ibrahim would not have been so willing to gather his meagre belongings and flee. It is no good. Try as she might, she can no longer twist herself to the paradoxical set of beliefs she adhered to for so long.

Another strand, like a band around her throat constricting her breath, is thinking *murderer*.

The Contessa leans down to examine the choice of ice creams more closely, and then her gaze flicks up and meets Liliana's. She waves excitedly and taps on the window, and Liliana waves back, and there is no time for preparation, to get their story straight, because here they are, the Contessa sweeping in, her perfume and her dazzling cerise lipstick, peeling off her gloves, exclaiming at the coincidence. 'Gosling,' she says, 'you look so well. I haven't seen you in an age. How long is it? A year? More? The sea air agrees with you.'

Liliana glances at Ugo just once. The smile he had outside

is still pasted on his face. No, not pasted. It is a genuine expression of feeling. He is amused. Ugo Montello finds something in this excruciating situation amusing.

'You know our little Liliana, don't you? Do you know our little Liliana?' the Contessa says.

Perhaps they will only stay a moment and buy an ice cream to take away. Perhaps they will not even notice Farida. They will just think she is a girl who happens to be at the same table.

'Oh, of course you do. You met in Rome, at the ball, didn't you?' the Contessa says, before he has even answered, and she turns to Ugo with a sort of conspiratorial smirk that twists a knife inside Liliana that is already twisting too much, contorting her so that she feels she might overbalance and topple from her stool. But then something in Ugo's face, something that the Contessa catches there or doesn't catch, something that does not exactly reflect back to her what she expected, makes her swivel her gaze between them. *Sotto voce* she says something else to him, but Ugo, half laughing, speaks at the same time. Then, 'Yes, we met in Rome,' he says, giving a little bow, 'and we have had the pleasure of meeting since. At the Roman ruins in Leptis Magna, when this young lady was with a tour party. How are you, Signorina Cattaneo?'

'I am well,' Liliana manages to say, as he takes up her hand and kisses the back of it. Did the Contessa really call him a dirty dog, or did she mishear?

'Oh, I see,' the Contessa says, and her gaze flicks between Ugo and Liliana and she smirks again. Then, seamlessly, she turns to Farida. 'And who is this young person with you? We haven't been introduced.'

And Liliana realises with horror that, like her, Farida is wearing one of the Contessa's cast-offs. There is no denying it.

Farida must have rubbed her chin, wiping away a smear of ice cream. The tattoo is showing through. Perhaps they will think it is a scar. She endures the curious looks of the Contessa and Ugo, but her whole body is quivering.

No one speaks and the silence stretches like a piece of elastic pulled to breaking point. And then, just before it snaps, Ugo says, 'Is this your sister-in-law, Signorina Cattaneo?'

'Yes,' Liliana says faintly. She can do nothing other than follow his lead. 'My brother's wife, Rosita.'

'I didn't even know your brother had got married! What a darling little creature. And where are you from?' the Contessa says.

'Sicily, didn't you say?' Ugo says helpfully.

'The island,' Farida says, finding her voice.

The Contessa titters. 'Oh, *that* Sicily.'

Farida shakes her head. 'The island of Ustica,' she says.

'Ustica,' the Contessa says. 'Isn't that one of the prison islands?'

'Ah, I knew there was a small community of Usticans here in Tripoli,' Ugo says, nodding sagely as if deeply fascinated. 'I would love to hear about it, but I am afraid I have a pressing engagement. Would you like to stay here and eat an ice cream with these young ladies?' he says to the Contessa.

'No, no,' the Contessa says. 'My husband is expecting me.'

'Come, then. Choose your flavour,' he says, taking hold of her elbow. 'A pleasure to meet you again, Signorina Cattaneo,' he says. 'And to make your acquaintance, Signora. I would love to hear more about Ustica. I have never been.' He bows to them both and steers the Contessa to the counter.

'What a strange accent,' she hears the Contessa say.

'Peasant stock,' Ugo says. 'She probably only speaks dialect.'

'I don't think I want an ice cream after all,' the Contessa says.

Liliana holds Farida's hand and leads her down Mercatelli Street in the direction of the cathedral. Farida's hand is hot and sweaty. There are beads of sweat on her brow too and her face, which rarely sees the sun, is even paler than usual. She cannot walk quickly because she is wearing shoes with heels and she is not used to them.

When they are safe inside the gharry and it is rattling homeward along the corniche, Farida looks out of the sea-ward side and does not meet Liliana's eye.

'What made you say Ustica?' Liliana says.

'It's where my grandfather was sent,' Farida says in a flat voice. 'In the early days of the occupation.' She keeps her eyes averted.

'What happened to him?'

'No one knows. Lots of people were deported. They didn't come back.'

Liliana knows that dissidents and opponents of the fascist regime sent into internal exile are put in penal settlements on Ustica and some other islands off Sicily. Angela, the girl at her work, was sent to Lipari, and is probably still there. But she has never heard mention of these deportations. She wonders if Farida has got it right.

Farida turns her head so she is facing into the carriage. 'We call them the souls lost on Italian soil,' she says.

The way she looks at Liliana, as if she is responsible for the loss of these souls, is hard to bear. 'I'm sorry,' Liliana says, 'I didn't know.'

She cannot think what else to say. She bites her lip and tries to sit still but Farida's gaze is making her squirm. She does not know and cannot control what blemishes and secrets, what dark things that are hidden from Liliana herself are being uncovered in the fierce light of Farida's gaze.

'Who is that man?' Farida says at last.

'A colonel in the air force,' Liliana replies. Her tongue has grown big in her mouth, making it difficult to form the words. That is a nice, neutral sort of reply, she thinks. Time enough for further revelations when she has worked out what and how much needs saying.

'What is he to you?' Farida says.

Liliana starts to cry. She can't help it.

Farida reaches across and presses her thumb into Liliana's forehead and gazes steadily at her. She ignores the tears.

No scrutiny has ever been worse.

'You told him about me,' Farida says.

'I didn't mean to,' Liliana manages to say. 'I never meant to.'

'But you did. You told him about me and you didn't tell me about him.' She is pressing hard, as if she wants to bore a hole into Liliana's brain.

'It wasn't like that,' Liliana protests.

'You brought me here, dressed like this' – Farida makes a gesture with her other hand, a sweeping downwards movement that takes in her green dress, her sheer stockings and her borrowed shoes – 'and you never told me.'

It isn't fair, this judgement, Liliana thinks. It's not the whole of it. And who is Farida to judge her anyway? She tries to twist her head away but the pressure of Farida's thumb is relentless.

'I thought we were friends,' Farida says. 'You and me, equal under the sun.'

Liliana closes her eyes.

Farida releases her thumb so suddenly that Liliana's head jerks forward.

When she looks across, Farida is pulling her barracan out of her bag. She tugs off her shoes. There is a mark across the top of her foot where the strap has dug in, and the second toe on each foot has been rubbed raw.

'Your poor feet!' Liliana says.

Farida, hidden now inside the barracan, clicks her teeth. She will not be side-tracked by talk of sore feet. She slides them into the flat slippers that she normally wears and packs the shoes into her bag.

They sit in silence as the carriage rattles through the streets. Liliana will explain to Farida when they are home. She needs to find the right words. That is all. And then Farida will stop being so angry. Together they will think of a plan, if they seem to need a plan. Her thoughts flicker here and there and cannot settle on any one thing. She keeps returning to the nature of the wilderness she might be cast out into, seeing it sometimes as desert, and sometimes as salt water with her adrift in a leaky boat, and other times, because she has heard stories of this fate for local women who have been used and discarded, of the brothel that she might be put to work in. Because surely now, once Farida knows the full tale, then Stefano will have to be told too. But wasn't she just the implement with which Ugo scratched his itch? But then she remembers again that the argument of serving a greater cause only worked when she thought the cause might be greater, if she ever truly did, and now she has no idea about causes at all. Perhaps they will not banish her because they will need her to help protect them from Ugo. Now Ugo knows that she has lied, that she has defied him and gone on 'Italianising' Farida, who is still with Stefano, she will have to use her body to assuage him, and she will have to go on doing that for as long as it takes.

But he no longer wants her. Then again, if he no longer cares about her, perhaps he will not care either about Stefano and Farida, because what harm is anyone doing, really? He is probably on a flying visit to Tripoli. He might already be on his way back to Cyrenaica. He was amused to meet them and now he has forgotten them. She will tell Farida the bare minimum, and Stefano need never know, and all will go on as before.

The gharry pulls up at Porta el Gedid. Before they alight, Farida says, 'That man is going to make us pay.'

Early the next day, not long after Stefano has left for work, a note comes, carried by Hamid. Liliana answers the door and holds out her hand, but the boy shakes his head and draws back. 'What?' she says. 'Give me the note.'

He says something in his guttural voice.

'I don't understand.'

He says it again.

It has never happened that there has been a verbal message as well as the written note. And she had no opportunity to tell Farida anything the evening before. Stefano was already home when they got back. There was dinner to be prepared. There was not a private moment.

She calls over her shoulder for Farida to come and decipher what the boy is saying. Farida appears beside her, and the boy hands her the note and runs away.

The two young women go back into the courtyard. 'He must have got it wrong,' Liliana says.

Farida mutely shows her the front of the folded piece of paper. It is addressed to Signora Rosita Cattaneo. She unfolds the note and looks at it, and then holds it so that Liliana can read out what it says. The date of the appointment is today.

The time is 4 p.m. beside the clock tower. 'Don't be late, Rosita,' Ugo has written.

Liliana snatches the note out of Farida's hand and turns it over, looking for another message, something else or more or different. 'He can't just mean you,' she says. 'Why would he want to send for you?'

Farida is looking at Liliana as if she must have an answer to that question and she is waiting to hear it.

She thinks of the body carried across the road, the beatings Ibrahim gets, the disappearance of Ali. She thinks of the other man, much earlier, bloodied and crooked that she saw being walked away, the smell sometimes in the flat when she arrived, the sweaty dirty blood smell. The way he flew low over the tented village and talked about bombing the people and about their treachery. She thinks of how she has lied to him and told him Farida had gone, and that her lie has been uncovered. She cannot pretend any more. And now he wants to punish Farida for daring to pretend to be Italian, or for some other thing that enraged him that she has not understood. It is her fault. All her fault.

If there were a proper chair, Liliana would collapse into it. She looks about her as if a chair might appear.

'What does it mean?' Farida says.

Liliana stands swaying in the middle of the courtyard. Can it be that Farida is now his chosen one?

'What does it mean?' Farida says again.

'He doesn't love me,' Liliana says. He never did.

'No,' Farida agrees. 'He loves her.'

'Who?'

'The rich lady.'

'Contessa Todino?'

'Yes.'

'No,' she says. 'No, because, because . . . ' She falters. She is thinking about how the Contessa offered her as a morsel for his delectation, as now she, Liliana, has offered him Farida.

'Oh,' Liliana says, but Farida has hold of her arm and steadies her.

'What does it mean?' she asks again.

'I don't know,' Liliana says, and she starts to sob.

Farida leads her into her bedroom, pulling the door to so that they are in darkness. She lights the lamp. They sit cross-legged on the bed, facing each other. 'I never meant for this to happen,' Liliana says. Farida lifts her head slowly, clicks her tongue, lowers her head again. She knows. She looks steadily at Liliana.

'I have brought this upon us,' Liliana says eventually. 'I will go instead. I will tell him that it was just that once. That you have now withdrawn back into your own society and will no longer come out disguised as an Italian. Isn't that what he wants?'

'That isn't what he wants,' Farida says.

'What then?'

'Not that.'

She knows that Farida is waiting for her to speak, but other than coming up with preposterous solutions, like running away, her mind is a blank.

'If I don't go, what will he do? What can he do? What is his power?' Farida asks.

'He is a very violent man,' Liliana says. She has never said that out loud before. She has never properly thought it. All the things she knows about him, that she has never articulated, that she has never allowed herself fully to think, jostle for prominence. 'He holds meetings with local leaders. They go to his apartment for talks. I don't know who they are, but I believe he is doing deals, negotiating, paying them off, buying their loyalty.'

'Yes?'

'And if they go against him, or refuse him, or if he thinks they have betrayed him, or won't tell him what he wants to know, he punishes them.' She needs to say it, but she can't because she's not sure that he kills them, or not deliberately anyway. 'He thinks the people here are ungrateful and treacherous and conniving, and that we are bringing civilisation, and they should submit. Not just pretend to submit.' How can she be justifying him even now? 'You see, for him it is a war.'

'It *is* a war,' Farida says.

THE ORIENTAL CAFÉ

Item: A postcard showing a line of Arab men smoking hookahs at the Oriental Café on the edge of the Tripoli souk.

Liliana and Farida have decided that they will both go to meet Ugo. That way there is no defiance, strictly speaking, and they will be able to look after each other. 'I won't let him hurt you,' Liliana says, thinking again that surely she has some residual power.

They will wear their most elegant European clothes, but they will take their barracans and flat shoes so they are pre-pared for any eventuality.

Muntaz is waiting. They slide into the back of the car and if he is surprised that there are two of them, he does not show it. He drives only a very short distance, not to Ugo's flat but to the Oriental Café on Souk al-Mushir, on the southern edge of the old town.

Ugo is standing at the bottom of the marble steps. He is dressed in civilian clothes, a grey suit with a white shirt and a navy tie with white spots, a grey fedora on his head. He is smiling, waiting to hand Farida out of the car and because of the blinds he has no idea, until Liliana steps out, that she is there too. His smile fades. He looks at her coldly. 'I didn't invite you,' he says.

Love makes her bold. 'Well I'm here now,' she says and she hooks her arm through his and squeezes his elbow into her side as if it is all a jolly game. Her heart is hammering and her mouth and lips feel dry.

It is a public place. He cannot be planning violence. He stands for a moment, as if thinking. 'No matter,' he says, 'your choice.' He leans into the car and gives Muntaz an instruction.

With one of them on each of his arms, they proceed up the steps and through the arched entrance, passing between guards in black robes trimmed with gold and leaving behind the bright afternoon light. They go down a corridor lit with electric lights where a huge black man dressed in kingfisher blue standing behind a wooden counter nods them past. They push through red velvet curtains into the café, and somewhere along the way Ugo shrugs Liliana off so that she is following behind and can see that he has moved his arm so that it encircles Farida's waist. On the other side of the curtains is a big space with a spotlit central area and darker shadowy recesses all around. In the very centre a woman in a low-cut red dress is singing in Arabic, a wistful-sounding song, accompanied by a small orchestra. The edges of the room melt away into darkness. Underneath the music Liliana can detect the low hum of muted conversations but the people speaking cannot be seen. She can smell perfume and candle wax and cigarettes and the fruity smoke smell from hookahs.

A hostess dressed as an exotic dancer approaches, and Ugo speaks to her in a low voice. They zig-zag after the woman in between partitions and curtained-off areas. Liliana glimpses a more brightly lit side room where people are gathered around a table and a black-suited man in a red bow tie is shuffling cards, holding the pack high in one hand and letting the cards cascade through the air to the other. They arrive at a space behind a wooden screen where there is a low table with two candles in yellow glass shades and a cushioned bench to either side. Ugo sinks with Farida onto one of the benches. Liliana stands watching as he leans in and whispers in Farida's ear. She doesn't know what to do. She looks about her and notices that the whole of the periphery of the vast room is divided up into these semi-private enclosures, each of which has a view onto the performance area.

She sits down on the other bench, opposite Farida and Ugo.

A bottle of sparkling wine and three glasses are brought. The waiter pops the cork, fills their glasses and then disappears. Ugo has gathered Farida to him, close into his side. 'She doesn't drink alcohol,' Liliana says. It is hard to make herself heard above the noise of the music, but Ugo does hear and he glances across. He puts his finger to his lips. 'Shh,' he says. Liliana cannot properly see Farida's face, but she can tell that she has retreated into stillness. Ugo picks up the glass, grabs Farida's chin, turns her face towards his and, holding her like that, lifts the glass to her mouth and seems to tap it against her teeth. She takes hold of it and drinks.

The music changes and Ugo twists in his seat to watch. A troupe of belly dancers come tripping into the light, waving ostrich-feather fans in unison. Ugo seems engrossed in the display, but it looks as though the hand that he has wound around Farida is squeezing her breast. It is hard to tell in the candlelight.

The waiter returns, bends and says something in Ugo's ear. He stands up, pulling Farida to her feet. 'Excuse us,' he says to Liliana. He leads Farida away and they disappear behind another screen. For a moment, Liliana sits paralysed and then she is on her feet, chasing after them through the smoke and the dimness and the barely perceived customers. She must not let this happen. She catches up with them as they are about to go through a door. She grabs at Ugo's jacket. 'Take me,' she says, 'please take me.'

He pushes her off. Farida shakes her head. There is no plea in Farida's eyes.

She turns to Ugo. 'No,' she says, 'Darling,' she says. 'Please don't do this.'

With Farida held in tight to his side he leans his big face down to Liliana's and he kisses her, pushing his fat tongue between her teeth and gnawing at her lips. She can smell his pine and lavender cologne and the pomade in his hair and the underlying scent of him. He has bathed and applied his various potions, but she can still detect it, his scent, his skin, his oily secretions. He pulls away. 'Don't be jealous, little bird,' he says breathily into her ear.

He turns and opens the door and tugs Farida after him. Liliana clings to his jacket, pushing through in their wake. 'Please, Ugo,' she says. 'I beg you. Take me.' They are standing in a narrow corridor dimly lit by lanterns fixed to the walls and with many doors leading off into what must be very small rooms, no more than cubicles. They stand there, the three of them, as if they are waiting for something, and a part of her is thinking, what is it, what are we waiting for, but the other part is still clamouring and pleading and pawing at him, and her voice now they are away from the music sounds shrill and pathetic. Someone from behind one of the doors shouts at her to shut up. Farida stands passively at Ugo's side.

The door behind Liliana opens, the handle catching her in the small of the back, and a hand is suddenly clamped over her mouth. That's what they were waiting for. Ugo bundles Farida along the corridor, away from Liliana, and into one of the little rooms, and the door clicks shut behind them. The hand that holds her is powerful and vice-like. Muntaz.

There is no point struggling.

He moves her clumsily along the corridor so they are outside the door where Ugo went. After a while he loosens his grip but does not entirely release her. She can move her jaw and so she sinks her teeth into his finger and tastes blood. He tears his hand away, slaps her hard on the side of the head so her ears ring and clamps her jaw shut again. A man comes out of one of the rooms hitching up his trousers. He pauses to look at them. She pleads 'help' silently. The man looks at Muntaz and at her, as if considering what to do. Then Ugo sticks his head out into the corridor and reaches for her, yanking her into the room.

The salty smell of sweat and sex makes the hot air in the little room almost unbreathable. As Ugo drags her into the corner Liliana takes in the only furniture: a wooden bed pushed against one wall with straps or ropes hanging down from the ceiling above. Farida is lying on the bed face down, unmoving, her head twisted towards the wall, her dress rucked up around her waist, stockings around her ankles.

'What have you done to her?' Liliana screams.

Ugo ignores her. His hair is stuck to his head and his forehead drips with sweat. He has pulled his tie loose and undone his top buttons, and is breathing heavily. 'Would I forget you, my little lying bird?' he says. He rams her against the wall and holds her there with one hand, tearing at her clothes with the other. 'No need to be jealous.'

She never has fought him off before, not since that first ineffectual time. And she wouldn't now except she needs to see if Farida is all right and so she keeps wriggling and squirming and flailing and shouting Farida's name, pinned between Ugo and the hard wall, trying to see around the great bulk of him, to see if Farida has moved. They are uneven, unbalanced forces, but she doesn't stop, even though now he has lifted her off her feet and her back is jammed painfully against the wall and he is pushing at her, into her. He is saying something over and over, but she can't make out what it is because she is still shouting and there is still a ringing in her ears. Her head jerks back and cracks against a ledge, and her vision swims as if she is about to pass out. Resistance leaves her.

Ugo finishes with a mighty roar and pulls out.

He lets go, and as Liliana's feet reconnect with the ground her knees buckle and she feels herself slithering down as if her bones have melted. She presses the palms of her hands against the wall to stop herself from puddling on the black tiled floor. As Ugo steps away she sees that Farida is sitting up on the edge of the bed, her dress still bunched around her middle, her bare legs dangling, her head hanging down.

Liliana walks her hands up the wall, pulling herself upright. Warm liquid spurts down the inside of her thighs. A hot searing pain inside prevents her from fully straightening. She leans crookedly against the wall. She doesn't yet trust her trembling legs to carry her those few steps across the room to Farida, and anyway Ugo is still there in the middle. He has pulled up his trousers and tucked his shirt back in and done up his belt, but now he is making angry snorting noises as he fumbles with the top button of his shirt. His great bull neck must have thickened because he is unable to fasten it. He gives up and pulls his tie to the centre. He has never been able to knot his own tie, even with the aid of a mirror, and here, in this cell-like room, there is no mirror. He stands for a moment, taking noisy nasal breaths. Then he steps to Liliana's corner, lifts his head and presents his throat. She notices the movement of his Adam's apple, the twitch in his jaw and the overripe fruitiness of his breath. She takes shallow breaths through her mouth. Her tongue is dry and swollen. It lies like a beached sea creature in the dirty cavern of her mouth. She reaches up and with clumsy fingers starts to knot his tie.

Out of the corner of her eye she sees that Farida has lifted her head and is watching them.

Ugo raises his left arm so he can consult his watch without lowering his head, and disrupting the tie-knotting process. 'Hurry up,' he says.

When she has finished, Liliana collapses back against the wall. Ugo reaches his fedora down from the shelf, smooths his hair back from his brow and jams the hat firmly on his head. He unhooks his jacket and slings it over one shoulder. 'You have five minutes to leave this room,' he says and slams out of the door.

Farida remains sitting perfectly still on the edge of the bed, her stockings pooling around her ankles, her bare thighs pressed against each other. Her gaze is still pointed towards the corner where Liliana stands but seems to be focused on something further away, as if there is a window in the wall and she is looking through it. There is no expression on her perfect oval face. To Liliana, in that dimly lit room, it appears that Farida has lost her sheen, as if she has been dusted with fine debris, or has turned to stone. She sits as still as a statue, small but monumental, and she looks straight through Liliana and out the other side as if she weren't there. Liliana's teeth start to chatter.

Then, all of a sudden, Farida moves. She leans forward

and rolls her stockings off. Clutching them in one hand, she gets to her feet and tugs her wrinkled dress down over her hips and her legs, down as far as her knees. She scoops her shoes up from the floor and advances on Liliana's corner of the room. She rummages in the bag that still hangs from Liliana's shoulder, fetching out their two barracans and their flat slippers, and placing her undergarments and heeled shoes in the bag instead. She thrusts a barracan into Liliana's hands. Then she drops both pairs of slippers to the floor and shuffles her feet into one set, takes a step backwards into the middle of the room and flips her barracan around her body. She spins round towards the door and stands with her back to Liliana and her hand on the doorknob. 'Are you coming?' she says. And Liliana, as if awoken from a trance, hoists up her own undergarments, tugs off her shoes and stuffs them in the bag, wraps herself in the barracan and follows.

They make their way down the dim corridor. At the far end there are two doors, the one that goes back into the café and another that opens directly to the outside. They step out into the bright afternoon sun, Farida leading the way. They cross the square and turn down into the copper-market street. They walk slowly, single file, along the narrow passageway between the hanging copper and brass lanterns, the mirrors and the frames, past the candlesticks, teapots and urns heaped outside the stalls. They limp through the dazzle and gleam and clatter of it and then take a left turn into another of the narrow, maze-like streets of the old town, heading for home. When they reach Sciara Sidi Hamura, where there is space to walk side by side, Liliana grips the cloth of her barracan in her mouth to hold it in place and reaches out to clasp Farida's free hand in hers. Farida, without pausing in her dogged, head-down shuffle, snatches her hand away.

FEEDING THE JACKALS

Item: A Tripolitanian stamp from 1930 showing a gazelle.

'Let's go and feed the jackals,' the pilot says, his heart dancing.

It is the final phase of the pacification. Fezzan has been quelled. Tripolitania is fully under Italian rule, and the rebel leaders in the west have fled, been captured or killed. Civilisation is continuing there apace. But in Cyrenaica, the third part of the territory, the rebels are still fighting. They get their supplies from their exiled brothers across the border in Egypt and from the treacherous and ignorant villagers who are in the hopeless thrall of the Senussi sect. They are led by an old man called Omar Mukhtar. They have been given every chance to submit.

Cyrenaica is where the most fertile land lies, and is the site of the Jebel Akhdar plateau, which offers rich rain-fed earth where cereals and vegetables, potatoes and trees might grow. It is an ancient Roman land – to scratch at the surface of the ground here is to unearth coins and relics of Roman antiquity – and it is crying out for the waiting thousands of Italian peasants, noble sons of the soil, to return and reclaim it, to dig and sow and plant and bring forth its bountiful fruit.

But before that can happen, the nomads with their anarchic existence that impedes agriculture, the enemies, must be removed. The forests of the Jebel Akhdar have provided cover and shelter for too long to the rebel army that is plunging ever further into poverty a land that is fecund and rich with promise. Pay, rations, information, arms: all find their way from the submitted ones to the rebels. They pay the Senussi agents a tax and give gifts of food and clothes and horses. The rebels have made of the Jebel Akhdar a vast natural fortress. The limestone tableland of northern Cyrenaica is covered with maquis and woods, ravines and caves, where a thousand fighting men hold the Italian fascist army at bay. It is time for different tactics. It is time for the forests to be emptied, for the way to be made clear for the new Roman civilisation, the new era.

Today he is on a reconnaissance mission. Another pilot reported fields of maize in this area but had no ammunition left to destroy them. Their crops must be eradicated, or they will be harvested and find their way into the bellies of the rebels.

Two days before, he bombed the Taizerbo oasis. At Taizerbo there were groves of palms, tamarind, acacia and cane, some herds of camels and a dozen or so villages of stone houses and tents. Intelligence told them that Taizerbo had become the base from which raiding parties of rebels set off.

It was a beautiful target. Twenty-five kilometres long and ten kilometres wide, cut through in the middle by a hollow containing the salty ponds and pools from which the population of the oasis drew their water and irrigated their crops. There were little houses clustered in the places where the palms were thickest and, near to them, many small green gardens where the people grew vegetables. There were not many cattle to be seen, just a few goats.

Four Romeo planes carrying a ton of explosives, including the mustard gas that has proved so effective, flew under his command, passing over the Giululat and the el-Uadi oases and then over the tents. They went in single file, flying low and dropping their loads and then banking, wheeling high into the sky. The shocks and jerks of the blasts made the air churn. They could feel it on the wings of their planes, and they needed all their strength and skill to hold the machines steady.

Beyond the furthest human habitation, they saw a caravan of a hundred-odd camels running away at great speed, their loose loads swinging and slopping from their saddles. The pilot flew very close to the ground, strafing the length of the caravan, from the tail to the head, emptying a whole magazine into the animals. Many collapsed to the ground, revealing their fat bellies and thrashing their long skinny legs in the air. The plane that followed finished off the stragglers.

The pilots have invented new rules to make the sport more challenging. How low can you fly? How few shots can you use? How much ammo can you save for the next time? None of them like saving ammo. They like the dust-cloud fireworks too much.

Today, he is flying alone.

Sometimes, when they have run out of enemy targets, they track gazelles. When the animals hear the sound of the plane approaching they pause, standing stock still and rigid on their slender legs. They stare up with their luminous eyes. They don't yet know to be frightened.

They put him in mind of Liliana, delicately made and brimming with energy, her eyes bright as if there was a flame alight behind them. She was not like the native girls he frequented or ordered in, who were hard-working when they were out in the fields, or collecting water from the well, or whatever tasks they were set, but had a kind of indolence in the bedroom. They lacked enterprise or verve. They were compliant, yes, always that, and unshocked, because so many unspeakable things had already been done to them, he supposed, and it was what they expected. They were like beasts of burden, waiting for the whip, a silent tremor when it came, and then plodding on, uncomplaining.

But Liliana wasn't like them. She was Italian for a start, and by definition of a different order. She deferred to him because she recognised that he was an important man. And she was willing to please him because of this. Well, at the beginning at any rate. Before she had thrown in her lot with the natives and shown herself to be no better than them, a traitor to her own race.

When the plane is overhead, its shadow cast over the gazelles, blotting out the light, all of a sudden the fear gets them. They start wildly running about, jumping and crashing into each other, scattering all around. Then, when nothing happens, they stand still again and look up.

There is something almost human about their imploring look. As if they are pleading for mercy. Or so one of his fellow aviators had once remarked. It wasn't the sort of notion that would have occurred to the pilot – too fanciful – but he liked it somehow and he remembered it. The human look in their eyes. The mute pleading.

The pilot hates pleaders, mute or vocal.

Liliana pleaded with him not to take the Bedouin whore, saying darling in her shaky voice, clutching at his arm. Please darling, no. Offering herself instead, as if he hadn't had her a hundred times already and couldn't have her again. And did, straight afterwards, to shut her up. Once was enough with the Bedouin, who looked hot but was cold and hard and unyielding inside. Like fucking a dried date.

They're funny, the gazelles, with their imploring eyes, but good for target practice.

MAKTUB

Item: A woven silk shawl, dark blue in colour.

Zaida has pulled her chair up close to the head of the bed and is stroking her father's face with the backs of her fingers. The bruises around his eyes are turning the yellow of plums. So there is change. The doctor has just been and gone. Healing is taking place. Blood is flowing to damaged areas, tissue is recovering. They are talking about waking him up on Saturday. They say his progress is good. She is starting to believe that her father might survive. She feels a flame of hope burning, but every time she remembers that Khal Abramo is dead the flame gutters and threatens to go out. Even if her father makes a complete recovery, it won't bring Khal Abramo back.

When she woke this morning and suddenly remembered about Abramo and that she hadn't even managed to talk to her mother yet, aloneness shrieked through her like a cold wind. She sat up in a panic, and there, on the other side of the bed, was Signora Jones, wrapped in a blue shawl and seemingly dozing. The shawl is made of a soft woven cloth in indigo blue that looks Libyan in origin, or North African at least.

She was so happy to see the old lady that she rolled out of her camp bed and came around the end of her father's bed to give her a hug, and Signora Jones, who must have been fast asleep, almost jumped out of her skin.

Signora Jones being there doesn't make things all right, but it makes them less awful. She stayed sitting with her father while Zaida ran down to the reception area to try to make a telephone call to Tripoli. She listened and offered tissues from her endless supply while Zaida wept after she had been unable to get through yet again. She told her she was a brave girl and that her mother would be proud. But when Zaida asked if Signora Jones could remember what her mother had been like when she was little, the old lady had twitched in that way she had and said 'Pardon?' and then 'Sorry,' and then lapsed into silence. Since then, she has been sitting with her head down playing with her rings, twisting them, occasionally shuddering as if beset by ghostly attackers. And each time Zaida has started to say something, Signora Jones has raised her hands, but not her head, in a gesture that has told Zaida to wait, to just give her a minute or two. Signora Jones wears two rings on the ring finger of her left hand, one with a diamond and one plain gold. So she is married, or has been. She seems to be thinking hard about what it is she wants to say.

It feels ominous. Zaida has noticed the suitcase in the corner of the room. Signora Jones must be intending to leave, and the thought makes Zaida feel small and scared, but she is not giving in to that feeling. She is thinking instead about what she might say to persuade Signora Jones to stay. When she gets a chance, when Signora Jones has said whatever it is she is gearing up to, Zaida is going to plead her case. Perhaps Signora Jones has not realised how glad Zaida is to have her here. She will tell her. She sits quietly, stroking her father's face, obeying the mute instruction to wait, and she watches the little twitchy lady with the wild white hair and it occurs to her that Signora Jones is the latest incarnation of the old woman who, according to the family legend, appears unexpectedly and saves the day. First, back when her grandmothers were young, there was Zohra, and then later there was Madame Simone and now here is Signora Jones. She turns that thought over in her mind. She has the sensation that there is another thread of connection and it thrills her even though she can't quite apprehend it. She calls to mind the story of Zohra, as recounted on many occasions by Grandma Farida. It was a time when Italian tanks were rumbling across the desert and the people of Cyrenaica were being marched to concentration camps. Zohra had been left behind when the soldiers came. She had been resting in a clump of tamarind trees on her way back from the well and remained hidden there for three days and two nights. When she returned to her home, a camel-hair tent on the edge of the ransacked village, thinking only to lie down and await her fate, she found two young women – one of them was Grandma Farida – strangers to her, and two newborn babies, in need of her aid. She ministered to them.

'There are a lot of French books in your apartment,' Signora Jones says all of a sudden.

'Pardon?' Zaida says. Her thoughts had drifted far away to the camel-hair tent in the deserted village and the kerosene lamp that lit it and to the two young women who lay inside. She doesn't know what she was expecting, but not a question about books.

'Does your father speak French?' Signora Jones asks.

'My father?' Zaida exclaims. She looks down at his poor battered face. 'He can hardly speak Italian and we have been here for four years. Isn't that right, Baba?' She bends to kiss his forehead. 'No, the books were already there. The apartment belonged to a French lady before, Madame Simone.'

The old lady starts, as if someone has crept up behind her and tapped her on the shoulder. The ghostly attackers are back. She shakes them off.

'She died two years ago,' Zaida says, and as she does so tears spring to her eyes, not just because of her dear Madame Simone being dead, but because of everything.

'I'm sorry. I didn't mean to upset you,' Signora Jones says, reaching for her tissues.

Zaida blows her nose and wipes her face. 'You haven't. It's nice for me to tell you about her,' she says, thinking how strange it is that she was wanting to talk about Madame Simone and now she has been given the chance quite naturally. But as she explains how Madame Simone was an old family friend who knew her grandparents and who used to turn up in Tripoli with treats from Italy for her Mama and for Abramo when they were little kids, a part of her mind remains with Zohra and the two young women that she rescued, and she feels a sense of mounting excitement, as if something is about to be revealed. The family lost touch with Simone during the war, she recounts to Signora Jones, because they moved away from Tripoli and everything was in chaos, and for several years there was no contact. And then one day, after the war was over, Abramo found an address in Rome for her and wrote and Madame Simone wrote back, and they went on from there. 'When me and my Baba ran away from Libya we went straight to her place. Where else would we go?' she says, watching Signora Jones.

The old lady shakes her head and presses her lips together as if to say, where else indeed? 'So they *did* lose touch,' she mutters. 'I see.'

Zaida pauses, wondering if Signora Jones wants to clarify what she has just said, but it seems not, or not yet. 'I miss her so much,' she says. 'We still have all her clothes and everything in the flat. We haven't got rid of anything.'

'No, you don't want to do that too quickly,' the old lady says, shaking her head. She is absorbed again in her ring-twisting. The rings are too big for her but Zaida cannot see how she could ever remove them because her knuckles are wider than the stretch of finger below. 'When would that have been?' she asks. 'When did they make contact again, I mean?'

Zaida doesn't know. These are legendary tales. They don't need dates. She wonders where this is leading, if anywhere. She searches her memory. Abramo and Nadia, her uncle and her mother, were teenagers. '1945?' she hazards.

Signora Jones nods and smiles as if with relief. Zaida nods back. They are nodding together and Zaida is glad they are in agreement, but not sure what about.

'Tell me more about your family,' Signora Jones says. 'I like hearing you talk.'

So Zaida tells her about her mother Nadia, who is a teacher, and her two big sisters, Salwa and Aisha, who are both married and who live in Tripoli. She mentions her aunts and uncles on her father's side, who are all in Benghazi, and her ancient great-aunt who lives in a high village in the Jebel Akhdar and her great-uncle Sadiq who died in the battle when Omar Mukhtar, the resistance hero, was captured. And Grandpa Saif, who died defending Kufra. She describes her grandmother Fatima, who is rotund and cuddly and a wonderful cook, and grandmother Farida, who is small and thin, but strong and full of wisdom. And all the while, as she is speaking, Signora Jones lets out little gasps or softly repeats a name and shakes her head in wonder.

'Salwa?' Signora Jones says. 'Your big sister is called Salwa?' Her eyes are wide.

'Yes,' Zaida says, and a funny feeling that she can't quite name shivers through her. Who is she, this Signora Jones? Why is she so affected by that name?

Signora Jones puts one hand to her heart. 'And is she well?' she asks.

'Who?' Zaida asks cautiously.

'Farida,' Signora Jones says. She places her other veiny little hand on top of the first. The diamond ring slips sideways.

'She is very well. She lives with Salwa and helps with her two little children.'

'*Alhamdulillah*,' Signora Jones says.

Zaida's eyes open wide. 'Oh,' she says, taken aback. She hasn't heard an Italian exclaiming in Arabic before.

Signora Jones, seemingly pleased by Zaida's reaction and diverted by it from whatever her more serious agenda is, explains how she can say just a few odd words in Arabic, a smattering of expressions that she picked up when she lived in Tripoli. She recites her repertoire of phrases, which are all either food-related or the kind of wise saying that Abramo and Grandma Farida favour.

Zaida's conviction that some truth is about to reveal itself strengthens.

'Thus it is fated. *Maktub*,' Signora Jones says.

'*Maktub*,' Zaida repeats, nodding. She has to sit and wait and be curious and expectant and it will emerge, this veiled thing.

'Where there is ruin, there is hope for a treasure,' Signora Jones says in heavily accented Arabic.

That was definitely one that Abramo liked to quote too, Zaida thinks, and is suddenly reminded of the conversation she had had with him about Italy's lack of awareness of its history in Libya.

'I remember that one because it's so optimistic. People

make mistakes and things collapse, but something good might still come of it,' Signora Jones explains in Italian. 'You just have to search through the ruins.'

Zaida understands that Signora Jones is doing the same thing that Khal Abramo did that time. She is making a generalisation about people and what they do, but she is actually talking about herself. And Zaida thinks, what's your secret, Signora Jones? What have you hidden in your ruins? She recognises the same sadness in Signora Jones that she felt in her uncle. Secrets stop you from knowing yourself properly, from being the whole of yourself, Abramo said. She hoped he had found a way of being the whole of himself here in Italy. Out loud she says, 'Khal Abramo used to say that thing about ruins and treasure. It comforted him about the state of our country.'

Her words seem to bring Signora Jones back to herself. She looks at Zaida and nods. Then she turns her gaze up to the crucifix on the wall and makes the sign of the cross. 'Oh for the solace of faith,' she mutters. Then she braces her shoulders and turns back. Zaida thinks, it is coming now, the question that Signora Jones really wants to ask. 'And Stefano?' the old lady says in a steady voice.

Stefano. Grandma Farida's Italian husband. Zaida still can't quite get the connection but its revelation is imminent, she knows it. A momentous thing is about to crack open. She concentrates to make sure she gets the facts that she has been told right. 'He died before the war. I don't know when.' She fingers the hand of Fatima hanging around her neck, trying to remember what else she has been told. 'Mama and Abramo were seven,' she says, recalling what her mother has said. 'Seven and a half.'

Signora Jones nods. She clears her throat. 'How did he die?' she asks.

'It was an accident at the race track where he worked,' Zaida says gently.

The two children were playing on the roof terrace of their apartment block when they were told the terrible news. Zaida knows where the building is: quite close to the beach, and not that far from the house that backs on to the sea where her Mama lives now, and where she too lived until she and her father fled here. Grandma Farida came up the stairs onto the roof and called their names. 'Abramo, Nadia,' she said. 'Come here.' Zaida can picture them, their bare brown legs, their short socks, their black hair. They ran to Grandma Farida and she sank to her knees to hold them. Everything changed for them after that. They had to leave because there was no money to pay the rent. Farida had been living as if she were an Italian, but she couldn't do that without Stefano. Abramo and Nadia were being brought up as Italian children and they went to an Italian school and all of that came abruptly to an end. Farida put her barracan back on. They travelled to Benghazi, where she had family. They took only what they could carry, one suitcase apiece.

Signora Jones is pushing her hands back through her curly hair as if to push something out of sight, but it either doesn't work or she changes her mind. She gets to her feet. 'Will you excuse me a minute?' she says. 'I need some air.' Clutching her handbag, she leaves the room.

She has left her suitcase, so will have to come back. When she returns, Zaida will tell her the story of Zohra.

CARDS IN THE AIR

Item: A hand-drawn design for a poster advertising Yaacov's emporium at the Tripoli trade fair of 1931.

Liliana is in her little room in the apartment. She is lying on her bed, staring at the ceiling. There is a stain there that looks like a man's head in profile. He has an enormous nose and a stubby curling eyelash. If she squints at him through half-closed eyes, she can make a nearby smudge seem to be a hat that has been blown off his head by a sudden gust of wind. But right now she is concentrating on the tip of his nose in the hope that the sick feeling in her belly and the constriction in her throat will go away and she will be able to doze.

She has been off colour for over a week. For a while she thought she had picked up a stomach upset from eating camel meat that was on the turn, but more recently the idea has crept into her mind that she might have been poisoned. It first occurred to her when she was bent over the toilet hole retching and she remembered Stefano doing the same thing back home in Monza after the Blackshirts had force-fed him castor oil. She cannot pinpoint when or how or by whom the poison could have been administered. She suspects Muntaz. Was it when she bit his hand in the Oriental Café? Did the venom that runs through his veins pass into her mouth? Or did he slip something into her drink? Or did Ugo?

The nausea began only ten days ago and it is nearly two months since the afternoon at the Oriental Café. Ugo is long gone. Word is that he has had a big promotion in Cyrenaica and will not be returning to Tripoli. But still the idea persists. Poison has entered. Perhaps it is not a real substance like the powdered roots and bark shavings and evil-smelling liquids and gummy ointments that are on sale in the market and which have all sorts of alleged powers to enchant or strike dumb or cure warts or avert the evil eye. Not one of those witch-doctor concoctions, no, but something less tangible, more vaporous. A malign spirit has breathed into her and her body is trying, fitfully and uselessly, to expel it.

The broad outlines of her life remain the same. She still lives in the Jewish quarter of the old town, around the corner from the synagogue, in the apartment she shares with Stefano and Farida. She continues to work three days a week at Signor Yaacov's shop on Souk el-Turk. But the detail, the colours that filled those outlines, have been rubbed over and have smudged. Farida no longer speaks to her. Farida has shut her out.

Her mouth is full of sin. It has the bitter taste of bile.

The best times are when she is at work. There, she is so taken up with the telephone calls, with supervising the packaging and dispatch of the orders, with entertaining the occasional Italian customers, that for whole minutes at a time, minutes that sometimes stretch into half an hour or more, she almost forgets her sorry state. She almost forgets that Ugo has torn her to pieces and thrown her away like yesterday's newspaper. She even almost forgets that Farida has retreated into a cold silence. Liliana has wept, she has explained a hundred times in all the ways she can think of that she never meant for it to happen. She has pointed out that she did not let Farida face Ugo alone. Farida is unresponsive. At most, she says, 'I know all this,' or 'stop now', and twice, when Liliana was mid-speech, Farida has held her right hand up, palm outward, as if to say 'hush', as if she wants now to speak, but has instead turned on her heel, gone into the bedroom she shares with Stefano and firmly closed the door. It is as if she has erected a fence around herself, or allowed a thick, impenetrable hedge to grow there, and Liliana cannot find the way through. Their private outings in European clothes, just the two of them, have ceased.

Liliana has taken to buying little things she knows Farida likes on her way home from work – grilled peanuts, sugary biscuits, dates and buttermilk, honey sweets flavoured with rosewater – and leaving them on the bench for Farida to discover. They are left untouched, or become part of the shared evening meal as if they were just groceries rather than carefully chosen treats for Farida's sole pleasure. With Stefano, Farida seems more affectionate than she used to be, caressing his cheek and reaching for his hand after dinner, so that they often retire early to their room. Their intimacy sharpens the sting of her own exclusion and loneliness.

But when Liliana is at Signor Yaacov's shop there is always something to keep her busy, even if there are no orders to fulfil. She has to learn about the merchandise so that she can satisfy the curiosity of Italian customers who call in and so that she does not always have to defer to Signor Yaacov. He has suggested that she develop an area of expertise and she has chosen textiles because she loves the different cloths. Yaacov agrees that their softness is befitting for a woman. So she has studied them, the wools and silks, the camel-hair blankets, the cloth made on hand looms, the weaving and the recurrent motifs. She now knows more than the layman about the old weaponry that hangs on the wall, the swords and the guns that mostly date from the time of the Ottoman rule of Libya, before the Italians ousted the Turks in 1912. She can talk too about the silverware and the brass, the filigree and the enamelled ornaments. But she is most confident when she flaps open a bedcover or shakes out a shawl or unfurls a rug woven in the southern province of Fezzan and describes its provenance and the workmanship to a potential buyer. She loves the indigo-dyed women's capes made by the Berber people. The geometric patterns are woven in cotton onto the wool and do not take up the dye so that they stand out against the dark blue. The shop sells a range of barracans too, from fine-mesh creamy white wool with silver silk borders to a rougher weave for everyday use.

Signor Yaacov has also given her the job of designing the literature for the stall they are going to have at the trade fair. There will be a poster, a leaflet to hand out and a notice that is to appear in the newspaper nearer the time. She is writing letters to some of their clients in Italy to ask about their experience of Signor Yaacov's emporium and these comments will be used in the leaflet. 'An Aladdin's cave of exotic delights,' says Signor Bragoli from Bergamo; 'An impressively wide range of authentic artefacts,' says Signor Modesto from Rome, and so forth. The fair will not be held until May next year, but these advance preparations are already under way.

If, in a quieter moment, the sadness and bitterness well up and she cannot prevent a sob, Signor Yaacov banishes her to the stockroom until she has composed herself. 'I do not want to be unkind, dear Signorina Cattaneo,' he has said, 'and my offer to run the villain who has wounded you through still stands, but we cannot present that miserable face to the customers. That glum look is not the look of Yaacov Djebali's emporium.'

He has taken to saying 'Bright eyes, Signorina,' and 'teeth and smiles' as he passes her seated at the ledger. And sometimes it does feel to her that the action of lifting the corners of her mouth helps lift her spirits a little too, as if things are not really as bad as she thinks.

Then she comes home and runs into the dense thicket of Farida's silence.

Liliana does not know what else to do. Her gifts go unappreciated, her pleading falls on deaf ears, her lapsing into silence to teach Farida how it feels has no effect. She is groping along in darkness, as if the light of her life has been extinguished. The edges of things are blurred and out of focus, and it is difficult to gauge where one thing starts and another finishes, so that sometimes she cracks her hip against a doorframe or a piece of furniture and, when she does, like a little child, she whimpers in distress.

A few times, on days when she is not working, she has wrapped herself in her barracan and gone wandering the streets of the old town, the ones where covered women go unnoticed, where she can move slowly and anonymously, unmolested. For some reason that is not clear to her, she does not put her barracan on inside the apartment, in front of Farida. She carries it in her bag down the dark corridor that leads to the front door, and only once around the bend does she wind it about her body. As soon as she does, her mind empties. She steps out into the little enclosed square with the white-painted tree in the middle and she sets off. She leaves the agitation and distress behind. She abandons Liliana Cattaneo. She is Salwa. She is no one.

She has taken to keeping the bag containing her folded barracan hanging from the hook on the back of her door, just in case.

Mostly, though, as now, she lies in her hot dead-end room with the door ajar so she can breathe, and hopes that sleep will claim her, or stares at the ceiling and tries not to think.

It isn't working. Her concentration on the outline of the man with the floating hat has wavered and the nausea can no longer be kept at bay. She rolls off the bed. She slings the barracan bag over her shoulder as she leaves her room and moves quickly on bare feet into the courtyard.

Farida is standing plant-like in a beam of sunshine.

Often, these days, Farida is to be found thus, upright and motionless in odd places around the apartment, in a doorway, facing a wall, behind one of the pink marble columns, in among the geometry of the shadow cast at certain times of day by the latticed screen on the upstairs veranda. Her eyes are focused on something Liliana cannot see. 'What are you doing?' Liliana has asked, more than once. When a reply comes, it is always the same: 'Nothing.' Farida's attention is elsewhere, as if she is listening to distant voices. Liliana has the idea that these voices comfort and sustain Farida and that, if only she could hear them too, and perhaps gaze where Farida is gazing, she might be able to join her and they might talk again, the way they used to do. Then together they would find an antidote for the poison.

As it is, Liliana is agonisingly alone.

She is careful not to cross directly in front of Farida's line of vision because when Farida looks through her as if she isn't really there some vital part, perhaps it is her soul, shrivels. She cannot forget the first time it happened, when they were in that smelly room with Ugo and Farida looked into the corner where Liliana was cowering but seemed not to see her. Of all the scenes from the Oriental Café that replay endlessly in her brain, it is this one that causes her the most pain.

Now, though, as Liliana pads past with her eyes cast down, Farida speaks. 'I have something to tell you,' she says.

'Back in a minute,' Liliana says, and her voice sounds childlike and excited. Farida has spoken to her and the rare pleasure of that attention creates a faint feeling of hope, a weak flutter within her chest.

In the toilet, she clutches at her belly and bends over the hole, but nothing comes out. She straightens and waits. She notices the dust motes floating in the fractured light that comes in from the high grid window, the dark edges of the white tiles on the wall, the rusty patches on the tin bucket full of water on the ledge. There are children playing outside. She can hear the scuff of their feet on the paving as they run about, and their shrieks and squeaky laughter. One has fallen and hurt himself and is whimpering. Another is comforting him. *Ma'lesh*, he is saying in a sweet voice. Never mind. *Ma'lesh*.

She is not going to be sick after all. She returns to the courtyard where Farida has lit the *kanoon* and is brewing tea. She makes a gesture towards the floor cushions. Liliana sits and for a while she observes the movements of Farida's hands, the flick of her slender wrists, the jingling sound that her bracelets make, in among them the one that Liliana bought and had engraved with the image of a bird. It is so nice and cosy on the cushion, with the afternoon sun shafting down into the courtyard and the fresh sweet smell of the mint leaves Farida adds to the tea and the coals on the *kanoon* sizzling. Liliana's limbs start to soften and relax. She rests her head back against the side of the bench and closes her eyes. Then she sinks further down into the cushions and curls up.

'Wake up,' she hears Farida say. 'Tea is ready.' She is standing over Liliana.

Liliana drags herself up to a sitting position. The tray containing the orange enamel teapot, two glasses and a bowl of peeled almonds has been placed on the floor at her side, but Farida remains standing. Liliana rubs her eyes to clear her vision and gets to her feet too. 'Yes?' she says, 'What is it?' She nearly says, 'Farida, dear,' but holds back. Not yet, she thinks.

'I am pregnant,' Farida says.

Liliana gasps. She hears herself exclaiming, 'How wonderful. A baby!' This must be the real explanation for Farida's withdrawal and pensiveness and increased affection with Stefano, she thinks; of course, this is all that it is. But even as she claps her hands to her cheeks as if in delight, she knows that something is not right.

Farida has not moved, nor has the stony expression on her face altered.

'A baby,' Liliana says again. She wonders if she should step forward and take Farida's hands, but the same thing that stopped her calling Farida 'dear' stops her now. Farida is looking at Liliana, as if waiting for her to say something else.

Realisation shivers down Liliana's spine. 'Oh,' she says, clutching the curve of her own stomach. 'Is it Stefano's baby?' She quakes in the searchlight of Farida's gaze. 'It is, isn't it?' she persists.

'How would I know?' Farida says. She narrows her eyes in a way that Liliana has only ever seen her do with people she doesn't trust. Perhaps she thinks that Liliana would tell her brother if the baby wasn't his.

'I wouldn't tell Stefano,' she says, shaking her head. 'He would never need to find out. And it's bound to be his, isn't it? The two of you have been so affectionate recently.'

347

Farida double-clicks her tongue against the roof of her mouth and rolls her eyes. 'How else would I persuade him that it is his?' she says.

'Oh.'

'I don't know which one of them is the father,' Farida says, staring at Liliana. 'Stefano is my husband. I love him. And now I must lie to him for ever.'

Liliana rocks back on her heels as if a great cold wave has hit her and threatens to knock her off her feet. She looks down. She swallows and then she starts to speak. She hardly knows what she is saying. She is telling Farida that she loves her, reminding her of their bond, that they are friends. She swings her head back up in time to see the eye-roll that accompanies Farida's single click of the tongue. No, Farida is saying without words. No. But what part of Liliana's statement is she contradicting? Or does Farida's refusal apply to something other than what Liliana has said. Or is Liliana misreading the gesture? 'Friends,' she repeats, lowering her eyes again and desperately trying to imbue her words with a certainty she does not feel.

'No,' Farida says.

'Excuse me?' Liliana says. She must have misheard.

What can that mean? A sudden image of the croupier in the side room at the Oriental Café comes to her. She seems to see the black and red cards tumbling through the air past her face, coming thick and fast, each one with a different picture:

Farida sold to Stefano by her father for fifty pieces of silver.

Her grandfather sent into exile to an Italian island, never to return.

Separated from her homeland, her family, her tribe.

Dressed as Rosita, thinking Liliana was her friend.

Force-fed alcohol and raped on a grubby bed.

Liliana puts her hand over her eyes but the images are still there. She tries to bat them away, because they are more than she can bear. They twist and turn as they fall so that she sees them from different angles. She gropes her way to the bench and sits down. She drops her head into her hands and presses her fingers into her eyelids. She is so weary. So sick and tired.

After a while, the giddiness subsides. She lowers her hands and opens her eyes. Steam is coiling from the spout of the teapot. 'Shall we have some tea?' she says. 'It will be getting cold.' What were they talking about before? The baby. Yes. 'Of course the baby is Stefano's,' she says.

Farida doesn't respond.

Liliana is never the one to pour the tea because Farida does it in a special way, lifting the pot and pouring from a height into the glasses so that a froth forms, but now she lowers herself to her knees next to the tray. She picks up the pot in one hand, a glass in the other. 'So it's good news,' she continues. She glances up. Farida is making the wobbly motion of her head that is always difficult to decipher, which might mean yes or no or something else entirely, but now the corners of her mouth have risen in what looks like the suspicion of a smile. She is going to have a baby and it will be Liliana's little nephew or niece. 'You're pregnant, Farida!' she exclaims again.

The sudden wailing sound of the muezzin at Gurgi mosque calling people to afternoon prayer almost drowns out Farida's soft-spoken words. 'So are you,' she says.

'Pardon?' Liliana says above the noise, kneeling there on the hard floor like a supplicant, the teapot raised high as if she is about to pour a libation. A spasm grips her stomach and she shudders. Tea spurts from the spout.

Farida repeats what she said before. Liliana's body con-
vulses again, as if she has been kicked in the stomach. The
teapot and the glass jerk out of her hands and fall, the glass
shattering as it hits the floor. She rocks on her knees and gasps
for breath. She clutches her hands to her ears to shut out the
drone of the muezzin. She can't think straight with that racket
going on. 'No,' she says. 'No, that's not right.' She is shaking
her head wildly from side to side.

Farida says it again.

The muezzin falls silent. The only sound in the courtyard
now are the moans and pants coming from Liliana. 'Oh,' she
is saying and 'no, no, no'. She's not a bad girl. She can't be
pregnant. 'I can't be,' she says. 'No, I can't be.' Nobody will
love her any more. Stefano will disown her. She will not be
able to live her life. 'I don't,' she says. 'I can't.' Her beloved
brother. He will know what she has been up to. But it's not
fair. Hasn't she been punished enough? 'Punished,' she says
aloud. She will never be able to go home to Italy.

She is shaking her head, genuflecting among the fragments
and the wet, moaning like a demented monk. She clutches
her belly as another spasm of nausea grips it. She clamps
a hand over her mouth but she can't stop it. She turns to
one side as a thin white liquid, like dirty milk, streams out
between her fingers and spatters onto the tiles, adding to
the mix of spilt tea and soggy mint leaves and splinters of
glass. 'No,' she says, wiping her mouth with the back of her
hand. 'I can't be.' She doesn't mean it is not possible. She well
remembers how when Ugo tore into her like a wild beast
in that dank corner he had not put on the sheath made of
animal skin that he always used. She already knew that no
man would ever have her now, tainted as she was. But a baby
will utterly ruin her. She will be an outcast. It will be the end

of her. It cannot be. She has already done her penance. 'It's all right for you,' she whispers, 'you've got Stefano. But I can't have a baby. I can't,' and she starts to shuffle on her knees across the floor. She drags herself along in her sopping dress and throws her arms around Farida's legs. 'Help me,' she says.

Farida reaches down to take hold of Liliana's arms and hauls her to her feet.

A whimpering noise over which Liliana has no control issues from her mouth and her breaths are coming very fast and shallow. She stands swaying and panting. Farida's eyes are ablaze. She is like an avenging angel. Liliana is exposed, every crevice and fault, every stain and blemish and meanness revealed. She is withering in that harsh light.

'Why should I help you?' Farida says.

Liliana tries to remember the words that Farida once said to her. Their pact to be friends in this unfair world. The effort is almost too much. A part of her just wants to disappear, to be swallowed up and cease to exist. With a huge effort she lifts her heavy arm and reaches forward to press her thumb to Farida's forehead. 'Because of you and me,' she starts to say, but before her thumb can make contact with Farida's forehead, Farida swipes her hand away. Liliana staggers.

'Friends love, enemies betray,' Farida says.

Liliana feels a fissure within her starting to widen. She sinks back down to her knees. Everything is crashing around her and she is wet through, as if the wave that nearly knocked her down before has drenched her. From somewhere up above, far away in her citadel, Farida is talking now, explaining something. Farida's words buzz meaninglessly around Liliana's head. She leans her head against Farida's legs for balance while she tugs her barracan out of the bag still hanging from her shoulder. It is awkward to remove it at this angle. When she does, she pushes off from Farida's legs as if they are the shore, pulling the barracan around and over her as she crumples.

YOUR SISTER IS SICK

Item: A ticket dated December 1930 for the steamer from Tripoli to Benghazi.

Stefano stood on the jetty, waving to Farida and Liliana up on the promenade deck, hoping the cheery smile on his face hid the uncomfortable mixture of relief and foreboding in his heart. It was a year and a half since he had been here at the port of Tripoli to welcome his little sister to Tripolitania. He remembered her loveliness and her simple joy that first day; now the sight of her little face, puffy from crying, was a sad contrast.

Liliana had not been herself for weeks. She had become listless. She kept retiring to her room and shutting the door, but at first he had not paid much attention. He was very taken up with the trouble at work. It was starting to look like the race would not even be held next year, and he feared for the future of the track and for his ability to provide. These concerns were pressing on him even more than usual because of Farida being pregnant. He had thought that whatever troubled Liliana was a passing thing, a physical ailment that she would shake off. It had taken Yaacov turning up with her on the doorstep, having closed his shop to accompany her home, a thing that had never happened before, to make him realise. 'Your sister is sick,' he said. 'You need to look after her.'

It was Farida who had come up with this strange solution. She and Liliana would travel to Cyrenaica, to a little guest house she knew of on the coast where the quiet and the sea air would restore Liliana. He needn't worry about the cost, because they were going to use Liliana's savings. Then, once Liliana was settled at the guest house, Farida would ask her kinsman in Benghazi, who ran a bakery, to take her home in time for the coming of the baby. It was necessary, Farida said, for her to visit her family. She had not seen them in two years. It was the right place for her to be when she gave birth. She would honour tradition, her family would meet their new little relation and then she would come back to him, with a restored Liliana, back to their life in Tripoli. All of Stefano's objections about babies and travel and hot sun and arid landscapes and sanitation and the lack of civilisation out there she brushed aside. 'It's where I'm from,' she said. 'It *is* my civilisation.'

'Is this what you want?' he asked Liliana. 'Yes,' she said in her new listless voice. 'Are you sure you wouldn't prefer to go back to Italy?' he asked, at which she started to weep uncontrollably.

It meant that they would be away for some months. It gave him a chance to work all the hours God sent. He could throw himself into saving his job.

Yaacov called Liliana's ailment the weeping sickness. His own wife had suffered from a bout of it earlier in the year. 'What brings it on?' Stefano asked. 'Grief,' Yaacov said. But Stefano did not know what it was that grieved his sister so. He hated to see her so empty and withdrawn. 'What cures it?' he had asked Yaacov. 'Rest. Gentle treatment,' Yaacov replied, 'and time.'

THE PARK ON THE HILL

Item: A jacaranda flower in full bloom.

Memories of Tripoli and her life there jostle in Liliana's head as she walks away from the hospital. That contradictory combination of fatigue and vitality, tired and yet pulsing with life, weak and on the verge of fainting, yet gripped by dreadful passions and nameless fears that she had often felt back then. There are echoes of it now coursing through her body, sending electric shocks to her heart, channelling through her veins, churning her insides, pressing on her bruise.

Stefano is dead. Stefano has been dead all along. He is dead. Her dear brother died. Her footsteps are the drumbeat and variations on those words are the refrain, as the knowledge comes shaking through her, setting up an internal avalanche. Of course he is dead. Only death would have severed the tie. She knew this in her heart. She had always known it. She knew it before Zaida said the words, but still she needed to hear them. She makes her way up a steep road under the shade of overhanging trees, pausing often to catch her breath, as the stories she has told herself, the things she imagined might be true, or invented to hide what she knew to be true, old certainties and near-certainties and foolish paradoxical beliefs are dislodged and topple.

She comes to an open gateway in the high white wall that edges the pavement. She sees it is the entrance to a park and goes in. She wanders its gravel pathways until, spying an empty bench, she sits.

She has done the sums. She did them in her head while Zaida was speaking. What a sweet smile that girl has. How able she is to be kind, even from within her own grief. Liliana has worked out that Stefano must have died towards the end of 1938, not long after she went to England and very soon after the arrival of the parcel she sent him from Monza. He would have died before he received her letter giving him her London address. Farida might already have left by the time that letter arrived, because without him she could not have stayed where she was. Not that Farida could have read the letter. But the children could have read it to her. The three of them would have had to leave that apartment. They could not have stayed.

When Liliana read about Ugo's death, she had been more surprised at the fact that he had been alive all those years than that he had now died. But Stefano's death did not come as a surprise. It was a shock, but not a surprise.

In all her imaginings about the fate of the family in Libya, she had always put them together, as a unit. They were either alive, but somehow hidden from her, or they were dead. She had not allowed for some interim state. She had not allowed for the impact on them of just one death, that of the provider, the man of the household, the Italian, the linchpin. She had considered only the extremes and failed to consider any intermediate possibility. It was what Stefano used to warn her about in his periodic lectures about the evils of fascism, his attempts to make her see complexity and ambiguity where she wanted only certainty. He used to insist it was not as simple as the slogans stated: black or white, with us or against us, the Duce is always right. There were a whole range of arguments and ways of thinking and possibilities in between. Poor Stefano, not knowing that it was futile and that she couldn't really hear him. He was up against Ugo. She could not believe both of them simultaneously and had to choose Ugo's way, or so she thought at the time. Otherwise she would have been lost.

And ultimately was, of course.

Her heart goes out to Farida. What anguish she must have endured losing the love of her life in that sudden and brutal way. What an impossible situation she had been left in.

But she had survived. Farida is alive and well and living in Tripoli.

And with that thought comes such a surge of joy that Liliana lets out a little cry and looks around to see if any passer-by has noticed and sees, for the first time, that she is sitting in a beautiful park, surrounded by lawns and flower beds, purple and white jacarandas and tall Mediterranean pines. There is the scent of blossom in the air and birds are chirruping in the branches above.

A gateway has been opened and a space has been created in her head, and from this new clearing she has a different perspective.

The conspiracy to exclude her, a conspiracy in which she made Simone complicit, vanishes as if in a puff of smoke. A hot feeling accompanies its disappearance. She loosens the shawl around her shoulders, as if the warm air in the park has overcome her, but she recognises the feeling as shame.

She concocted a story in which she was the victim and all

these years she has chosen to hang on to it, because it was easier than facing the truth of what happened.

She thought she had left the hospital and sought solitude finally to face up to the difficult questions, but instead what is arising in her mind is the moment when Farida said she was pregnant. For the first time she understands that by abandoning herself, she abandoned Farida too. She has been blind to this. She has never thanked her for scooping her up, poor broken thing that she was, and caring for her, even though she did not deserve it. And she has never, properly, said sorry.

Liliana, wittingly or not, betrayed the best friend she ever had and then she ran away. It should have been unbearable to face this sorry truth, but it was not. It was a release.

Did she have a baby? Or didn't she? She doesn't know. If she had one, did she kill it? Of course she didn't. Farida wouldn't have let such a thing happen. Did it die? But when she allows herself to think that, consciously to connect that thought with the awful grief that she has carried like an unhealing bruise all these years, the feeling is not that the baby died, the baby girl with bright blue eyes. The feeling is that *she* died. Liliana died.

But she didn't. Alan died. Ugo died. Stefano died. Abramo, whom she had not known, died. But she, Liliana Jones, née Cattaneo, is alive and sitting in the sunshine in a park in Rome. Farida is alive too. And Nadia. And, most importantly in this moment, Zaida.

It is time to make an honest reckoning of what she might have to offer. She is sixty-nine years old, but with few and only niggling ailments – her tinnitus, the twinge of arthritis in her left hip, a tendency to get headaches. She owns outright a small house in London. She is in receipt of a pension. She is a widow and has no dependants. She is quite ridiculously free.

She could still go back, pick up her suitcase, make her excuses and return to her little London life.

But she will not.

Farida's son has just died and she isn't going to abandon her a second time, whatever that means. She thinks it might mean staying here in Rome and looking after Zaida and the man in the bed.

She gets to her feet and sets off back down the hill to the hospital where Zaida awaits. She needs to say sorry, and she needs to say thank you. That's how simple it is.

SALWA

Item: Two twists of black baby hair wrapped in a scrap of cloth.

They leave Benghazi in the pre-dawn darkness. The man who is known to Farida, her kinsman, leads them to the place on the edge of town where the camel train waits. He brings them hot tannour bread from his bakery. They walk behind him, wrapped in their barracans and he carries their bags.

They are to ride in a small striped tent mounted behind the camel's hump. The camel kneels down in the dust and they clamber aboard, one on each side. There is a wooden ledge to sit on and wool cushions to lean against. They unwrap their heads and breathe inside the brown and yellow cloth, the golden glow it casts on Farida's face. They hold hands.

They pass a place called Soluch where a vast camp of tents is surrounded by a barbed-wire fence and where ragged children with crusted eyes hold out their hands.

They arrive at the town of Ajedabiya where there is a fort and more barbed wire and an open space, which on some days is the market square but on this day is used for hangings and where two men hang from the gallows. The camel train can take them no further. They lodge in a stone hut attached to a family's house on the edge of town. Salwa does not go out. They stay there many weeks. There is no one to take them further. Italian soldiers go past in tanks and armoured cars.

The people speak rarely, and when they do Salwa does not understand the words because although she feels herself to be a creature of the desert, she does not speak the desert people's language. Words are the surface and she is travelling at a lower level, in the beneath, in the undercurrent. Perhaps she has learned to breathe under water. Or perhaps she is holding her breath.

Sometimes she comes up for air and finds Farida, always there, who talks in whispers so that she cannot be overheard, so the language she is using cannot betray them.

A man called Reth comes. He is on his way to Kufra in the southern desert and he will take them to Farida's town.

They move at a camel's pace across an arid plain.

Once, high above, a plane passes overhead in the unbroken blue of the sky and they see something drop from it and cower. But they are in the lee of a giant sand dune, sheltering in its shadow. They pass unnoticed. The plane's dropped load does not explode. Soon afterwards, they pass the body of a man, lying on his back in the sand with his hands and his legs bound.

A hyena crouches behind a boulder.

Mostly Salwa dwells in the place below words, where she sees but does not comment. She has been told to stay silent so that the camel-driver and the other men in this caravan do not know that she is not of them. If they knew, they would refuse to take her. It suits Salwa to be quiet. She has nothing to say.

Her life before the desert is shadowy, partial and fragmented. She used to have a different name. Glimpses of canopied walkways, shafts of sunlight streaming down, the hindquarters of a donkey, the sound of the muezzin calling to prayer, the shouts of the market traders, the slap and hiss of the sea lapping Tripoli's shore. All that has been left behind.

The days start early, in freezing cold and darkness when the moon is still in the sky, their numb fingers fumbling to fasten their clothing inside their sleeping sacks. They never get fully undressed but keep their clothes on as an extra layer against the chill of the desert night, only loosening their undergarments for greater comfort, and to ease their swollen bellies. She lies on her back under a mound of blankets and the last things she sees before she goes to sleep are the stars, hanging in the big black sky.

In the starlit, sand-encrusted pre-dawn they stumble upright, wrapped in barracans and blankets, and sit beside the little fire that the camel-driver has lit. Reth is sinewy and muscled, with the calm, clear eyes that life in the desert gives. He is on a mission for the Italian authorities, carrying supplies to the troops near Kufra. They sweeten the coffee with sugar he breaks off from a slab he carries in his knapsack. They sit next to the small glow of the fire and drink the bowls of syrupy coffee and eat the squashed dates that are the only food. Then Reth stamps out the fire and covers it with sand, and when the wind has come and gone and wiped away the prints it will be as if they were never there.

They mount the camels again, wrapped in their barracans and blankets, and the unrelenting onward motion resumes, rocking and swaying. Dawn brings light but no heat, not at first. There is a slit in the fabric of the tent that she looks through, but there is nothing to see, nothing new to see. She looks out and it is the same as before, the same monotonous landscape stretching out to the horizon, and if it weren't for the motion of the camel it would be as if they hadn't moved. As the sun mounts, the hoar-frost covering the grey-green desert sand disappears. She sleeps a lot in the day, even though it is uncomfortable.

There are two of them. The other one leads and Salwa follows. The other one speaks but Salwa stays silent.

Sometimes Reth sings to the camels.

When the sun is on the ascent it warms them through. When it is high in the sky it reaches a burning intensity and they overheat, encased in their moving tent, lolling there. They fold back their outer garments. The dry air scorches their lungs. They are small and at its mercy. The gritty air cleanses.

Senussi horsemen with prayer beads in one hand and ancient rifles in the other gallop by. Reth looks the other way. If anyone were to ask, he hasn't seen them.

Twice the *ghibli* comes. The camels know it first. They start to sniff and twitch and flare their nostrils. When it arrives, all the people lie down in the sand with the camels and wrap themselves in their cloths and they wait for it to pass.

Farida's pains begin and Reth leaves them in a village. He will collect them on the way back if they are still alive. In a month's time. Or six weeks.

They are alone. They walk down dirt paths strewn with debris in between ancient stone huts and dusty patched tents. Farida calls out but no one answers. All the people have departed. All the animals too. When her pains come, Farida stands still, turns to face Salwa with her hands on her shoulders, gripping them. She closes her eyes, her breath rasping, and Salwa takes some of her weight. When it passes, they

363

move on, Farida shouting out words that evoke no response. Salwa holds Farida's hand and walks beside her.

They have only one skinful of water. They find a well, but it has been filled with concrete.

They enter one of the black conical tents. There is a rug in the middle, sheepskins and a straw mat. Farida stands in the middle, resting her head against the central pole, and she cries. Salwa stands as close behind as her own big belly allows. She puts her hands on Farida's hips. Farida cries and moans and mutters in the desert tongue. When her next pain comes she turns and leans on Salwa.

The gaps get shorter. Farida squats near the entrance to the tent where some light comes in. Salwa kneels opposite and holds her arms. Salwa cannot squat. Her body never learnt how. Farida groans and her eyes roll back in her head and she makes a low grunting noise and she pushes the baby out. He is a slippery one, but Salwa catches him. Farida lets herself fall back onto the mat and Salwa places the child on her stomach, but Farida continues to groan. She thrashes her head from side to side and wails as if she is dying. Tears ooze out of the corners of her shut eyes and roll sideways down her cheeks and into her ears.

Salwa goes to the doorway.

Help, she calls, but no one answers.

Take me, she says. Take me instead. She cannot hear her own voice. She doesn't know if she speaks the same language as God any more. Take me, she shouts. She raises her prayer hands to the sky and the unrelenting sun beats down on her head.

A great drenching occurs. An internal river undammed. She is soaked through from the waist down and her waters flow into the sand.

God has heard. He will take her instead.

When she crawls back into the tent she sees that Farida has hoisted herself up and put her son to her breast.

Salwa wakes to shocking pain. All the blinding desert light is prising her open. The central part, that should not crack – the kernel – it is cracking. She drags herself to her knees. She rests her head against the tent pole and leans there. Farida lays her baby down and comes to help. Salwa kneels on the ground on all fours and she grunts. The blood-red pain has her in its teeth and it shakes her as if she were a rag doll. It shakes her until her bones rattle and start to come loose. 'Push,' Farida says. Salwa pushes and the last brick in the dam comes away. She rolls onto her back.

Farida holds the baby in her arms, all smeared and bloody and beautiful. She hands her to Salwa, who takes her in her arms, holds her, sniffs her peach scent, the sweet skin on her nape, and kisses the top of her head, the perfect circle of her fontanelle. The baby opens her brigand-blue eyes and they look at each other. She kisses her cheek and the baby makes a little noise. My special girl, Salwa says. She lifts the baby up and Farida takes her. Salwa's life blood is pumping out, soaking through the floor covering and into the sand below. She slides the bracelet from her wrist. She watches as Farida pushes it over the baby's foot and up her leg. Keep her safe, Salwa says, but not out loud, because there is no need.

Tears are running down Farida's face. 'Stay with me,' she says, but Salwa has done a deal with God and cannot stay.

She wakes to new pain. Where Farida was, there is now an old woman, a crone, kneeling. Salwa's feet are pressed against the woman's knees. The woman reaches up inside Salwa, into Salwa's bleeding torn body, and she grapples with something, pulling and clawing as if she wants to drag Salwa's innards out. The old woman tugs, something gives and more blood gushes. The woman places a great bloody part that she has wrenched from Salwa on the tent floor and forces her hand back inside. She leans forward and puts her other hand on Salwa's belly, one hand inside and one outside. She presses and holds, presses and holds. The pain now is black and purple and bigger than Salwa, pulsing out from her, spilling out, overflowing from her body and filling the tent with its darkness. Her head drops back to the ground and a sleep as sweet as death comes to claim her.

READY FOR TOMORROW

Item: A silver bracelet engraved with the image of a bird with raised wings.

Zaida sits waiting for Signora Jones's return, brimming with anticipation. When she comes back, Zaida is going to ask her a question, and if the answer is yes she is going to tell her the story of Zohra and the two young women she helped. 'Long ago, when tanks were rumbling across Cyrenaica,' it begins.

Zaida used to love listening to that story, and all the other stories that Farida used to tell and probably still does when she is tucking Salwa's children up in bed for the night.

After Stefano died, Farida explained to Nadia and Abramo that Nadia's real mother was Stefano's sister, and that Farida only had her for safe-keeping. So Zaida and her sisters had also always known that Farida was not their real grandmother, but they loved her and so they had never minded. The only thing Nadia had that had belonged to her real mother was a silver bracelet that she had passed on to Salwa, her eldest daughter, and Salwa had passed on to her first daughter, Leila. Zaida wishes she had it here with her because she would like to show it to Signora Jones.

Zaida and her sisters used to clamour for Farida to tell the story again. Tell us the bit where the old lady of the desert uncovers her store of water. Tell us about the tamarind trees and the vultures circling, they would say. Their favourite part was always at the end, when Farida would say, 'and those two girls were my best friend and me. She gave me her baby to look after and I promised to keep her safe.' Then she would say, 'Did I keep her safe?' and the children would roar back, 'Safe and sound and ready for tomorrow.'

The door clicks open and Zaida looks up. 'Signora Jones,' she says, 'is your name Liliana?'

ACKNOWLEDGEMENTS

I owe a debt to the British Library, a place of wonder and mind-expanding resources, where much of the research for this novel took place. I am also grateful to the Elsa Morante library in Ostia, Italy, for providing a space overlooking the sea in which to write.

My thanks and gratitude go to my agent Nicola Barr for her guidance and unwavering belief in my writing as well as her colleagues at the Bent Agency and too to my wonderful editor Ursula Doyle and all at Fleet and Little, Brown.

A special mention goes to Kate Smiley who read and listened and reflected ideas back to me in a way that helped shape the book. Thank you too to my family and friends for their love and their encouragement, especially Ben and Harry, my mother, Jill Baily, an early reader, who helped iron out anomalies and my aunt Paula Macnamara for always providing a home from home for me in Italy.

NOTE ON SOURCES

There is scant information on Italy's colonisation of Libya and the period is little discussed. This reticence is part of what drew me in, but it also posed challenges.

The history books and academic commentaries that informed me include *L'Africa del Duce* (*The Duce's Africa*) by Antonella Randazzo; *Genocidio in Libia* (*Genocide in Libya*) by Eric Salerno; *Italian Colonialism*, edited by Ruth Ben-Ghiat; *Journeys through Fascism* by Charles Burdett; *The Making of Modern Libya* by Ali Abdullatif Ahmid; *A History of Libya* by Peter Wright; *The Italians in Libya* by Angelo del Boca; *Staging Memory* by Stefania del Monte; *How Fascism ruled Women* by Victoria de Grazia; and *Fascist Voices* by Christopher Huggens.

But this is a work of fiction and not at all a history of this forgotten period. As such, I read widely but not systematically: contemporary memoirs, novels, poems, song lyrics and even a PhD thesis. I watched old Italian newsreels available online from the Istituto Luce archive and scrutinised dozens of images, postcards and luggage labels.

For the flavour and detail of local Italian life in Libya in the 1920s I read *Magic Gate of the Sahara* and *The New Italy Overseas* by Angelo Piccioli, chief of education in Tripoli at the time. From *Tangier to Tripoli* by an intrepid American traveller Frank G. Carpenter brought the markets, food and camels of 1928 Tripoli to life. Vincenzo Biani's memoir, *Ali italiane sul deserto* (*Italian wings over the desert*), offered a picture of a pilot's life, the attitude towards local resistance, specific bombardments, planes and air bases. I consulted too *Libia Redenta* (*Libya Redeemed*) by Rodolfo Graziani, variously known as 'the Pacifier of Libya' and 'the Butcher of Fezzan', depending on where you were looking at him from.

The wonderful illustrated history of the Tripoli Grand Prix by Valerio Moretti, *Grand Prix Tripoli 1925–40*, provided information on the cars and races, while *Architecture and Tourism in Italian Colonial Libya* by Brian McLaren did the same for buildings and tourist trails.

I drew on the British explorer Rosita Forbes's *The Secret of the Sahara*, as well as *Desert Encounters* by Knud Holmboe, a Dane who converted to Islam, for an impression of how desert travel was for Westerners at the time.

Finally, two Libyan novels that had an impact and are available in English are the epic *Maps of the Soul* by Ahmed Fagih and *Al-agaila: The Camp of Suffering* by Ali Hussein.

POEMS AND SONGS

The quotation from Nizar Qabbani is my reinterpretation of existing translations from the Arabic. An English version can be found in *On Entering the Sea: The Erotic and Other Poetry of Nizar Qabbani*.

The translations of Giuseppe Ungaretti and Charles Baudelaire are my own, as is the quote from the 1927 song '*Lucciole Vagabonde*' – Vagabond Fireflies – by Bixio Cherubini.